"I LOVE YOU, NICKI,"
HE WHISPERED HOARSELY.

She closed her eyes, fresh tears spilling from them.

"Don't cry." He took her damp face between his hands. "Please don't cry. I swear to God I love you." He pressed his lips to her cheek, salty sweet. An agonizing gladness welled within him; it squeezed his throat, stung his eyes. "Don't cry."

"You love me?"

"Always and forever." He rubbed his cheek, wet now with his own tears, against hers, the oath her husband had extracted from him echoing in his ears. *You'll endeavor to sire me a son. . . . You'll keep your true purpose from Nicolette, and when it's done, you'll leave here and never contact her again.*

"I never stopped loving you," she whispered, her hands in his hair. "But it was wrong. It still is."

**"A finely crafted tale of bittersweet love . . .
poignant, remarkable, unforgettable."
—*Old Book Barn Gazette***

BREATHTAKING ROMANCES YOU WON'T WANT TO MISS

Wild Wind

by

Patricia Ryan

A TOPAZ BOOK

TOPAZ
Published by the Penguin Group
Penguin Putnam Inc., 375 Hudson Street,
New York, New York 10014, U.S.A.
Penguin Books Ltd, 27 Wrights Lane,
London W8 5TZ, England
Penguin Books Australia Ltd, Ringwood,
Victoria, Australia
Penguin Books Canada Ltd, 10 Alcorn Avenue,
Toronto, Ontario, Canada M4V 3B2
Penguin Books (N.Z.) Ltd, 182–190 Wairau Road,
Auckland 10, New Zealand

Penguin Books Ltd, Registered Offices:
Harmondsworth, Middlesex, England

First published by Topaz, an imprint of Dutton Signet,
a member of Penguin Putnam Inc.

First Printing, February, 1998
10 9 8 7 6 5 4 3 2 1

For my sister,
Janice Kay Burford,
with love

And first, in the security bred of many harmless marriages, it had been forgotten that Love is no hot-house flower, but a wild plant, born of a wet night, born of an hour of sunshine; sprung from wild seed, blown along the road by a wild wind. A wild plant that, when it blooms by chance within the hedge of our gardens, we call a flower; and when it blooms outside we call a weed; but, flower or weed, whose scent and colour are always wild!

—John Galsworthy,
The Man of Property

The de Périgeaux Family

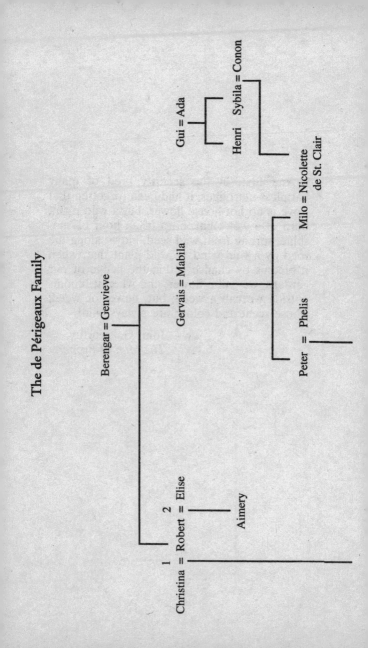

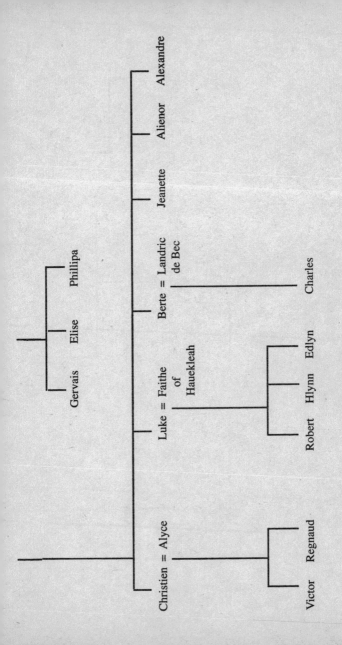

Chapter 1

"Alex, who is that woman? Do you see how she's looking at you?"

"Which one, Faithe? Is she pretty?" Alexandre de Périgeaux shielded his eyes against the morning sun and scanned the sizable crowd assembled in the courtyard of the Tour de Rouen, grateful for some diversion from such a long wait in such hellish heat.

Faithe of Hauekleah, Alex's sister by marriage, shifted the babe on her shoulder and cocked an eyebrow. "I thought all women were pretty," she teased, flinging his own, oft-repeated words back at him, "if you but looked at them from the right angle."

"Cheeky wench. So they are." Alex studied the multitude of lords and ladies—the flower of Norman aristocracy—garbed in peacock-hued finery, fanning themselves restlessly as they anticipated the upcoming ceremony. Some had gravitated around a *jongleur* accompanying himself on lute, who serenaded them with a long and lyrical *chanson* about knights going in search of the Holy Grail. At the outskirts, clerics chattered in small groups, like clusters of blackbirds.

"She's wearing white," Faithe offered. "An exquisite silken tunic."

"No lady in white is looking this way." Worse luck.

A little harmless flirtation—and perhaps a bit more, if the fates favored him—was just what he needed to adjust his bodily humors, unbalanced by having re-crossed the English Channel for the first time in seven years. It should gladden his heart to stand on Frankish soil, the soil that had bred and nurtured him, after so long an absence. And it wasn't as if he was alone here, his brother's family having journeyed with him from their Cambridgeshire farmstead for this great occasion. Yet he missed England—missed it terribly—and had from the moment he'd left its shore.

Perhaps he should have stayed there. Having little tolerance for court life and less for standing about waiting, Alex wondered how he would bear up under the full week of royal celebration to come.

Faithe peered into the crowd. "She must have turned back round. Her mantle is blue."

"Little help there." The courtyard was a sea of blue-cloaked backs.

Faithe patted the squirmy infant Edlyn. "She turned and stared at you, with the most curious expression. I thought she must know you."

"There you are, brother!" Luke of Hauekleah greeted Alex with a slap on the back that he felt in his bones. "Do you never tire of flirting with my wife?"

"Never. You'd best stop wandering from her side, lest I resolve to steal her from you."

Faithe rolled her eyes. Luke guffawed. Even five-year-old Robert, perched high on his father's shoulders, smirked at the familiar empty threat. Luke and Faithe's middle child, Hlynn, oblivious to the adult banter, gripped her father's hand and sucked her thumb as she gazed with wonderment at the grand noblemen and their ladies milling in the courtyard. The three children were identical in coloring, with their Saxon mother's creamy skin and calm hazel eyes, and the distinctive blue-black hair that Luke shared with Alex and the rest of their swarthy kin.

"Steal her from me, eh?" Luke exchanged an amused but softly intimate look with his wife. "You'd have to kill me first. And I don't die easily."

"The Black Dragon didn't," Alex conceded. "But the Cambridgeshire farmer standing in front of me hasn't defended himself with a weapon in years. I, on the other hand"—he patted the hilt of his broadsword, sheathed on the belt buckled over his ankle-length ceremonial overtunic—"have been honing my skill in the service of our liege for fully a decade now."

"Almost a decade," Luke corrected with an ostentatious yawn. That was true. The de Périgeaux brothers, knights of Aquitaine, had been recruited by William, Duke of Normandy, when Alex was seventeen and Luke four-and-twenty, which would be but nine years ago. They both served their Norman master—Alex with his sword and Luke with his crossbow—through the conquest of England and the duke's ascension to the throne of that kingdom. But whereas Luke had eagerly traded his crossbow for Hauekleah, Alex continued to reject King William's offer of honorable dismissal and an English estate in recompense for his service—to the puzzlement of all, save perhaps for Luke and Faithe.

"*Almost* a decade then," Alex said. "And before that, I did naught but study the arts of war—I was swinging a sword when I was smaller than Robert here. So I daresay I could take you, brother. And then I'd have your lady wife all to myself." He bowed with mock formality in Faithe's direction.

"Let's settle this now." Grinning, Luke handed Hlynn to her mother and bent over to lift his son down. "Like men—with our fists."

"Suits me." Alex slammed his fist in his brother's stomach as he was rising, earning him an answering blow that stole his breath, if only for a moment. The two men grappled in their long, elegant tunics, laughing breathlessly, as people turned to watch and the children rooted loudly for their father.

"Stop that!" A furious yank on his hair made Alex turn to find his sister, Berte, scowling at her younger brothers and casting anxious glances toward their audience. A formidable personage, Berte had inherited the de Périgeaux height, making her half a head taller than her round and balding husband, Baron Landric de Bec. He hovered behind her, clucking in sympathy with her outrage. "Have you two no sense of decorum whatsoever?" she demanded.

"Nay," Alex answered.

"None," his brother concurred.

" 'Tis my fault, my lady." Faithe looked as if she were fighting a smile. "I should have stopped them."

Berte shook her head, her expression doleful. "One may as well try to stop a raging storm. These two have always done just exactly as they please, and living on that barbaric island seems only to have made it worse."

"Quite so," Landric agreed.

Faithe raised an eyebrow at the slur to her homeland, but wisely kept her counsel.

"Now everyone is staring," Berte fretted. Alex followed her mortified gaze toward the onlookers, chuckling as they disbanded.

One figure, a woman, stood perfectly still amidst the swirls of multicolored silk, the ripple of veils and glint of jewels. Pale and slender, as unreal as a church statue carved of pearly marble, she met his eyes across the courtyard. . . .

Across the years, for she'd looked much the same the first time his gaze had fallen upon her nine long summers ago. Her beauty had a transfixing harmony to it—high, wide cheekbones, sharp little chin, willowy throat. She'd worn white that day, too, although then her hair had flowed in a gleaming flaxen stream down her back. Today it was plaited in two braids over which a veil of gossamer sendal silk trembled in the sultry breeze. Then, as now, her sea-green eyes were large and quiet and intent.

"That's her," Faithe said. "The woman in white. The one I told you about."

From the corner of his eye, Alex saw Luke turn toward the woman in question. Recognizing her instantly, he shot an apprehensive glance toward Alex.

Faithe noticed this. "You do know each other."

"She's Nicolette de St. Clair." Alex fingered the worst of his scars from that misbegotten summer, a puckered little rivulet that snaked down his forehead, carving a small bare patch through his right eyebrow. "My cousin's wife."

He definitely should have stayed in England.

As he watched, the lady Nicolette smiled tentatively, eyes alert and wary. The civil thing would be to return her smile, but his maelstrom of conflicting emotions—shock at seeing her, loathing, yearning—so confounded him that all he could do was stare. Presently her expression began to waver uncertainly.

A fanfare of trumpets startled him. He glanced toward the sound and saw a procession of youths descending the steps of William's private chapel. A volley of cheers greeted them.

"They're coming!" Berte exclaimed. "The young knights."

"They're not knights yet," Luke pointed out.

Alex returned his attention to the lady Nicolette, only to find her turning away, eyes downcast, mouth tightly drawn.

"They soon will be," Berte said. "There's my Charles, third in line. Do you see him?"

"Aye," Luke said, frowning at the red-haired lad and his comrades. "God's eyes, how many are there?"

"Four-and-twenty altogether," Berte answered. "Come, we must follow them to the sporting field. That's where the dubbing is to take place."

Alex allowed himself to be swept along in a slow surge of humanity toward a field of mown grass on the right bank of the Robec, near where the small river fed into the Seine. Unable to wrest his thoughts from Nicolette, he searched the strolling horde for her as he walked, but didn't see her.

"I've never known so many young men to be dubbed at once," Faithe said as she herded her two older children along in front of her while cradling Edlyn. " 'Tisn't the English way."

" 'Tisn't generally the Norman way, either," Luke said, taking the baby from her to free her hands, "unless, as today, a man of unusually high rank is bestowing the honors. Few families would pass up the opportunity to have their sons knighted by a king."

The candidates for knighthood came to a halt at the base of a carpeted platform on which had been erected a long table displaying a dazzling array of armor and weapons—gifts from their families and invited guests. King William and his queen, Matilda—crowned and draped in ermine-trimmed mantles despite the heat—sat on grand thrones in the center of the dais, flanked by courtiers and high churchmen. To one side, a band of minstrels played a lively canso on flute, harp, and castanets.

Berte squinted into the crowd as it settled into position facing the platform, her rouged bottom lip caught between her teeth, rings glittering as she wrung her hands. "Where's Christien? I knew he'd be late."

"Merciful heavens," Landric muttered. "Christien."

The eldest of Alex's siblings, Christien had inherited the family's Périgeaux estate in its entirety upon their sire's death, prompting his landless younger brothers to leave the southern duchy of Aquitaine and take up arms for William in the hope of earning holdings elsewhere. Christien boasted many virtues of character, but punctuality was not among them—a potential complication today, inasmuch as he, along with Alex,

Luke, and of course, Landric, was sponsoring young Charles for knighthood, and was expected to participate in the rites to come.

"Don't trouble yourself, Berte," Alex soothed. "He traveled all the way from Aquitaine for this. He wouldn't miss it."

"Aye, but did you see how much he drank last night? He might still be abed."

"Not if Alyce has anything to say about it," Alex said. "She wouldn't let him sleep through his nephew's initiation into knighthood."

The music ceased. The audience quieted as the king rose to his feet.

"Find him," Berte ordered her husband in an agitated whisper.

Landric darted like a fat squirrel through the crowd as King William stepped forward to address his vassals. Having expected long-winded and tiresome preliminaries, Alex was relieved when, after a brief word of greeting, William gestured for the first candidate and his sponsors to ascend the platform.

Everyone watched in silence as the young man's male relatives outfitted him in his newly forged mail and presented him with his sword. Then the king delivered the *colée*—the ritual open-handed slap that transformed its recipient from callow youth to chevalier. Unfortunately for the chevalier in question, the *colée* knocked him off his feet, and he landed with a clank of armaments on his back. Crimson-faced, he allowed the king to pull him up.

When the second youth was summoned onto the dais, Berte began to mutter anxiously under her breath. "Charles is next. If his eldest uncle isn't up there with him, what will people think?"

Alex and Luke exchanged a look. Berte hadn't changed much in the years they'd been gone.

During the second lad's initiation, Berte frantically searched the onlookers, finally gasping in relief.

"There he is! He and Alyce and their two boys. Landric's found them." She returned her husband's wave. "Who is that with them? By the saint's bones! Is that Nicolette de St. Clair?"

Alex whipped around, tracing his sister's line of sight to a small group near the front of the crowd, by the platform. Landric pointed proudly toward Christien while Christien's wife, the lady Alyce, spoke into Lady Nicolette's ear. The two women had met when Nicolette came to Périgeaux nine years ago. He recalled that they'd become fast friends, but they couldn't have seen much of each other in recent years, what with Alyce living in Aquitaine and Nicolette up here in Normandy.

Whatever Alyce was saying made Nicolette smile— that cryptic half-smile that had always intrigued him so. Her air of mystery had enchanted him, drawing him to her like a bee to a tightly closed blossom full of promise—a promise never fulfilled.

The flesh around Berte's eyes tightened. "What is *she* doing here? Did Alyce ask her? I certainly didn't."

"Why not?" Alex asked. "After all, she's married to our cousin."

"Milo?" Berte plucked at her wimple. "He's the reason I didn't ask her—or them, rather. Hardly anyone invites them anywhere anymore, considering what's become of him."

"What do you mean?" Alex asked.

"You don't know?"

"I've heard naught of him since I left Périgeaux nine years ago."

"You never thought to write to him? You two were such good chums."

"I was trained to wield a sword, not scratch away with a quill like some soft-bellied monk."

"You could pay some clerk to do it."

"Berte," he ground out impatiently. "What did you mean? What's 'become of' Milo?"

His sister glanced around with feigned nonchalance and lowered her voice. "I'll tell you later—best not to air such matters here. Suffice it to say he declines what few invitations still come their way, and it's just as well. I hear he hasn't set foot outside Peverell Castle in two or three years. She's never seen, either, since it would hardly do for her to go larking about on her own. From what I hear, she spends all her time writing those long, tiresome poems about ancient battles and tragic lovers—a shameful occupation for a girl of her breeding."

"Then what do you suppose she's doing here today?"

"I can't begin to imagine. And I must say I'm surprised to find her showing up here unescorted. Not like her to ignore propriety—not like her at all." Returning her attention to the dais, Berte gasped and shoved Alex toward the stage. "It's Charles's turn! Go! You, too, Luke. Go! Go!"

Banishing thoughts of Nicolette from his mind, Alex mounted the platform, along with Luke, Christien, Landric, and young Charles.

First, Lord Landric, as his son's primary sponsor, endowed him with a hauberk and gaiters of fine chain mail, which Alex and his brothers helped the boy to don over his gold-embroidered red tunic. The boy was flushed and sweating by the time Alex pulled the hauberk's mesh coif over his head. It took a strong young constitution to tolerate a full suit of mail in midsummer. At Berte's insistence, every one of the double-woven iron rings had been silvered, causing them to gleam like white fire in the bright sun. Alex turned from the sight, blinking. . . .

And saw her again, gazing directly at him from the front of the audience, as doe-eyed and motionless as before. She quickly looked away.

"Alex," Luke hissed as he buckled the lad's sword-belt around his waist. "The sword."

Quickly Alex crossed to the table and retrieved the broadsword he'd commissioned for Charles, the honor of giving it having been granted to him in light of his own renowned swordsmanship. The blade, of brilliant Poitou steel, shimmered in the sunlight. In the knob of the pearl-encrusted hilt could be seen a bit of dried blood of St. Romaine encased in transparent crystal. Alex handed the weapon to his nephew, who kissed the holy relic before sheathing it.

Alex watched Christien present his jeweled helmet and Luke his shield and lance, all too aware of Lady Nicolette's gaze upon him. His skin prickled beneath his clothes; his body felt oddly large and unwieldy.

He'd thought he would never see her again, nor had he wanted to. He'd never expected her to be here. According to Berte, no one had.

He wondered about Milo. Despite everything that had transpired that last, eventful summer in Périgeaux, Alex harbored no ill will toward his cousin. What happened wasn't his fault, not really. And he and Milo had always been, as Berte pointed out, the best of chums, the ten-year difference in their ages inconsequential—especially once Alex reached adolescence and could tag along with Milo and his mates as they hunted and caroused. Life was carefree and exhilarating and golden, and Milo was at the center of it all. Educated for Holy Orders as befitted a second son, but lacking the temperament for a religious vocation, Milo dedicated his considerable intellect to the pursuit of pleasure. Intensely charismatic, he possessed the striking de Périgeaux looks—the height, the raven hair—combined with a quick wit and an amiable disposition that earned him many friends.

Trumpets blared. Shaking off his memories, Alex joined the other sponsors as they stepped aside for the king. William approached the youth, who bowed his head. Fully armored and equipped, young Charles looked every bit the soldier awaiting battle. The last

Alex had seen him, before leaving for England, he'd been a small boy. Now, at sixteen, he was taller than his father, although Alex and Luke still towered over him.

The *colée* was swift and hard, but Charles remained standing, although he stumbled back a step or two. Cheers rose from the onlookers.

William embraced the novice knight. "Go in strength and courage, Sir Charles. Be of generous spirit and stout heart, and honor God and your sovereign with your faithful service."

"Heartfelt thanks, my liege," Charles recited, his voice on the edge of cracking. "May the lord God hear this oath of fealty, and may I serve and love both you and Him until my soul embraces the fountainhead of peace."

More cheers arose from the crowd. Alex clapped his nephew on the back. "Well done."

It took the remainder of the morning for all of the candidates to receive the *colée*. Then came the war-horses, four-and-twenty destriers beautifully groomed and harnessed, which the armored knights mounted simultaneously from running leaps—a feat that drew an elated roar from the crowd. The lads tilted at quintains and engaged in mock duels through the early afternoon, by which time Alex's old hip injury was throbbing like a drum. Generally it only troubled him on wet, chilly days. All this standing still must have aggravated it.

Almost worse was the grousing of his empty stomach. His gaze strayed frequently to the river's edge, where banquet tables had been arranged beneath a pink-and-purple-striped canopy. Savory aromas drifted toward him on the warm breeze, making his mouth water—yet still the games persisted. Only after two of the young knights had fainted dead away from the heat was it announced that the celebratory feast would now be served.

* * *

"I've asked Lady Nicolette to join us," Alyce announced to her husband and his siblings as they seated themselves at one of the long trestle tables beneath the canopy.

Pink-stained sunlight filtered through the striped cloth above their heads, suffusing Nicolette with a rosy glow; she might almost have been blushing. She *should* blush, Alex thought, at the prospect of facing him again.

"Lady Nicolette," Alyce said, "you've met my sons, Victor and Regnaud"—the well-trained boys bowed—"and I trust you know my sister by marriage, the baroness Berte de Bec, and her husband, Lord Landric."

Cordial greetings were exchanged.

"Do you remember my husband's brothers?" Alyce asked. "Luke and Alexandre. You met them in Périgeaux that summer you came—"

"I remember," Nicolette said, in a voice so soft Alex could barely hear her, her hands tightly clasped. Stiffly she inclined her head toward the two men in turn. "Sir Luke . . . Sir Alexandre."

"My lady," Luke responded with a small bow.

"My lady." Alex forced a polite smile, but she turned away too quickly to see it.

"And this," Alyce said, "is Luke's lady wife, Faithe of Hauekleah, and their children. . . ." She hesitated, clearly struggling to recall their names.

"That little devil"—Faithe nodded toward her son, picking bits of spiced bread out of his trencher and stuffing them into his mouth, something Alex was tempted to do himself—"is Robert." Faithe introduced Hlynn, propped up next to her with unfocused eyes and her thumb in her mouth, and the infant Edlyn, nursing at her mother's breast. Faithe had drawn her mantle over the babe, a gesture of modesty lost on Berte, who looked away in disgust.

Nicolette did not appear shocked. Indeed, she

smiled with seemingly genuine delight at the sight of the children and insisted on sitting between Hlynn and Robert—which placed her almost directly across the table from Alex. He hoped he wouldn't be forced to engage her in strained conversation.

She leaned close to Hlynn. "Tired?"

The child nodded, her eyes half-closed.

"Me, too. 'Twas a long ceremony—especially for a wee little girl like you."

"I'm a big girl," Hlynn said groggily without removing the thumb.

Nicolette smiled. "My apologies, Lady Hlynn. Are you as hungry as your brother?"

Hlynn shook her head. Her mother said, "I brought some bread and fed it to the children a while ago. Luke warned me it might be a long and trying morning."

"I wish someone had warned me," Nicolette said. Did Alex just imagine it, or did she glance uneasily in his direction? Returning her attention to Hlynn, she whispered conspiratorially, "I would have tucked some bread into my sleeve if I'd known."

Hlynn giggled drowsily, again without extracting her thumb.

The obvious joy Nicolette took in Hlynn came as a surprise to Alex. He wouldn't have thought her the nurturing sort, yet she displayed a warmth and ease with the little girl that couldn't have been feigned. Seeing her like this reminded Alex that there were two Nicolettes, or used to be—the cool, formal public Nicolette, well trained in decorum by her mother, and, hidden beneath that facade, the spirited young woman to whom he'd once lost his heart. Unfortunately, her more decorous—and calculating—side, incapable of real human affection, seemed to be dominant.

Robert paused in his methodical decimation of his trencher. "Will we eat soon?"

"That one's always hungry," Faithe explained, "regardless of when he last ate."

"Alas, we must all strive for patience," Nicolette counseled the boy. "King William hosts grand and wonderful banquets—often twenty courses or more—"

"Twenty?" Robert said excitedly.

"But there are some matters of ceremony to attend to first." She nodded toward the high table, at which the king and queen sat with the four-and-twenty newly dubbed knights. The king's banquet master made a show of presenting an ornate salt dish to the royal couple and their guests.

Robert sighed. "Now can we eat?"

"Patience," Nicolette murmured as the banquet master summoned the pantler, who unwrapped a saffron-hued loaf from its *portpayne* of fringed cloth, sliced its upper crust, and presented it to the king. Next came the laverers, who made the rounds from table to table with their basins of herb-scented water, embroidered towels looped over their arms.

Hlynn, clearly struggling to keep her eyes open, swayed slightly on her bench. She tried to lean on her mother, but the nursing baby was in the way. "Wait until Edlyn's gotten all the milk she wants," Faithe instructed the sleepy child, "and then you may put your head in my lap."

"She's overdue for her nap," Luke explained to the company at large.

"I've got a perfectly good lap that's going to waste," Nicolette told Hlynn, adding, to Faithe, "If your mama doesn't mind."

Faithe hesitated fractionally, then smiled. "Not at all. Hlynn, would you like to—"

But Hlynn was already curling up contentedly on her new friend's lap, thumb firmly in place. Robert, meanwhile, rested his weight on Nicolette as he nibbled his trencher into nothingness.

"Do children always take to you so readily?" Faithe asked her.

"I like them. I think they sense that." Nicolette's smile struck Alex as sad.

"A pity you never had any children of your own," Berte said.

The smile vanished. "Aye, well . . . we were not so blessed."

"Not yet," Berte said. "But you're not too old to quit trying—not quite. How old are you—thirty? A bit older, perhaps?"

Nicolette met the older woman's gaze impassively. "Eight-and-twenty, my lady. And yourself?"

Reddening slightly, Berte ignored both the question and Alex's little huff of spontaneous laughter. Nicolette was never easily cowed, a trait he couldn't help but grudgingly admire. "Well, then." Berte nodded resolutely. "There's plenty of time. You haven't given up hope, I trust."

Alex and Luke exchanged a look. Their sister could be monstrously bothersome with all her probing and prying.

Nicolette merely lowered her gaze to the sleeping child in her lap, threading her fingers through the little girl's sweat-dampened black hair. Alex speculated on her thoughts: After nine barren years of marriage, a child now would be nothing short of miraculous.

"Perhaps," Berte counseled, in unctuously maternal tones, "if you spent less time at that writing desk of yours, and concentrated on more feminine pursuits—needlework, say—'twould realign your womanly aspects, and facilitate the planting of a babe."

With an incredulous little cock of her head, Nicolette said, "Are you suggesting that I'm childless because I compose verses?"

Berte smiled indulgently. " 'Tis a man's avocation, is it not, my dear? I'm sure they're much cleverer at it than a mere woman could hope to be, even one with such a . . . plethora of education as yourself. And for a woman to engage in men's work causes an imbalance in the vital fluids that regulate"—she glanced awkwardly at the men and lowered her voice—"generative matters."

Nicolette's mouth twitched, just slightly. "What a remarkable theory. I shall take it under advisement."

Berte nodded with self-satisfaction. "Do. No doubt my cousin, your lord husband, will be most grateful to see you set aside your parchment and quill."

Alex wondered if there might not be some truth in that, recalling his own uneasiness with Nicolette's learning, the product of a rigorous convent education. Granted, like most young knights, he'd been relatively unschooled, incapable of reading or writing anything but his own name. Although Nicolette's intellect—and her facility with verse—had impressed him immeasurably, his admiration had been tainted with a vague sense of inadequacy. Milo, on the other hand, was a man of letters, having been brought up at the Abbey at Aurillac. He'd always seemed to enjoy Nicolette's erudite perspective on things, and they shared an interest in literature and philosophy—disciplines of which Alex was largely ignorant, having a smattering of military history and little else. Perhaps Milo appreciated his wife's mind as much now as he did back in Périgeaux. Or perhaps he'd grown weary of her epic verses, and longed for a simple woman with a fertile belly.

"Speaking of Milo," Berte said silkily, "I must say I find it odd that he allowed you to travel from St. Clair all by yourself." Eliciting no response from that, she said, "You did come here alone, did you not?"

"Nay, my lady," Nicolette responded with a placid smile, and offered no further elaboration, to Berte's evident frustration. The fates conspired to Nicolette's advantage, for at that moment a laverer came up behind her and offered his basin. Nicolette turned toward him, rolling back the trailing sleeves of her tunic, then stilled, her gaze on something beyond their canopied enclosure—two men walking toward them from the direction of the palace.

Berte craned her neck; her jaw dropped. "Is that—?" She squinted hard. "Blessed Mary. It is."

Alex focused on the two men as they advanced slowly—excruciatingly slowly—across the cropped lawn. The dark-haired fellow was tall and burly, with a massive chest and limbs like tree trunks. He supported his gray-haired companion, almost as tall, but gaunt and stooped over a cane, his legs quavering as he walked. Alex recognized the first man, but couldn't place the older fellow until he looked up.

"Sweet Jesus," Alex whispered when he saw the familiar face.

Chapter 2

Alex glanced at Luke, who returned his stunned expression. At six-and-thirty, their cousin Milo looked as frail and sickly as an old man.

Nicolette watched her husband's unsteady gait with anxious eyes. Alex suspected that she would go to him, did she not have a sleeping child on her lap. Rising, he said, "Perhaps I can be of some—"

"Nay." Nicolette waved him back down without wresting her gaze from Milo. "He wouldn't want your help—'twould shame him. Gaspar and I are the only ones he'll let touch him."

Ignored by her, the laverer moved on.

"He told me he was going to stay inside, where it's cool," she murmured.

"Forgive me, my lady," Berte said, "but 'twas my impression that your husband . . . well, that he's . . . not fit for travel."

"Nay," Nicolette said distractedly, gazing at Milo, who raised a hand when he spied her. "He's not. But he insisted on coming here. I couldn't talk him out of it. He wouldn't even listen to Gaspar."

Alyce reached over to touch Nicolette's hand. "I wouldn't have asked you if I'd known how ill he is."

Nicolette shook her head wearily. " 'Twould have made no difference. He was determined to come even before we received your invitation. I don't know why—he's never cared much for court functions."

"Curious," Berte muttered.

When the two men were under the canopy, Milo shook Gaspar off and made a show of walking up to the table with only his cane for assistance. The closer he got, the clearer it became that something was dreadfully wrong with him. His emaciation was evident not only from the way his tunic hung on his skeletal frame, but from his face. Milo had always been handsome, but in a singular, even odd, sort of way, his prominent eyes and nose and mouth all vying for attention. Now those oversize features looked almost grotesque, cloaked as they were in shrunken, yellowish skin that sprouted patches of broken veins. His overgrown hair was lank and on its way to going completely gray.

Milo grinned when he saw Alex, and came directly to him, his free arm held wide, while Gaspar hovered solicitously. "I heard you'd be here," he said, his voice as deep as always, but indistinct, as if he'd just awakened, or was in his cups. "Welcome to Normandy, cousin."

Rising, Alex returned Milo's embrace with great care. He felt as if he'd shatter in a heap of bones from the slightest pressure. The sweet, musty odor of old wine filled his nostrils. " 'Tis . . . good to see you, Milo."

"Liar." Milo backed off, his smile touched with gravity now. "I'm a *gargoille*. Children run when they see me."

Quietly Alex said, " 'Tis always good to see you, cousin. I'm only sorry it's been so long."

"As am I."

Alex introduced Milo to Faithe and the children as he circled the table to greet Luke. "I'll sit here, right across from Alex," he informed Gaspar, who helped him struggle onto the bench. "The better to catch up on old times."

When Milo instructed Gaspar to sit next to him,

Berte cleared her throat. "Servants are being fed in the palace kitchen."

Gaspar stared stonily ahead, his meaty hands curling into fists and then slowly releasing.

"Cousin Berte." Milo executed a small, mocking bow, his lips stretched over his teeth in what might have been either a smile or a grimace. "As imperious as ever, I see."

Berte scanned the faces of her dinner companions, as if trying to discern whether she'd been insulted.

Nicolette spoke up. "Gaspar is . . . more a retainer, my lady. He's Peverell Castle's most important man-at-arms. My husband relies on him—"

"I know who he is." Berte fiddled with her bracelets, turning them to display their jewels to best effect. "And, as I said, I'm sure they can find something for him to eat in the—"

"Gaspar stays with me," Milo said. "I need him." His eyes lit with devilment. "Unless, when it's time for me to visit the privy, you'd care to assist me yourself."

Berte gulped air, her face flooding with hot color. Landric coughed behind his hand. Alex suspected that he did not completely share in his wife's outrage. She offered no further protest, and the object of her scorn coolly took his seat.

Gaspar le Taureau looked much the same as ever. Although he and Milo were about the same age, one would never know it. His tanned face was unlined, and his dark hair, shorn close to the scalp, devoid of gray. As brawny as the bull for which he had been named, he carried himself with a sense of military readiness, radiating great power held in check. Nevertheless, Alex remembered him as an affable fellow, a man whom other men respected for his brute strength, but genuinely liked as well.

Gaspar's gaze briefly skimmed every face at the table before settling on Alex. "You were a lean young whelp last I saw you, Sir Alex. Put on some height, you have. Grown some shoulders, too, from the looks of you." He grinned. "Soldiering can make a man out of anyone, it seems."

Alex shook his head ruefully. "You haven't changed a bit, Gaspar."

The big man regarded him for a moment, his smile fixed. "Yes, I have."

Milo lifted the silver goblet in front of him, frowning to find it empty. He grabbed that of his wife, sitting next to him, but it was empty as well. "Wench!" he called to a passing servant girl. "Bring me some wine."

"I'm terribly sorry, milord, but I can't," the girl replied, pointing toward the king's cup-bearer, filling an ornamental gold beaker from a barrel near the high table. "It hasn't been tested yet."

" 'Twill be served soon," Nicolette assured him softly.

"Did I ask you?" Milo demanded in a burst of snarling wrath. "I know damn well 'twill be served soon. I want it now!" All around them, conversations ceased. The only sound at their table came from Hlynn, who let out a somnolent little growl at having been disturbed. Nicolette, placidly ignoring her husband's outburst, quieted the child by stroking her hair and whispering soothing words.

Gaspar laid a hand on his master's shoulder and murmured, "Calm yourself, milord."

"I will be calm," Milo said between clenched teeth, "when I am shown the courtesy due any guest who makes a simple request—"

"I'll take care of it." Picking up his master's goblet, Gaspar set off in the direction of the wine barrel.

A ponderous silence ensued, terminated to the relief of all when Alyce said to Nicolette, "He seems an agreeable sort, your Gaspar."

"He is that. And . . . well, he's indispensable."

"So I understand," Berte put in. "They tell me he exercises quite a firm command over Peverell. Does it

never trouble you to have a man of such . . . humble
origins acting as castellan in your husband's stead?"

With a sneer, Milo turned to Landric. "Tell me, old
fellow, does it never trouble *you* to have a wife who's
got bigger ballocks than—"

"We're very grateful to Gaspar," Nicolette said
quickly, darting a warning glance toward her husband.
Milo looked away pointedly, as if the conversation
bored him. "He's been of immense help to us."

"Yes," Berte said, pinning the dissipated Milo with
her wintry glare, "I imagine he has. I think it only fair
to warn you, though, that people do talk. You know
what they call this 'indispensable' Gaspar of yours,
don't you?"

Nicolette met Berte's gaze squarely. "Yes, I know."

"The apothecary castellan." With a furtive glance
toward Gaspar, muscling the cup-bearer aside to fill
the silver goblet from the untested barrel, Berte confided to all, "He's merchant stock. He grew up over
a shop in St. Clair."

"That's right," Nicolette replied matter-of-factly.
"He apprenticed as an apothecary to his widowed
mother, but his heart wasn't in the trade. When she
died, he sold the shop and hired on as one of my
uncle's men-at-arms."

"Ah, yes. Henri de St. Clair—Peverell's old castellan.
I remember him well. What was he thinking, to take
on a man with no military training?"

"I gather Uncle Henri was impressed with Gaspar's
size and fighting skills. He was famous in St. Clair for
his prowess with his fists. Also, his mother had taught
him to read and write Latin—it's a rare soldier who
can read. Uncle's instincts were excellent. Gaspar has
proven himself a leader among his men."

"He's coming," Alyce whispered.

Silence fell over the table as Gaspar returned and
set the goblet, now full, before his master. "Here you

go, milord. They tell me it's the finest Bordeaux has to offer."

Milo lifted the goblet with a palsied hand and swiftly gulped its contents down. Handing it back to Gaspar, he said, "Be a good fellow and fill that up again."

The banquet's fourteenth course, in honor of the new knights, was a giant warhorse sculpted of marzipan and spun sugar, which servants paraded between the rows of tables while myriad jugglers tossed lit torches into the air. Alex half-expected the canopy to burst into flame at any moment, and was relieved when the spectacle came to an end and the horse was chopped up and served.

Milo refused any of the ludicrous confection, having consumed nothing but wine all afternoon—goblet after goblet of it. Upon draining his own goblet, he would reach for his wife's and drink that, an appropriation that had the look of longstanding habit to it. His head wobbled slightly on his shoulders; his voice grew thick and slurred. The drunker he got, the more fixated he became on Alex, telling him over and over again how pleased he was to see him, and that they must talk—just the two of them—soon.

King William and Queen Matilda, evidently having limited taste for marzipan horses, chose this opportunity to visit with some of their vassals, beginning with Alex's table.

"I'm so glad you could come, Lady Nicolette," said the queen after the royal couple had been formally greeted—with Berte fawning obsequiously—and taken their seats. "I wanted to thank you in person for doing such a splendid job on that poem." To the others she explained, "I had asked her ladyship for a piece about the search for the Grail—something a jongleur could put to music and play for us today, a sort of tribute

to the young knights. 'Twas performed in the courtyard before the ceremony. Did anyone hear it?"

"I did!" Berte piped up. " 'Twas exquisite, Highness. What an inspired subject. The audience was
captivated."

Luke caught Alex's eye and shook his head, smiling.

" 'Twas the verse itself that so enchanted them, I
think," Matilda said.

"I was going to say that," Berte claimed. "A triumph. But then, my lady cousin is so clever with
words, is she not?"

"How kind of you." Nicolette seemed to be stifling
a smile. "Yet, recently," she confided to the queen,
"I've begun wondering if all the time I spend at my
writing desk isn't disrupting my vital humors."

"Who put such rubbish into your head?" The queen
laughed dismissively, and the others followed suit—
including Berte, looking decidedly ill at ease. "Your
talent is a gift from God, and I'm grateful to Him for
bestowing it on you." She sighed. "Would that you
were a man. Then I could bring you to England as a
court poet."

Alex saw Nicolette's eyes light briefly at that prospect, and then dim. Little wonder it seemed so entic-
ing, considering what marriage to Milo must be like.

" 'Twouldn't do, I'm afraid," the king pronounced.
"The English would regard me as even more of an
eccentric foreigner if I established a lady bard in my
court. I want them to accept me, not think me mad."

"You look more like an Englishman every day, my
liege," Alex commented. "Your hair is almost as long
as mine now." Emulating his conquered countrymen,
Alex had allowed his hair to grow out of its severe
Norman cut, but it was not yet long enough to bind
into a queue, as Luke wore his.

William grinned. " 'Twas your idea, was it not?" To
the rest, he explained, "Sir Alex thinks 'twill endear
me to my English subjects if I look like one of them."

"Did you convince him to grow the beard as well?" Queen Matilda inquired archly.

"That I did not, my lady. 'Twas your lord husband's own misguided notion, that."

"She doesn't care for how it feels against her face," the king announced.

"My lord!" Matilda scolded.

Her husband blinked. "Is that not what you said?"

She stared him down with a rigid lack of expression that spoke more eloquently than words. He cleared his throat and muttered an apology—the great William the Conqueror reduced by a diminutive female to a groveling penitent.

Yet one more reminder of how wise Alex was to hold out against the dubious blessing of marriage.

"Alex de Périgeaux," William said, "is the most anglicized of all the knights in my private retinue, yet he steadfastly refuses to let me grant him an English estate. I've offered him one in Cambridge, near his brother's, but he wants no part of it."

" 'Twould mean being released from your service," Alex said.

The queen frowned in puzzlement. "But you've earned that release. My lord husband tells me you're among his finest swordsmen. Aren't you the one they call the White Wolf, for the silence with which you approach your prey?"

"They call him the Lone Wolf now," Luke taunted. "For his refusal to marry and settle down."

Nicolette looked up from the chunk of marzipan she was breaking up and feeding to Hlynn, who'd awakened.

"What quarrel do you have with the state of matrimony?" the queen asked him.

Alex wished the conversation hadn't followed this particular curve in the road—especially with Nicolette present. "None in theory, my lady. 'Tis a holy institution, and I've the greatest reverence for it."

Luke choked on his wine. Faithe nuzzled baby Edlyn in an effort to hide her smirk.

Her eyes sparking with amusement, Matilda said, "Your avowal rings hollow, Sir Alex. Tell me, is it women you object to?"

Chuckling, Luke said, "Alex has never met a woman he objected to."

Milo laughed uproariously at this. With some measure of discomfort, Alex noticed Nicolette quickly drop her gaze.

"Is it children, then?" the queen persisted. "Do you not care to sire offspring?"

" 'Tis a task I can't say I'm eager to face."

"Task!" King William exclaimed, to much laughter from the men. "The production of children is, indeed, a task for women—the curse of Eve, you know. But for men it's, well . . ." He cast a careful glance toward his wife. "Not a task."

"Until the children are born," Alex said, aware of Milo studying him purposefully as he drained yet another goblet of wine.

"You don't care for children?" Matilda asked.

Alex shrugged. "I don't despise them, but nor do I seek out their company. I find them . . . an irritation."

Faithe laughed. "Then why, pray, do you come laden with gifts for your nieces and nephew whenever you come to call at Hauekleah?"

Alex grimaced. " 'Tis but a sop so they'll leave me in peace."

"If that be so," Luke said, "how come you to spend all that time teaching Robert to hunt small game?"

"He's good with the dogs," Alex grumbled.

"You told me I'm too easy with them!" the boy protested. "You always handle them yourself."

Alex glared at his nephew with mock ferocity, his ears filling with yet more laughter at his expense.

"Are you truly a lone wolf, Sir Alex?" Queen Matilda asked quietly. "Do you never ache for home and hearth, as the rest of us do? Do you never hunger for a pair of warm, familiar arms? Never long to have a son of your own to take hunting?"

In the silence that followed this soft challenge, Alex fancied that he could hear his own blood coursing through his head. Everyone was staring at him, including Nicolette. Why hadn't he stayed in England?

"I swore an oath of fealty, my lady queen," he replied soberly—not a complete answer, but the only one he was willing to offer. "An oath to God and your husband, on this very sword." He clasped the hilt of the broadsword sheathed at his side, which contained a lock of hair of St. Augustine of Canterbury— a proper holy artifact for a man with such a fondness for England. "I swore to serve my sovereign until the day I passed from this world."

"Or until I chose to dismiss you," William said.

"That wasn't part of my oath."

The king smiled. "That damned soldier's honor of yours means everything to you, doesn't it?"

"An oath is an oath."

"You vowed to obey me. I could order you to leave my service, and you'd be obliged to do it."

" 'Twould fill me with melancholy, Your Highness." Alex was proud to be part of the retinue of battle-tested, fiercely loyal men whom the king considered not just his finest knights, but his closest friends.

"I know it," William replied thoughtfully. " 'Tis why I can't bring myself to do it. That," he added, grinning, "and your skill with the steel. There will always be room for a swordsman of your caliber in my corps. You may continue in my service."

"I'm relieved to hear it, sire."

"After Christmastide."

Blood thudded in Alex's brain again. Someone snickered. "After Christmastide?"

"You hardly ever take leave," William said, "and when you do, 'tis for but a week, a fortnight at most.

I hereby order you—and by that precious oath of yours, you must obey—to withdraw from my service until . . ." He waved a hand absently as he pondered the precise parameters of Alex's furlough. His queen whispered in his ear and he perked up. "Until the first day of the year of our Lord one thousand seventy-four."

"But that's . . ." Alex calculated swiftly on his fingers. "That's six months, sire! You're granting me six months' leave?"

"Why, yes." King William looked inordinately pleased with himself. "I suppose I am. Mind you put the time to good use."

"How the devil am I—" Alex shook his head in frustration. "How am I supposed to . . . keep myself occupied for half a year?"

The king raised his arms in a grand and meaningless gesture. "Take up hawking. Learn to play the gigue."

"What the devil is a gigue?"

" 'Tis a sort of . . ." William drew a shape in the air that put Alex in mind of a voluptuous female. "Stringed instrument."

"Long and slender," the queen elaborated.

"And it makes a most mellifluous sound," Berte put in. "You really ought to heed His Highness and try your hand at—"

"Yes, fine," Alex gritted out, quite overwhelmed. "I shall take the . . . what is it?"

"Gigue," Luke offered, snickering.

"Gigue . . . under serious consideration." He drew in a deep, pacifying breath. "Many thanks for the suggestion, Highness."

"Not at all!" Beaming, William rose, offering a hand to his queen. "We've tarried here longer than we ought to have, my plum. The next course is about to be served, and if I'm not mistaken, 'tis a fish jelly. Your favorite."

"Ah." Beaming in anticipation, the queen leapt to her feet. "Mustn't miss that."

"Why so melancholic?" Milo inquired blearily after the royal couple had hastened back to the high table to savor their fish jellies while minstrels pounded their drums and rang their bells.

"I'm not melancholic, merely" —Alex shook his head at the impossibility of the situation— "perplexed as to what I'm supposed to do with myself for the next six months."

Milo's smile struck Alex as almost sly. "Perhaps I can be of some assistance there."

"What do you mean?"

Milo lifted his wife's goblet to his mouth, spilling a fair measure of wine down his chin. "Blast!" Wiping his chin with his tunic sleeve, he said, "We must talk. Just the two of us."

"Yes, you've been saying that."

"Have I?" Milo frowned and shook his head. "Can't recall . . ."

Nicolette and Gaspar exchanged a glance.

"Yes, well, you know . . ." His head quivering, Milo slid his gaze first toward his wife, and then Gaspar. "Just the two of us. Catch up on old times."

"Very well," Alex said carefully.

"That sounds right jolly," Gaspar said, "but as for now, milord, I think you'd best let me take you inside for a little nap. The heat and all . . ."

Milo did not acknowledge the cordial summons. "Come to my chamber at compline," he implored Alex. "We'll take a walk along the Seine and watch the sun set over the water."

A walk along the Seine? Thinking it unlikely Milo would be up to such an outing, Alex nevertheless agreed to meet him. Gaspar and Nicolette flanked Milo and gently urged him up from the bench.

"They gave us the worst chamber in the whole cursed keep," Milo griped as his wife and retainer began leading him away. "Dismal little cell at the top of the north tower. All those stairs . . . damn their eyes . . ."

"Well!" Berte huffed when the three were out of earshot. "Have you ever in your life—"

"I need to stretch my legs." Alex stood abruptly.

"As it happens, so do I." Rising, Luke asked his wife, his gaze flicking almost imperceptibly toward Berte, "Will you be all right here alone for a bit?"

Faithe regarded him balefully. "For a bit."

Alex and Luke strolled upstream along the bank of the Robec until the babble of music and conversation from beneath the canopy faded into blessed silence. Pausing at a curve in the river, Alex picked up a rock and skipped it across the water. His brother followed suit. They occupied themselves in this manner until Luke said, "Rather a nasty surprise, eh? Finding the lady Nicolette here."

Alex shrugged as he inspected the stones at his feet, looking for one of just the right shape. "Life is mad. One deals with it."

"So you've said many times. I've long envied you your phlegmatic temperament. But can you really be so unmoved by the reappearance of a lady who once brought such misery down on your head?"

Alex flung two more rocks, his aim so poor that they sank ignominiously. "I had been rather enjoying this peace and quiet. Must we fill the air with conversation?"

Luke smiled crookedly. By wordless consensus, they continued on.

Some distance farther upstream, half hidden by an overgrowth of wild shrubbery, they stumbled upon an abandoned longship. Delighted with their find, they whipped off their confining overtunics and investigated the dilapidated boat like boys, leaping from bench to bench and searching through debris in the musty, low-ceilinged cabin until they wearied of stooping over. All they found were bits of rope and the occasional shard from a broken barrel, the vessel having long ago been stripped of oars, mast, sail, and whatever goods it might have contained.

Having explored as much as he cared to, Alex picked the sturdiest looking of the oarsmen's benches and lay on his back to contemplate the clouds scudding across the azure sky. Luke sat cross-legged on the bench next to his, took out his little knife and the piece of wood he was currently carving—which was to be a crucifix for Hlynn, if Alex wasn't mistaken—and bent his head to his work.

" 'Tis the worst case of wine sickness I've ever seen," Alex said, breaking the silence he'd requested.

"Aye, he can barely walk."

"Why do you suppose he came here?"

Luke kept his gaze fixed on the little chunk of wood, which he sculpted with great precision. "I should think he made that fairly obvious."

Alex just looked at him.

"He came here because of you. He heard you'd be here, and he wanted to see you."

In his mind's eye, Alex conjured up images—some dreamlike, some nightmarish—of that fateful summer in Périgeaux. "Why?" he asked with a vague sense of dread.

Luke rubbed his thumb thoughtfully over his handiwork, then raised his eyes to his brother. "That might be worth finding out."

Chapter 3

Alex couldn't shake his sense of disquiet as he climbed the narrow, winding stairwell within the ducal castle's north tower. He fisted his hand to rap on the oaken door at the top of the stairs, but muffled voices from within made him hesitate. Drawing on his uncanny hearing—as keen as any wolf's, and a valuable asset in the field—he concentrated on making out the words.

"Eat some of this—please." A woman's voice: Nicolette.

"I don't want it! My stomach's in a twist. I told you that."

"Just a little, Milo. You haven't eaten in—"

"Because I haven't wanted to. Damn you, you meddlesome bitch, get that away from me."

Alex turned and had descended halfway back down the spiraling stone passage when a rattling crash—as of something hurled against the door—made him spin around. He paused only briefly before sprinting back up the stairs.

When he was within sight of the topmost door, it opened. He heard the whisper of silk as Lady Nicolette backed out of the chamber. "You'll have to clean it up yourself this time, Milo," she said, her voice quiet but strained.

"Send up a maidservant to clean it," came Milo's gravelly voice from within. "And tell her to bring some wine."

She shut the door and turned to lean back against it, eyes closed, her chest rising and falling slowly as she took several deep breaths. The warm torchlight burnished her face, igniting it with a golden luster. Alex frowned when he saw the brown spatters that marred the otherwise pristine white silk of her tunic.

Her eyes opened, and then grew wide. "Alex," she breathed.

"Hello, Nicki," he said quietly, his heart racing in his chest.

They regarded each other in charged silence. Presently Alex said, with a glance at the door, "Is this a bad time? I can come back later." He kept his voice low, lest Milo hear.

She didn't seem to hear him, absorbed as she was in studying his face. Her gaze lit on his jaw, his chin, his nose, and finally his forehead. The scars were so old and well healed as to be nearly invisible in the light of day, but in this torchlight, he knew, they would stand out in sharp relief.

He stood rooted to the spot as Nicki descended the stairs. She was fairly tall for a woman, and when she paused on the step above his, they were nearly eye to eye. She stood close enough for him to inhale her spellbinding scent—roses mingled with a faint spiciness and the lure of warm skin—so astonishingly familiar to him after all these years.

Her gaze riveted on his forehead, she brushed her fingertips over the most visible of his scars. He stiffened, and she quickly withdrew her hand.

After another moment of silence, she said softly, "Is the life of a soldier all you'd thought it would be?"

He took a deep breath. " 'Tis everything to me. 'Tis what I live for."

"But do you like it?"

"Do you like being married to Milo?"

She nodded slightly, as if conceding a point, but said, " 'Tisn't as bad as it may appear. He's never struck me, and I know he never would." With a glance at the door she added, in answer to his initial question, "This is no worse a time than any other. You can go in. He's been looking forward to your visit."

She swept down the stairwell in a fragrant rustle of silk, her shoulder grazing his as she passed.

Alex climbed once more to the doorway and paused, feeling the cool, airy touch of her fingertips on the snakelike little scar. *Is the life of a soldier all you'd thought it would be?* Could she really think these scars had been earned in battle? Didn't she know? Perhaps she was toying with him.

Alex knocked, and the door swung open. "Cousin!" Milo, supporting himself with his cane, embraced him and waved him into the room—not the "dismal cell" he'd made it out to be, but a pleasantly cozy little chamber, with a sizable window. A far cry from the straw pallet Alex, as a single man, had to make do with in the great hall, and nothing to complain about. The bedcurtains were tied back; a lady's night shift of white silk lay neatly folded on a red brocade pillow. The sight only served to further unsettle Alex.

Turning deliberately from the bed, he saw, strewn over the rushes near the door, a wooden tray, a white-bread trencher, and some slices of meat. A brown liquid—the meat's sauce, he supposed—was sprayed across the door and wall.

Noticing the direction of Alex's gaze, Milo said simply, "I wasn't hungry." He was slurring less, presumably having slept off his inebriation. Looping two empty wineskins over his shoulder, he motioned Alex to follow him out of the chamber. "We'll have our walk, but first I must get these filled."

"How do you expect to walk all that distance," Alex ventured carefully, "if you're sotted?"

"A damn sight better than I could if I were sober." Milo began his quavering descent of the twisting stairwell, one hand braced on the wall while the other clutched the cane.

Alex reached out to assist him, but hesitated, remembering what Nicki had said about his not wanting anyone but her and Gaspar to do so.

"It's all right," Milo said. "You can help me. A tumble down these stairs would finish me off for sure."

After stopping at the buttery to fill Milo's wineskins, the two men began their torturous trek toward the Seine, Alex staying close enough to his cousin to grab him if he fell. The setting sun cast a glaze of gold over the rooftops of Rouen and the trees fringing the path on which they walked. Insects hummed; birds giggled and sang. Alex smelled the river up ahead, an elusive undercurrent in the balmy breeze.

"Are you certain you want to do this?" Alex asked after his cousin had stumbled for the second time.

"Have to talk to you alone," Milo muttered breathlessly as he squeezed some more wine into his mouth. "Blasted castle is too damned crowded. Too many sets of ears."

"You must be used to that. Isn't Peverell crowded?"

"Soldiers mind their own business." The castellan of Peverell—at one time an appointed position, now hereditary—served as a sort of constable for William, maintaining an active force of fighting men at his ready disposal.

"The men-at-arms live in the castle with you?"

Milo shook his head. "Gaspar quarters them in barracks, but they have the run of the great hall during the day." He took another swallow of wine. "They keep to themselves, for the most part. 'Tis an adequate arrangement."

Alex squinted at the water in the distance, glittering as if it had been showered with gold dust. His chest hurt; he grieved in his heart over what had become of his cousin. "We've got six more days of feasting and tournaments ahead of us. Think you're up to it?"

"What do *you* think?" Milo sneered as he tottered along, grimacing.

"I think you must be half-mad to have come here at all."

Laughter rattled in Milo's bony chest. "After this evening, I daresay you'll think me a raving lunatic."

Alex was about to ask what he meant by that when Milo said, "Aye, I'll stay the entire week if need be."

"If need be?"

Milo offered his wineskin to Alex, who shook his head, having resolved to keep his wits about him this evening.

"Why did you come here, Milo?" Alex asked.

Shrugging, Milo avoided Alex's gaze. "Perhaps I merely thought it would be a pleasant diversion from Peverell. Have you ever been there?"

"You know I haven't." Alex was growing impatient with Milo's obvious stalling.

" 'Tis a gigantic old stone keep, twice the size of the Tour de Rouen, and ten times as drafty. A crypt for the living. Or," he added, indicating himself with a shuddering sweep of his hand, "the barely alive."

"A crypt, eh? Isn't that a bit . . . dramatic?"

"Wait till you see it."

"I've no plans to go there."

"Yes, well . . ." Milo squirted some more wine down his throat. "I suppose I haven't painted a particularly attractive picture of it, have I?"

"Hardly."

" 'Tis a dreadful old place, but at least it's mine— more or less."

"I assume Nicolette inherited it from her uncle?"

Milo sighed uneasily. "In a manner of speaking. Along with the castellany, which became my responsibility when the old man died, six weeks after our wedding." His gaze slid toward Alex. "I know what you're thinking. What should have been my duty has become Gaspar's."

"I make no judgments."

Milo smirked. "Lying cur. You think me an idle, wine-soaked knave. Duty is your lifeblood. Honor and allegiance and all that military trumpery. If you'd ended up master of Peverell, you'd have been castellan in more than name—you'd have seized the office with both hands and done right by it. Tell me I'm wrong."

The only way Alex could have ended up master of Peverell would have been by marrying Nicki. He wondered how much, if anything, she'd told her husband about the summer that had culminated in their betrothal.

"I'm sure you're happier at Peverell than you were in Périgeaux," Alex said in an effort to redirect their conversation to safer ground. "I know how much you resented living under Peter's roof." Unlike Alex and Luke, who'd committed themselves as youths to mastering the arts of war, their erudite cousin had cared no more for soldiering than for the Church. His destiny, he maintained, was to be the lord of a great manor, and he resented that the new system of inheritance gave his sire's entire estate to his older brother, Peter.

" 'Twas living under Peter's thumb that was so vexing. The burden of matrimony seemed a small price to pay for the privilege of becoming Lord of Peverell."

"You were so certain Henri had named her as his heir?"

"Her mother confided in me about the terms of Henri's will."

So Milo had married Nicki for Peverell, but still . . . Despite her shortcomings, she was, quite objectively, a woman of exquisite beauty and grace. And, given her learnedness, she had much in common with Milo. To think of marriage to her as a burden struck Alex as extraordinary.

"Does her mother still live with you?" Alex asked.

"Lady Sybila?" Milo shuddered. "She met her maker a while back. Three, four years ago. Perhaps five." He rubbed his forehead. "My memory isn't what it could be. I recall the night it happened, though. She was dressing down her daughter for venturing outside the solar with her hair uncovered. 'Twas late, and Nicolette had simply run down to the hall to fill the bed warmer with coals, but Sybila never did put much stock in excuses. Hissing and sputtering like a wet cat she was, then all of a sudden she simply keeled over. Dead as a stone, just like that. Damnedest thing you ever saw." Grinning and shaking his head, Milo filled his mouth with wine.

Alex made a quick sign of the cross—an automatic and meaningless gesture. It would be self-delusion to pretend that he honestly regretted the lady Sybila's passing.

By the time they arrived at the bank of the great river, the sun was but a gleam on the horizon of a violet sky, and Milo was trembling with fatigue. Alex helped his cousin to sit on a boulder, then leaned against a tree to watch him empty the first skin and start in on the second.

"I don't think you came here to get away from Peverell," Alex said, "no matter how big and dreary it is."

Milo wiped his mouth with the sleeve of his tunic. "Nay?"

"Luke seems to think you came here to see me."

Milo paused with the wineskin halfway to his mouth, then slowly lowered it. "He's too perceptive by half, that brother of yours. Sees everything. Gaspar's much the same. For all that he's a godsend, the bastard really gets on my nerves. You know why I always liked *you* so much?"

Alex rubbed the bridge of his nose. Milo was delaying again.

"With you," Milo said, "everything's on the surface.

I don't have to crack open your armor and go digging for your secrets. There are none."

"Everyone's got secrets." Was Milo just tormenting Alex for sport, or did he honestly not know about him and Nicki?

"Not you." Milo snorted. "You wear your soul on your chest. You're tediously honest, disgustingly forthright. Ever in a good humor. I remember, back when we were drinking companions in Périgeaux, wanting to punch you in the nose just to erase that idiotic smile from your face."

"I never knew my contentment troubled you so greatly, cousin," Alex said dryly.

Milo wheezed with laughter. "You were so . . . comfortable with yourself. So satisfied with your lot. Quite the opposite of me in that respect. Things were simple for you. If something was the right thing to do, you did it. If it was sinful, you didn't. If something was on your mind, you said it. If you made a promise, you kept it. You're still that way. I can tell."

"What do you want from me, Milo?" Alex asked quietly.

"I loved you like a brother," Milo said, his voice rawly ernest. "I still do."

"Milo . . ."

"There's a favor I want to ask of you." His appealingly sheepish smile reminded Alex of the old Milo, the charming, good-natured companion of Alex's youth. " 'Tis a rather . . . unusual favor. I couldn't ask it of just anyone."

"Out with it."

Milo fortified himself with a quick gulp of wine. "I want you to father a child for Nicolette."

Chapter 4

The blood rushed in Alex's ears. "Did you say—"

"I want you to get her pregnant." Milo's gaze was direct and sincere.

"You want me to get your wife pregnant."

"Aye."

Alex pushed roughly away from the tree, astounded that Milo would ask him, of all men, to perform this extraordinary "favor." "You don't know what you're saying."

"I know damn well what I'm saying. I want you to lie with her, and plant your seed in her belly, and get her with child."

In his mind, Alex saw the shift of white silk folded on the scarlet pillow . . . breathed in the scent of roses and spices and warm womanflesh. He shook his head, raking his fingers through his hair. " 'Tis the wine talking. It's deranged your senses."

"I told you you'd think me mad before the evening was over." Milo smiled sadly. "In truth, I came to this decision during one of my few drearily sober moments—if it's any comfort to you."

"Comfort? This whole bloody notion makes me feel sick. Does Nick—" Careful. "Does your lady wife know what you're asking of me?"

"Nay. She'd be horrified."

"Quite rightly. What you're proposing is . . . it's abominable. How can you ask this?"

"I thought you might be a bit put off."

"Put off?" Alex was quivering. "God, Milo, what kind of a man are you?"

"You want to know what kind of a man I am?" Rising from the boulder with some difficulty, Milo took a faltering step toward Alex. "I'm a man who can't even sit astride a horse anymore without falling off. I rode here in a covered litter, Alex, like an old woman, while my wife rode on horseback. I'm a man who can't summon up even the pretense of respect from his own subordinates. The soldiers under my command—or, more accurately, under Gaspar's— laugh at me behind my back . . . and sometimes to my face. I've been known to wake up soaked in my own piss, like an infant."

"Christ, Milo."

"Do I disgust you?"

"Your self-pity disgusts me."

"You'd pity yourself, too, if you couldn't even remember the last time your cock got stiff enough to—"

"I've heard enough." Alex turned and began striding back up the path toward the castle.

"Nicolette has a little over a year to produce a son," Milo called after him. "Or she loses Peverell."

Alex paused, hands fisted at his sides. Grudgingly he turned around. "You're making no sense. Peverell belongs to her. She inherited it. You told me so yourself."

" 'In a manner of speaking,' I said." Milo took another unsteady step in Alex's direction. "My wife's uncle was childless, you see, and he left a rather . . . complicated will . . . which Duke William approved, of course. There's no way to contest it."

"Get to the point."

Milo licked his cracked lips. "Nicolette is not Henri de St. Clair's heir. Her firstborn son is. By the terms of his will, she must produce a son by the ten-year anniversary of Henri's death—that's fifteen months from now—or forfeit Peverell to the Church. There's an abbey in St. Clair that is to assume control." He drew in a shaky breath. "We need a son, Alex."

Alex felt as if his brain were swelling inside his skull. "And you expect me to sire him?"

"I'm afraid I've proven myself . . . unequal to the task." Milo made his way back to the boulder and sat down, as limp as a rag doll that's lost half its stuffing. "Not for want of trying—in the beginning, that is. When we were first married, I made a gallant effort to start a babe growing in her belly. 'Twas a doomed enterprise, though, and one to which neither of us brought the slightest shred of enthusiasm. Do you want to know something?"

"Nay." Alex turned his back, but he did not walk away.

"I could only rouse to her when I closed my eyes and imagined she was Violette."

Squeezing his own eyes closed, Alex swept from his mind the disconcerting image of Milo diligently tupping Nicki, and thought instead of Violette, whom his cousin had loved since his youth. The daughter of a saddle-maker, she was too far beneath him for marriage, and uneducated to boot, but they were devoted to each other all the same. Alex remembered her easy laughter, much like Milo's. The laughter ceased for a time when the babe she bore him, a girl, perished of a sudden fever within days of her birth. It ceased for good, Alex was told, after Milo married Nicki and left for Normandy.

"Then," Milo said hoarsely, "about a year into my marriage, Peter wrote to me that Violette was dead."

Alex turned to face his cousin, nonplussed to find Milo looking at him through a sheen of tears.

"He said she died of a broken heart." The tears spilled down Milo's jaundiced cheeks; he didn't seem to notice. " 'Twas the truth, but only part of it. I found out later she'd traded all the jewels I'd given her to

some old crone for a vial of powdered hemlock root—"
His voice broke.

"Milo," Alex said gently, "don't torment yourself
with your memories."

"They're all I have left." Milo rubbed away his tears
and swallowed some more wine. "Or they soon will
be, if Nicolette doesn't produce an heir by October
of next year. We'll be homeless, Alex—homeless and
destitute, both of us."

"Milo, for God's—"

"After Violette died," Milo said, gazing at nothing
with his yellowed, rheumy eyes, "I lost interest in everything, even making a son so we could keep Peverell. I drowned myself in wine. Thank God for Gaspar,
or who knows what would have become of Peverell.
When I finally tried to bed my wife again, 'twas at
her insistence. Not only was she desperate to produce
the requisite heir and protect our rights to Peverell,
but she'd always longed for children. Unfortunately,
by the time I took up the cause again, I'd become
incapable of performing."

"The wine?" Alex asked.

"Aye, that, and . . . I kept dreaming of Violette, her
shrouded body lying in the cold earth. Who knows? I
just couldn't. I was too ashamed to tell Nicolette the
truth, though. I let her think it was her fault—that I
found her unattractive."

The notion was so absurd that Alex laughed, but
with little humor. How could Milo have grown so
weak and craven? Alex wanted to feel smugly gratified
that Nicki had gotten herself bound in such sorry wedlock, but couldn't summon up any pleasure in the
situation.

"It's been . . . I don't know . . . six or seven years
since I even attempted my husbandly duty, knowing
how futile it would be." Milo was slurring his words
again. "Time's running out, though. We both know it,
and we're both terrified of what will become of us

should we be forced to leave Peverell. Can you imagine me trying to provide for us in my condition?"

Alex honestly couldn't.

"I began to entertain the hope that she'd take a lover and get with child from him. Unfortunately, she seems to be a paragon of marital fidelity. Finally I suggested it outright."

"You didn't."

"Don't underestimate my desperation, cousin. I presented it quite rationally—explained that our only hope was for another man to father a child for her. She was appalled, of course, and unwilling to compromise her marital vows. Begged me to try again, although she said she knew she repulsed me, if only for the sake of an heir." Milo sighed and tilted the wineskin to his mouth. "I finally had to tell her the truth about my . . . inadequacy. 'Twas a shock to her, of course, and quite sobering, but still she refused to let another man do that which I'd failed so miserably at. 'Twould be dishonorable, she said."

"Curious. I don't think of honor as being a particularly feminine trait." And certainly not a trait Alex would ascribe to Nicolette de St. Clair.

"Oh, she takes her marriage vows quite seriously," Milo said with obvious contempt. "But mind you, it's not just the sinfulness she's concerned with. There's her reputation as well. She's very fretful about what people will think if she suddenly becomes pregnant after nine years without children. Damn that mother of hers for making her such a monster of respectability!"

"This is the first time," Alex said, "that I can recall hearing a man bemoan his wife's good character."

Milo evidently had a mouthful of wine, because he choked on it. "Aye, well that good character of hers," he gasped out, "might well be our undoing. Fat lot of good her fine qualities will do her—or me—if we end up begging on the streets."

"That's ridiculous. You can always go back to Périgeaux and live with Peter."

"Never!" Milo proclaimed with startling vehemence. "Nothing could make me return to that house."

"Easy." Alex sauntered over to the tree and leaned against it again. The sun had set, drawing with it a dusky veil of twilight studded with innumerable winking stars, yet the heat was as oppressive as ever. The river lapped softly; frogs grunted in the lazy chant of a summer evening. "If not Peter, then there must be relatives somewhere who'd take you in."

"You don't understand," Milo spat out. "It's not just Peter. I couldn't bear living that way again, an interloper in someone else's home, someone who's tolerated—as long as he makes himself inconspicuous and submits to his host's will in all things. At best, it's like being a child under the rule of his parents. I may not be much of a man anymore, but at least I've got my own home, and I damn well intend to keep it."

"Even at the expense of your wife's honor?"

Milo sneered. "You sound like Nicolette. Claims to be just as anxious as I am to keep Peverell, but refuses to barter her precious virtue for it. She came up with some idiotic scheme to keep us on as stewards after the Church takes title, but—"

"Why is that idiotic?" Alex challenged. "Seems a sensible solution if the Church would agree to it."

" 'Tis the abbot of St. Clair who'd have to agree to it, and he's a spiteful gelding who feels that sots such as I are undeserving of such earthly rewards as Peverell."

"The lady Nicolette must feel she can sway him."

"She can't. To the good Father Octavian, all women, especially beautiful ones, are but the Devil's handmaidens. He'd never let us stay on, and even if he did, I hardly care to spend the rest of my life as a bloody caretaker for what I was once lord and master of. I've forbidden her to pursue the matter. 'Twould do naught but compound our humiliation."

"Well, then." Alex shrugged. "Perhaps some convent would take in the lady Nicolette. And if you could accommodate yourself to monastic life—"

"Jesu!" Milo slammed his cane against the boulder. "If I had a spiritual bone in my body, I would have taken Holy Orders twenty years ago and avoided this whole bloody mess! You're not listening to me, Alex. I won't give up Peverell! Not while there's a breath left in my body."

Alex sighed. "Then I advise you to find yourself a nice little tin cup for collecting alms after you've been tossed out onto the street. The cane should prove helpful, but you might consider putting an eye out, or chopping off a limb or two."

"How can you make light of my dilemma? Mine and Nicolette's. She'll be ruined same as me."

"Come." Alex crossed to his cousin and held out his hand. "Night is falling, and you're soused. We'd best be getting back."

Alex tried to help Milo off the boulder, but his cousin jerked out of his grip, throwing himself off balance. Grabbing him and standing him upright, Alex said, "Can you make it back all right?"

"I made it here; I'll make it back." The drunker Milo got, the slower his speech became. Alex supported him with a hand on his shoulder as they set off for the castle. "I'll pay you a hundred marks."

"What use have I of your money?"

"Does William the Bastard compensate his Lone Wolf so well for his services?"

"As a matter of fact, he does." Since Alex refused to accept land, King William insisted on rewarding him with gold, and generously. He'd earned more in the recent Scottish campaign than the most capable mercenary might amass during an entire military career.

"I thought this all through, you know," Milo said thickly. "And I was sure you'd help us. You were always willing to lend a hand, always ready to do the right thing."

"That's just it, Milo. What you're asking is as wrong a thing as I can imagine."

"Not if it saves two people from a life of penury and disgrace. You've got to help us, Alex. I'm pleading with you."

"On the subject of disgrace," Alex ventured, "aren't you at all concerned with what people will think when your wife gets with child after nine barren years? Especially considering the inheritance situation."

"Nobody knows about that." He frowned. "Not many people, anyway."

"Regardless. It won't look good. People will suspect that the child isn't yours."

"Look at me, Alex. I'm well past the point of caring what people think of me." Squeezing wine into his mouth, Milo veered drunkenly toward the edge of the path. It was all Alex could do to keep him walking in the right direction.

"Nicolette obviously cares."

"She shouldn't. A few tongues might wag—what of it? Most people won't give a damn. There are bastards in every noble house. Look at your great William— Count Robert's by-blow by a tanner's daughter, and now both duke of Normandy and king of England!" He shook his head disgustedly. "Nicolette's a fool. Peverell's all she's got, and this is the only way to save it. She shouldn't be so uncooperative."

"But she is, and therein lies your scheme's fatal flaw. Even if I agreed to it—and I assure you I won't— your wife would never consent to let me . . ." Alex shook his head at the madness of this conversation. "It wouldn't work."

"Not if she knew about it. You'd have to keep your true purpose from her. You'd have to seduce her."

"Seduce her. Without letting her know that I'm in league with you to get her pregnant."

"Exactly." Milo tripped over something in the dark. Alex righted him. "You can come visit us through Christmastide. That should give you enough time to plant a seed that will take—that's all the time we've got, in any event. Once she's with child, you may return to England and forget the entire thing—in fact, I'll insist that you do."

"Just ride away, leaving a pregnant woman behind."

"You'll have done her a favor, cousin—the greatest boon imaginable."

"There's yet another flaw," Alex pointed out, envisioning again the glimmer of white silk against scarlet brocade. "Seduction takes two willing partners. If your lady wife is so virtuous, who's to say she'll cooperate?"

Milo's teeth flashed in the dark. "If anyone can breach her defenses, you can. I've heard about your way with those English wenches. They say the Lone Wolf likes to spread his seed. Alex the Conqueror, some call you."

Alex sighed. "I hadn't heard that one."

Milo chuckled raspily. "Quite a switch from the innocent young lad I knew in Périgeaux. As I recall, you'd little interest in the fairer sex."

So, thought Alex. *He doesn't know about Nicki and me.*

"All you cared about back then," Milo continued, "was perfecting your skill with the sword—the one on your belt. The weapon between your legs had not yet been bloodied in battle, as far as I knew."

"That's why you chose me for this . . . service?" Alex demanded. "Because women have been known to lift their skirts for me?"

"They don't seem to be able to help themselves, but that's not the only reason. I told you—I've thought this all out carefully." Within sight now of the castle—

a dark, turreted stone box rising against the night sky—Milo stopped in his tracks and turned to face Alex, who had to hold him up with both hands. Even in the semidarkness Alex could see how unfocused his cousin's gaze was. His head shook like that of a jointed toy soldier.

"It doesn't matter what your reasons are," Alex said tiredly. "I won't do it. Let's get back so you can go to—"

"We're of the same blood, you an' I," Milo said, enunciating slowly in an apparent effort to counteract his muddled speech. "Thas' important. We look a bit alike, don't you think? Or we used to—at least in coloring. The baby would be of de Périgeaux stock, and he'd look it, by God."

"You're wasting your time, Milo. Let's go—"

"You're unmarried," Milo interrupted. "I wouldn't ask this of a wedded man. They say you've no attachments, nor do you want any."

"Nor do I want any children," Alex pointed out.

"Precisely, which means it's unlikely you'll claim any that come from my wife." Milo grinned blearily, clearly pleased with himself. "Thought it all out—I told you. Another thing—you live far away. You're practically an Englishman now. You won't be always about, inspiring bothersome speculation about who really sired Milo de St. Clair's son."

"So you do care what people think."

"I would spare Nicolette her cherished reputation if I could. 'Twill make everything simpler, in any event, if such conjecture is kept to a minimum. Legally, it makes no difference whether folks think he's legitimate or not. Henri's will merely stipulated that Nicolette must bear a son—it didn't specify whose."

"Since you've thought this all out so well, tell me— what will you do if she gives birth to a daughter?"

"Find some healthy newborn boy and negotiate a trade with his parents, I suppose. The baby girl and a

handful of silver for their son and a promise to keep
mum. Or, if Nicolette refuses to part with the girl, I'll
simply buy a boy outright and claim she had twins."

"You've become quite an unprincipled wretch, you
know that, Milo?"

"A man doesn't beg to be cuckolded without coming to that realization, cousin."

"Well, unfortunately for you, my principles are still
quite intact. I won't do it."

"Not even for Nicolette?"

"Especially not for her." *Damn—that was careless.*

In a quiet, almost sober voice, Milo asked, "What
is that supposed to mean?"

A dozen different inane prevarications occurred to
Alex, but he didn't have the stomach for any of them.
Finally, on a heavy sigh, he said, "You'd best ask her."

Milo nodded slowly, then turned and lurched
toward the castle. Alex took hold of him and fairly
dragged him through the entrance. By the time they
reached the north tower, Milo's legs were buckling
beneath him, and Alex wondered how he was going
to get him upstairs to his chamber.

Hearing footsteps from behind, Alex turned and
saw Gaspar coming toward them. "There you are, milord! I was beginning to worry about you. Here, Sir
Alex. Let me give you a hand with him." Squeezing
three abreast in the narrow stairwell, Gaspar and Alex
supported the insensible Milo between them and half-
carried him up the steps. When they got to the door
at the top of the tower, Alex knocked.

"Milo?" Nicki called from within.

Gaspar opened the door. "Aye, milady, but he's . . .
oh. Beg pardon, milady."

Nicki was seated on the edge of the bed, drawing a
big ivory comb through her hair. She stood up quickly,
and Alex saw that she wore the white sleeping shift
that had been laid out for her. The shimmery silk

highlighted her feminine contours and left her arms and lower legs completely bare.

Alex averted his gaze, as did Gaspar—if not quite so swiftly—while Nicki grabbed a wrapper off a hook and hurriedly tied it over the shift. "Oh, Milo," she murmured, shaking her head. "Put him here." She folded down the bed covers.

"I've got 'im." With seemingly little effort, Gaspar lifted Milo like a baby and deposited him on the bed. "You can be on your way, Sir Alex," he said over his shoulder as he tugged Milo's boots off. "I'm used to this."

Circling the bed, Nicki leaned over Milo to un-buckle his belt, her great swath of golden hair gleaming in the light from the horn lantern dangling overhead. She slid the belt beneath her husband's inert form, tossed it aside and set about wrestling him out of his tunic.

Pausing in her task, she raised her head and met Alex's steady gaze, her eyes enormous in the mellow lamplight. "Thank you for your help," she said softly, "but Gaspar and I can handle the rest."

Alex withdrew from the room and sprinted down the steps, but lingered at the bottom of the stairwell, uneasy to have left Gaspar up there with Nicki. Absurd; he was a trusted retainer. Yet something about the way he'd looked at her in her night shift had raised Alex's hackles. Within a minute, however, he heard the big man's heavy tread on the stairs, and feeling very much the fool, retired to his pallet in the great hall.

Alex knocked softly on the door to the guest chamber allotted to Luke and his family. It was late—nearly matins—and he didn't want to awaken the children.

The door squeaked on its hinges and Faithe peered out, cradling baby Edlyn in one arm and holding a candle aloft. "Alex." She opened it all the way and

stepped aside for him to enter, whispering, "What are
you doing up at this time of night?"

It was obvious what *she* was doing up, for her voluminous night shift was untied to allow Edlyn to suckle.
Setting down the candle, she draped a linen towel over
her exposed breast, but in a leisurely way that implied
no sense of shame. Alex liked it that she felt so at
ease with him, as friends should. How very remarkable
to have a woman for a friend. How fortunate for both
of the brothers de Périgeaux that Luke had married
Faithe of Hauekleah.

"I'm looking for something to drink," Alex said—
very softly, so as not to awaken the others. The small
chamber held—just barely—a bed, a pallet, and the
cradle and trunk they'd brought with them. Luke lay
facedown in his drawers on one side of the bed, an
arm dangling off the edge, his inky hair loose and
disheveled. Robert and Hlynn shared the pallet—
rather unequally, for the little girl was stretched out
luxuriously, with her brother curled up on the edge.
All of them were coated with a sheen of sweat; it
hadn't cooled down much after sunset.

"Can't you sleep?" Faithe asked him.

"Nay. 'Tis hot as blazes in that hall." What little air
crept through the arrow slits was kept steamy from
the body heat of the hundred or so other men obliged
to bed down there. Alex's wool chausses itched un-
mercifully. Even his shirt felt oppressive, despite his
having untied it halfway down his chest and rolled up
the sleeves. In truth, it wasn't just the heat keeping
him awake, but this was hardly the time or place to
unburden himself. "Luke has some fortified wine,
doesn't he? I tried the buttery, but it's locked."

"Little wonder, with all these soldiers about."
Faithe slid a finger into Edlyn's mouth to release her
hold on the breast, and adjusted her gown to cover
herself. The baby yawned, little fists quivering, as milk
trickled down her chin. Arranging the towel over her

shoulder, Faithe burped the infant with a few efficient pats and laid her gently in the cradle. Free at last of her sweet burden, she stepped over the pallet so that she could kneel before the trunk in the corner.

"Sorry to be such a bother," Alex said.

"You're not a bother." She opened the lid of the trunk, which creaked, causing Robert to awaken with a groan of protest. "I take that back." She smiled in a resigned way as she rooted through the contents of the trunk.

"Hlynn's taking up the whole pallet," the boy whined.

Faithe sighed. "They've been at this all night." To her son she said, "I'll move her in a—"

"Move over, piglet!" Robert shoved his little sister aside, roughly awakening her.

"Mummy! Robby hit me."

"Did not. I just—"

"Not again," Luke groaned. "Quiet, both of you! Go back to sleep."

"But, Papa." Hlynn grabbed at her father's dangling arm. "Robby—"

"I don't care what he did. It's hot. I just want you two to stop this nonsense so we can all get some . . ." Lifting his head, Luke blinked at his brother. "What are you doing here?"

"I'm trying to talk Faithe into running away with me."

"Hmph." Luke settled back down and closed his eyes. "Take the children, too."

Faithe retrieved a leather flask and closed the trunk. As she stepped back across the pallet, she said, "The next child who speaks tonight will eat nothing tomorrow but bread and broth. No sweetmeats of any kind. No herb cakes. No fruit tarts. No marzipan anythings, I don't care how clever. Do you both understand me?"

They nodded dolefully, glowered at each other, and settled down facing in opposite directions.

"You can sleep in here if you'd like," Faithe offered, prompting Alex to snort with laughter. This was no better than the great hall.

Accepting the flask of strong wine, he said, "Thanks all the same, but this castle's an oven. I've got to get out of here."

"You're going to sleep out of doors?"

"Luke and I found an old longship this afternoon on the banks of the Robec. It has the advantage of no roof. If a cool breeze happens to pass through Rouen tonight, I'll be ready for it."

"Clever you," she said, and bid him good night.

By the time Alex arrived at the boat, he was drunker than he'd been in years, having methodically drained the flask as he walked.

He should have stayed in England. England didn't have heat like this—not often, anyway, and never in the middle of the night, for pity's sake. More important, England did not have Nicolette.

Setting the half-empty flask with inebriated care on an oarsman's bench, he stripped and went for a swim, grateful for the chance to cool off. Afterward he donned his loose linen drawers, but wadded up the shirt and woollen hose and shoved them in the crook where the hull met the bench, a sort of pillow for later.

His money pouch lay on the deck of the boat where it had fallen when he undressed. He retrieved it and, on impulse, dug around in it until he found, at the very bottom, something he'd put there nine years ago and never removed.

It was a ribbon, a slender band of white satin that had once, in another lifetime, been woven through the hair of Nicolette de St. Clair. Finding it creased and wrinkled from its long confinement beneath heavy coins, he stretched it out on the bench and flattened it with his palms. It looked to be perhaps a yard and a half in length.

Luke frequently chided Alex for his carelessness

with his things, for he was forever misplacing items of importance. This ribbon and the purse that housed it were the only possessions Alex had ever taken pains not to lose.

Alex lifted the ribbon and wrapped it around his hand. It looked like a bandage in the moonlight. Bringing it to his nose, he fancied that he could detect just the faintest hint of roses.

Idiot. He uncorked the flask and quickly finished the job of emptying it. Reeling from the wine and the day's events, he lowered his head to his makeshift pillow, pressed his ribbon-wrapped hand to his chest, and gazed into the starry heavens.

And remembered a sweet and sultry summer afternoon nine long years ago, an afternoon that bound him for all eternity to Nicolette de St. Clair.

Chapter 5

A feverish heat held the world in thrall that day, spawned by a sun that burned like a torch in a cloudless Aquitaine sky. The air shimmered in waves above the sheep meadow through which Alex and Nicolette strolled on their way to the cool shadows of the woods to the south.

Alex couldn't believe his good fortune in persuading her to take a walk with him alone. Her mother would have been outraged, but Lady Sybila had taken to her bed after the noon meal, having succumbed to the heat—and she wasn't the only one. When Alex had arrived at his cousin's home, adjacent to his, for his daily visit—a habit born several weeks ago, when the lady Nicolette had come to spend the summer there—he found that most of the household had chosen to sleep away the afternoon rather than put up with the scorching heat.

Happily, he'd discovered Nicolette by herself beneath an old oak, rereading one of the books she'd brought with her. He wondered, not for the first time, how she could be content deciphering page after page of ink scratchings for hours at a time. Joining her beneath her tree, he had pleaded with her to slip away for a walk. She'd balked at the impropriety of being alone with him, finally consenting when he swore a solemn oath not to take advantage of their solitude;

she knew already that he did not take oaths lightly.
And she'd made him promise not to tell anyone, lest
her mother find out.

She looked extraordinary that day, in a pale green
tunic of the most delicate, filmy silk trimmed in heavy
bands of silver braid. A demurely shapeless garment
when she stood still, it drifted around her as she
walked, clinging intermittently to a slender thigh . . .
a graceful hip . . . a tantalizing swell of breast. It took
every chivalric instinct Alex possessed to keep from
staring openly.

The heat imparted a bloom of color to that extraordinary face of hers, highlighted by the unaccustomed
austerity of her hair, which she'd pinned up in deference to the warmth of the day. She glowed as if from
within, an ethereal creature, not of this world. Not of
this region, at any rate, her particular brand of pale
Norman beauty being a rarity this far south. She was
an exotic creature, strange and elegant and full of mystery. From the moment she'd arrived in Périgeaux to
visit her cousin Phelis, Alex had been obsessed by her.
As long as he could remember, his sword had been
the focal point of his life. Now his every waking
thought was of Nicolette de St. Clair. He lived for
those brief moments when he could exchange a few
words with her—always under the watchful eye of others. But this afternoon, for the first time ever, he had
her all to himself!

As they approached the edge of the meadow, they
noticed something curious; actually, it was Nicolette
who pointed it out. A group of sheep had abandoned
their grazing and ventured into the woods, where they
could just be seen, all gathered in one place. They had
never left the meadow before.

"Come," she said, "let's go see what's drawn
them there."

She reached for Alex's hand, and his heart stopped.
Looking abashed to have been so forward, she stilled

just as her fingers brushed his palm, and turned quickly away. His heart hammered wildly; his palm tingled where her fingertips had grazed it. He looked after her as she strode toward the sheep, wondering how she would react if he should run after her and take her hand in his. Would she welcome the gesture, or consider it a violation of his vow to keep his distance?

"Come along," she called over her shoulder. Realizing the moment had been lost, and rebuking himself for his childish indecision, he sprinted after her. As for what had prompted her to reach for him in the first place, it seemed to him that she was unusually relaxed this afternoon. In fact, the farther they got from Peter's house—and her mother—the more light-hearted she seemed.

"Look at this, Alex," she said, squeezing among the placid sheep to investigate. They were all clustered together near an outcropping of rock that rose high among the snarled foliage and ancient trees.

"Here, let me." He muscled his way through the dusty animals. "You'll soil that beautiful tunic."

What he found, emanating from the rock through a blanket of thorny vegetation, was a current of deliciously cool air. The sheep were basking in it as a respite from the brutal heat.

"Perhaps there's a spring in here, or an underground stream," Alex suggested as he set about tearing the concealing shrubbery away from the rock—sweaty work despite the cool draft.

"You'll get *your* tunic dirty," she said. "And ripped."

Envisioning his stepmother's fury should he present her with yet another shredded tunic—an unfortunate consequence of swordplay—Alex took off his belt and tunic, hanging them over the branch of a tree. As he rolled up the sleeves of his damp linen shirt, he noticed Nicolette's gaze light on his forearms. He glanced at her and she swiftly looked away.

Gradually stripping away the prickly growth—and

earning scores of scratches in the process—he revealed an opening in the rock, small and low. But deep.

" 'Tis a cave!" she exclaimed, joining him in pulling away the last few branches. Her delight was infectious. They both trembled in anticipation as they squatted down to peek into the cavern's dim interior.

She grinned at him. "I didn't know we were going to have an adventure!" She had an oddly beguiling mouth, her lips naturally rosy and rather wide, but not full. He loved it when she smiled, yet her smiles had always seemed oddly restrained—until now. There was something so rapturous in her expression of happy triumph that it made his heart ache.

Alex cleared his throat and said manfully, "I'm going in."

"I'm going with you."

"Nay. It could be dangerous."

"Nonsense." With an airy wave of her hand, and bending low, she ventured into the dark aperture. "This cave has been closed off for a very long time, considering how troublesome it was to clear away all that old growth. There will be no bears to eat us— and I'm not afraid of spiders."

"That's fortunate." Following her at a crouch into the cave's cool interior, Alex grinned. "Watch out for the bats, though."

"Where?" She bolted upright, thumping her head on the low ceiling of rock overhead.

He winced, feeling like a drooling lackwit. " 'Twas a jest. I'm sorry. Are you hurt?"

"Aye!" She rubbed her head, but she was laughing, thank the saints. "I'll have a lump the size of a swan's egg—see if I don't."

I'll kiss it for you. That's what he wanted to say. Instead, he said, quietly, "I am sorry. I'm such a dunderhead."

She graced him with an astonishingly luminous smile. "I don't go on adventures with dunderheads."

He grinned in absurd gratification as she turned and continued deeper into the cave. "Here, let me go first," he said, hurrying to catch up.

"We'll go side by side," she said. "That's fair enough."

It seemed to Alex that "fairness" had little to do with safeguarding the weaker sex, but as he saw no real danger at hand, and was eager to be as close to her as possible, to revel in her warmth and spicy-sweet scent, he graciously let her have her way.

The cave opened up several yards in, the floor dipping down somewhat and the ceiling rising over their heads, enabling them to stand fully upright. What they saw in the dim interior when they did so stole the breath from their lungs. For long moments, all they could do was turn in slow, measured circles, staring incredulously at the cave walls.

They had been painted, embellished with myriad images in tones of rust and black and sepia. Most of the pictures seemed to be of animals. Alex recognized a deer and some sort of bull. Some of the others were less identifiable. Small figures of men with spears were interspersed among these creatures, as if hunting them.

"Look." Nicki pointed to the dark outline of a tiny hand, her expression wistful. "A child."

"Who did this?"

"I can't imagine." She crossed herself, shrugging self-consciously to find him watching her. "It makes me think of a church, somehow."

Alex nodded and followed suit. There was something almost holy about this long-empty chamber, a sort of rustic sacredness.

"These pictures must be at least a hundred years old," Alex said in his most authoritative voice.

"Older than that," she murmured, then pointed. "The cave continues that way."

They followed a sort of narrow, meandering corridor until they reached the apex of another downslope, steeper than the last, and peered into the vast darkness beyond. From somewhere up ahead came the gentle slapping of water against stone—the source of the cool airstream that had drawn the sheep, and which was raising goose bumps on his sweat-soaked body.

"How far in do you think it goes?" Her soft inquiry resonated in the great empty space. He could barely see her, the light from the small opening through which they had entered having almost exhausted itself.

"I don't know." Wild to go exploring, but mindful of her feminine limitations, he said, "I suppose we should go back."

She chuckled. "You want to search further."

"I'm thinking of you. It's so dark, and we don't know what the footing's like. I'm wearing boots, but you've just got your slippers, and your skirts might get in the way. . . ."

"Here." Kicking off her kid slippers, she lifted her skirt above her ankles, holding it with one hand as if she were about to dance the *tourdoin*. Something about her girlish smile and those pale, bare feet on the cavern floor touched him deep inside his chest. She was so different this afternoon—not the pale, enigmatic beauty he'd adored from afar all these weeks, but a real human being, lively and vital and full of childlike wonder.

"All right," he said quietly. And then he tentatively reached out and took her free hand in his. "In case you fall."

She contemplated him for a moment, and he feared she would pull away from him. But presently her lips curved in a slow, sweet smile, and she murmured her thanks.

Alex guided her with careful steps down the slope, grateful when it leveled out. He could barely manage to put one foot in front of the other. The very rock seemed to shift beneath him, so overwhelmed was he to be touching her. Her hand felt like the cheek of a baby, inconceivably soft, and it was warm, and it was hers, and she was letting him hold it. Nothing that had happened to him in his seventeen years had given him such dizzying joy.

The darker it got, the more cautiously they trod, until at last they stood in near-total blackness in the midst of what felt like a great fathomless void. The soft sloshing of water was closer now.

"Must be an underground stream," he said.

"Aye."

The absence of light was so complete that he couldn't see Nicolette standing right in front of him, although he sensed her gaze searching for him through the darkness, as his searched for her.

"We'd best go no further for now," he said. "We can come back tomorrow with a lantern."

"Aye." Her voice had a shivery quality he'd never heard in it before.

"Are you afraid?" he whispered.

Her breathing quickened. "I don't know."

"I'm right here." He reached for her other hand, and held both; they felt wonderfully warm in this cool abyss. The ragged rhythm of their breathing echoed off unseen walls of rock, until the sound of the stream faded away and it was all he could hear. He didn't know which breaths were his and which were Nicolette's.

"Do you want to go back?" he asked her.

"Nay. Not yet."

The coupling of their hands felt like his tether to earth. Should she release her grip on him, he might fly off into the infinite blackness, lost for all eternity.

But she didn't release him. Indeed, she chose that moment to tighten her grasp, her fingers achingly soft against his callused flesh. A drop of water rang in the darkness.

They stood for some time in breathless silence, in this cool, dark, strangely hallowed place, indifferent to the slow and steady passage of time in the mortal world above them, just being there, together.

Something was happening, Alex realized, inside of him—inside both of them. Their souls were splintering apart and merging together into a new and marvelous pattern, like ice crystals melting and reforming on a frozen lake.

He was changing. They were both changing, profoundly and for all time. He felt it in the depths of his soul, and he knew she felt it, too.

They'd been united, always and forever, in a spiritual bond that could never be broken.

They were one.

"I'm in love with her," Alex whispered to his brother.

"Which one?" Following Alex's gaze, Luke peered at the three young women chatting before a window in the great hall of their cousin Peter's manor house.

"Lady Nicolette, of course!" The other two were married, Phelis to Peter and Alyce to their brother, Christien. And both were large with child, for pity's sake!

"Hush!" Luke scolded, darting a wary glance toward their father and stepmother, being greeted by Peter not two yards away. "Do you want the whole world to know?"

"Yes!" Alex watched as Nicki, unaware of his scrutiny, smiled politely at some comment of her cousin Phelis. She wore her favorite tunic today, a silken gown of snowy white. Backlit as she was by the midday sun streaming in through the window, she looked like an angel who'd floated to earth just for him. Her radiant hair, crowned with a circlet of gold, hung in two long braids interwoven with white ribbons, exposing the pearl earrings dangling from her delicate ears. "I want to shout it to the heavens. I can't, but, God, how I want to! I love her, Luke. I'm unbearably in love with her. I used to laugh at the jongleurs and their silly romantic cansos. Now, finally, I truly know what it means to be in—"

"Oh, hell." Luke expelled a great and weary sigh.

"What's the matter?"

"Have you told her how you feel?"

Three weeks had passed since his revelation the day they'd stumbled across the cave, but he hadn't yet been able to work up the courage to declare himself. "I will, soon. I just—"

"Don't. Have you told anyone else?"

"Nay. Well . . . just Father Gregoire. Her mother would be—"

"Good. See that you keep your mouth shut."

Alex frowned at Luke's sharp tone. He'd waited weeks to confide in his beloved brother, conscious of the danger—mostly to Nicki—should they be found out. Now he wished he'd kept his counsel.

From across the hall, Nicki glanced in his direction, then abruptly looked away. Her mother must be close at hand. He scanned the hall, swarming with servants setting up tables and the guests mysteriously summoned by Peter that morning for dinner and a "special announcement." Presently he spied Lady Sybila de St. Clair, who dominated her otherwise strong-willed daughter's actions—even her thoughts, it seemed—with steely authority. Ever the grim widow, Nicki's mother was enshrouded in one of her several black tunics, her hair concealed beneath a white *couvrechef.* The severe hooded headdress, and that dour expression, ruined any beauty she might once have possessed and added years to her age. How could a girl as incandescently lovely as Nicki have been born of such a creature?

"That's why you've lost interest in your training

this summer," Luke muttered disapprovingly. "You've been mooning over a girl."

"I'm not just 'mooning over' her. I love her. And I haven't lost interest in my training." Alex was already celebrated for his mastery of the sword, despite his youth—perhaps because of it. He would not let his skills rust away. "I've simply taken some time to myself this summer, before we have to report to Duke William."

"Does Lady Nicolette know that you'll be leaving Périgeaux in two weeks to wield your sword for the duke? That you have no home and no immediate prospects of one?"

"Of course. I tell Nicki everything. I can talk to her—"

" 'Nicki'?" Luke grimaced. "Don't let anyone else hear you call her that. For God's sake, Alex. What are you thinking of, courting a lady of her rank when you can offer her nothing? Have you lost your senses entirely?"

"Absolutely. I'm in love. Have you never been in love?"

"I'm a soldier."

" 'Tisn't an answer."

Luke's expression sobered. "Yes, it is. We're landless knights, both of us. 'Tis best that we form no attachments of any kind—I've told you this a hundred times. Some day your sword and my crossbow may earn us property, but until then we're unmarriageable, and you'd best remember that."

"I know I can't marry."

Luke's eyes flashed. "Then you have no business dallying with a highborn lady like Nicolette de St. Clair."

"I'm not 'dallying' with her, for God's sake!" Alex whispered furiously. "I love her. I respect her. She's a pure young girl, and I've done naught but hold her hand." Luke would probably laugh if he knew how deeply it had moved Alex the first time he'd closed his hand around hers—how it moved him still, just to touch her in that chaste and simple way.

"Young girl?" Luke said. "She's older than you."

"By only two years," Alex said defensively. "And she looks younger than nineteen." He watched her smile at some jest of Alyce's. It was a smile he hadn't seen before—reticent, almost melancholy. But then, she still tended toward an almost grave sort of decorum when other people—notably her mother—were hovering about. It was only when they were alone together in their cave that she seemed truly at ease, not the proper and unapproachable Nicolette St. Clair, but Nicki—his Nicki.

The lantern they'd brought to the cave had revealed yet more mysterious paintings in the giant cavity through which the water ran—and from which, it turned out, there was no further passage. It was this chamber that became their secret refuge. They stocked it with blankets to sit upon, wine to drink, and cheese to eat, and met there nearly every afternoon. They scrounged up tallow candles and lit them at the edge of the stream—dozens of them, reflecting the water onto the ornate cave walls in iridescent waves of light. Sometimes Nicki would bring along a book of verse, or one of her own poems, and read aloud to him. Oftentimes they would lie on their backs, with only their hands touching, and speculate on what the paintings meant, and who had executed them. Most of the time they talked—or rather, he did. She questioned him endlessly about himself and his fierce dedication to soldiering, but seemed reluctant to reveal much of her own past. All he really knew about her was that she lived in the castle of her uncle, a powerful Norman castellan, and was visiting her cousin Phelis to avoid a difficult family situation.

"She seems older than nineteen to me," Luke murmured. "Not in looks, but there's something about her, a shadow of something . . . as if she's keeping a part of her under lock and key. 'Tis almost as if she has something to hide."

"She does—her love for me. Her mother disapproves of soldiers."

"A sensible position. If I had a daughter, I wouldn't let her anywhere near us. Has she told you she loves you?"

Alex hesitated. "Not as yet." Like him, she was probably afraid of saying it out loud. And one couldn't discount the stifling influence of her mother. "If you knew the lady Sybila as I do, you'd understand. 'Twould be disastrous if she found out about us. We meet in secret, in a . . . a place we found near Peter's sheep meadow to the south."

"You do realize you're risking her reputation if you're found there alone with her," Luke warned. "And what if temptation proves too much, and you do something you oughtn't?"

"Never. She's an innocent, an untouched maiden. And my interest in her transcends lust. I wouldn't dream of compromising her."

Luke smiled roguishly. "Oh, surely you've dreamt of it."

Alex looked away, his face warm. Dreamt of it? He'd lain awake nights, rigid with need, imagining her body, soft and slender, beneath his, filled with a dark, unrelenting hunger for her even as he worshipped her purity. To defile that purity would be unthinkable. He'd confessed his base desires to Father Gregoire, prayed for deliverance from them—yet they grew more ungovernable with every breath he breathed.

Dinner was announced. Phelis invited her family and guests to be seated at the three long tables, which had been arranged in a horseshoe. Alex was grateful for the respite from his brother's censure, which he hadn't expected and found unsettling. But as he started toward the tables, Luke seized his arm, pinning him with that damnably astute gaze of his. "What you need is a woman who's not quite so innocent." He lowered his voice. "Tempeste mentioned you last night."

Alex groaned. "I don't want some unwashed tavern wench."

Luke's mouth quirked. "Washing is overrated."

"That's as may be, but I still don't want her."

"She seems to want *you*," Luke said, grinning. "No sooner had I lowered her skirts back down than she started in about you again. Said you were almost too comely, that it was—how did she put it?—painful to look upon such beauty in a man. Asked me for the hundredth time who you were saving yourself for."

"She said all this while she was lying in bed with you?"

"Lying in sawdust on the floor of her tavern, actually."

"Perhaps I don't want a woman who gives herself quite so freely."

Luke looked genuinely perplexed. "Why the devil not? For the price of two tumblers of wine, she'll make you a man." He grinned salaciously. "A very happy man. She really knows what she's doing. Ask any of the fellows."

Alex envisioned the voluptuous Tempeste, with her copious bosom and unruly auburn hair, and felt a momentary spark of lust, but swept it aside. He loved Nicolette, adored her with a reverence that left no room for other women, no matter how tempting. If his body must ache without relief to protect the purity of their love, so be it.

"You're a bit long in the tooth not to have tasted the pleasures of the flesh," Luke said. "By the time I was seventeen, I'd been wenching for two years. Come on—give Tempeste what she's been begging for. 'Twill cure you of your Lady Nicolette, I'll wager."

"My love for her is a blessing, not an affliction. It needs no cure."

Luke studied Nicolette thoughtfully as she took her seat. "That remains to be seen."

Nicki evaded Alex's gaze all through dinner—or so it seemed to him. She and her mother had been seated, along with Peter and his family, at the table that formed the crosspiece of the horseshoe, Alex and Luke along one of the legs. From where he sat, he had an unobstructed view of her, which made it easy to catch glimpses of her over his cup, or while he was talking to Milo, who sat next to her. He only wished she would glance in his direction, just once. If their eyes could but meet for a moment, it would keep his fierce longing at bay until they could be together again.

Milo, in exceptionally high spirits today, held forth over dessert about Charlemagne's nephew, the legendary Count Roland, who'd lost most of his army in a disastrous encounter with the Moors.

"Roland was a fool," Milo said, eyes sparking with mischief as he glanced toward Alex. "He should have summoned help sooner, but his idiotic pride got in the way, and his men suffered the consequences."

"Roland was a superb military strategist," said Alex, rising to the bait. "He got bad advice, that's all."

"But the final decision rested with him," Milo countered. "He ought to have sounded his horn for help, not stood about fretting over it."

" 'Twas a matter of honor," Alex retorted.

Milo smirked. "I doubt the men who perished under Roland's command that day would forgive him because of his fine display of military honor. What you call 'honor,' cousin, I call arrogant pride. 'Tis more often a curse than a blessing, I would say." Turning to Nicki, he asked, "You've read the new interpretation of the incident, have you not, my lady?"

"Aye. It's beautifully written."

Alex was pleased that Milo had chosen to draw Nicki into the exchange, relishing the opportunity to talk to her. Unfortunately, their conversation digressed to this new literary treatment, about which Alex couldn't begin to comment, his knowledge of Roland's tale having come from troubadours and jongleurs. It was not the first time his inability to read had kept him out of such discussions. Alex envied Milo his intellectual rapport with Nicki. He might even have been jealous, were it not for Violette, to whom his cousin was passionately—and exclusively—devoted.

Eventually Alex's father and brothers joined the conversation, refocusing it on current military matters—specifically, the rumor that William of Normandy planned to invade Brittany.

"It must be true," Christien said, "considering how eagerly he's been recruiting mercenary specialists. They say he's snapped up every crossbowman and engineer in Aquitaine."

Luke nodded. "Flanders and Auvergne as well."

"If he was only interested in crossbowmen and engineers," Peter said, "how come he to sign you up, Alex?"

"Because Luke insisted." Duke William had been eager for Luke—the ruthless Black Dragon who'd served him so valiantly during his invasion of Maine last year—to rejoin his corps of elite mercenaries for the Brittany campaign. But now that Alex was old enough and proficient enough for battle, the brothers were loath to be separated, and Luke had urged William to consider Alex as well.

"That's not the way I hear it," said Alex's father. Tall, silver-haired, and imposing, Robert de Périgeaux emitted an air of wisdom and authority that inspired a kind of awe in everyone who knew him—even his own sons. "They say 'twas your brilliant demonstration of swordplay, rather than your brother's influence, that earned you a place in William's army. 'Twas the duke himself, they say, who dubbed you the White Wolf, for your sneakiness.''

"He called it stealth," Alex corrected with a proud grin. He stole a glance at Nicki to gauge her reaction to his renown, only to find her gazing into her goblet, expressionless.

"When will you and your brother be leaving to join Duke William?" Phelis asked Alex.

"A fortnight from now, my lady."

"I wish we knew exactly what the duke has in mind," groused Alex's sire. "But all we get this far south is heresay and conjecture."

Phelis turned to the lady Sybila. "Your brother Henri recruits and trains soldiers in Normandy for Duke William, does he not, my lady? He might know of the duke's plans."

Lady Sybila cleared her throat daintily. "If so, he has not shared such plans with me—but then he wouldn't. Gaspar reports directly to my uncle. He would know. He knows everything."

"Gaspar!" Peter called across the room.

Gaspar le Taureau looked up from the corner table at which he dined with his two brutish underlings, Vicq and Leone. One of Henri de St. Clair's most trusted soldiers, Gaspar, along with his men, had escorted Sybila and Nicolette on their journey from Normandy. He attended them—in particular Lady Sybila—like a huge, good-natured bear trained to anticipate needs and follow orders to the letter. He was especially adept at concocting the many tonics she was forever dosing herself with—sleeping potions, headache powders, infusions of chamomile to soothe her nerves, decoctions of anjelica to ward off evil spirits.

"Join us, won't you?" Peter invited.

Gaspar looked toward his mistress. Lady Sybila nodded, and he rose obediently to his feet. Vicq and Leone stood also, which did not surprise Alex. They followed Gaspar around with the slavish constancy of dogs, while in appearance they more closely resembled a pair of hulking apes Alex had seen once in a cage at the Poitiers court. That their weapon of choice, like Gaspar's, seemed to be the club, only reinforced their air of brutality.

Waving his men back down, Gaspar crossed the hall.

"Have a seat." Peter indicated a vacant spot on the bench next to Luke. Sybila nodded, and Gaspar sat.

"We were wondering," Peter began, "whether you might have been privy to any conversations between your lord Henri and Duke William regarding the Brittany matter. Mind you, we're not asking you to betray any confidences. . . ."

"He's going to invade," Gaspar said, "if that's what you're asking, sire."

This statement was met with a collective murmur. Alex whooped, eager to test his mettle in a real battle. Nicki looked sharply in his direction, then dropped her gaze once more.

His father shook his head. "I fear for the success of this endeavor. 'Tis particularly troubling, in that my sons will be participating in it."

"Fear not, Father," Luke soothed. "We're skilled knights—no harm will come to us. And 'tis an opportunity to prove ourselves to Duke William before he assumes the throne of England."

"They tell me England is a green and fertile land," Alex said.

" 'Tis a cold and rainy island," sniffed the lady Sybila. "Populated by barbarians. I've been there once, and would never set foot there again."

Alex nodded in a cursory way to acknowledge the sour sentiment, but said, " 'Twill suit me, I'm sure—and my brother. We could stay here, but then we would remain landless. If we follow the duke to England and serve him well, he'll most likely grant us English holdings."

"Eventually," their father sighed. "It could take a very long time for you to earn estates. I might not see you for years."

" 'Tis our best hope for land," Luke gently reminded him.

When the family's patriarch, Lord Berengar, died, the old system of partible inheritance called for his substantial property in Périgeaux to be split into two contiguous estates under the control of his two sons, who eventually had sons of their own. But while Alex's generation was growing to manhood, primogeniture—succession by the eldest son—was swiftly replacing the old system, which had fragmented the Frankish empire's great holdings among numerous offspring. Therefore, the two adjacent estates in Périgeaux were to be split no further; they would be inherited in their entirety by Christien and Peter, respectively. The younger sons—Alex and Luke, and their cousin, Milo—knew from infancy that they would one day be left landless.

Alex and Luke had prepared for this day by training to become stipendiary knights, in the hope of earning estates elsewhere. Milo, having rejected first a religious, and then a military, vocation, was left with no prospects other than to live under his brother's roof, which Alex knew he found vexing. He'd been stewing about his predicament quite a bit in recent months, robbing him of his usual good humor. Alex was gratified to find his cousin so animated this afternoon. Perhaps he'd found some way out of the situation. More likely he was simply learning to live with it.

"An impressive scheme for earning land," Milo said, executing one of his mocking little bows toward his cousins. "Unfortunately, it all hinges on William the Bastard actually rising to the throne of England."

"Of course he will," Alex said. "Edward of England

has promised him the throne. Then England and Normandy will be united under the rule of one man—a man my brother and I will have served faithfully, and who will no doubt reward us with rich English estates."

"It might take years, as my sire suggests," Luke said soberly. "Probably so. But 'twill be worth it."

Milo waved a serving wench over to refill his goblet. "Luke might settle down if he earns an estate, but not you, Alex. Soldiering is in your blood. If you were granted a choice holding tomorrow, you'd still go off and fight for your almighty William."

Alex couldn't suppress a grin. "I won't deny I'm anxious to try my hand at some *real* fighting. I've grown weary of mock sword fights. 'Tis high time I christened my blade in blood."

From the corner of his eye, he saw Nicki hold her goblet up to be filled, looking strangely pensive.

"Gaspar," Luke said, turning to the brawny retainer sitting silently next to him, "why don't you join us? Lord Henri might release you into William's service if you requested it, and then you could earn some land of your own, even if it *is* in England."

"Preposterous," muttered Lady Sybila under her breath.

Gaspar shook his head. "I'm no wellborn knight, like you fellows—just the humble son of an apothecary."

"Duke William is the grandson of a tanner," Milo said, "born on the wrong side of the bed, no less, and he may end up king of England."

"I've been happy at Peverell, serving my lord Henri," Gaspar said, adding, with a bow toward his mistress, "and my lady Sybila. I've come far, for a man of my station, and I'm not about to give it up for the chance to earn a patch of earth in some dreary foreign land. No offense to those who choose to, but it ain't what I want for myself."

With Gaspar's zeal for following orders, it surprised

Alex to hear him speak of what he wanted for himself. But then, he supposed every man must have some sort of ambition, even a lowborn man-at-arms such as Gaspar.

"Milo, why don't you join us?" Alex asked. "Come with us and seek your fortune in England."

Milo toyed with the stem of his goblet. "I have . . . other plans," he said cryptically. "Besides, I'd stay out of it anyway. England isn't a private estate, like Normandy. King Edward can't simply promise it to his chosen heir. England's witan chooses their king, and they'll probably choose Harold Godwineson, Earl of Wessex, over the Bastard of Normandy—they revere Harold in England."

"The witan will choose the king whom Edward recommends," Luke said, "and since Edward has promised the crown to William, 'twill go to William."

"Perhaps," Milo suggested, "Edward made his promise unthinkingly, or perhaps William misinterpreted some comment of Edward's. Or perhaps he invented an interpretation quite unlike what Edward had intended—"

"What are you implying?" Alex demanded, shocked as much by his own wrath toward his beloved cousin as by Milo's base insinuation. "William is a man of honor. He'd never stoop to such underhanded—"

"Easy, Alex," Luke placated. "Milo didn't mean any—"

"But I did!" Milo's devilish grin dissolved quickly, replaced by an expression of fraternal concern. "I don't much mind you fighting for this bastard, Alex, but don't deify him, for God's sake. If you're going to throw in your lot with him, do it with your eyes open. He's botched things up in the past, and he's about to do so again in Brittany—and perhaps in England as well. God forbid the witan should decide to crown Harold. William will go rushing across the Channel in an unthinking frenzy—"

"Unthinking!" Alex pounded a fist on the table. Luke rested a hand on his shoulder. "He's a brilliant military leader!"

"That's what you said about Roland," Milo reminded him drolly. "And his folly cost thousands of lives."

"William of Normandy is destined to be king of England," Alex declared, "and I intend to support him no matter what. If I have to fight the English for his right to rule, then I'll fight them. At least I've got the stones for it, which is more than you can—"

"Alex . . ." Luke's grip tightened on his brother's shoulder.

"Cousin." Peter rose, stabbing Alex with a censorious scowl. "This conversation has gone on long enough, I think. The ladies are growing weary of it."

Abashed, Alex wondered how Nicki had reacted to his outburst. He glanced her way to find her looking at him, very still and quiet. He chanced a smile, and her features softened.

"When I asked you here this morning," Peter said, "I told you I had an announcement to make."

Nicki abruptly looked away.

"I do," Peter continued. "A very special one, which greatly gladdens my heart." He grinned broadly. "This morning, my wife's beloved lady cousin, Nicolette de St. Clair, honored my brother, Milo de Périgeaux, by consenting to be his wife."

Blood roared in Alex's head, overwhelming the swell of voices raised in exclamations of pleasure. It was a struggle just to fetch his breath as he watched Milo accept the congratulations with cordial good grace. Nicki was subdued.

"Nay," he rasped.

Luke's fingers dug painfully into his shoulder, quelling his impulse to bolt to his feet. "Be still."

"Nay." Bracing his hands on the table, he tried to

rise, but Luke slammed him down, hard. In the tumult of excitement, no one seemed to notice.

"Not now," Luke ground out as Peter called for silence so that he could finish his announcement. "Not here."

"When, then?" Alex whispered harshly.

"Never."

"I entreat you all to join us at the chapel door to-morrow morning at terce to witness the joining in holy wedlock of—"

"Tomorrow!" Alex's outcry was drowned out by a chorus of astonishment.

"The wedding must needs be hasty," Peter said with exaggerated patience, having evidently anticipated this uproar, "for word arrived late last night that the bride's uncle, Henri de St. Clair, has been stricken with a stoppage of the liver. The ladies Nicolette and Sybila are compelled to return posthaste to St. Clair. My brother, as Lady Nicolette's lord husband, will accompany them."

"Christ." Alex wrested himself out of his brother's grasp and stalked out of the hall.

So deeply shaken was he that, when he found himself in the middle of the sheep meadow, he could not recall having walked there. As he gazed across at the woods that hid their little cave, a torrent of rage and loss rose within him, ripping out of his lungs as a raw animal howl. The sheep scattered, bleating. He dropped to his knees, fists clenched, and screamed every foul oath he knew as loud as he could.

A hand on his back made him whip around, trembling. "Jesu! Luke."

Luke sat next to him. "Didn't you notice me following you?"

Sinking down, Alex rested his arms on his updrawn knees and shook his head.

"Come on." Luke patted him on the shoulder. "Let's go home."

"You go ahead," Alex said raspily, his throat sore from screaming. "I'm going to wait and talk to her."

"Alex . . ."

"I just need to talk to her. Don't worry about me, brother. You're always watching out for me. I feel smothered. I'm not a child anymore."

"I know that, Alex, but you're upset. 'Tis best if you come home with me—"

"How could she do this?" Alex dragged shaking fingers through his close-cropped hair. "I love her. She knows it, she must. I've shown her in a thousand ways. I've treated her like a princess. I've been gentle and chivalrous and . . ." He shook his head helplessly. "Why?"

Luke hesitated, as if choosing his words. "Perhaps you've been . . . a bit too chivalrous."

"What's that supposed to mean?"

"Perhaps she didn't want a gentle chevalier. Perhaps she wanted . . . a man."

It took Alex a moment to grasp his brother's meaning. When he did, he leapt to his feet. "She's an innocent maiden. She knows naught of such things." Turning away as Luke stood up, he added, "I'm going to go talk to her."

Luke grabbed his arm and came around to face him. "Alex, think about it . . . a rushed wedding and all. Have you considered the possibility that . . . they had to get married?"

Alex hauled back and slammed his fist into Luke's face. His brother fell to the ground, blinking in astonishment, blood oozing from beneath the hand cupped over his nose.

Stunned at what he'd done—he'd never struck his brother in anger, only for sport—Alex felt his knees buckle. Finding himself kneeling in the grass, it only seemed right to whisper a brief prayer of forgiveness.

Luke sat up, chuckling to find Alex executing a solemn sign of the cross. "You'll have to work on your punch if you expect to do enough damage to pray over."

"I broke your nose."

Luke prodded his swollen nose, from which blood trickled. " 'Tisn't broken, just angry." Gently fingering the reddened flesh around his left eye, he said, "I'll have a black eye tomorrow, though. 'Twill give me an excuse to visit Tempeste. She's good with poultices and such. And when it comes to giving comfort, she's without equal."

Alex shook his head mournfully. "I'm an animal."

Luke slapped him on the back. "I spoke without thinking, said things I shouldn't have, especially with you so upset. I suppose all I really meant was . . . well, Milo is older than you, and . . . women tend to be attracted to a more mature man. And, of course, they've much in common. There's a sort of affinity of the mind between them. Surely you've noticed."

Steeped in misery, Alex could only nod.

"It really shouldn't surprise you that she chose him," Luke said gently.

"But it does," Alex said hoarsely. "It astounds me. You don't understand, Luke. You don't know . . . what's transpired between us."

Luke frowned. "You told me you'd done naught but hold her hand."

"I don't mean physically. I never . . . I wouldn't have . . . I love her! It doesn't make sense. None of this makes sense. She loves *me*. I know it!" Rising to his feet, Alex offered his brother a hand up. "I'm going to talk to her."

Luke sighed. He started to say something, then shook his head. "Do as you must. But don't make this a public event. Find some way to speak to her privately."

"The things I need to say to her," Alex assured his brother, "I could hardly say in front of an audience."

Chapter 6

A lex spent the rest of that afternoon lying on the
floor of the cave, studying the mysterious paintings and feeling very juvenile and inept for having let
things come to this pass. His heart pushed against his
chest as if it were trying to burst through. Part of him
wished it would, just to put an end to this torment.

When night fell, he made his way undetected to the
little guest house in which Nicki and her mother slept,
a thatched stone cottage across the flagstone courtyard
from Peter's main house. Anxious not to be seen, he
slipped around back, jimmied open the shutters on the
single window, and crept inside.

By the watery moonlight he found a lantern and lit
it. The one-room cottage was homey and well kept,
with a fresh coat of whitewash on the walls and herb-
strewn rushes carpeting the clay floor.

A bowl of fragile little wild roses sat in the middle
of a linen-draped table. They were from the edge of
the sheep meadow, near the cave. Alex had picked
them for Nicki yesterday. He lifted one to smell it,
but a thorn bit into his thumb, drawing blood. Slipping
the blossom back into the bowl, he licked the blood
absently.

On a little table next to the washstand he found a
tidy arrangement of toiletries on an embroidered
cloth: a lump of soft soap on a clay dish, a comb of
bird's-eye maple, a boar's-hair brush. He unstoppered
a tiny bottle of thick, bubbly blue glass and sniffed; it

contained rose oil. A little pot of some sort of balm smelled spicy. He opened a small ivory case carved in an intricate pattern and found that it housed a polished-steel looking glass. Fancying that it retained Nicki's image in its silvery depths, he entertained a reckless urge to slip it into the leather pouch on his belt. In the end, he replaced it where it had been.

From hooks on the wall hung an assortment of ladies' tunics. He counted four of plain black wool—the lady Sybila's, of course—and half a dozen silken gowns in the delicate hues that her daughter favored—ivory, dove gray, lavender, icy blue, a pink as muted as a blush . . . and the pale green trimmed with silver that she'd been wearing the day they discovered their cave.

Alex touched the green gown, rubbed the liquid-smooth silk between his fingers. It was nearly the same sea-green as her eyes. Perhaps that's why she looked so devastatingly beautiful in it.

His throat spasmed. Taking deep breaths, he forced his anguish deep inside. He hadn't cried since he was a child. He'd be damned if he'd let Nicki find him weeping over her.

Against the back wall stood a large bed. Alex crossed to the trunk at its foot and opened it. A white silken garment lay on top, as if tossed in carelessly. Lifting it, he found it to be a sleeping shift—a rather scanty one, obviously designed with warm summer nights in mind. The detachable sleeves had been removed at the shoulders, and the bodice dipped low in front; it was surprisingly short. He envisioned Nicki wearing this slick little layer of silk and nothing else, and the breath caught in his lungs.

Gathering the shift in his fists, he brought it to his face and breathed in the warm, tantalizing scent that had held him in a bewitched haze all summer. His mind reeled with the provocative thoughts and images that had haunted his nights—damp flesh . . . secret places . . . dark, unyielding needs.

A faint rattling came from the door—a key being turned in the lock. Alex threw the shift into the trunk and slammed it shut as the door swung open.

Nicki took one step into the room and drew up short, eyes wide. An enormous key slipped from her fingers, disappearing into the rushes. "Alex!"

"Nicki."

The lady Sybila stepped out from behind her, gaping in shock. She stalked into the room, looking back and forth between the two of them, nostrils flaring. "Jesus have mercy," she whispered, her eyes igniting with comprehension.

"Mama . . ." Nicki began.

"Nicolette, didn't I warn you?" her mother asked in a quavering voice. "Do you never learn?"

"Mama, please—"

"He's got to leave! If he's found here, you'll be destroyed." Turning to Alex, she held the door wide and pointed rigidly toward the courtyard. "Get out! What were you thinking, coming here? My daughter is to be married tomorrow morning. If anyone saw you come in here, she'll be ruined."

"No one saw me," he said with as much calm as he could muster. "I came in through the window."

"Merciful God," Sybila muttered.

"I'm not going," he said. "You are."

Sybila's face twisted into a mask of outrage. "And leave you alone with her? Are you mad?"

"I mean to speak to her, nothing more. If you don't go now, I'll let my presence here be known to one and all."

"You wouldn't."

"I assure you I will," he said gravely.

"Go, Mama," Nicki implored. "Please. I'll be all right. He just wants to talk."

Sybila pinned Alex with a look of loathing so intense that it chilled him. "You have made a grievous error, coming here," she said softly.

Whether that was intended as a threat, Alex knew not, for she didn't elaborate, merely departed quietly. Alex fetched the key from the rushes and locked the door. Tossing the key onto the table, he turned to Nicki. "Are you carrying his child?"

Her hand flew to her bosom. "Nay! How can you ask that? He's never touched me! I swear it!"

She seemed sincere, but that wasn't the only reason Alex believed her. Milo had always said he found Nicki too thin and pale and delicate for his taste. He liked buxom, earthy women like his Violette.

"Then why?" Alex demanded. "Why, Nicki?"

"He . . ." Nicki's voice shook. "He proposed last night. 'Twas after the letter came, about my uncle. Mama told him we had to return to St. Clair, and he found me and asked me to marry him."

"He doesn't love you. He loves a woman named Violette."

"I know. He told me last night."

"Did he tell you he's only marrying you to get out from under his brother's thumb?"

"I know why he's marrying me, Alex," she said quietly, her voice a bit more steady. "I'm no fool."

"Then why are you doing this?" he roared.

"Alex, please!" She darted an anxious glance toward the door.

Resting his hands on his hips, Alex stared into the rushes and concentrated on slowing his breathing. In a more subdued voice he asked, "Are you hoping he'll transfer his affections from Violette to you? If so, you're deluding yourself. He'll love her till the day he dies."

She turned away from him slowly, her arms wrapped around herself. "You're so young, Alex."

"I'm only two years younger than you."

"Aye, but there are so many things you don't understand." The back of her long neck, revealed by the braids draped over her shoulders, was graceful and perfect and luminous as white marble. Oftentimes he'd been tempted to kiss it.

He took a step toward her. "I understand more than you think. I know you set your sights on Milo, encouraged him even as you spent every afternoon with me—"

She pivoted to face him. "That's not true, Alex."

"I may be young, but I'm not a fool, Nicki." He stalked toward her and she backed up, eyes wide. "Milo is a man—a man of learning—and I'm just an uneducated boy. That's it, isn't it?"

"Nay!"

"A harmless puppy who follows you around slavishly, lavishing you with attention—"

"Nay!" she cried, stumbling backward. "Alex, please—"

"Desperate for some morsel of affection. Irritating, but slightly amusing. Is that how you think of me?"

She tried to sidestep him, but he seized her by the arms and backed her roughly against the wall. His heart drummed in his ears; his chest heaved.

"Is that what I am to you?" His gaze traveled from her face downward, lighting on the thick plaits of golden hair resting against her chest. Letting go of her arms, he wrapped one hand around each braid, high up, and slid them down slowly. The slick ropes felt heavy and cool against his palms; the white satin ribbons tickled slightly, making him shiver.

"A harmless, smooth-faced boy?" he murmured, stroking the braids downward. Against the backs of his hands, he felt the birdlike racing of her heart, the soft rise and fall of her breasts. "A boy who's content to merely hold your hand . . . who would never think of doing more . . ."

His knuckles grazed her nipples through the sleek tunic. Her indrawn breath stirred a quickening in his loins. Moving fractionally closer to her, he glided his hands upward, back over the little crests, and down again, feeling them stiffen as he stroked them.

She closed her eyes; her throat moved as she swallowed. "Alex . . ."

"I think about it all the time." Releasing the braids, he closed his hands over her breasts, all the while watching his actions from above, as if it were not he, but another man, taking such scandalous liberties with the undefiled Nicolette de St. Clair. He felt the weighty resilience of warm flesh through silk, the rigid peaks so sensitive that she gasped every time he touched them.

It was a kind of panic driving him, he realized, a frantic dread of losing what he'd shared with her—and the bitter awareness that what had been the fiercest passion to him might only have been a summer's diversion to her. Panic turned to hunger as he fondled her—a primitive hunger, a desire to possess her, make her his.

"I lie awake at night thinking about it," he said gruffly, lowering his head. "About you."

"Please go," she whispered raggedly. "You shouldn't be here. Mama's right—I'll be ruined if anyone knows that you've been—"

Alex silenced her by closing his mouth over hers, his hands trailing upward to hold her head still when she tried to evade him. He kissed her hard, not knowing or caring whether he was doing it right, just needing the hot, sweet pressure of her mouth against his. The time for gentleness was over.

She shoved his chest. Grabbing her wrists, he pinned them against the wall. "I love you," he breathed against her lips. "As a man loves." He pressed himself against her, aching with need. Let her feel what she'd done to him; let her know.

She grew very still and quiet, in that way she had. "You want me. It's not the same thing."

"I want you and I love you."

"Alex, I . . ." She shook her head. "I'm not the woman you think I am. There are things about me you don't know. You're better off without me."

Alex backed away a bit, his grasp on her loosening. Rubbing her wrists, she stepped cautiously away from him and crossed to the big bed, where she sat with her head in her hands. He thought he heard her say, "And I'm better off without you."

"How can you say that?" he asked incredulously as he approached her. "How can you possibly think it? We belong together."

Kneeling on the floor in front of her, he lifted one of her braids and untied the white ribbon woven through it. Sliding it out, he tossed it onto the bed, and then he did the same to the other braid.

"You belong on the battlefield," she said.

"You've been listening to your mother." He combed his fingers through the heavy satin tendrils, crimped from having been plaited. Lifting a handful of hair, he stroked his face with it, inhaled its scent.

"I've been listening to you," she countered. "Soldiering is in your blood. You love your sword above all else."

"You're in my blood." Cupping the back of her head, he pulled her head down, kissing her thoroughly but taking his time, trying to do it right this time. His other hand stole to her breast. "I love you."

She looked earnestly into his eyes. "Don't say that."

"I do. And you love me, too." He kneaded her breast, rubbed his fingertips over the pebbly little nipple.

Squeezing her eyes shut, she said breathlessly, "I can't afford to love you."

"You love me." Reaching down with his other hand, he slid it under the hem of her skirt.

Her eyes flew open. "I'm going to marry Milo." She scrambled backward on the bed in an effort to get away from him. He pounced in a blur, leaping onto the bed and trapping her beneath him. Her hair sprayed out around her in a breathtaking halo of gold.

Taking her face in his hands, he said, "I know you've got your heart set on being Milo's wife, but he'll never love you. You'll never steal his heart away from Violette. It can't be done. He doesn't love you and you don't love him. You love me." He shifted his weight on top of her, nestled his hips against hers. "You belong to me." Compelled as before by a primal need—the urge to take her, to claim her as his—he moved against her in an intuitive rhythm.

"W-what are you doing?" she asked.

"What I should have done long ago."

She pushed futilely against his shoulders. "I belong to Milo now."

"He can't have you." Whipping her skirt up, he wedged a knee between her legs and reached his hand between them. She cried out softly at his first light touch on her most sensitive flesh.

"He'll never have you," he vowed, his voice low and rough. "You don't want him. You want me."

Alex lowered his mouth to hers as he explored the hidden mysteries he'd so often imagined during long, sleepless nights alone on sheets damp with sweat. He knew his touch was awkward, inexperienced, but he didn't care, driven as he was by brute instinct. He was rigid as a sword beneath his tunic.

"Oh . . . oh, God, Alex . . ." She closed her hands over his shoulders, gripping him tightly.

Her breathing became erratic as he caressed her, his fingers growing marvelously slick. From things Luke had told him, he knew this was a sign of her arousal. "You do want me," he murmured into her ear. "Say it." He thrust against her, never pausing in his intimate caress. She moaned, her hands skimming down to press against the small of his back.

"Say it." Kneeling between her legs, he tore off his

belt and threw it on the floor. "You want me." She shook her head, her face stained with a feverish flush of excitement. "Admit it." Yanking off his tunic, he threw it aside. "You want me. You love me."

Holding himself stiff armed over her, he pressed himself against her, letting her feel how hard he was through his thin shirt and chausses. She lifted her hips with a defenseless little whimper. "This isn't fair."

"I don't care." He fumbled beneath his voluminous white shirt to untie his chausses. "Say it."

"Don't make me," she begged him breathlessly.

"Say it. Say you want me. *Me.* Not him. Say it!"

"I . . . please, Alex." She writhed beneath him, her expression of anguished desire mirroring what was in his heart. They both wanted this. And by laying rightful claim to her, he was rescuing her from a calamitous mistake. She'd be miserable with Milo.

And she was his. *His.*

Freeing his straining shaft, he lowered himself on her, investigating her tentatively to locate the place of entrance. "Yes," she whispered when his finger probed the tight little passage, so wet and ready. He groaned, his body pulsing with the need to drive itself into hers. He hoped he'd last long enough to do the job properly. Luke had always counseled him to avoid virgins in general, but in the event he felt impelled to take a maidenhead, to be exceedingly tender and patient. On the verge of release even now, all he wanted was to ram himself into her and explode.

"Say it, Nicki." Reaching between them, he positioned himself for entrance.

"I . . . I want you." Her arms went around him. "I do, Alex . . ."

Rising onto his elbows, he flexed his hips, pressing her open, just slightly. "And you love me. And you're mine, and you won't marry him. Say it."

"Alex, please." She arched upward, her body closing around him, hot and damp.

Summoning all the strength at his disposal, he withdrew from the snug embrace. *"Say it!"* he commanded, his cock on fire, every muscle in his body tight.

"I can't," she cried, her eyes shimmering. "Alex, please." With a trembling hand she caressed his cheek, whispering hoarsely, "We'll never have another chance. Please." She tilted her hips again, slowly, drawing him into her intoxicating heat. He fisted his hands in her hair, searching within himself for the strength to resist her until she said the words he needed to hear. "Please," she whispered, "just—"

Hurried footsteps sounded on the flagstone outside, followed by the frantic rattling of the door handle.

"Mama!" Nicki clambered off the bed with breathless speed, yanking her skirts down. "She's got her own key!"

"Christ." Alex knelt on the bed with his back to the door, frantically tying his chausses, arousal plummeting as he heard the metallic snick of Sybila's key in the lock.

"Nicolette!" Sybila burst into the cottage, key in hand. "Phelis is on her way. . . ." The words died in her throat. Looking over his shoulder, Alex saw her take in her daughter's state of dishabille—the loose, disheveled hair, the rumpled tunic, her telltale flush. Then she turned her frigid gaze on him, crossing herself at the sight of him adjusting his chausses and pulling his shirt down. "Holy Mary, Mother of God."

"Mama," Nicki began.

Sybila slapped her daughter's face, a sharp openhanded blow that made Nicki's head whip around. "Have you learned nothing?" She aimed her hand to strike again, but Alex jumped down from the bed and caught her wrist in a solid grip.

"Are you all right, Nicki?" he asked.

She nodded, rubbing her reddened cheek, her chin quivering. He despised Sybila for having the power to reduce her daughter to this sorry state. If only Nicki could be a stalwart with her mother as she was with everyone else.

He released Sybila's hand. "Leave her be, my lady. If anyone deserves a beating for what happened here, 'tis I."

"I daresay that's true." When she raised her hand to him, he did not attempt to stop her. She dealt him a stinging crack across the face, which he accepted passively, determined to deprive her of the satisfaction of a response.

"Mama, stop it!" Nicki beseeched tearfully as her mother struck him again, and yet again.

Alex calmly turned toward the bed. Sybila rained frenzied punches on his back as he gathered up his tunic and belt, stuffing them under his arm. "So you just wanted to talk to her, eh?" she spat out. "I should have known you couldn't be trusted. You brazen young knights are all alike. No woman is safe around any of you."

"Mama, for pity's sake," Nicki said, wiping the tears form her cheeks.

Sybila let off beating Alex and turned to her daughter. "How could you give yourself so cheaply, Nicolette? Does it mean nothing to you that you're to marry Milo tomorrow morning?"

"She won't," Alex said. "Not if I can help it. I won't let you marry him, Nicki. I'll do whatever it takes to stop the wedding."

Sybila sputtered in outrage while her daughter shook her head slowly, her face tearstained, her eyes red. "It can't be stopped," Nicki said quietly. "I have to marry him. Go, Alex. Please!"

"She'll be ruined if you're found here," Sybila declared. "If you cared about her, you'd leave, and you wouldn't be threatening to interfere with the wedding. It's what's best for her."

Desperate, Alex seized Nicki's arm. "Come away with me."

"What?"

"Meet me at dawn at our—" He eyed the lady Sybila warily. "At our secret place. I'll take you away."

"And make her your whore?" Sybila demanded. "You're not free to marry. Nicolette, he's a landless soldier. He can offer you naught but shame."

A knock came at the door. "Nicolette?"

"Phelis!" Sybila whispered, and shoved Alex toward the window. "Go!"

"I've brought my wedding tunic for you to wear tomorrow," Phelis said through the door. "May I come in?"

"Alex, go!" Nicki pleaded, tugging on his shirt.

"I won't always be landless, Nicki. I love you. Come away with me."

Sybila made a sound of derision. "And what do you propose to do with her while you follow Duke William from Brittany to England to God knows where?"

Alex tried to ignore Phelis's knocking as he groped for a solution that would give him the two things he most desperately wanted in life, the only things he truly cared about: Nicki and soldiering. "There are convents. . . ."

"Oh, for God's sake," Sybila muttered.

Nicki regarded him mournfully, clearly sobered at the prospect of cloistered life.

"Oh, God, Nicki," he moaned, alarmed at the possibility of losing her, "I know I'm doing everything wrong, but I love you, and I'll make everything right. Come away with me. Meet me at dawn."

Phelis's knocking grew more insistent. "Nicolette?"

"Just a moment!" she called, then whispered, "Go, please!"

"Not until you promise to meet me tomorrow at—"

"I can't."

"Nicolette?" Phelis called. "Is anything wrong?"

"N-nay!" she called. "I'll be right there. Please, Alex." Nicki pulled him toward the window. "I can't. Just go!"

He stroked her face, warm and soft and damp, reluctant to leave her like this but not really seeing as he had any choice. "Perhaps you'll have changed your mind after having had the night to think about it."

She closed her eyes and rubbed her cheek against his palm. "Perhaps you'll have changed yours."

"Never." He curled a hand around her neck to draw her toward him, kissing her deeply and urgently as her mother battered him with her fists.

"I love you," he whispered into her ear, "and he doesn't. Sleep on that tonight." With a final lingering caress of her cheek, he opened the shutters and leapt out of the window.

When he'd gotten far enough away not to be seen, he stopped and shook out his tunic. Something fluttered to the ground, and he bent to pick it up. It was one of the white satin ribbons he'd pulled out of her hair, which had evidently gotten tangled up with his tunic. Thinking it a good omen, he rolled it up carefully and tucked it away in his money pouch before heading home.

Alex prayed nonstop the next morning as he rode along the little track through the woods that separated his father's estate from Peter's, pleading with God to let Nicki be at the cave when he got there. Surely she'd changed her mind about the marriage, given time to ponder the fact that he loved her and Milo never would. Perhaps she'd intended to meet him even last night, but knew better than to admit it in front of her mother. In any event, he mustn't panic if she wasn't already there when he arrived, for it wasn't quite the appointed hour yet. The first silvery glow of dawn was only now washing the darkness from the sky.

Mounted on his best stallion, he led two other horses by the reins—a gentle mare for Nicki and a packhorse heavily laden with provisions for a journey. If they left forthwith, they could be many miles away by the time their absence was discovered. Beyond that, he had no firm plans. Nicki seemed averse to living in a convent until he could provide a home for her, but perhaps he could change her mind. Or perhaps something else would come to him. He'd think of something. It would work out. It had to.

As he rounded a curve in the path, about fifty yards from where it opened out into the sheep meadow, he saw a shadowy figure sitting on a fallen log. His heart slammed in his chest. He almost called Nicki's name out loud, thinking she'd decided for some reason to meet him here instead of at the cave, when he realized it couldn't be her. The figure was a man, and a large one. Only one man carried that kind of bulk—Gaspar le Taureau.

Gaspar did not rise as Alex drew up, merely nodded at him and squeezed a wineskin into his mouth. Alex's scalp tightened.

"What brings you this way at this hour, Gaspar?" Alex asked as he reined in the horses.

"I've a message for you, Sir Alex," Gaspar said, wiping his mouth with the back of his hand. "Two, actually. One from the lady Nicolette and one from her mother."

Crushed that Nicki hadn't come, Alex said, "I care naught what the lady Sybila might have to say. What news of my lady Nicolette?"

"She asked me to tell you that she has not changed her mind. Her wedding to your cousin Milo will take place as planned, and she prays you do nothing to interfere with it."

Alex clenched the reins in a white-knuckled fist. "I will do everything in my power to prevent that wedding. She knows not what she's doing."

Gaspar rubbed the back of his neck. "In that case, I'm obliged to deliver the lady Sybila's message as well." He held the wineskin toward Alex. "Have some. 'Twill make the message easier to bear, I think."

Struggling to hide his grievous disappointment, Alex dismounted and tethered the horses, then took the wineskin and drank. He tried to hand it back, but Gaspar wouldn't accept it. "Have some more, young sir. You'll need it."

"I'd rather have the message."

Gaspar regarded him somberly. "Suit yourself." His big body unfolded slowly as he stood up from the log. Reaching beneath his short cloak, he produced a club, which he hefted in his meaty hand.

Shit.

A rustling came from behind. Alex turned to find Gaspar's churlish subservients, Vicq and Leon, emerging from the woods brandishing clubs of their own. Alex wished he was wearing his sword, or at least a dagger. Without a weapon, he was defenseless against three armed men.

Gaspar tapped his club against his boot. "Lady Sybila asked me to tell you that her daughter's wedding is of the utmost importance to her, and you're not to try and meddle with it." He sighed. "And she instructed me to make sure you wouldn't be able to."

"I don't suppose there's any way to change your mind. Silver, perhaps?"

The big man shook his head. "An order is an order. You're a knight. You understand."

"Aye."

Gaspar closed both fists around the handle of the club and took a sweeping practice swing. Nodding toward the wineskin in Alex's hand, he said, "You'd best finish that off. She said I was to do a thorough job of it."

Alex drained the wineskin and tossed it aside. "Do

me one small kindness if you would, Gaspar. Don't damage my sword hand."

Gaspar smiled. "Only too happy to oblige." He stepped forward and swung, slamming Alex in his midsection. Bone crunched. He hit the dirt. Two more jolting blows came from behind. One got him in a kidney; he swallowed down a roar of pain.

Don't yell. Keep your mouth shut and take it.

They struck him in the legs, the back, the stomach. He wrapped his arms around his torso to keep from using his precious hands to shield his face when they started in on that. Pain surrounded him, consumed him in blooms of white fire. He swallowed dirt and blood.

In his mind's eye, a face materialized, backlit by a haze of searing light—the smooth, pale, coolly innocent face of Nicolette de St. Clair. He fixed his entire being on that face, studied it, focused on its every detail as a way of transcending the hot bursts of pain that erupted again and again and yet again.

At long last, the pain receded, the face faded, the light dimmed, and a dreamless night descended upon him.

Alex swam in and out of consciousness for a timeless interval, aware mostly of pain—everywhere there was pain—but also, dimly, of hands tending to his wounds—the hands of a woman, for he heard her voice, and sometimes that of his brother. The hands were cool and slightly work-roughened, the voice throaty. She smelled of cooked food and sweat and some cloyingly sweet scent. Another odor—turpentine?—made his nostrils flare, but it didn't come from her; it seemed to come from him.

When he came fully awake, he found himself in bed in his own chamber at home. He tried to sit up, only to groan in agony and frustration. Both arms and one leg were splinted, his ribs tightly swaddled, and the rest of him—from the head down—heavily swathed in bandages and poultices. All he could move were his hands and feet. He flexed the fingers of his right hand slowly, relieved to find that it appeared to be intact. Gaspar had been as good as his word.

"You've been doing that for the past three days," came a voice from somewhere behind him.

"Luke?" Alex rasped through parched lips.

A chair squeaked. The face of his brother appeared above him. "Your eye," Alex moaned contritely when he saw the fading bruises surrounding Luke's left eye.

Luke smiled weakly and touched his black eye. "You've got two of these, and your nose looks like a great white turnip. But that's the least of it. Your right hand is the only part of you've that's moved since I found you."

"What is that stink?"

"You."

Luke brought him a cup of water and held his head up so he could sip it. Alex saw that his brother had something wrapped around his hand—the leather thong attached to the wooden crucifix he'd carved as a boy, and which he wore around his neck. It was his habit to hold it this way, with the cross in his palm, while he prayed. "Were you that worried about me?" Alex asked.

Luke's expression sobered. His eyes, Alex noted, were red rimmed. He'd never known his brother to cry.

"I thought you . . ." Luke's voice snagged; he cleared his throat. "I wasn't sure you were going to make it." He drew in a breath and released it. "When I couldn't find you the morning of the wedding, I remembered what you said about some secret meeting place by Peter's sheep pasture. On my way there, I found you on the path. . . ." He shook his head. "I recognized you by your tunic. The rest of you was . . . Christ, Alex. Was it bandits?"

Alex tried to shake his head, but pain thudded from within. "Gaspar," he whispered. "And those apes of his."

Luke stared at him in disbelief. "Why?"

Alex licked his lips. Luke gave him another sip of water. "To keep me from stopping the wedding."

Luke swore softly. Unwrapping the leather cord from his hand, he draped the crucifix around his neck. "It worked. Father Gregoire married Milo and Nicolette that morning."

Alex felt the room tilt. He had to look away from the sympathy in Luke's eyes. "Ah."

"They're on their way to St. Clair now, along with that shrewish mother of hers. And of course Gaspar and his thugs. When we go up north to join William—assuming you're still up to it—"

"I will be."

Luke smiled. "That's the spirit. When we arrive in Normandy, we can seek Gaspar out and teach him a lesson."

Alex tried to shake his head again, and winced. "Nay. He was following his mistress's orders. 'Twas only right that he do so."

"Look at you. He had no call to give you such a savage beating. He nearly killed you."

"I deserved it. I was a fool. 'Twas a useful lesson to me." Wondering exactly how much of a fool he'd been, Alex said, "Do you think she was deliberately encouraging Milo behind my back?"

Luke's expression of contempt said it all.

"Then why did she keep coming to the cave with me? Why would she have let me think she cared?"

"I'll tell you," Luke said with a hesitant smile, "if you promise not to deal me another black eye. Not that you could, in your fix, but—"

"Tell me," Luke demanded, unamused.

"Women have been known to use one fellow to

make another one—the one they're really interested in—jealous."

Alex digested that, finding it all too plausible. But . . . "Milo loves Violette. He couldn't have been made jealous over me."

"She doesn't know about Violette."

"She does. He told her."

Luke blinked. "Verily? He's not as clever as I'd thought. But he didn't tell her until he proposed, so she might have thought it would work."

Alex's head pulsed. "God's bones, do you really think—"

"She wanted Milo," Luke said. "And she saw you as a way to get what she wanted."

"Christ." Could it be true? If so, then the passion he'd inspired in her that night in her chamber, when they'd almost made love, had been nothing more to her than a physical craving, an itch that had needed scratching. "It's all so damned complicated and sordid and—"

"Welcome to the domain of the heart." Luke turned and crossed to the little window, opened the shutters, and leaned out. When he spoke, his voice was so soft and measured as to lull Alex into drowsiness. " 'Tis a hard life, that of a soldier. We're not like other men. The things they cherish—a home, a loving wife, children— are denied us. No woman of any worth wants to be united with some great lout in bloody chain mail who never knows where he'll be or who he'll be killing tomorrow. Falling in love is not an option for us. We must make do with our laundresses and whores and tavern wenches."

"No attachments," Alex murmured languidly, repeating the advice Luke had tried with so little success to drum into him. "I was an idiot. I shall not make the same mistake again."

Turning back around, Luke leaned against the window frame and crossed his arms. "Until you're landed. Then you can—"

"Never again," Alex breathed, his eyes closing of their own volition. "No attachments."

Alex awoke some time later to the sensation of pleasantly rough fingertips gliding over his lips, anointing them with some sort of fragrant salve. Drawn for some reason to taste it, he touched his top lip with his tongue, brushing it across a fingertip in the process. A woman's low chuckle made him squeeze his eyes open.

"Oh." He squinted to bring the face into focus—dark eyes, lush lips, a snarled mane of auburn hair spilling out of the rag in which it was tied. Tempeste; she sat on the edge of his bed, holding a tiny jar. He'd just licked her finger. "Terribly sorry."

She smiled and leaned closer, her bosom resting heavily on his chest. "You may do it again," she offered, nudging his lips open with the slick fingertip. "Do you like the taste? 'Tis violet water and oil of sweet almonds in duck's grease."

He heard the creaking of the chair behind him, and then Luke appeared in his field of vision. "Awake again, are you? Tempeste has been caring for you. I sent for her as soon as I brought you home."

"I see," Alex managed.

"Didn't I tell you she's handy with poultices and the like? Three days and not one wound has festered."

" 'Tis the turpentine that keep them from putrefying. One of my many little tricks." Tempeste smiled coyly at Luke as she rose and went to set the little jar on the corner table, which was covered with vials and bottles and stacks of clean bandages.

"Tempeste's talents are myriad and varied." Luke lowered his voice. "I've paid her well to tend to your needs—all of them. See that you let her. I hate wasting my silver."

"Are you serious? I can't even move."

Luke smiled slowly. "Tempeste can."

*   *   *

"That's it, then," Tempeste announced after she'd removed the last of Alex's bandages. His nakedness seemed to trouble her not in the least, so he didn't let it trouble him. The only services she'd attempted to render him since he'd regained consciousness several days ago were of the healing variety, which was just as well, all things considered.

"I'll have to rebandage some of them bad ones," she said, dipping a cloth in a bowl of warm water and wringing it out. "But I reckon it's high time I cleaned you up a bit."

She started with his face, dabbing the cloth with great care over forehead, cheeks, and nose. As always when she tended to him, she sat snugged up against him on the bed, breasts and hips and fleshy arms pressing against him as she worked, her earthy scent enveloping him. "Some of them scars will stay," she said. "But the way I see it, that's all for the good. You were almost too perfect before. A man shouldn't be more beautiful than the woman he's with."

Alex gestured toward the wall behind her. "There's a looking glass hanging over the wash basin. I use it for shaving. Bring it to me."

"What do you want to shave for?" she asked, rubbing a hand over his youthful stubble. "I like a man with a rough jaw."

"I want to see my face."

Quietly she said, "No, you don't."

"I do." He wanted to brand his wounds into his memory before they healed. He wanted never to forget what his unchecked infatuation had wrought. "Bring it to me."

She did. He kept his expression neutral as he inspected the ravaged remains of his face, knowing he would never look quite the same again. The boy who had lost his heart to Nicolette de St. Clair was gone, replaced by a man who would bear the scars of his encounter with her for the rest of his life.

Tempeste hung the looking glass back up and set about washing him from head to toe, expounding all the while on his beauty—the squareness of his shoulders, the hard muscles of his belly, his lean hips and long legs.

She saved one attribute for last. "You're quite as sizable in your privities as your brother," she observed, thoroughly bathing the parts in question, which responded by stirring to life. Although far from modest by nature, Alex couldn't help but feel nonplussed to be growing hard under such close scrutiny, even by a woman who spoke of men's privy parts as if discussing the qualities of beets.

"It's obvious you and Sir Luke were sired by the same stallion," she cooed, rubbing the warm cloth over him with increasingly firm pressure.

He rose painfully onto an elbow. "You really needn't—"

"Lie back down before you hurt yourself!" she scolded. He did so. "That's better. You must let Tempeste tend to you." Dropping the cloth in the bowl, she slid her damp fist up and down his length, watching intently as the object of her fascination swelled and rose.

He clutched the sheets as she stroked him, her palm deliciously raspy against his taut flesh. "Look at that," she marveled softly as he became fully erect. "What a shame for such a lovely thing as that to go to waste. Don't you think so, milord?"

Alex swallowed hard. "I suppose."

"Your brother said as how I was to take away all your aches and pains." She pumped him faster now; his breathing grew harsh. "All of them."

He thrust into her hand, which incited a bolt of pain in his right hip. "I . . . I don't know as I'm capable of . . ."

"You just lie still," she soothed as she began gathering up her skirts. "I'm capable enough for the both of us."

Alex closed his eyes and lay unmoving as Tempeste climbed atop him and set about ridding him of the last shreds of his innocence. "That's right, Sir Alex . . . just relax. Let me do all the work."

He hitched in his breath when she lowered herself onto him. So did she.

He saw the burning white light again, and Nicki's ethereal image, her smile serene, her eyes cool and unblinking as the pleasure mounted within him. And he promised himself this would be the last time he allowed himself the agonizing luxury of gazing upon her face, even in his imagination.

Chapter 7

"Alex? Alex, wake up." Nicki crouched over Alex, sleeping on an oarsman's bench in this forsaken longboat, wondering why the devil he wouldn't awaken. She must have said his name a dozen times.

"Alex," she said more loudly. Still no response. She began to wonder whether she ought not to go get some water from the river and dump it on him, when he stirred, stretched . . . and looked at her.

Her heart lurched.

God, those eyes. How many times over the years had she dreamed of looking into them again? Sometimes, as now, she could see right into them, as if they were polished chunks of amber. Other times, it was like gazing into pools of ink.

Alex glanced around—at the boat, the bright morning sky—as if he couldn't quite remember where he was or how he got here. Meeting her gaze again, he mouthed her name. And then he reached for her.

Nicki held her breath as Alex trailed a callused fingertip lightly down her cheek. It was as if he didn't quite believe she was really there, or that it was really her. His touch rekindled something in her—a heat, a longing, a need for him that had never completely gone away, just lain dormant for nine cold years.

A band of white wrapped around his knuckles caught her eye. "What's that? Are you hurt?"

He glanced at his hand, then quickly withdrew it

and sat up, pivoting so that his back was to her. That seemed to upset his equilibrium, for he sank his head in his hands and groaned.

She stood up. "Are you all right?"

Alex grunted in what she took to be affirmation. From his movements, she could tell he was unwinding the bandage from his hand. She couldn't wrest her gaze from the powerful slope of his back, layered with muscle. In the summer heat, Peverell's men-at-arms would sometimes train without their shirts. On such days, the athletic field would be a sea of naked backs, yet she couldn't recall ever having seen one worth staring at.

What would Mama have thought if she knew her daughter had deliberately awakened a man asleep in a boat in his underdrawers? She would have been appalled—especially considering that the man in question was Alexandre de Périgeaux, whom she'd despised with a virulence bordering on madness.

And whom Nicki, God help her, had loved to distraction.

She could scarcely believe her eyes when she saw him yesterday in the castle courtyard, tussling with his brother—not just because he was there, but because he'd changed so dramatically. Gaspar was right; Alex had grown up, filling out that lanky adolescent body with dense muscle. In proportion, he reminded her of that tiny marble statue of a Roman warrior that Mama used to make Uncle Henri hide from her. Of course, she'd found it and studied it at every opportunity, entranced not only by its naturalistic beauty, but by its aura of potent masculinity.

Alex looked every bit the seasoned soldier. His body had the well-used look of a wooden shield that had been nicked in too many battles. He had scars everywhere, and some were ghastly. It chilled her to think how many times he must have come close to death.

He leaned over to pick something up off the deck of the old boat, stuffing the bandage into it. "How did you find me?" he asked groggily. His voice had deepened considerably since adolescence, but retained the slight raspiness she'd always liked.

"The lady Faithe told me where you'd be. I tried to wake you up for the longest time. I got worried something was wrong with you."

He rose unsteadily and stumbled over something, which rolled into her field of vision—a leather flask, the type men liked to keep strong drink in when they went out and about.

"Ah." She should have recognized the symptoms of a morning head. She'd lived through Milo's often enough, back when he still had them. They seemed to be a thing of the past now that he reached for his wine immediately upon awakening.

Alex leaned heavily on the boat's sloping hull. He rubbed his forehead as if it ached. " 'Twasn't the wine. I sleep very deeply. 'Tis a common source of complaint, not being able to rouse me. It usually takes a few hard kicks. A fellow I was quartered with once cracked two of my ribs trying to wake me for battle."

Nicki flinched.

He shrugged. "It worked. Women don't use enough force, so they have less luck."

This oblique reference to the women who'd shared his bed did not escape Nicki. It made sense that he would have found success with women. Alex de Périgeaux was more than merely handsome. His face had a quiet drama to it that was extraordinarily compelling. His most striking feature had to be those eyes, not so much because of their shape and color—although they were quite beautiful, and set off by sharply slanted black eyebrows—but because of their intensity. They didn't just look at you—they focused in, as if you were the only person in the universe, and Alex's sole desire in life was to plumb the depths of

your soul. They drew you in, those eyes. Drew you in
and never let you go.

Women must find him utterly irresistible. Just as
she had.

A cloud of regret passed over her soul; she would
have been his first, had things been different. She
didn't respond to his comment about women, resolved
to maintain a prudent distance from him—after all,
she was married to his cousin, and the past was dead
and buried—but he frowned slightly, as if sensing her
discomfort. He used to do that a lot, she reminded
herself. He always seemed to know what was in her
heart. No one had ever seen all the way inside her
the way Alex did.

Alex's morning stubble rasped loudly as he rubbed
his jaw. She remembered his eyes as having shone
with the unclouded innocence of youth, but that guile-
lessness was long gone, and the intent focus she'd
found so mesmerizing had changed character. He studied her with a gaze as penetrating as that of the wolf
for which he'd been named.

His face had lost the boyish softness that had made
him almost pretty, the years having imparted a rugged-
ness to his features that his nearly imperceptible facial
scars only served to enhance. And of course his hair
was longer now, as shaggy as an Englishman's. Yesterday it had been neatly combed, but this morning it
hung in stray tendrils over his forehead.

Silence hung heavily between them. She'd come
here with a purpose, but somehow this seemed an
inopportune moment to say what she had to say. Instead, she said, inanely, "You have so many scars."

He looked down at the old, well-healed injuries that
marred his body. "No more than most soldiers."

She sat on the bench next to the one he'd slept on.
"Yesterday, His Highness mentioned you as being
part of his private retinue. I'd always thought you

were a stipendiary soldier—a mercenary who fought for pay."

"I started out that way—Luke and I both did. William recruited us right before . . . before you came to Périgeaux that summer, for his Brittany campaign." Chuckling humorlessly, he rubbed the back of his neck. "What a disaster that turned out to be."

"Your father was a wise man—he predicted the Brittany defeat."

"Aye," he said. "Just as Milo predicted that the English witan would choose Harold over William."

"And that William's army would respond by rushing across the Channel."

"We didn't rush," Alex said testily; she'd struck a nerve. " 'Twas a well-planned invasion, and we conquered England with a single battle. A good day's work, even if I didn't walk away completely unscathed."

"Is that where you got . . ." she began, eyeing the worst of his scars, a jagged gash on his side that disappeared beneath the waist of his drawers. "Nay, I don't want to know."

"This?" She froze in astonishment as Alex casually untied the drawstring and lowered his drawers, maintaining the barest coverage for modesty's sake while displaying his mangled hip in its entirety.

"Blessed Mary," she whispered, taking in the deep and disfiguring gouge, as if his flesh had been torn off the bone by wild beasts. "I'm surprised you can still walk."

"It did take a bit of work to get back on my feet after this one," he said, hiking the drawers up and retying the cord. "It still seizes up on me if the weather's cold and damp. 'Tisn't from Hastings, though. It happened a few months later, while we were under the command of a sheriff in Cambridgeshire, subduing rebellion. Luke and I were on the way to Hauekleah, for his wedding to Faithe, when two Saxons ambushed us in the woods. One of them had this . . . well, it's a farm tool, really, but peasants use it as a weapon, and it's a good one—a great mallet with a spike on it—"

She shuddered. "I don't think I want to hear this."

He smiled slightly, and she saw something in his eyes, a glimmer that reminded her of how it had once been between them, when they used to meet in their cave and talk for entire afternoons. He was still easy to talk to, she realized with some measure of surprise. Despite everything, she found herself relaxing in the presence of this half-naked, hung-over, ravaged soldier she had loved as a boy.

"What about that?" She pointed to a gash on his calf.

"Wolves."

"Wolves?"

"Well, one wolf. The whole pack was after me, but—"

"I don't suppose any of your wounds were actually earned in battle," she said.

He surprised her by laughing. "This"—he pointed to a deep crease in his right forearm— "is my memento of Hastings. A Saxon with a fistful of throwing axes."

"Ah." She rubbed her arms.

Alex bent over to retrieve the wad of clothes his head had been resting on, which caused him to squeeze his eyes shut briefly, in evident pain. Extracting a pair of chausses, he sat on the bench—facing her this time—to insert first one foot and then the other into the woollen hose. "This arrow wound on my thigh is from the northern expedition a year or two after that. William paid off most of his mercenaries at the end of that campaign, thinking things would settle down and he wouldn't need them again. I refused to go, which seemed to impress him at the time. He drew me into the ranks of his personal corps, and I've been there ever since. He still pays me, but that's only because I won't take land."

He stood to pull up his chausses and tie them off, his keen gaze fixed on her the whole time. "You always did have a way of making me go on and on about myself," he said quietly. "What of Nicolette de St. Clair? How has she fared these past years?"

Nicki looked off toward the river. "I think you know how I've fared."

She entertained the rash urge to tell him about her and Milo's predicament—that they were going to lose Peverell if she failed to bear a son by the appointed date. But she barely knew him anymore. How could she disclose something so personal, so potentially calamitous? Moreover, he'd pity her even more than he did now, and she didn't think she could stand that.

When she looked back at him, he was studying her with an oddly intent expression that she fancied held a trace of sympathy. She smoothed the skirt of her pale blue gown. "There were two northern campaigns, weren't there?"

He gave her a look of amused indulgence that let her know he was aware of her effort to direct the conversation back toward himself. She supposed he'd had enough experience with that tendency of hers to know it when he heard it.

"Aye," he said, shaking out his big, wrinkled shirt, "we headed up north again in the winter of sixty-nine, to rout the Danes out of Yorkshire. They fled over the Humber River, meaning to gather supplies, so we . . ." He frowned uneasily. "You don't want to hear this."

"I do."

He gathered up the shirt and lowered it over his head. It was partially open, displaying the smooth planes of his upper chest, the topmost ridges of his belly. "We burned them out," he said. "We followed them past the Humber and gathered all the farm implements and foodstuffs into giant piles and set them on fire. We slaughtered cattle, torched houses . . ."

"What about the local people? You were destroying their property, their means of sustenance. Didn't they object?"

"Of course." He dragged his fingers through his hair. "They screamed and wept as we razed their villages. Five shires in northern England are barren and desolate to this day."

"How could you have . . . I mean, didn't you feel bad about—"

"I was consumed with remorse," he said quietly. "But my king ordered it done, and so I did it."

"Yes," she murmured, comprehension dawning. He'd sworn an oath of obedience to William, and he did not take oaths lightly.

"If we sinned in what we did," he said, fetching a leather pouch from the deck and tying it around his waist, "our punishment came during the march back to York. 'Twas a bitter winter that year, and we had to travel on foot through steep mountain passes. Some of the men lost their toes and fingers. Many of them took ill. My closest friend, Hugh, died in my arms."

"I'm surprised you didn't ask to be dismissed from the king's service after that."

"I'm a soldier," he said, sitting to pull on his boots. "Luke warned me when I embarked on this life that I might have to follow orders that didn't sit easy with me. 'Tis a hard life, but there's a certain freedom in it. I'm responsible only to myself and my liege—and, of course, to God. I've no estate to maintain, no villeins depending on me for their livelihoods, no wife and children to be responsible for. William tried to release me again last year, after our campaign against Malcolm, king of Scots, but I turned him down."

"There was a time when you craved the land you now turn your back on. 'Twas the very reason you put in with William in the first place."

Looking up, he met her gaze. "I changed my mind," he said tonelessly. Before she could summon a response, he stood, wincing, and made his way down the weathered board that served as a sort of makeshift gangplank between the boat and the riverbank. "I can visit Hauekleah whenever I'm on leave. 'Tis adequate to satisfy my rare urges to envelop myself in the noisy bosom of family life." Kneeling by the river, he cupped his hands in the water, filled his mouth and spat it out.

Lifting her skirts, Nicki stepped cautiously onto the dilapidated board. "Is that what you'll do during this six-month leave the king has imposed on you? Spend it at Hauekleah?"

"I imagine so." Turning, he saw her inching her way down the steep incline, but he made no move to assist her. There was a time when he would have rushed to offer his hand. His gallant streak had been part of the youthful charm that had stolen her heart that summer in Périgeaux.

"I'll stay with Luke and Faithe," he said, rising and drying his hands on his chausses, "while I petition the king to allow me to come back earlier."

"Even as a boy, you were fiercely dedicated to soldiering. I always knew you would never give it up, not for—" *Not for me.* That's what she'd been about to say. Instead she said, " 'Twas a consuming passion with you."

"It was," he said quietly. "Now, it's . . . just a way of life." Spearing her with a look that made her shiver, he said, "It's all I've got anymore."

She couldn't mistake his hostility as he turned abruptly and squatted down by the river to splash water onto his face. It seemed he blamed her for the lonely and unsatisfying course his life had taken. True, she might have tried harder to discourage him that summer in Périgeaux, knowing they had no future together. But she'd been young, and she'd adored him;

how could she have been expected to turn him away? And, too, considering his knightly vocation, he knew as well as she the futility of pursuing her.

Perhaps she'd been unwise in coming here. Given their history, she should be avoiding him, not seeking him out; had experience taught her nothing? She decided to broach the subject she had come here to discuss, and then leave. "Milo woke me up in the middle of the night. He asked me if I might have any idea why you . . . why you might hate me."

He stilled, crouched down with his back to her. After a long moment he stood and turned to face her, lifting his shirt to dry his face. "What did you tell him?"

He could have denied any animosity toward her, but he didn't. That stung in light of her feelings for him, which had lingered tenaciously all these years. How he would laugh at her if he knew! Straightening her back, she said, "I told him that nine years ago in Périgeaux, you'd . . . wanted me to become your mistress. And that I'd refused."

Incredulous anger flashed in his eyes. "That can't honestly be how you remember it."

Her gaze dropped to the muddy riverbank. "I know there was more to it. But I didn't think it wise to share . . . everything with Milo. Just the basic facts of what—"

"Facts?"

"You can't deny that you tried to . . . that we almost—"

"And you can't deny that it was more than mere lust that drove me."

"Don't you understand, Alex?" She forced herself to meet his eyes. "It doesn't matter what drove you. The fact is, you knew you were leaving to join William."

"And that meant I couldn't fall in love?" He took

a step toward her; she took a step back. "I loved you, Nicki. You knew how I felt. I told you."

"I know."

"I asked you to run away with me, for God's sake!" he exclaimed, his hands fisted, a cord bulging on his neck.

"I know," she said softly, "but you never asked me to marry you."

He stared at her, a hint of what looked like self-doubt eroding his expression of outrage. That he was so clearly taken aback made Nicki almost pity him. How deluded he'd been. "I . . ." He raked his hair off his face, but it fell right back. "I wasn't in any position. . . ."

"You wanted me to be your leman," she said, with as even a temper as she could muster. "You wanted to keep me tucked away in some nunnery until you found yourself between battles and came to call—"

"You're twisting things around," he said, but there was a note of uncertainty in his tone, and he seemed to have a hard time meeting her gaze. It was as if he were struggling to remember all that had transpired, all he'd claimed and offered and promised, during their last, eventful encounter. "The convent was supposed to be a temporary refuge until I earned some property of my own."

"You weren't in a position to marry me," she said, quoting his own words back at him, "but you wanted me to run away with you." She shook her head solemnly. "Mama was right. You could offer me naught but shame."

He spun around, grinding his fists against his temples. "Damn, I wish my head would stop pounding, so I could think."

"You wanted me to be your whore." She chanced a step toward him. "Milo wanted me to be his wife."

"Milo wanted Peverell!" he thundered, whirling around.

"Who are you to judge him?" she demanded, her own voice rising in righteous anger. "You, who were willing to ruin my life just to possess me."

"Christ, Nicki, you knew me." His eyes glittered with sincerity. "Do you think I had it in me to be that inhuman, that coldly calculating? I was too young for any of that. I loved you. I wanted you. 'Twas that simple."

"Perhaps so," she conceded, seeking forbearance and understanding within herself. "But you wanted the soldier's life, too. Didn't you know you couldn't have both? Your brother offered you counsel on everything else. He must have told you this."

He closed his eyes, rubbed the bridge of his nose. She barely heard his whispered, "Aye."

"Regardless of your intentions," she said, "if I'd left with you, 'twould have been a nightmare, especially for me. You would have led me into a life of disgrace . . . clandestine meetings when you could manage it, long months of loneliness in between. You would have grown weary of the secrecy, the complications, my unhappiness. When it all became too much, you would have been compelled to discard me. I don't think I could have borne that."

"I bore it when you discarded me." Alex's voice seethed with a bitterness cultivated over nine long years. "Or don't you recall having done so?"

"I . . ." She remembered how wretched she'd felt during Peter's announcement of her betrothal to Milo, how she'd wanted to run to Alex and throw her arms around him and weep and scream and explain and . . .

"I was the one who was tossed aside, Nicki. You led me on for weeks, letting me lose my heart to you, letting me think you cared, when all the while you had your sights set on Milo. You were using me to make him jealous. I was but the bait for the trap you laid—"

"Trap! How can you—"

"And it worked. Congratulations," he said nastily.

"I hope you're happy with the quarry you snagged." Stalking past her, he climbed back up to the boat and grabbed the leather flask. When he stepped back onto the improvised gangplank, his foot slipped and he stumbled, the flask falling to the ground as he regained his bearings. He rubbed his eyes with trembling fingers, his face pale as chalk.

She retrieved the flask and handed it to him when he got to the ground. Sympathy for him warred with hurt that he could think so ill of her. "If this is what's become of you," she said, "I daresay I'm no worse off with Milo than I would have been with you."

He wheeled on her, advancing with swift steps that forced her back against the hull of the longship. She tried to push him away, but he threw the flask aside and seized her hands in a painful grasp. "Don't compare me to that withered old hen." His gaze lingered on her body as he moved closer. "You wouldn't want to goad me into demonstrating how wrong you are."

She rammed her heel down hard on his instep. He spat out a ripe oath as he released her. "I daresay you're right about that," she said, moving aside to put some distance between them.

He pressed his forehead to the hull of the boat. "Nicki, I'm . . ." He shook his head. "That was . . ." He sighed. "Go away, Nicki. 'Twas ill advised, you coming here."

Her heart ached, remembering those long, enchanted afternoons in their cave. She mourned for the boy who's shyly taken her hand the day they'd discovered their haven, and held it in the dark while a secret awareness passed between them, heady and exhilarating. He'd been so young, so fervent, so eager—not just for her, but for his future and the glorious battles that would shape it. Now, by his own admission, soldiering was simply all he had anymore.

"You've changed, Alex," she said. "You were so . . . unsullied. Such a good, sweet boy."

"I wasn't a boy, not really, Nicki," he said quietly, turning to face her. "Not in any way that mattered. And I'm certainly not now. Nor am I particularly good and sweet." Wearily he reached down and picked the flask up off the ground. "Go away."

"Why were you and Milo talking about me, Alex?"

He blinked at her. "We . . ." He shrugged carelessly, but consternation darkened his eyes. "I don't know. He happened to mention you. I don't remember—"

"Hear me well, Alex. I don't like being talked about. And I certainly don't want anyone to start speculating about things that happened nine years ago. If Milo or anyone else happens to mention me again, just you keep your counsel."

He shook his head scornfully. "Always looking out for your precious reputation, eh, Nicki?"

"And why not?" she asked as she turned to leave. " 'Tis all *I've* got anymore."

Halfway through the noon meal—another lavish feast, this one provided in the Tour de Rouen's great hall rather than outdoors—Gaspar set before Alex a beaker containing something noxious.

"What the devil is this?" Alex pushed the tall goblet away, his stomach roiling. All that fortified wine had poisoned not only his head, but his stomach. He'd neither broken his fast nor partaken of the sumptuous dinner being served to the many guests staying on at the ducal palace for the days of celebration to come.

" 'Tis a physick, milord," Gaspar said. "Pimpernel boiled in wine. 'Twill purge your morning head and cool the heat in your belly. My lady Nicolette instructed me to make it for you."

Alex glanced down the table to find Nicki looking at him. How stunned he'd been to be awakened this morning by her scent tickling his nostrils . . . roses and some elusive spicy note. He'd opened his eyes to find a face blocking the worst of the sun's scalding rays. Shielding his eyes for a better look, he'd seen her, crouching over him. Her face, despite its being cast in shadow, had been luminous as alabaster, her eyes translucent. Her diaphanous white veil, anchored by a silver circlet, billowed in the breeze from the river, giving her an angelic aspect. Nothing could have kept him from reaching for her.

And then they'd quarreled, badly. Christ, he'd all but molested her, inexcusable regardless of how much he'd drunk the night before. Given that, it astounded him that she would bother to do him this kindness. He imagined she'd ordered many such elixirs prepared for her husband through the years. Thinking of Milo made Alex wonder where he was. He hadn't seen his cousin all day.

"Alex has a morning head?" Faithe asked skeptically.

Luke, sitting next to Alex, clapped him on the back, making his gorge rise. "Overdid it last night, did you, brother? That's not like you."

"Not at all," Faithe said. "In all the years I've known you, I don't think I've once seen you truly in your cups."

It gratified Alex on some petty level for Nicki to hear this and know how wrong she was to have compared him to Milo.

"Go ahead, Sir Alex," said Gaspar, standing behind him. "Drink it. 'Twill do you good."

"I hate tonics," Alex groused, knowing he sounded like a petulant little boy. "They taste awful."

Gaspar chuckled. "This one's no worse than the taste that's already in your mouth, I'll wager."

Everyone was looking at him. Grimacing, he grabbed the beaker and swallowed the vile stuff down in a few swift gulps, then excused himself from the table and left the hall.

The midday sunshine, although it stung his eyes and made his head pulse, was a refreshing change from the dimness of the keep. Moreover, he was spared the suffocating press of humanity, the only other person in the courtyard being a jongleur. Alex recognized him as the fellow who'd sung Nicki's tale of the Holy Grail yesterday. He sat on a step beneath the wide stone archway that provided entrance to the ducal chapel, absently strumming his lute.

Alex slowly crossed the courtyard, shielding his eyes against the sun until he reached the cool shadows beneath the chapel arch.

"Good day, milord," greeted the jongleur as he looked up from his lute. Eyeing the coin Alex withdrew from his pouch, he asked, "Is there anything in particular you'd care to hear?"

Alex flicked the coin to the young fellow, who caught it with practiced ease and slid it into his boot. "You sang yesterday of the search for the Grail."

The jongleur brightened. "Ah. You've a good ear. 'Tis a remarkably beautiful *chanson*. You don't mind if I sing it sitting down, do you? I've got blisters from all this standing."

"Not at all." Alex leaned against the arch, his arms crossed, and lost himself in the tale of a holy quest in a far distant time. The jongleur was right. It was an exceedingly fine song, lyrical and moving and told for the most part with an elegant economy of words.

Nicki wrote this, he thought, as the song danced around him, entered him, transported him. Her gift with verse had always vaguely perplexed him, given his lack of learning. Now he felt not so much confused as awed. There was a kind of magic in sitting down with a quill and a horn of ink and turning a blank sheet of parchment into such a marvelous tale.

Little wonder she'd preferred Milo to him. *A good, sweet boy,* she'd called him. Good and sweet and pathetically ignorant.

By the time the song ended, Alex's headache had dissipated, and he no longer felt quite so woozy. Perhaps Gaspar's physick actually worked; after all, he had trained as an apothecary. Or perhaps it was the tranquilizing effect of the music.

The young musician bowed and excused himself, explaining that he was expected to perform in the hall during the final course. As he left, Alex turned and discovered Milo leaning on his cane not two yards away, nursing a wineskin. How long had he been standing there?

Milo made his halting—and obviously drunken—way to the steps and lowered himself with a grunt of effort. He took a leisurely swallow of wine and said, "You wanted her nine years ago. You can have her now, with no obligations at all."

Alex turned in disgust and gazed out at the bright courtyard. Except for a goat that had wandered in from one of the merchant lanes surrounding the castle, prowling for food, he and his cousin were completely alone.

"Your wife doesn't want me discussing her," Alex said. "I'm just as happy to oblige."

Milo's eyes looked very dark and wide in the shadowy archway. "You've spoken to her?"

"Aye."

"You didn't tell her . . . what I asked of you, did you?"

"Hardly. 'Tis an unholy proposal. It sickens me."

Milo raised an eyebrow. "Since when has it made you ill to bed a beautiful woman?"

"Since the moment her husband broached the idea," Alex shot back.

" 'Twould hardly have affected you so nine years ago, would it?" Milo's gaze was too sharp, too discerning for Alex's comfort. "You wanted her then. She told me so." His eyes sparked with amusement. "Chaste young pup though you were, you tried to make her your leman. I'm impressed!"

Alex shook his head. "That's her version of it."

"You didn't want her?"

Alex rubbed the little scar on the bridge of his nose. "I didn't say that. But . . ." *Careful, now. Don't reveal too much. Nicki is right; 'twill only make matters worse.* "Wanting her . . . 'tisn't the whole story."

Milo smiled wryly. "It never is."

Alex had been stunned at the riverbank when Nicki pointed out the implications of his not having asked her to marry him. Why hadn't he? He'd loved her, considered her spiritually united to him ever since that first day in the cave. The simple answer was that landless young knights were unmarriageable. But if he'd been willing to give up soldiering, could he have found a way to make her his wife and provide a home for her? Possibly; probably. He could have learned a trade, or become a master at arms, teaching swordplay to other young men. But he'd never once paused to consider such alternatives, hungry as he was to test his mettle in battle. What an arrogant, misguided young fool he'd been, to think he could avoid the painful choice between his two passions—Nicki and soldiering.

"You can have her," Milo said, his voice low, almost seductive, "with no ties or responsibilities of any kind. Isn't the Lone Wolf tired of tumbling serving wenches and whores? Think of it. You could have Nicolette de St. Clair, with her soft skin and her golden hair, and you wouldn't have to give up anything for her. I'm offering you a liaison with a woman of exceptional beauty, a clever, learned, highborn woman, and when it's over, you can simply return to your former life as if the whole thing had never happened."

Alex watched the goat as it snuffled and searched. In his mind he saw a white silk shift neatly folded on a crimson pillow. " 'Tis an ill-conceived plan, you know. You claim to have thought it all through, but . . . well, what if your wife is barren? After all, you tried at one time to get her with child, but it didn't work.

You did have a baby with Violette, though, so the problem can't be yours."

"Nicolette is fertile," Milo said shortly.

"How can you possibly know that?"

Milo regarded him speculatively for a moment, as if weighing his answer. Finally, with a sigh of resignation, he said, "On our wedding night, when we lay together for the first time, it felt—"

"Christ, Milo." Alex turned away. "I'm leaving. I don't need to hear—"

"There was no resistance, no blood. And she didn't even try to pretend there was pain."

Alex turned slowly back around.

"I questioned her, and she admitted the truth. Not only had she lost her virginity years before, but she'd already been with child."

Chapter 8

"**W**ho's next?" bellowed Vicq, the biggest of Gaspar's two apes, at the audience of men who stood gathered around a circle of beaten earth in the sporting field. Alex sat in the grass on a nearby knoll, where he had a good view of the fighting circle below.

"Who's man enough to fight Gaspar le Taureau this fine afternoon?" yelled barrel-chested Leone.

Gaspar himself stood unmoving in the middle of the circle, his bloodied fists resting nonchalantly on his hips, as his underlings paced around him, goading the crowd. A pair of sweat-soaked linen braies covered his legs to the calves, and his feet were encased in heavy boots. Half-naked, he was a daunting specimen, and Alex didn't wonder why so few men were willing to take him on. His chest was a wedge of pure brawn, heavily furred. He had the back of an ox, arms bulging with veined muscle. Sweat and blood dripped from him, soaking the packed dirt beneath his feet. Alex would not have stepped forward. He marveled that several already had.

"He's taking on all challengers!" Vicq shouted. "Come on! Where are your ballocks?"

"I've got a pair," came a voice from the spectators. Alex sighed and shook his head.

The fellow stepped into the ring, peeled off his tunic and shirt, and threw them to a companion. He was young and strong, but he'd be no match for The Bull.

The youth put up his fists. Gaspar slugged him in the head and he hit the dirt. The crowd groaned as one. Laughing, the big man kicked him in the side as he shielded his bloody face with his hands. "Come on, get up. Give us a fight. You said you had a pair. Prove it."

The young contestant tentatively uncovered his face. His nose was misshapen, and blood stained his lips. With a shaking hand he reached into his mouth and extracted a shard of tooth. "You win," he said nasally.

"So soon?" Gaspar said with exaggerated disappointment. "Wasn't much sport to that. Are you sure you've got anything in here?" he asked, yanking on the drawstring that secured his opponent's chausses.

Some of the onlookers laughed nervously. Others just watched in silence as Gaspar untied the hose and pulled them down. When he reached for the underdrawers, the poor fellow began to struggle, so Gaspar ordered Vicq and Leone, howling with laughter, to pin him to the ground.

Alex had seen enough. Rising to his feet, he cupped his hands around his mouth. "What a noble display, Gaspar!"

Heads turned. Gaspar, hunched over his writhing victim, glowered up at him.

"Three against one!" Alex yelled. "But, then, that's the way you like it, isn't it?"

The audience looked toward Gaspar. Grimacing, he backed away from the young man and ordered his underlings to do the same. The fellow's friends helped him to his feet and hauled him, his chausses around his ankles, from the ring.

Gaspar nodded to Vicq and Leone, who set up the appeal for more challengers. To Alex's dismay, another youth stepped forward. Alex turned away in disgust, thinking he'd walk to the river and seek out the solitude of the old longship, when a glimmer of yellow in a nearby meadow caught his eye.

It was a woman, sitting with her back to him in a saffron-dyed silk tunic—Nicki, for he'd seen her earlier in that gown. Faithe, with whom she'd become friendly, sat across from her on a blanket spread on the grass, baby Edlyn at her breast. Robert and Hlynn flanked Nicki, the three of them bending their heads over some activity that seemed to engross them.

Shielding his eyes against the afternoon sun, Alex studied the distant figure in yellow as he ruminated over Milo's astonishing revelation yesterday. Thinking back to that summer in Périgeaux, he recalled his excruciating chivalry with Nicki, his reluctance to take liberties that would shock her. Just holding her hand had thrilled him immeasurably. How utterly laughable she must have found him. Of the two of them, he'd been the blushing virgin. She'd lost her innocence three years before.

She'd become pregnant at sixteen, she confessed to Milo, and lost the babe. With tears in her eyes, she'd begged him not to tell anyone, lest she be ruined. Milo had agreed not to reveal her secret to a soul, and he hadn't, until yesterday. He'd made Alex promise not to tell anyone, including Nicki, what he confided beneath the shadows of the chapel arch.

Judging by Milo's account, he'd been remarkably sanguine about his bride's past, and certainly more understanding than Alex would have been. Milo hadn't pressed her for details, and she had not seemed disposed to offer any. When Alex asked his cousin how he could have taken it so calmly, Milo replied that he was in no position to judge her, having hardly been a paragon of chastity himself.

Milo's worldliness about such matters had always mystified Alex. It struck him as unfathomable to regard women—women of their own class and position, at any rate—as being entitled to the same sexual liberties as men. A man had a right to expect his bride to be pure and untouched on their wedding night. A high-ranking maiden's virtue wasn't something a man should ever feel compelled to question. He had certainly never questioned Nicki's. In retrospect, although he knew she'd been no angel, having used him to manipulate Milo into proposing, he'd been as certain of her virginity as he was of his own.

How well he'd thought he'd known her; how foolish he'd been. Luke had realized something was amiss. Alex remembered his brother remarking that Nicki looked like a woman with a secret. Hadn't she as much as told him so herself? *I'm not the woman you think I am. There are things about me you don't know.*

Out in the meadow, Faithe noticed him and waved; he waved back. Nicki turned toward him, but offered no greeting. Robert and Hlynn leapt to their feet and raced toward him. Faithe called after them, and started to rise—awkwardly, given the baby she was nursing—but Nicki waved her back down and strode across the grass after the children.

When little Hlynn tripped over the hem of her tunic, her brother helped her up and held her hand the rest of the way. Alex smiled, remembering how combative they'd been the night he came looking for Luke's wine flask.

"Look, Uncle Alex!" Robert exclaimed, waving something—a wax tablet. Hlynn carried one, too. "Aunt Nicolette's been teaching us to write!"

"Little Hlynn as well?" Alex asked doubtfully. She hadn't yet seen her third birthday.

The children scampered up the knoll, Hlynn thrusting her tablet proudly into Alex's hand. "She's still learning her alphabet," Robert said, pointing to the crudely scribbled letters gouged into the wax. "Aunt Nicolette says she's doing very well for her age."

Hlynn beamed. Alex ruffled her hair as he returned her tablet to her. "Good work, Mouse." She giggled, as she did whenever he called her that.

"She's a very quick-witted little girl," Nicki said as

she joined them, slightly out of breath, her cheeks flushed. Her gaze connected with his for a breathtaking moment before she looked away; in that brief instant, he sensed a universe of feelings roiling beneath the surface. Her hair was caught in a snood of golden gauze today. She glowed like the sun. "Her brother is very clever as well. He wrote a poem today!"

"Mummy had already taught me the alphabet," Robert confided, handing his tablet to Alex. "And Aunt Nicolette told me how to spell the words. But I made it up all by myself."

Alex looked down at the little rows of words— meaningless to him—inscribed with painstaking care into the wax.

"Aunt Nicolette says it's excellent," the boy bragged. "Do you like it?"

Heat crawled up Alex's throat. Feeling Nicki's gaze on him, he would have given anything at that moment—*anything*—to have been able to read what was on that tablet. "I'm sorry, Robert," he said, giving the tablet back, "but I can't—"

"Here," came a breathless voice from behind. "Let me have a look."

Alex turned to find Milo toiling with his cane to ascend the little hill. He was surprised his cousin had made it this far from the castle without help.

Robert handed over the tablet to Milo, who squinted at it, swaying slightly; drunk again. "Why, this is splendid." Clearing his throat, he recited, " 'We sing our praise, For summer days, And almond cakes, With honey glaze.' "

Alex couldn't help but smile at the things a five-year-old boy found worthy of extolling in verse. "That's excellent, Robert."

"Come," said Nicki, rounding up the children. "Robert, you may return to your mother. Hlynn, I promised Mummy I'd take you back to your chamber and put you in for a nap."

Hlynn held her chubby arms up beseechingly. Nicki smiled and hefted the little girl, who promptly shoved her thumb into her mouth and went limp.

Quietly Nicki said to Milo, "You shouldn't have walked all this way. You'll exhaust yourself."

"I'm sick to death of that blasted castle," Milo griped. "You know that, damn you. Leave me be."

She looked as if she wanted to say more, but after a brief glance toward Alex, she left. The two men watched her carry the child across the field toward the castle.

"She's good with children, is she not?" Milo asked, speaking slowly in an apparent attempt to counteract the thickness of his speech. "Patient, understanding."

"Almost as good as she is with you," Alex said. "And you're a damned sight more trouble."

Laughing raspily, Milo lifted his ever-present wineskin to his mouth and took a drink. "She'd give her soul to have a child of her own."

Alex sighed wearily. "Well, she won't get one from me."

" 'Twould mean the world to her," Milo said. "And you'd be saving her from homelessness in the bargain."

Alex reflected on Robert's charming little poem, indecipherable to him until it was read aloud. "What do you think of me, Milo?"

Milo seemed to be struggling to focus his gaze on Alex. "I love you like a brother, Alex. You know that."

Alex nodded. "A slow-witted little brother, good for a bit of company now and then . . . or the occasional very special favor. Is that it?"

"What are you driving at, cousin?"

"I'm no more than breeding stock to you, am I?"

Milo made a face of derision. "Alex—"

"A stud bull. Witless, to be sure, but he'll mount

any female put in front of him. Good for his seed
but—"

"You *are* witless," Milo said, choking with laughter,
"if you think that's how I view you."

"What else am I to think?"

Milo clamped a bony hand onto Alex's shoulder.
"Don't you remember how it was, back in Périgeaux
those last few years? You were more than my
cousin—you were my confidant, the friend of my
heart. I needed you. You had a way of looking at
things straight on, where I was always peering around
corners, making everything vastly more complicated
than it needed to be. I questioned everything. I
needed your clear vision, your sense of rightness and
honor, to remind me what was important. You kept me
from all my little dishonesties and self-indulgences."
Grimly he said, "If you'd been around these past nine
years, I doubt I would have deteriorated into the sorry
wastrel I am today." He was slurring badly, having
abandoned his effort to appear sober.

"But that's just it, Milo. I wasn't around. For almost
a decade you made no attempt to contact me. When
you finally sought me out, 'twas to ask the most ob-
scene 'favor' imaginable."

"I needed you then, and I need you now. More
than ever."

"I'm sorry, Milo, but I can't stomach what you're
asking of me. Find someone else."

"Actually," Milo said, "I already have. If you won't
do it, Gaspar will."

Alex gaped at him. "Gaspar?"

A roar from the crowd around the fighting pit made
both men turn to see what had prompted it. It was
the arrival of a new opponent, a monstrous brute—
some sort of infidel judging from his dark skin and
the gold ring in his ear. He was entirely as tall and
broad as Gaspar, every muscle on his torso clearly
defined. The spectators cheered wildly as the savage

dodged two punches, landing Gaspar a punishing blow to the stomach that doubled him up. He turned to acknowledge the hurrahs of the crowd, only to have Gaspar leap on him from behind and tackle him to the ground.

Gaspar and Nicki? God's eyes . . . "He wouldn't do it," Alex said.

"He already offered to," Milo retorted. "And if I need him, I'll order it. He may be the apothecary castellan, but he hasn't forgotten how to follow an order."

"Christ, Milo." Down in the fighting circle, the competition had evolved into a wrestling match, with the two sweaty behemoths grappling furiously for dominance. "Was it his idea?"

"Nay," Milo said quickly—too quickly, perhaps. " 'Twas mine. We were drinking one evening, after supper. I was . . . perhaps a bit loose tongued."

Alex grunted; easy to imagine.

"I confided in him about the inheritance problem, the need for a son. And he offered . . ." Milo frowned uncertainly, as if trying to remember. "But mind you, the idea came from me. He offered to sire the child. For the sake of all of us. If we're forced to leave Peverell, he might have to leave, too. At best, he'd lose the authority he wields now, and one can hardly blame him for wanting to hold on to it—a man of his humble origins."

"I daresay," Alex murmured, wondering how much of this scheme had come from Gaspar. "She'll never allow it. She'd never let him seduce her."

Another chorus of cheers rose from the crowd. The barbarian had Gaspar pinned on his back. Gaspar thrashed and grunted. Finally he hooked a leg around the other man's and, with a howl of effort, wrested him loose and flipped him face down. Throwing himself on the dusky giant, he pinioned his flailing limbs. "Surrender!"

The infidel twisted and writhed.

"Surrender, you black beast." Gaspar ground his opponent's face into the dirt. "Surrender!"

"You're right, of course," Milo said, swaying slightly on his feet. "Nicolette would never submit to Gaspar. I told him as much. He took offense, I could tell. He's rarely angry, but I could see it in his eyes. I probably worded it poorly—I was in my cups." Milo paused, squinting at the two sweat-slicked, writhing bodies in the fighting ring. "He does, however, have other means at his disposal—means that wouldn't depend on my wife's permission."

The dark-skinned man screamed invective in his native tongue while he bucked and rolled. Gaspar held on tight, grunting as he struggled to keep his foe immobilized. Grabbing a fistful of hair, he lifted his opponent's head, slamming it hard into the packed earth. "Give in, you godless pagan!"

"You can't mean . . ." Alex began. "You wouldn't let him . . . take her by force."

"Rape her? I'm not quite that depraved, cousin. Nay, but there's a way he could do it that wouldn't require her cooperation . . . or even her knowledge."

"What are you talking about?"

"He knows how to make a potion that will induce a deep sleep."

"Oh, for God's—"

"Nicolette wouldn't even know what was happening."

"Jesu! You're capable of such . . . Milo, have you descended so low?"

"Desperation drives men to low acts, cousin. Yes, I'm capable of ordering my lovely lady wife to be so ill used. Absolutely. I'm at the end of my tether. I'll do anything."

The crowd was pleading with Gaspar, who continued to pound the now-insensible wretch's head against the earth, to stop. Finally, dripping sweat, his chest heaving, he climbed off the unconscious man and raised both fists in the air, beaming. A smattering of applause and a few cheers, mostly from Vicq and Leone, acknowledged his victory. The onlookers dispersed.

"Of course," Milo said, "I would rather avoid such unpleasantries. My feelings for Nicolette may not run as deep as a husband's should—we never had that kind of marriage—but I've always been fond of her."

"Doesn't seem that way at times."

"When one loathes what one has become," Milo said with drunken solemnity, "that loathing tends to break free from time to time and seek the most convenient target. In my heart"—he tapped his chest with a palsied hand—"I care for her almost as one would a sister. She has a good soul, and she's remarkably gifted, and . . . well, 'tis a rather unsavory business, his drugging her wine and . . ."

Alex closed his eyes and saw Gaspar, grunting and straining atop his helpless opponent.

"But make no mistake, cousin," Milo said softly. "If it comes to that, I'll order it. Don't doubt that for a moment."

"I don't," Alex whispered, rubbing his eyes.

"Do you see why I asked you to father this child?" Milo squeezed the wineskin into his mouth, frowning to find it empty. " 'Twould be ever so much more civilized, having you do it—much better for Nicki. And, of course, there are all the reasons I pointed out before—the de Périgeaux blood, and our resemblance, the fact that you live so far away . . . That's important. Gaspar would always be about, and what if the baby looked like him? Not good, not good at all."

Alex watched Gaspar wipe down his face and chest with a rag, which he then traded to Leone for his shirt.

You haven't changed a bit, he'd remarked to Gaspar yesterday.

Yes I have.

"Does Gaspar know you're asking this of me?"

Milo's eyebrows drew together. "Nay." He tried again to make the wineskin produce wine, grimacing when he remembered he'd run out. " 'Twould irk him, I think, that I chose someone else over him. As I said, he took offense when I told him Nicolette would never have him. I was too soused at the time to realize why, but I understand now. He doesn't like reminders of his station, and he assumed the only reason I rejected him is that he's baseborn. I told him I'd decided entirely against the idea of another man siring her child."

Gaspar donned his tunic, buckling his belt over it, and ran his hands over his close-cropped hair. He noticed Milo and waved, and Alex was struck by how tame and civilized he appeared. Alex looked away to find Faithe, carrying the baby and accompanied by Robert, crossing the field toward them.

"Whatever you do," Milo said in a heated whisper, "don't let Gaspar know that I've asked this of you. He wouldn't take it kindly if he found out I chose you over him. I only hope you'll get the task done and neither he nor Nicki will ever know it was by my design. They'll think it . . . just came about."

"Just came about . . ." Alex muttered, musing on this elaborate and ignoble scheme.

Milo gripped Alex's shoulder; his breath stank of sour wine. "Cousin, I know this business doesn't sit well with you. I can appreciate your misgivings. But think of what will happen to us if we're cast away from Peverell. Look at me. I've no skills, no trade. I never learned how to fight, and my hands shake too badly to hold a sword even if I had. I've turned into an old man, and old men like to stay where they are. Take pity on both of us."

They descended the knoll to greet Faithe, and were soon joined by Gaspar, whom Milo congratulated for his defeat of the black giant. The big man greeted Alex coolly. Alex merely nodded.

Alex observed with interest Gaspar's transformation from bloodied brawler to cheerful retainer—his deference toward Milo, his politeness toward Faithe, his easy way with Robert. Gaspar's gaze, however, kept straying toward something in the direction of the castle, which seemed to absorb him. Alex doubted he would have noticed this had not his own attention been fixed on Gaspar. Turning casually, he found the object of Gaspar's covert preoccupation to be Nicki, walking toward them.

"Hlynn was fast asleep by the time I put her on her pallet," she reported to Faithe as she joined them. "Your maid is watching over her."

During the ensuing small talk, Alex noticed Gaspar's gaze crawl over Nicki very briefly, almost imperceptibly, when he thought no one was looking. Alex's hands curled automatically into fists.

Milo broached the subject of Alex's furlough, prompting Faithe to say, "The children will be thrilled to have their Uncle Alex for such a long visit. As will Luke and I."

" 'Tis most gracious of you," Milo said in the measured way that meant he'd resumed caring about appearances. "But I was thinking perhaps my young cousin might prefer a change of scenery." He turned to Alex, his bleary gaze sharpening, becoming almost smug. "I thought perhaps you'd like to come stay with us at Peverell. My lady wife and I would relish the company . . . wouldn't we, my dear?"

Nicki blinked at her husband, and then at Alex. "I . . . yes, of course. But I'm sure Sir Alex would prefer—"

"You see, Alex? We'd love to have you. You can return with us to St. Clair and remain there through Christmastide. We've got a nice, private guest chamber for you," he added significantly, "very quiet and cozy. What say you, cousin?"

Faithe smiled and shrugged. "We'll understand if

you choose to spend your leave at Peverell, Alex. I'm sure you've missed your cousin."

Gaspar stared at him with a cool lack of expression. Nicki studied him in that still, wide-eyed way of hers, her arms wrapped tightly around herself.

" 'Tis a kind offer," Alex said tightly. "And one which I find myself . . . helpless to refuse."

Grinning broadly, Milo landed Alex a good-natured but feeble punch to the arm. "I knew I could talk you into it."

"More wine, milord?"

Milo lifted his face from the table to gape at Gaspar, standing over him with the wine jug, in the jittery, open-mouthed way that meant he'd long since forgotten where he was or what he was doing. The sorry sot would be out cold soon enough, Gaspar knew, but that didn't mean he didn't want a refill. Milo de St. Clair always wanted a refill.

The lady Nicolette, sitting next to her husband, caught Gaspar's eye. "He's had enough," she said softly. Judging from the expressions of the others at the dinner table—the de Périgeaux brothers, the lady Faithe, that witch Berte de Bec and her fat toad of a husband, even those blasted children—they concurred with her ladyship's assessment.

Gaspar couldn't wait to get back home, where he wouldn't have a dozen pairs of eyes scrutinizing his every action. He liked things as they were at Peverell. He particularly liked not having to play the fawning lapdog, except perhaps with the lady Nicolette, who still fancied that she exercised some measure of authority over her subordinates—even him.

Of course, things wouldn't be quite the same, with that irksome young cousin of Milo's spending the next six bloody months with them. Milo wouldn't be so hospitable if he knew the bugger had almost stolen his bride away before he could marry her. Gaspar could share that fascinating bit of de Périgeaux family history with his "master," but then he'd question why his trusted retainer had waited so long to do so. If Gaspar were to reveal the truth—that he made it a practice to tell Milo only enough to keep him from interfering with Gaspar's authority—it wouldn't go well for him. He would tell Milo about his wife and his cousin if and when it became useful to do so.

"Gaspar," said Lady Nicolette, "my lord husband is tired. Perhaps you'd like to help him to—"

"Meddling bitch!" Milo slammed his open palm on the table, his face contorted in a drunken rictus of indignation. "Jus' need s'more to drink." Milo tried to push his half-full goblet toward Gaspar, but it toppled over, soaking the oaken table with wine. "Damn. Fill that up." He grabbed his wife's goblet, as he was wont to do, and gulped down its contents.

Alex de Périgeaux stood. "I'll take him to bed, my lady."

"Thank you," she replied, "but Gaspar doesn't mind. Do you, Gaspar?"

God's bones, but he wished she wasn't so bloody beautiful. When she looked at him like that, with those haughty eyes and those silky pink lips, he felt something wind up tight inside, coiled for release. He wanted to slap her; he wanted to grind his mouth against hers and shock the chilly complacency out of her.

Patience . . .

"Certainly not, my lady." Hauling his insensible master off his bench, Gaspar dragged him up the tower stairs to his chamber and dumped him unceremoniously on the bed.

Her ladyship's night shift had been laid out, he saw, folded up all nice and tidy on a pillow. Gaspar rubbed his hand across it, his calluses snagging on the delicate silk. It got him hard, remembering how she'd looked in this the other night, her tits as round as a young girl's, and those long, shapely legs—the kind that could wrap good and hard around a man's back.

He could filch the shift. It would be easy, just shove it into his tunic and bring it out later, when he was alone. Take it back to Peverell and keep it hidden in his quarters with the other little souvenirs he'd been squirreling away all these years—the garnet earring, the satin slipper, the beaded girdle, and his favorite, the chemise sleeve. He liked that one, because it smelled like her. This shift would smell like her, too, he reckoned. He could rub it on his face, his body . . .

Milo mumbled something. It sounded like "Violette."

"She's dead, you pathetic souse." To ravage yourself with grief over some chit from the past when you had a woman like Nicolette de St. Clair in your bed struck Gaspar as the height of lunacy. Setting himself to the task of undressing this drunken wretch, he pondered his role in bringing about Milo's marriage to Nicolette nine years ago.

It was obvious that Nicolette had taken a fancy to young Alex that summer in Périgeaux. Nothing about her escaped Gaspar's notice for very long. Still, he'd been astounded when Lady Sybila had come to him in one of her dithers, screeching that Alex was threatening to steal her daughter away before she could wed Milo.

Gaspar had shared in his mistress's alarm. It was imperative that Nicolette's marriage to Milo proceed as planned. Not that he was happy about it. He'd wanted her for himself, of course—he always had— but given his station, she'd been unattainable. Since it was inevitable that she marry, better Milo than Alex de Périgeaux.

Despite his youth, the young knight had all the hallmarks of a natural soldier and leader of men. If he were ever to become castellan of Peverell, he would command with an authority Gaspar could never hope to usurp. Not so the weak and harmless Milo.

Just as galling, a marriage between Nicolette and Alex would have been a union of passion, not property. It was clear that she was well on the road to falling in love with him, if she hadn't already. He represented a threat not only to Peverell, which Gaspar aspired someday to command, but to Nicolette's affections, which he'd been determined—in his foolish naiveté—to capture.

She would eventually come to care for him, or so he'd thought, when she accepted that he was the true lord of Peverell, and her equal in spirit if not by birth. Not that she would ever agree to marry a lowborn apothecary's son, sensitive as she was to the opinions of her aristocratic peers. But if she lost her heart to him, she could most likely be persuaded into his bed— perhaps even consent to become his mistress, if he promised secrecy. That had been his plan, and he'd intended to see it to fruition. Alex de Périgeaux could not be allowed to ruin it.

When Lady Sybila had launched into her fit of rage over Alex's plan to run away with Nicolette, Gaspar promptly mixed her up a sedative tonic—extra strong. Not only would it make her stop shrieking in his ear, but she'd be all the more receptive to his solution to the dilemma of Alex de Périgeaux. As it happened, she suggested the beating even before he could plant the idea in her mind. *And if he never wakes up from it,* she'd drawled as the tonic took effect, *so much the better.*

In the end, he'd chosen to stop just short of killing the boy, though it had taken some doing to call Vicq and Leone off. Once they tasted blood, those two were damnably hard to rein in. Lady Sybila had been peevish upon hearing that the object of her wrath had survived, but the trouncing had served its purpose.

Alex had ceased to be a problem. Indeed, for almost a decade, it was as if he'd never existed.

Until now.

Having stripped Milo down to his drawers—Jesu, but he was scrawny as an old man—Gaspar drew the sheet up to his chin, thinking how very much he looked like a corpse in a shroud. It would be a simple matter to turn appearances into reality . . . stir a bit of poison hemlock and white hellebore into his wine, and that would be that. If Milo's death would solve anything, Gaspar would have brought it about long ago, but Nicolette as a widow was a dangerous prospect. William the Bastard would marry her off instantly, to preserve the castellany, and her new husband might not be the meek and pliable puppet that Milo had proven himself.

Gaspar watched in disgust as Milo muttered unintelligible things in his drunken torpor. Pathetic bag of bones. A far cry from the man he'd been in Périgeaux, yet even then Gaspar had detected a frailty of character hidden deep within his façade of urbane good humor. He'd sensed Milo's weakness as any good predator should, and once they were settled in at Peverell, he'd set about nourishing it. This he'd done for the most part by encouraging his new master's dependence on wine. After Violette's suicide, it had taken little urging for Milo to steep himself in it.

Milo grumbled and turned onto his side, disturbing the little red brocade pillow, which slid to the floor, taking the shift with it. Gaspar replaced the pillow on the bed, but held on to the shift, stroking the silk that had caressed her body so provocatively.

Gaspar had grown to relish the power he'd carved out for himself at Peverell—just as he'd grown increasingly consumed by his need to possess its mistress, although his desire for her had taken on a bitter taste over the years. Not once had that cold-hearted bitch ever looked at him as a man. He was her subordinate, her apothecary castellan. He always was and always would be beneath her.

Gaspar gripped the silken garment in his fists, wondering how it would feel to throw her onto a bed and yank it up—or better yet, tear it off her until it hung in shreds. He'd drive himself into her like a battering ram, fuck her till she screamed. She'd notice him then, by God.

Looking down, he saw that he'd ripped the shift in two along a seam. Now he'd have to take it with him; how could he explain the damage?

He wondered if Nicolette even suspected the depth of his hunger for her. What would she think if she knew how often he'd imagined finding her alone in the woods and forcing her to strip for him . . . she'd weep and plead as he shoved her down on her hands and knees. Often he pictured Vicq and Leone there with him, watching. Sometimes he even imagined letting them have a go at her while *he* watched.

How many times, in his waking dreams, had he done things to her, or forced her to do things to him, that a woman like her couldn't begin to imagine, things even whores balked at. He'd humble her, degrade her, and then she'd know how he'd felt all these years. Then she'd know.

Patience . . . he'd have her soon enough. His only regret—and it was a major one—was that she'd be in a drugged stupor while he took her, unaware of what she'd be made to submit to.

But at least he would have her, at long last . . . with or without her lord husband's permission. Milo had been so tractable at first, letting Gaspar foster in his inebriated mind the logical solution to his lack of an heir . . . *Of course, if another man were to sire the child . . . but surely you've thought of that, milord . . . no doubt you've considered me for this service, and if you order it, it shall be done, with the utmost discretion. . . .*

Only, once he'd sobered up, Milo had rejected the scheme on the grounds—all too sound, but vexing nonetheless—that Nicolette would never voluntarily take Gaspar to her bed. And so Gaspar had suggested the sleeping draught, but Milo seemed squeamish about such measures. That drunken fool might be willing to let Peverell slip through his fingers, but Gaspar had no intention of allowing it. Losing Peverell would destroy everything he'd worked for all these years, and what's more, he'd never have Nicolette.

He *would* have her; he would. If it must be without her knowledge, so be it. He didn't need Milo's approval to dose her wine with a sleeping draught. And once his seed was sprouting in her belly, Milo would be so relieved that he wouldn't care how it came about.

Patience . . . wait for the right moment.

Gaspar wadded up the torn shift and stuffed it beneath his tunic and shirt. It felt slippery-smooth against his chest. Her naked flesh would feel this way against his, smooth and warm and arousing.

The hell with patience, he thought as he left the little chamber and descended the tower stairs. He'd dose her wine at the first convenient opportunity after they returned to Peverell. He'd waited long enough for Nicolette de St. Clair.

No more waiting.

Chapter 9

"Is there a relic in that sword?" Milo demanded of Alex as he struggled to sit up against a mound of pillows in his narrow, curtained bed. He spoke quietly to avoid being heard by the people at the opposite end of Peverell's enormous great hall—two serving wenches clearing away the last of the supper dishes and some soldiers playing draughts. Alex could barely hear him over the rain pattering against the window shutters.

"Aye." Standing next to the bed, Alex reached for the hilt of his sword, his hand closing over the knob that contained the hair of St. Augustine.

"Swear on it."

Alex shifted to take his weight off his bad hip, which the weather had set to throbbing. "For pity's sake, Milo, I don't need to—"

"Swear on it!" Milo sat forward, his goblet clutched in a quivering fist. "I want to know that the thing will be done!"

" 'Twill be done," Alex whispered, glancing uneasily at one of the wenches, who'd looked toward them at Milo's outburst. "Why do you think I'm here?"

In truth, Alex had been asking himself what he was doing here ever since their arrival early that afternoon. After a full week of dazzling sunshine in Rouen, the steady rain that had plagued their journey to St.

Clair—and that had persisted past sundown—struck
him as a bad portent. He'd found Peverell Castle to
be entirely as huge and dismal as he'd been warned,
although it had clearly been modified somewhat for
comfort during the century or so since it was built.

The vaulted ground floor, through which entrance was
gained to the keep, had once housed a kitchen. When
a freestanding cookhouse was constructed in the inner
bailey, this undercroft was partitioned via walls of stone
into guest chambers for important visitors. One of these
chambers, a modest corner cell with a feather bed and
two window slits, Milo had assigned to Alex. Upon discovering the other chambers to be empty, Alex had
asked for the large one with the fireplace, but his cousin
had smiled cryptically and insisted that he'd find the
corner chamber more to his liking.

A stairwell in the keep's single turret provided access to the raised hall, a cavernous space with a hearth
at one end and a cluster of smaller rooms—buttery,
pantry and dairy—at the other. Here meals were
served on collapsible tables to the scores of soldiers
quartered, along with Gaspar, in barracks located in
the outer bailey.

The level above the great hall was a solar that
served as a great chamber for Peverell's lord and lady.
However, immediately upon their arrival today, Milo
had ordered his bed to be disassembled, carted downstairs, and rebuilt in front of the hearth in the great
hall. His wife's bed would remain upstairs, but until
further notice, he would sleep in the hall. The visit
to Rouen and the journey back had drained him, he
explained, making the trek up and down the turret
staircase a torturous prospect. Milo did appear particularly pale and shaky of late, but Alex suspected his
new sleeping arrangements had less to do with his
health than with a desire to provide Nicki with as
much privacy as possible during Alex's stay.

"We both know why you're here," Milo said under

his breath, "and I know your intentions are good. You're a man of honor, after all, but still—"

A huff of disgusted laughter rose from Alex. "I used to be a man of honor. I don't know what I am anymore."

Milo waved a bony hand toward the hilt of Alex's sword. "Swear to it, so I can rest easy."

With an exasperated sigh, Alex gripped the hilt of his sword. "I swear to Almighty God and all the saints that I will . . ." Christ, but he couldn't bring himself to say it out loud, even to Milo.

"That you'll endeavor to sire me a son," Milo provided.

"I so swear it."

"And that you'll keep your true purpose from Nicolette, and when it's done, you'll leave here and never contact her again—or the child, of course."

"Fear not," Alex assured him. "I've no desire for such attachments. I do have one condition, though. You mustn't attempt to trade the babe away, if it's a girl. I don't mind your procuring a boy and claiming your wife bore twins, but—"

"Yes, very well." Milo waved a hand dismissively. "Swear to it—all of it."

Alex hesitated as he pondered the implications of this oath . . . *You'll leave here and never try and contact her again.*

"Cousin?" Milo prompted.

Alex squeezed his eyes shut. *Women have been known to use one fellow to make another one jealous . . . Not only had she lost her virginity years before, but she'd already been with child.* "I swear it," he said quickly. "I will do all that you've asked of me."

"And what is that?" came a soft voice from behind. Alex wheeled around to find Nicki standing in the turret doorway.

Milo greeted her with a mild smile. "Nicolette, my dear. I thought you'd retired for the evening."

"It occurred to me that you might need . . . a few things during the night." Nicki set a candle on the little table next to him and placed a chamber pot beneath his bed. She still wore the tunic she'd had on earlier that day—a pink one—but she'd freed her hair of its veil and brushed it out of its braids. It swayed in a rippling sheet as she moved, reflecting the light from the low fire that crackled in the hearth. Nicki had ordered the fire built in an attempt to ward off the damp chill of the hall for Milo, who got cold easily, but Alex appreciated it, too. The warmth eased the pain in his hip.

"The servants who sleep in the hall can tend to my needs," Milo assured his wife. "Go back upstairs. I'm fine."

Her gaze lit on Alex's hand resting on his sword hilt. "You were swearing some sort of an oath when I came down." Her eyes reflected the firelight, too, sparkling like pale green crystals.

"I . . ." Lying had never come easily to Alex; he groped for words. "I was merely . . . I wasn't really . . ."

"He was promising to instruct the men in swordplay while he's here," Milo said easily, and brought the goblet to his mouth.

Nicki's elegant eyebrows drew together. "You made him *swear* to do it?"

Milo shrugged. "Seemed like the thing to do. Perhaps my thinking was muddled."

Her consternation appeared to deepen. Little wonder; Milo's memory lapses and confusion had gotten worse over the past few days, no doubt from the stress of the trip.

"I want you to eat something before you go to sleep," she said.

He made a face. "Don't start trying to shove food down my throat again."

"You haven't eaten since we got home. I'm going

to go out to the cookhouse. There may be some of that stew left. If there is, I'm going to sit here and see that you eat it."

"Damnable harpy! You can bring it back, but you can't make me eat it."

"It's raining," Alex said as she turned to go. "I'll get the stew."

"I'll be fine—I'll wear my mantle," she called out as she disappeared into the stairwell with her husband hurling threats and insults at her back. Milo didn't seem to notice when Alex bid him good night and retreated to the undercroft.

Alone in his candlelit chamber, Alex sat on the edge of the bed and rubbed his hip until the band of pain loosened a bit. He tugged off his boots and hung up his tunic, and had started pulling his shirt over his head when he noticed a small oaken door tucked into a corner. Perplexed at not having noticed it earlier, he realized that it had been concealed by a tapestry, now gone. His first thought was that the door must lead to an adjoining chamber, but that was impossible, seeing as how it was positioned at the juncture of two outside walls. Perhaps he had his own private garderobe!

Lowering his shirt back down, he opened the door and ducked his head into it, discovering a dark shaft with narrow stone steps winding steeply upward—a secondary stairway, probably intended for servants, hidden within the thickness of the keep's massive walls. Wondering where it led, Alex took his candle and climbed awkwardly up the musty, spiraling passage until, halfway up, it opened onto a tiny landing with another small door. He had to push the door hard to get it to open, sacks of something heavy having been piled against it. Inside he found a small, whitewashed room lined with benches on which were stacked loaves of bread and various other foodstuffs; dried fruits and meats hung from the ceiling. It stood to reason that there would be access between the pantry and the undercroft, since the lower level had once been a kitchen.

Withdrawing to the landing, he gazed up the stairwell, which rose to the keep's third level—the solar, now Nicki's private domain. Alex wondered if it was as unrelentingly grim as the rest of Peverell Castle. After a moment's hesitation, he made his way up the stairs to the topmost landing, silent in his stocking feet. Pausing at the door, he listened for sounds from within. Nicki was out fetching her husband some stew, but her personal maid might be puttering about. On hearing nothing, he cautiously turned the door handle. It opened without resistance.

Alex stepped into the spacious, lamplit room, remembering the other time he'd stolen into Nicki's domain uninvited, the night before her marriage to Milo. Part of him felt like the lowest form of knave for trespassing on her privacy, but he found he could not stifle his curiosity. As it happened, Nicki's solar was a far cry from the rest of Peverell Castle.

The windows were large, the walls whitewashed and festooned with colorful, exotic rugs. One was draped over a long bench, on which a dozen embroidered pillows had been scattered, along with a book that had a white ribbon hanging out of it. He recalled that Nicki sometimes used to undo her braids when she was reading to him in their cave, so that she could use her ribbons as bookmarks. There was an empty spot where Milo's bed had apparently been. Next to it, coming out from the wall, stood another narrow bed, curtained in pale yellow. The insides of the window shutters and turret door had been painted the same summery color. Sunflowers with long, crooked stems sprouted from a clay pot on a writing desk.

Rain drummed on the oak-shingled roof overhead, rattled the shutters. Yet the solar felt snug and cheerful, bearing as it did Nicki's intimate stamp. It looked like her—like the best of her, the sweet and girlish Nicki he'd known in their dreamy afternoons together in Périgeaux. Or rather, the girl he'd thought he'd known—untouched, unspoiled. Reality had been a different matter entirely, he reminded himself.

So this was why Milo had insisted on giving him that little corner chamber downstairs—because it connected, very discreetly, with his wife's private sanctum. No doubt he had ordered the tapestry removed, so that Alex would not be long in discovering his chamber's most significant amenity. Shaking his head, Alex prowled around a bit, peeking into a chest, opening a bottle and sniffing its contents. Did Milo expect him to be her up here, he wondered, or take her downstairs? Alex had tupped married women on occasion, but never with their husbands sleeping beneath the same roof. This arrangement felt increasingly unsavory by the moment.

The slanted writing desk with its attached chair drew him. She must have had two dozen ink-stained quills of varying types and sizes all laid out in an orderly row. Alex lifted one that looked as if it had come from a raven and stroked his lips with the glistening black feather. Picking up her bone-handled penknife, he scraped its blade against his cheek; it was sharp enough to shave with. A sheet of parchment, blank but neatly ruled, was pinned to the desk next to a wax tablet and stylus. On a table next to it sat a small wooden chest, its lid open to reveal a stack of heavily inked pages—her poems. The stack was untidy, as if she'd been searching through it—apparently with success, for one page had been removed and set aside.

Alex lifted this page, mystified by what was written on it, of course, but intrigued by the delicate little drawing above the title: two hands clasped within a thorny wreath that bore a single delicate rose.

The door to the turret staircase squeaked as it

opened. "Alex!" Nicki stared at him from the doorway.

"Nicki. I . . ."

"Give me that!" Crossing the room swiftly, she snatched the sheet of verse from his hand. "You had no right to read this."

"I didn't. I . . . can't."

"Ah . . . yes." Seeming both chagrined and relieved, Nicki returned the page to the box and locked it with a key that she retrieved from the pouch on her girdle. Avoiding his gaze, she unpinned her blue mantle, drenched from the rain, and hung it on a peg, then kicked off her sodden slippers and stepped into a pair of dry ones. Her hair shimmered enchantingly in the lamplight.

"Has Milo finished his stew already?" Having been caught snooping in her things, Alex decided he'd rather brazen it out than slink away with his tail dragging.

"He dumped it in the rushes." She lifted her chin, but her smile wobbled slightly. "I'm not sure how to get food into him anymore, short of tying him down."

Alex's chest ached. "Nicki . . ." he said softly, taking a step toward her.

Footsteps shuffled up the stairs. "Edith!" Sprinting to the turret, she called down, "I won't need you tonight, Edith. I'll undress myself."

A pause, and then came the reedy voice of her elderly maid. "As you wish, milady," and the footsteps receded.

Nicki shut the door and slumped bonelessly against it. "How did you get in here?"

Alex nodded toward the small door in the corner. "That stairway leads to my chamber. I was exploring, and I ended up here."

She frowned. "Milo put you in that little corner chamber?"

"I don't mind." The lie came all too easily to his

lips—or perhaps, now that he knew of the secret passageway, he really didn't mind.

"Nonsense," she said. "There's a much larger chamber down there, with a fireplace."

"It's July. What need have I of a fireplace?"

"Perhaps, but it's twice the size of the one you're in." Turning toward the door, she said, "I'll have your things moved right away."

"Nay!" Leaping across the room—at considerable expense to his hip—Alex seized her arm. "I don't mind." He gentled his voice, rubbed her arm soothingly where he'd grabbed it. "Truly. Don't trouble yourself."

" 'Tisn't any trouble." She eyed him guardedly, almost suspiciously. She was an intelligent woman, he reminded himself, very intelligent. He must tread carefully, lest the purpose of his visit become all too obvious.

"Aye, but you've got enough on your hands just dealing with Milo."

At the mention of her husband's name, she backed away, disengaging his touch. "I hate to think of you pitying me."

"I don't pity you, Nicki. I might if you seemed overwhelmed, or hopeless. But you handle him as best you can. I admire you for it." That just came out, but it was no more than the truth.

"You're different than you were . . . at the boat that morning," she said, studying him in that intent way of hers.

He laughed sheepishly. "I don't have a head full of wine now. Some of the things I said . . . and did . . . that morning . . ." He shook his head.

"Me, too," she offered quietly.

For the moment their gazes connected, and he knew that the spell that had bound them together nine years ago had not completely lost its power. "I said some things," he said, "about what happened between us that summer that I wish I hadn't—"

"Perhaps it's best if we don't talk about that summer."

She was right. They were getting along, and if they tried to analyze what had passed between them before, they would surely start arguing again. His point in being at Peverell, he reminded himself, was to entice her into his bed, and he could hardly do that if she had her defenses up, waiting for him to accuse her of past wrongs.

"All right," he said, taking a step toward her. "Let's pretend it never happened."

"Good." Turning abruptly away, she crossed to her writing desk and tidied up the row of quills he'd disturbed. Alex didn't know whether her nervousness in his presence boded well or ill for the success of his mission. Noticing the locked box on the table, she took it and knelt gracefully next to the bed, sliding it underneath.

"You wrote all those poems?" Alex asked, just for something to say; he didn't want to leave yet.

"Aye—over the years. Some are from when I was a child." She braced a hand on the bed to rise. Alex crossed to her in two strides and offered his hand, which she hesitantly accepted. He helped her to her feet, but kept her hand, rubbing his thumb on her palm.

"You have the smoothest skin I've ever touched," he murmured.

She tugged her hand from his and hugged herself. "You should go. You shouldn't be here."

There had been a time when she would let him hold her hand for hours. Perhaps he'd erred in remarking that hers was the smoothest skin he'd ever touched—a reminder of all the other women he'd touched over the years. Yet what he'd said was true—none of them had felt as enticingly soft as Nicki, or smelled like her, or been her. Had he thought, somewhere deep inside, that if he sampled enough women's favors, he would eventually find a replacement for the lost love of his youth?

From outside the door came the scrape of feet on stone, and old Edith's voice. "Milady? I've come to help you get ready for bed."

Nicki closed her eyes briefly. "It's all right, Edith. I can undress myself."

A pause. "Oh. Yes. Very well." She shuffled away.

Alex cast a puzzled look at Nicki, who sighed. "Edith is getting old. She forgets things. I'd replace her, but 'twould break her heart."

"Then, even if she *had* seen me here," he said with a smile, "she might not remember."

Nicki didn't smile. "Someone else would. You should never come up here again. Please don't."

Stalling, for he was loath to leave, he said, "What was that poem about? The one with the two hands drawn on it?"

Spots of color bloomed on her cheeks; she averted her gaze. "It's just something I wrote a long time ago—'The Thorny Rose.' I . . . don't care for it."

"Then why do you keep it?"

" 'Twouldn't do any good to discard it at this point. Milo came upon it while I was finishing it. We'd just gotten married, and I was . . . he thought 'twould cheer me up if . . ." She sighed. "He took it and had it put to music by one of the knights, a fellow named Marlon, who's something of a trouvère—he sings beautifully. He still sings it from time to time. It makes me cringe."

"Why?"

Her back still to him, she shook her head. "You should leave, Alex," she said quietly.

"Nicki, I'd really like to know—"

"Please leave." She turned to face him, melancholy darkening her eyes. "Leave."

Alex crossed grudgingly to the small doorway in the corner. This was not going as well as he had hoped. "Come for a ride with me tomorrow, if the rain lets up," he said as he reached for the door handle.

She stilled. "I . . . I don't . . ."

"You can give me a tour of Peverell," he suggested.

"I'll ask Gaspar to show you around."

"I want you to do it."

She folded her arms. "Gaspar could show you the barracks, introduce you to the men."

"Nicki . . ."

"No, Alex. Please—you should go."

He raked a hand through his hair. "I thought we were going to put that summer behind us."

"This has naught to do with that summer. I just don't think it would look right, me going off alone with you for a ride."

Alex gritted his teeth. Damn her sense of propriety—and the memories that lingered stubbornly, defying banishment. This was going to be more of a challenge than he'd anticipated.

An idea occurred to him. "If it's all right with Milo, will you come riding with me?"

"Milo's judgement isn't what it should be. Nay. I won't go riding with you."

"Nicki . . ."

"Good night, Alex."

"Nicki, can't we just—"

"Go, Alex." She held his gaze for a moment, looking very sad and very determined. "Go. Please."

He opened the door. "Good night, Nicki."

"Good night."

He muttered a string of raw oaths as he limped ignominiously back down the twisting little stairwell, berating himself for his ineptitude. He couldn't even talk her into a ride. How the devil was he supposed to seduce her?

Alex the Conqueror, indeed.

Chapter 10

"Why did you invite Alex here?" Nicki asked her husband the next morning as she sat on the edge of his bed, coaxing spoonfuls of porridge into him.

"What do you mean?"

Nicki scanned the great hall. Servants were breaking down the breakfast tables, and a few soldiers were laughing in the corner, but no one was within earshot. "You know what I mean."

Milo stared at her. "I'm afraid I don't." He seemed so guileless, but then he had the gift for displays of mock sincerity. Lying didn't trouble him, as long as he could justify it to himself.

Nicki sighed in irritation and spooned some more porridge into his mouth. As eager as she was to question him, she also wanted to take advantage of his good mood and relative sobriety—he was his most clearheaded upon awakening, his worst at night—to get him to eat.

Milo watched her as he swallowed his porridge, something half-amused, almost sly, in his eyes. "I'm sorry if my inviting him has troubled you, my dear. I know you and Alex don't care for each other, and perhaps I should have taken that into consideration before asking him to stay. But he's my cousin, and we were always close."

" 'Tis he who doesn't care for me," she said. "My feelings for him are . . ." *Careful.* "He's my cousin by marriage, and I'm endeavoring to be hospitable. But that's not what I meant. I want to know why you invited him."

"Must there have been some reason, other than merely wanting his company?"

She stirred the porridge thoughtfully. "There might have been."

"Such as?"

She tried to feed him another spoonful, but he swatted her hand away. The porridge plopped onto her apron, which she'd taken to wearing while attempting to feed him. Even her most utilitarian wool tunics, such as the one she had on, were troublesome for Edith to clean.

"I need some wine to wash the taste of that sewage out of my mouth," he growled.

Nicki wiped off her apron with a napkin. "Not yet, Milo. Can't you wait a bit till you start—"

"If I could 'wait a bit' for my wine, do you think I'd have turned into this?" he snarled, holding out his arms—as frail as sticks in his too-big shirt. A few faces glanced in their direction, then turned away. Everyone at Peverell was used to Milo's sporadic outbursts by now.

Nicki studied him, discouraged by what she saw. He'd grown even more gaunt and jaundiced since the Rouen trip. She never should have allowed him to go. "Milo." She laid a careful hand on his shoulder, heartsick at the feel of sharp bone through the linen. "Please. I know you hate it when I talk about your drinking, but—"

"Then don't," he said wearily. "Just bring me the wine jug and a goblet."

She shook her head resolutely. "I told you a long time ago, I won't give you any more wine. I'll bring you juice, water, fresh buttermilk—"

"Buttermilk, for pity's sake." He grimaced. "I'd rather drink fresh piss."

"But don't ask me to help you kill yourself with wine, because I won't."

"Thank God Gaspar is more accommodating than you. He'll be in soon. I'll get it from him."

Nicki had tried to forbid Gaspar and the rest of their staff from giving her husband wine, but Milo had overruled her, his prerogative as castellan—if only in name.

"You didn't answer my question," he said, his good humor returning as precipitously as it had fled. "Why do *you* think I invited Alex here?"

"I don't know." She evaded his shrewd gaze, unsure enough of her suspicions to feel embarrassed about voicing them. "I was thinking about . . . what you proposed."

He cocked his head slightly, as if puzzled as to her meaning.

She took a deep breath and glanced around to make sure no one was near. "About my . . . having another man's child."

His eyebrows shot up. "You think that's why I brought Alex here?"

"Nay! I . . . I don't know. I thought perhaps—"

"But you rejected the idea outright."

"Aye, but—"

"I took you at your word," he said, his look of mild indignation transforming to interest. "Why? Have you changed your mind?"

She slammed the porridge bowl on the little table. "You know I haven't changed my mind. The idea disgusts me." To open her legs for a man, any man, for the coldblooded purpose of getting with child . . . it made Nicki shudder.

"Well, then." Milo shrugged his skeletal shoulders. "I took you at your word, and that was the end of that."

"Aye, but . . . but I thought perhaps you had hopes of . . . changing my mind, or . . . I don't know. You might have come up with some scheme—"

"Would it do me any good? After all, you'd have to consent for . . . anything of that sort of happen, would you not? And you've already made it clear that you won't."

"I most certainly won't!"

Chuckling, Milo took the napkin from her and wiped his mouth with it. "My dear, I do hope you don't fly to such conclusions every time one of my relatives comes for a visit."

She swore at him, but the novelty of hearing such words from her lips only made him laugh harder. "Milo, have you given any more thought to my idea?"

"Your idea?"

"Our staying on here as stewards."

Now it was his turn to swear, which he did far more colorfully than she had. "I told you, Father Octavian would never allow it. He mistrusts women, and he despises me. And, as abbot of St. Clair, he'd have to appoint us himself—"

"But I've thought of a way—"

"I ordered you to abandon this idea, did I not? 'Twill only shame us, to have you begging favors of that malicious bastard."

"Will it be any less shameful to be tossed out of here on our ears?"

He smiled inscrutably. "It won't necessarily come to that."

"It most certainly will come to that, unless we take measures to prevent it—something you seem curiously unwilling to do."

"I did come up with a solution."

"Ah, yes. I'm to save Peverell by playing the whore. Do you honestly think that's less shameful than asking to remain here as stewards?"

"Your outrage at my proposal strikes me as a bit much, my dear. After all, 'twouldn't be the first time you've bestowed your favors on a man to whom you weren't wed."

Nicki stared at her husband in shock, heat scalding her face. This was the first time in nine years of marriage that Milo had taunted her with her youthful indiscretion. The hurt she felt took her breath away.

Leaping to her feet, she grabbed the bowl of porridge and thrust it into Milo's hands. "Here!" She whipped the bed curtains closed around him, turned and strode out of the hall. "Feed yourself! I'm going to go dump all the wine into the moat!"

Alex, astride Milo's sorrel gelding, found Nicki's mare exactly where her husband had said it would be—on the bank of the stream that meandered through the woods to the north of the castle, at the top of a rugged declivity that produced a waterfall. She always fled to the same little refuge in the woods when they had words, Milo had assured him. Alex would be certain to find her there—alone.

The day was clear and sunny—a relief for his hip after yesterday's downpour—but little of that sun filtered through the dense canopy of foliage overhead, producing the effect to twilight in midmorning. It was pleasantly cool here, the air still redolent with the wet, green scent of rain. Most of the forest floor was thickly carpeted with ferns, but the rest had turned to mud. His mount's legs were coated with it by the time he found the stream.

Dismounting, he tethered his horse next to Nicki's and went in search of her. He spied her about a hundred yards downstream, leaning over a patch of mud with her back to him—although at first he didn't believe it could be her.

She had on a humble gray tunic—nothing like the gleaming silks she'd worn at William's court—and her hair was bound up in a white scarf twisted around her head rather like a Moorish turban. Her skirts were gathered up in one hand, exposing her bare, mud-splattered feet and ankles. In the other hand she held a twig, which she scraped purposefully on the ground. She was writing, he realized, etching words into the mud as if it were a tablet. So absorbed was she in this activity that she didn't hear him approach. Of course, with his instinct for stealth, only those with the keenest hearing ever detected his presence from behind.

"What are you writing?"

She spun around, dropping her twig. "Nothing." Turning back around, she dragged a foot across the mud, obliterating the carefully scratched words.

"I can't read it, remember?" Alex said quietly.

She paused with her back to him; her shoulders slumped. "I forgot."

He stepped closer to her. "What was it?"

"A . . . a poem. The beginnings of one. The words came to me, and I had no tablet with me."

"What was it about?"

She hesitated. "Nothing. 'Twas just a poem." Yet she picked up the twig and began scratching in the mud again, her brow furrowed. "Oh, blast it, I can't remember." She hurled the twig into the stream. "What are you doing here, anyway?"

He cleared his throat and tried for a nonchalant tone. "I was bored, and—"

"How did you find me?"

"Milo told me where you'd be. He said this is where you always come after . . . that is . . ."

"Did he tell you what we quarreled about?"

Damn. Sometimes he wished he had Milo's gift for easy deception. He wanted to shrug carelessly and say, "Nay, was it anything of consequence?" but in fact, Milo had warned him about her suspicions and cautioned him to deny everything if she voiced them . . . *Learn to lie! You're a grown man, for pity's sake.*

So preoccupied was Nicki with her stewing that she paid no heed to Alex's telltale hesitation. "Nay, he wouldn't have told you," she muttered. "Even he knows better than to air such matters openly."

Anxious to change the subject, Alex smiled at her

muddy feet. "You look like a little girl who's gotten into something she ought not have."

She bent over to inspect her feet. "It washes off."

"The hem of your tunic is muddy in back."

Nicki groaned. "Edith will give me *that look*." Hiking her skirts up to her knees, she waded into the stream.

"Why do you . . ." Alex shook his head. "Nay, you'll think it a foolish question."

Crouching over, she scrubbed at her submerged feet with her hands. "Why do I what?"

He rubbed his neck. "I know naught about . . . writing and such. I was just wondering . . . why you would go to this trouble to do it. What compels you?"

She splashed water onto her legs and wiped the mud from them. "What compels you to fight for your king?"

" 'Tis no longer a labor of love, if that's what you mean. 'Tis simply all I know how to do."

Straightening up, Nicki regarded him with that hushed alertness of hers. "Have you ever considered . . ." She bit her lip.

"Have I ever considered what?"

She waded out of the water, pausing at the edge of the mud with her skirt still clutched in her hand, and looked around. "Would you bring me my shoes so I don't get my feet muddy again? They're over by that tree."

Alex fetched the soft kid slippers, stained with mud, but held them out of her reach when she tried to take them from him. "Have I ever considered what?"

She took a deep breath. "Have you ever considered learning how to read and write?"

Alex couldn't stop his bark of harsh laughter. "Don't you think I'm a bit old for that sort of thing?" He knelt before her. "Lift your right foot."

"I can do that, if you'll just give me those slippers."

He looked up at her. "Do you fear me?"

Her eyes were fiercely luminous in the forest halflight. "Of course not."

He stroked her ankle lightly. "Then why are you so skittish with me?"

"It's just that . . . it's unseemly for you to be touching my feet."

He felt goose bumps rise beneath his fingertips. "I've touched you in more intimate places than your feet."

"I thought we were going to forget that summer."

"I'll never forget that summer," he said softly, holding her gaze as he caressed her calf. "We merely agreed not to talk about it."

"Then don't," she said tightly.

"As you wish." Reaching up, he took her free hand and placed it on his shoulder. "To help you keep your balance," he explained, lifting her right foot and cradling it while he wriggled the slipper onto it. Even her feet were soft, he marveled, and strangely pretty—as small and delicate as a child's.

"So you think you're too old to learn something new?" she challenged.

"Probably." He slid the other shoe onto her left foot and took her hand before she could remove it from his shoulder. Holding it, he rose, standing far too close to her, but making no move to back away.

"Is that so?" Wresting her hand from his grip, she stepped around him. "If someone handed you a new form of weapon, some wonderful advance—say, a machine that shoots missiles—"

He propped his hands on his hips and smiled. "It exists already. It's called a crossbow, and I know how to use it, even if I don't have Luke's skill with it."

"Not a crossbow, a . . ." She drew a small shape in the air with her hands. "A device you can hold in your hand. 'Twould expel tiny little iron balls very quickly."

"Tiny little iron balls?" He laughed skeptically. "The point of a weapon is to kill the enemy, or at least cause serious injury. A little iron ball might take out an eye if one could aim it well enough, but—"

"I'm not sure exactly how it's supposed to work,"

she said. "It's my friend's idea. He invents things. On parchment, that is. He makes drawings—tools, weapons, scientific instruments . . ."

"Your friend?" Foreboding crawled over Alex's scalp. Did Nicki have a "friend" of whom Milo was unaware—a lover she entertained in secret while protesting her fidelity? Considering Milo's longstanding impotence—not to mention Nicki's history of manipulating men's affections—the possibility seemed all too likely.

"Sometimes, if it's a particularly promising design," she said, "he'll actually build one of these inventions, or a model of it."

"Does Milo know about this friend?"

Her expression of puzzlement gave way to outrage as she digested his meaning. "My friend is a monk," she said acidly. "An *old* monk. Brother Martin, the prior of the St. Clair Abbey. And of course Milo knows about him. I've been visiting him since I was a child."

Alex executed a sheepish little bow. "I apologize if it seemed I was implying—"

"It didn't 'seem as if you were implying' anything," she spat out. "You all but accused me of adultery."

"Nicki, I'm—"

"A fat lot of nerve you've got, being so self-righteous, considering . . . what they say about you."

"What do they say about me?"

Her cheeks pinkened in the cool, dusky light. "They talk about . . . all the women you've had."

"It's true, I've known many women." Gravely he added, "I only ever loved one, though."

A breeze swept through the forest, rattling the leaves overhead. Some of them broke loose, spinning and twirling around Nicki as she gazed at him.

"I have to go." She turned and strode away.

Alex sprinted to catch up with her. He grabbed her shoulder. "Would you teach me how to read?"

She pivoted to face him, her eyes immense. He could see right through them, as if looking into the clear green depths of a tidal pool. "You really want to learn how to read?"

"And write, I suppose. Yes," he said, astounded that he really meant it. "Yes, I do. Will you teach me?"

Her eyes searched his. "What changed your mind?"

"You."

She frowned. "Alex . . ."

He closed his hands around her upper arms and implored her to meet his gaze. "I mean the fact that you write such extraordinary poems, and I can't even read them. Milo can. Luke can read and write, and so can every woman I know—they all learned in convent schools. Christ, even little Robert wrote that blasted poem about honey cakes—"

"Almond cakes," she corrected with a little laugh. The music of it tickled his chest deep inside. He didn't think he'd heard her laugh since Périgeaux.

"Almond cakes," he chuckled. "With honey glaze." He still had his hands around her arms, he noted happily. She hadn't recoiled from his touch—not yet, anyway. "Will you teach me?" he asked, gliding his hands down to capture hers. "Please?"

She withdrew her hands from his, but gently, without the agitation she'd shown before. "I suppose I could talk Brother Martin out of another writing desk. We could put it in front of a window in the great hall, and I could instruct you there."

Alex moaned. "That awful hall? It's so dank and gloomy." And crowded. He'd be sacrificing an opportunity to have her all to himself if he agreed to take his lessons anywhere in the keep. "Can't you teach me . . . well, out here?"

"Here?" She looked around doubtfully. "In the woods?"

"Or in a meadow . . ." He smiled. "Perhaps we could even find a nice little cave."

She did not return his smile.

He raised his hands placatingly. "Sorry. That was . . . sorry. I *would* rather we did this outside, though—anywhere you'd like. I can't stand being in that gloomy old castle. How can you bear living there?"

The shadow that crossed her face said it all: She bore it because she had to. "All right. I'll teach you out of doors. No reason we can't bring tablets with us."

"And a blanket."

She hesitated, then shrugged. "Yes, I suppose we'll need a blanket."

Thank the saints. Progress.

"What about your oath to Milo?" she asked.

"My . . . my oath?" Alex stammered.

"You swore that you'd teach swordsmanship to the men. Will you have time for that?"

Alex let out a sigh of relief. "I'll do that in the mornings. We can take our lessons in the afternoons."

"Very well." She caught her lower lip between her teeth. "One thing, though. It might not look good, our spending so much time alone together. Milo won't care. He's . . . well, he won't care. But others might talk."

"I'll be discreet," he assured her, irritated as always by her fixation with propriety, but thrilled at the prospect of long hours alone with her. "We can leave the keep separately and meet at some agreed location. Is this a good place?"

"As good as any, I suppose."

"Excellent." This was a secluded spot, deep within the woods. The likelihood of unwanted company was minimal. Alex pictured them on a blanket beneath the sheltering trees, their heads bent over their tablets, her arm brushing his, her scent drifting around him. A sweet ache rose within him, speeding his heart.

He did want to learn to read and write; he also wanted to be with her, to touch her, to finally claim

that which he'd let slip away nine long years ago. He
shouldn't desire her—even just her body—after all
that had transpired between them, all she'd done to
tarnish his ardor. Yet he could no more stop wanting
her than he could stop breathing. "Shall we meet this
afternoon, then?" he asked, trying to contain his eagerness. "After dinner?"

"I can't this afternoon. I must supervise the changing of the rushes in the great hall."

"Tomorrow, then?"

"Aye. Tomorrow." She addressed him with a stern
look that made him want to laugh. "You promise to
apply yourself to your studies?"

"I assure you," he said with a slow smile of anticipation, "I approach this endeavor with the utmost
enthusiasm."

Alone in his quarters, Gaspar uncorked a tiny vial
and tapped a few grains of pungent white powder into
his mortar, being very judicious as to the amount.
Hemlock was among the most formidable of his many
herbal remedies, but it was by far the most dangerous.
A pinch in a sleeping draft could bring on a deep,
almost deathlike sleep. Too much produced a mindless
frenzy, during which the heart seized up and stopped.

Satisfied with the dose he'd chosen, Gaspar unfolded a parchment packet on which he'd written *Valerian* and poured a little drift of the brownish powdered
root next to the hemlock in the mortar. He paused,
wondering whether to add more. Lady Nicolette was
tall for a woman, but of a slender build.

Valerian, being governed by Mercury, had warming
properties, which made it useful for nervous conditions, seizures, and headaches. But, as with so many
potent herbs, too much could produce symptoms similar to those for which it had been employed—searing
headaches, wrenching spasms, even hallucinations.

For his purposes, Gaspar sought an amount sufficient to soothe the nerves, but not enough to cause any alarming side effects. He wanted merely to complement the sedative effects of the hemlock. There would be little harm in the lady Nicolette's awakening with a headache, but hallucinations might raise suspicions.

Too bad he had to sedate her with the hemlock. How he'd love to look into her eyes, wide with terror and mortification, as he did all the things to her he'd yearned to do for so long. How he longed to hear her cry and beg, to feel her thrashing beneath him in a panic as he pounded into her . . .

The hemlock would rob him of such pleasures by inducing a deep sleep. Did he have to use it? Excitement mounted within him as he reflected on the potential of dispensing with the hemlock and giving her valerian alone—but far more than would be prescribed for its curative properties. Bereft of her senses, she'd be easier to control. And, deranged or not, as long as she remained conscious—and no woman could sleep through what he had in store for her—she would be completely aware of what she was being made to endure, a tantalizing prospect.

Quite possibly the valerian would affect her memory, and she would not even recall her ravishment afterward. If she did, her mind would be so dazed, and her account so confused, that she would most likely be deemed ill and suffering from delusions. The only real risk would be if her report was believed and she could identify Gaspar as having been the one to force himself on her, but if he wore a bandit's mask, she'd never know it was him. Most likely some hapless cutpurse would be hanged for the deed.

It would never come to that, though. Even if she did remember, they'd think she was imagining things, perhaps going mad. He could take her night after night, and no one would be the wiser.

Gaspar tossed out the contents of the mortar and

replaced it with a generous mound of valerian. He hesitated, then added yet more. Hallucinations might actually be rather intriguing, and he didn't much mind spasms; he was certainly strong enough to hold her down. Or he could tie her to the bed; he'd probably have to gag her, anyway, so she wouldn't awaken the household. As for headaches, he cared not how much she suffered upon awakening. Let the bitch suffer, as he had. Let her writhe in agony, her mind a chaos of nightmarish memories, wondering what was real and what was imagined. It was only just, after all the years he'd striven to prove himself to her, hoping that she'd eventually view him as a man, only to have her regard him as dispassionately as she did the rest of her inferiors.

As an afterthought, he added to the valerian a handful of other herbs known to affect the senses, crushing them together with his marble pestle. He winced at their noxious odor, the kind of smell you could taste in the back of your throat. He'd have to grind the stuff fine and mix it well into something strongly flavored, or she'd never swallow it. She liked spiced wine with her dessert; he could give it to her after supper tonight.

The rest would be easy. Milo had moved out of the solar; she was all alone up there. After the household had retired for the evening, he could slip into the pantry and climb the little service stairwell to the solar. She'd be feeling woozy by then, perhaps even have begun seeing visions and hearing things. Or perhaps she'd be insensible. He'd slap her awake.

And then she'd pay, he thought, grinding the brown powder into dust, grinding and grinding until sweat beaded on his forehead and his hand ached. She'd pay for ignoring him all these years. He'd show her she wasn't so high and mighty.

He'd show her.

Chapter 11

"**S**piced wine, milady?"

Nicki looked up from her peach tart to find Gaspar hovering over with a flagon. Having drunk more wine than usual at supper, she was tempted to wave him away, but he'd be disappointed. Given his facility with herbcraft, he liked to mix up the spiced wine himself and serve it at the end of the meal—to the family, of course, not to the dozens of soldiers supping noisily at the rows of tables that filled the great hall.

"Thank you, Gaspar."

Smiling, he set a fresh goblet before her and filled it from his flagon, which he then recorked.

"What about me?" Milo demanded thickly. "I'd like some."

"This bottle is empty, milord," Gaspar explained as he headed toward the buttery. "I'll fetch another."

Obviously disgruntled, Milo lifted his wine goblet and drained it. This was the first he'd gotten out of bed since they returned home yesterday, and it seemed he was back to his old habits. To her knowledge, he'd eaten nothing since those few spoonfuls of porridge this morning, but he'd drunk steadily all day. "So, Alex," he said to his cousin, who sat across the table from them. "I understand you're going to learn how to read and write."

Alex looked at Nicki as he took a slow sip from his own goblet. She evaded his gaze, as she frequently did, fearful that he'd see it all in her eyes, the stubborn passion that had never died, but which could never be—a passion, moreover, that he evidently didn't share. He'd never denied hating her, she reminded herself. Although his feelings may have mellowed into ambivalence since their encounter at the longboat, any interest he might have in her—beyond her ability to teach him to read—could only be of a purely carnal nature. His love for her had died nine years ago, when she'd chosen to marry Milo. Now she had to live with that choice.

"Aye," Alex said. "Lady Nicolette is most kind. I hope she's patient as well."

Milo smiled. "I think I can attest to her patience. I must say, I was delighted when she told me you'd asked her to be your teacher." He chuckled. "I should have thought of it myself."

Alex looked down at his untouched peach tart, frowning. Nicki wondered what had discomfited him.

"You two are getting on quite nicely, then. Excellent." Milo lifted his goblet, grimacing to find it empty. Unsurprisingly, he reached for Nicki's, swallowing down half of her spiced wine in a single tilt.

"Milord!" Nicki turned to find Gaspar hurrying toward them from the buttery, another flagon in his hand. "I poured that for your lady wife."

"You can pour her another." Milo brought the goblet to his mouth, but Gaspar snatched it from him before he could drink any more. "What do you think you're—"

"That was from the old batch," Gaspar said soothingly. "It might have begun to turn." He filled Milo's empty goblet from the flagon in his hand. "There you go, sire. This will taste better, I wager."

"It *is* better," Milo pronounced upon taking a sip. "Much better."

Some time later, as the serving wenches were clearing the tables, one of them reached for Milo's goblet, which still contained some wine. He yanked it out of her reach, then, swaying on his bench, set it down awkwardly, its contents sloshing onto the table.

"Milo," Nicki said quietly. "Perhaps you've had enough."

Shaking his head, he reached for the goblet again, but knocked it over, spilling wine onto the table. Nicki blotted it with a napkin.

"The hell . . ." Milo muttered, waving a hand in front of his eyes. "I'm seeing double."

Nicki looked toward Gaspar, who observed all this with an expression of inexplicable alarm, his face ashen. Curious; one would think he'd be used to this sort of thing by now. "Gaspar," she said, "my husband is ready for bed, I think. Would you please help him to—"

"Damn!" Milo lurched to his feet, his eyes wild. "What in bloody hell—"

"Milo?" Alex stood up, his brow furrowed with concern. "What's the matter?"

"He'll be all right." Nicki rose and put her arm around her husband. He was shivering. "Milo, Gaspar's going to help you to—"

"Something's wrong," Milo said in a quavering voice as his hands began to shake. "Can't you see something's wrong? I'm sick, damn your eyes! I think I'm dying."

"Come along, sire," Gaspar coaxed as he helped Milo over the bench.

"I'll help him." Shouldering Gaspar aside, Alex put an arm around him. Gaspar looked on stonily as Alex led his cousin across the hall, with Nicki following closely. The soldiers ignored them, for the most part, accustomed to seeing their castellan being helped to bed.

"I'm dying!" Milo wailed, squirming against Alex's grasp. "You're trying to kill me."

Nicki patted her husband's back. "Alex doesn't want to kill you, Milo."

Milo peered at his cousin, evidently struggling to focus on his face. "I thought you were Gaspar. Gaspar's trying to kill me."

Nicki's heart sank; she'd never seen him so bad. "Nobody's trying to— *Milo?*"

Spasms racked his body, head to toe. Alex called his name as he eased him down onto the rushes, where he convulsed for a few moments before going limp.

"Milo?" Nicki took his face in her hands. "Milo! Milo, talk to me!"

"Let me get him into bed." Alex lifted his insensate cousin as if he were a rag doll and carried him to his bed by the hearth. His concern for Milo was touching.

Every soldier in the hall, and all of the staff as well, watched in wide-eyed silence. Thank the saints for Gaspar. He cupped his hands around his mouth, bellowing, "Supper is over. Everyone back to the barracks."

As the men filed out amid a buzz of murmurings, Alex pulled off Milo's boots and tunic. Milo's head whipped back and forth, a guttural groan rising from him. He clutched at the bedcovers as shudders coursed through him.

"Milo." Nicki stroked his hair with trembling fingers. "Milo, look at me. Milo!"

She didn't hear Alex saying her name until he grabbed her by the shoulders and turned her to face him. "Nicki, did you hear me? He needs a physician. Tell me where to find one."

"There's a barber-surgeon in St. Clair." She gave him directions to the home of old Guyot. As he turned to leave, she seized his arm. "What do you think is wrong with him, Alex?"

"I don't know." He looked toward the high table at the other end of the hall, empty now save for Gaspar, studying them with his arms folded. For a moment, she thought he was going to say something, but he just shook his head as if to clear it. "I really don't know. It could be . . . anything. Some sort of fever, probably." He squeezed her hand. "I'll be back soon, with the surgeon. Stay with Milo."

*   *   *

"That's it, then," said Maître Guyot as he set his little knife in the bucket of blood and bandaged the vein he'd opened in Milo's arm. Guyot nodded to Alex, who'd taken on the unpleasant task of holding his cousin down for the procedure. "You may release him. There's naught to do now but pray."

Nicki, kneeling next to her husband's bed, closed her eyes and murmured another in a long string of prayers as Milo tossed and moaned. The praying served a dual purpose—to influence God to release Milo from this dreadful infirmity and to keep her mind off what the surgeon was doing to treat it. Her husband's sudden attack had thrown her into a kind of panic, but now that his stomach had been purged and he'd been bled, she had to believe that the worst of the virulent humors had been expelled from his system.

When she opened her eyes, she saw Alex kneeling on the other side of the bed and crossing himself. He looked at her, his gaze dark and sober. "Are you all right? You're so pale."

"I'm fine, I just . . ."

Alex cocked an eyebrow. How useless, to lie to the one man who could see into her soul. "Nay," she admitted. "I loathe bloodlettings. I feel faint just thinking about them, and to have to be present at one . . ." She shook her head.

" 'Tis true," old Guyot interjected, untying his blood-spattered apron. He wore a green coif over his sparse white hair; Nicki always thought of a lizard when she saw him. "She's quite irrational about them. Won't submit to them herself. Once, I had her tied down so I could bleed her for a fever, and she fought so hard against the ropes that they cut into her wrists. Her husband made me release her."

"I would have, too," Alex said quietly, his gaze still trained on her.

" 'Twas a mistake." Guyot unrolled the sleeves of his tunic. "And one that might have cost her her life.

Bleedings can be critical. Take his lordship here. He would have died for sure if we hadn't drained the tainted blood from him."

Gaining his feet, Alex said, "What do you think the problem is?"

"I know what the problem is," replied the old man testily as he packed up his satchel. "His lordship is suffering from a cephalical ailment."

Nicki and Alex exchanged a look of puzzlement as she rose from the floor.

The surgeon made a face that implied only the barest toleration of their ignorance. "His brain has been afflicted with hot vapors."

"Ah," Nicki said. "So, does that mean he's—"

"Being situated at the top of the body, the brain—which is by nature temperate—is exceedingly vulnerable to overheating." Guyot lifted his bloody knife from the bucket and wiped it off on a rag. "Since it is the seat of sense and reason, when the brain is overcome by heat, the afflicted party may experience such dementia as his lordship displays."

"But what caused this overheating?" Alex asked. "Is he ill, or . . . is it something else?"

"Of course he's ill," the old man snapped. " 'Tis a contagion brought on by a flux in the atmosphere. 'Twill strike others, mark my word—especially if they stand close enough to his lordship to breathe in the malignant vapors as they're driven out of him."

Nicki and Alex both backed away from the bed.

"Will he be all right?" Nicki asked.

"That's for the Almighty to decide." Guyot pinned his mantle over his shoulders.

"Isn't that anything more we can do?" she asked, dismayed at the notion of just sitting around and waiting for fate to take its course.

The old surgeon nodded. "Boil a red onion in a mixture of verjuice, honey, and mustard. Hold it under his nose twice a day, while it's hot, and make him smell it. Do you need me to write it down?"

"Verjuice, honey, and mustard," Nicki said. "I'll remember."

"Very well, then." Maître Guyot cleared his throat and held out his withered old hand, palm up. "Then all that remains is the matter of the—"

"Oh, yes." Nicki dug in her pouch for the requisite payment and pressed the coins into his hand.

"Twice a day," he barked on his way out. "While it's hot. I won't be responsible for the consequences if you forget."

Nicki and Alex stood in silence over Milo's bed as he writhed and muttered.

"I'll sit up with him tonight," Alex offered, his old instinct for gallantry having reasserted itself. She almost wished he would avoid any such chivalric gestures; it would help to dampen her feelings for him.

"Nonsense. I've already ordered a pallet made up for me right here, next to the bed. I'll stay with him."

"You shouldn't be anywhere near him. You might catch his illness."

"So might you."

"I'm a man," Alex protested. "I could withstand it better. I should take care of him. He's my cousin, after all."

"He's my husband," Nicki said, quietly but firmly.

Alex looked at her. She saw a muscle jump in his jaw. Softly he said, "Won't you let me do anything for you, Nicki?"

"I won't let you do this. It's not your place. It's mine."

He rubbed the back his neck. "Promise you'll summon me if . . . he becomes difficult to handle."

"I will. Good night, Alex."

"Good night."

"Where are you? Christ, woman, where are you?"

Nicki sat bolt upright on her pallet, her heart racing.

"Milo?" It was dark; the candle must have burned down. She hadn't meant to fall asleep, only to rest her eyes, but she must have been more tired than she realized.

"Are you there?" Milo's voice was groggy and breathless.

Nicki stood up and saw the dark shadow of her husband sitting up in bed. "Here I am, Milo. Lie down."

"Thank God." He sank back down onto his pillow. "You're here. You're here." Nicki smoothed the damp hair off his forehead. He'd been sweating; that was probably good, because it would cool the hot vapors ravaging his brain. Most likely he'd slept as well, for if he'd been consumed all this time by the delirium he'd suffered earlier, she never could have fallen asleep. That had to be a good sign.

"Go back to sleep, Milo. You've been sick. You need your sleep."

He reached for her, pulling her onto the bed. "Lie with me. Please. It's been so long."

It *had* been a long time—years—since they'd lain together in the same bed. Neither of them had much missed that physical intimacy, but now he was ill, and in need of the comfort of another warm body next to his. And surely comfort was all he was after. He was incapable of anything else.

"Take this off," he said, tugging at the wrapper she wore over her night shift. "I'm cold. I want to feel your warmth." She slipped it off and laid it at the foot of the bed, then got under the covers next to her husband—who was shivering, despite the balmy night—pulling the bed curtains closed around them in case she dozed off here. Servants slept in the rushes nearby, and soldiers would start straggling in around dawn. It wouldn't do for them to see her in bed in a sleeveless shift.

Milo gathered her in his arms, and she cautiously returned the embrace. Maître Guyot would disapprove of such close contact, but if God intended for her to be stricken with this malady, she would be stricken with it. Regardless of the course their marriage had taken, Milo was her husband, and he needed her.

"You were always so warm," he murmured, his shivers abating. "So soft. How it pleased me just to hold you." It frightened Nicki to hold Milo, and she did so carefully. She could feel his ribs through his shirt, and the bandage on his arm where he'd been bled. He smelled of wine and sickness, and his skin was clammy to the touch.

Closing her eyes, she remembered him as he'd been back in Périgeaux—the charming, funny, erudite older cousin of the boy she loved. Alex had adored Milo, and for that reason, so had she. He was immensely likeable; who could help but be fond of him? When he'd proposed, she knew she could have done far worse.

Of course, she hadn't known how he would deteriorate. It made her ache inside to think what had become of him. He'd lost the best part of him. And she . . . she'd lost Alex.

"I've missed this." He stroked her hair with a palsied hand. "I've missed you. Do you remember the last time we made love?"

She shook her head. Their couplings had been all too forgettable, and they'd ceased so long ago. She did recall trying to talk him into bedding her after he'd lost interest, for the sake of an heir. And she remembered the night he'd finally admitted the truth—that the problem lay not with her, but with him, and that they'd never have children and she'd best accustom herself to the idea.

" 'Twas in your father's shop," he breathed into her ear, "after your family had gone to bed. I came and woke you up in the middle of the night, remember? You all slept in that one room, so we had to go in back, where he made the saddles."

Oh, God. Nicki closed her eyes. "Milo . . ."

"I remember the smell of the leather." He pressed his lips to her temple so tenderly it made her eyes sting. "And the smell of you, and the little sounds you made, and the way your breasts felt through that rough homespun shift of yours. You made some silly jest in the middle of it, and giggled—I felt it deep inside you. You asked why I didn't laugh."

He kissed her hair, her forehead. Never, even when they were first married and trying to make a go of it, had he been so gentle and loving. She hadn't known he had it in him. To discover it now, in this way, consumed her with sadness.

"I couldn't tell you," he murmured hoarsely, "what I came to tell you that night—that I'd be marrying someone else in the morning. I'm sorry, Violette. 'Twas weak of me, and cruel, to let you find out afterward. I know you never—" His voice caught. "You never forgave me," he finished in a quavering whisper.

"God, Milo." Nicki's throat felt as if a fist were squeezing it tight. "Milo . . ."

"Shh." He kissed her eyelids, damp with unshed tears. "Let me tell you now what I couldn't bear to tell you then—that I had to do it, or thought I did. I thought it was my only chance for happiness." His little rasp of laughter was grim. "God, what a fool I was. And you paid the price."

She stroked his face—skin stretched over bone. "It's all right, Milo," she managed as hot tears spilled down her cheeks. "You did what you thought you must. I forgive you."

"How can you?" he whispered.

Nicki thought of Violette, who'd sacrificed her life rather than go on without Milo. "Because I love you. I always have. That hasn't changed."

"Oh, God, Violette." He held her tighter than she would have thought possible, given his frailty. "I love you so much. I love you. I love you. I'll always love you."

"I know." She was weeping now, and holding him as tightly as he held her.

"I'm sorry. I'm so—"

"I know. It's all right. You can go to sleep now. I'm here."

"Will you be here in the morning?"

She took his face in her hands. "I'll always be here. We're together now."

He smiled in the dark, and for a moment he looked like the old Milo again, the jocular, carelessly agreeable fellow who was everyone's friend.

She kissed his cheek, snuggled up against him. "Good night, Milo."

"Good night, my love." His breathing grew steady, his arms around her heavy. As he drifted into the darkness, so did she.

Just as sleep was claiming her, she thought she heard him whisper, "Thank you."

"Damn!" Daybreak glowed through the narrow slits that served as windows in Alex's tiny chamber. He'd overslept.

He grabbed his chausses off the floor and pulled them on, berating himself; he'd meant to check on Nicki during the night. That is, he meant to check on Milo and see how Nicki was doing with him.

He threw on his shirt as he leapt up the turret stairs. Servants were setting up trestle tables when he strode into the great hall. A few soldiers loitered about, waiting for breakfast. The hall was vast and dim, lit only by a few shafts of dawn light squeezing through the arrow slits.

Nicki's pallet was empty. Milo's bed curtains were closed. She must have arisen early and gone up to the solar to wash up and get dressed.

Hoping Milo had managed to get to sleep, Alex stepped silently over the pallet and pulled the bed

curtains aside. In the dark, womblike shelter of the
bed he saw that Milo was, indeed, sleeping.

With Nicki, also sound asleep, curled in his embrace.

Alex stared, shaken on some level he hadn't known
existed. Nicki and Milo asleep together, their arms
around each other.

Like lovers.

Like husband and wife.

She had her back to Alex, but her face was tilted
up. Her mouth was slightly open. A strand of golden
hair was stuck to her cheek, in the salty trail of what
could only have been a tear.

Would she have cried for him, he wondered, if he'd
been the one who'd succumbed to this mysterious affliction? For it must be an illness of the brain, caused
by atmospheric upheavals, as that withered old surgeon had insisted. Alex had briefly suspected Gaspar,
but the pieces didn't fit. Gaspar's scheme had been to
dose Nicki with a sleeping draft, not a poison that
caused lunacy and convulsions.

Nicki's incredible hair spilled off the side of the bed,
cascading to the floor. Her bare shoulder and arm
looked creamy in the semidarkness.

Alex wondered how it would feel to wake up in the
morning with Nicki's arms around him. At that moment he would have given anything to trade places
with Milo.

No attachments, remember? He was here to plant a
babe in her belly, nothing more. He'd sworn an oath
to do it, so he'd damn well do it—and without wasting
any time about it. The sooner she quickened, the
sooner he could get away from here—which he was
suddenly very eager to do.

He started to draw the curtain closed, when Nicki's
arm moved. She shifted restlessly, as one does upon
awakening.

And then she opened her eyes and looked at him.

Chapter 12

Nicki was taken aback to find Alex staring at her when she awakened, standing over the bed with the curtain held aside. His gaze was steady, his eyes very large and dark.

With the poor light, she couldn't see his hard edges, the faint scars. He looked almost boyish, or would have were it not for the morning stubble that shadowed his jaw.

Alex looked toward Milo, still sleeping peacefully, and back at her. It felt strange for him to see her this way, in bed with Milo's arms around her. But for the immodesty of it, it shouldn't. Milo was her husband, after all. And yet . . .

She'd loved Alex. If the truth be told, she loved him still—a sinful love, given her marriage to Milo, and foolish, given his lack of regard for her, but there it was. To have this man for whom she harbored this illicit, barely suppressed passion looking on as she awoke in another man's embrace confounded her utterly.

Don't let him sense your discomfort, she counseled herself. *Don't let him know you care. All you've got left is your dignity.*

He cleared his throat softly. "Milo is better, I take it?"

It helped her composure that he seemed to find nothing awkward in the situation. "Aye," she whispered, trying not to disturb Milo.

He looked back and forth between them again, his expression almost grim. "I'll be gone for most of the morning. I'm going to saddle up Milo's horse and give myself that tour of Peverell. "

"Ask Gaspar to go with you."

He grimaced. "I plan to keep my distance from that blackguard. You'd best do the same."

"Blackguard? I admit he's rather rough, but he's always been trustworthy."

"I think he's changed." Alex looked as if he wanted to say more, but he merely shook his head. "Just stay away from him."

"Alex . . ."

"Good day, Nicki."

He closed the curtain and she heard his soft footfalls fading away.

"Here you are, milady." Gaspar handed Lady Nicolette the goblet of wine he'd dosed with his strongest headache remedy. "This'll set his lordship straight." How he loathed playing the servile attendant. But it was fitting enough, considering how badly he'd bungled things last night. He knew Milo liked to drink from his wife's cup; he should have taken that into account.

She put aside the boiled onion she'd been holding under the nose of her husband as he lay in his bed by the hearth. "Thank you, Gaspar," she said as she took the goblet.

"Yes, a thousand thanks," Milo rasped, "for making her take that nauseating thing away from my face. Stinks like the very bowels of hell."

Peering into the goblet, Nicolette frowned. "Did you have to put it in wine?"

"Wine?" Milo perked up for the first time all day. He'd been listless since awakening, lying unmoving in his bed while his wife bathed him and changed his clothes. She hadn't left his side all morning except to attend to her own toilette in the solar while Milo's manservant, Beal, shaved his chin and held the chamber pot for him. She'd eaten her dinner at his bedside while he took a midday nap. Now, at the mention of wine, he struggled upright, his wife hurriedly bolstering his back with pillows. "Where?"

"I asked you to put the headache powder in juice," she reminded Gaspar tersely.

"His lordship asked for wine, milady." A patent lie; Milo had been too consumed all morning by his aching head and terrible lethargy to ask for anything.

"Did you?" Nicolette asked her husband.

"I suppose I must have." Milo reached for the goblet, but his hand quaked so badly that his wife had to hold it to his mouth so he could drink.

"He's having trouble remembering things," she told Gaspar as Milo sipped from the goblet. "He can recall nothing of last night. I had to tell him he'd been sick."

Gaspar smiled, elated by this news. In a way, it was a stroke of luck, Milo having drunk the potion intended for his wife. Now Gaspar knew that it did, indeed, affect the memory. This evening, when he dosed Nicolette—and this time he'd make damned sure she drank the stuff herself—he'd have the peace of mind that came from knowing she'd remember nothing that transpired in her solar during the night.

She was looking at him strangely.

"Is something amiss, milady?"

"I was just wondering," she said evenly, "what it is about my husband's condition that could prompt you to smile."

Gaspar thought fast. "He underwent a terrible experience last night, milady. Who would want to remember it? Forgetfulness can sometimes be a blessing, don't you think?"

She waited too long before answering; it made him nervous. "I suppose." She returned her attention to her husband, setting aside the half-emptied goblet and holding a bowl of eel soup to his mouth. "Your favorite, Milo. I had Cook make it up just for you."

Her apparent distrust sat ill with Gaspar. Regardless of her coolness in the past, she'd always had the utmost faith and confidence in him, of that he was sure. What had changed to influence her? Could it be the presence of her husband's cousin at Peverell? On the surface, Alex de Périgeaux treated him civilly enough, but there could be no mistaking the resentment that seethed beneath the surface—no doubt a result of the clobbering Gaspar and his men had dealt him nine years ago. Most likely his antipathy toward Gaspar was rubbing off on Nicolette. Gaspar knew that bastard would be trouble. Perhaps he was still sweet on her—and she on him. Best to keep an eye on those two, the better to foil any budding romantic intrigue before it had the chance to spoil his plans.

He didn't deserve her, the conniving little whoreson. She was rightfully Gaspar's. Gaspar had waited years for her, biding his time while he planned and positioned himself. Now that his machinations were on the verge of yielding fruit, he'd be damned if he'd let that cocky young upstart steal the object of his fixation out from under him.

Milo sipped obediently from the bowl, to his wife's obvious delight. "This is just what you need to help you get your strength back."

An idiotic sentiment, to Gaspar's way of thinking. It had been years since Milo could lay claim to strength of any kind.

"I'm going to stay by your side until you're completely better," she promised him, tilting the bowl carefully to his mouth.

Milo turned his face to the side, letting soup spill down his chin for his wife to wipe up. "I don't want you to."

"But you need me to—"

"Whatever I need, Gaspar can attend to. Isn't that right, Gaspar?"

Gaspar bowed his head in the servile way that he despised, but which the highborn seemed to find reassuring. "Of course, milord."

Lady Nicolette cut her gaze briefly toward Gaspar. "But what if he's not here when you—"

"Then some other servant can help me."

Gaspar's hackles rose at being lumped in with the other servants.

"I know you want to feel indispensable, my dear," Milo said soothingly, "but you do have other duties to attend to."

"Naught of any importance."

"Aren't you supposed to be giving lessons to Alex in the afternoons?" he asked. "You should be doing that right now instead of pouring soup down my throat, which anyone could do."

"Alex wasn't at dinner," she said. "I assume he's still touring Peverell."

"Perhaps he's waiting for you, eager to begin his studies."

She caught her bottom lip between her teeth. Gaspar liked that nice, wide mouth of hers; he'd wondered if she'd ever used it the way he'd make her use it tonight.

"Go," Milo urged, patting her cheek with a jittery hand. "I'm really much better. And, in truth, I'd rather enjoy the solitude."

"All right," she said, her eyes lighting with devilment. "But only if you finish the soup."

He groaned. "My belly's in a—"

"Your belly's always in a twist." She brought the bowl to his mouth again, smiling when he drank from it. "It's probably because you don't eat enough."

Milo finished the soup with surprising speed, whereupon he ordered her gone.

"Stay with him for a bit, won't you?" she asked Gaspar as she tidied up.

"As you wish, milady."

"You won this bout," she informed her complacent husband, "but there's no way you can keep me from sleeping down here on the pallet until you're entirely well again."

Down here? "That's not necessary, milady," Gaspar said.

They both turned to look at him.

Bloody hell. His plans depended upon the privacy of her solar. "Beal can sleep on the pallet. 'Tis too much of a burden for your ladyship."

"Gaspar's right," Milo put in. "You'll be more comfortable upstairs."

"It's not a matter of comfort," she said crossly. "You're my husband! Does no one understand that?"

Neither Gaspar nor Milo could offer a response to that.

"I'm sleeping down here tonight," she declared as she turned to leave. "And every night until you're better."

Gaspar ground his teeth as he watched her go. This was a vexing development. He could drug her wine, but he couldn't very well tup her on a pallet in the great hall! He'd have to wait to make his move. He'd do it the very first night she went back to the solar.

But damn it all, he'd waited long enough. He was sick to death with waiting for her. His craving for her had become a live thing, a beast that needed to be fed. It strained at his seams, threatening to split him wide open.

"Bloody hell," he muttered as he glared at the turret doorway, through which she'd disappeared. "Bloody, bloody hell."

"Anything wrong?" Milo inquired.

Gaspar grabbed the goblet off the table and thrust it at the pathetic bastard. "Here. Drink."

*   *   *

Nicki dismounted in her usual place, at the apex of the waterfall, and tethered her beloved dappled mare, Marjolaina, next to Milo's sorrel gelding. If Atlantes was here, it meant Alex was, too. He had come after all, although it was already midafternoon, and they'd agreed to meet right after the noon meal. She wondered if he'd been waiting for her all this time.

She untied her saddlebags, which contained a blanket, a tablet, a stylus, a Latin primer, and some leftovers from dinner, and carried them down the rugged slope toward where they'd agreed to meet. She squinted through the trees. There was no sign of him up ahead, in the designated spot. Frowning, she turned in a circle, scanning the woods and the stream.

And saw him.

The saddlebags thudded to the ground. He was standing under the waterfall with his back to her, skimming his hands over his hair.

And he was naked.

Chapter 13

Nicki watched in shock as Alex turned toward her, his eyes closed, his head tilted back into the water that crashed behind him, scrubbing at his face. The stream came up only to his calves, so she could see nearly all of him, and, God help her, she couldn't wrest her gaze from the sight.

She'd never seen a man entirely naked before, even in bed. Milo had always blown the candle out and kept his nightshirt on. And thinking back before that, to Philippe—well, their joinings had been clandestine and frantic. He'd untie his chausses and throw her skirts up, and it would be over within moments.

Water coursed over Alex's broad shoulders and chest, meandered in rivulets over the densely packed muscles of his stomach. He stood with his weight on his good hip, the damage to his injured one all the more striking for his nudity. It was as if God, having judged him too perfect, had ripped a piece from him to make him as flawed as the rest of mankind.

Watching him like this recalled all the times she'd stolen into Uncle Henri's chamber to dig the Roman statue out of his chest of valuables, which she'd learned to unlock with her eating knife. She'd sit cross-legged in the rushes and turn the little marble soldier over and over in her hands, marveling at its masculine proportions, its air of virility . . . and wondering what the devil was hidden underneath that tiny leaf.

Alex's vital part could never fit under a leaf of any kind—and it was at rest. Nicki shuddered with a certain nervous fascination, imagining what it must be like to lie with such a man. She'd almost found out nine years ago. Would it have been a union of pain or pleasure? Pain most likely, despite her lack of a maidenhead; he'd been young and inexperienced.

Not so anymore.

He opened his eyes and looked at her.

She wheeled around and stumbled over her saddlebags.

"Nicki!"

Gaining her feet, she seized the saddlebags with one hand and her skirts with the other and fled toward her horse. She passed a boulder she hadn't noticed before, on which his clothes were carelessly tossed.

"Wait!"

She heard the ripple of water as he waded out of the stream, and quickened her pace.

"Nicki, don't go." He was closer.

She threw the saddlebags over Marjolaina's back and stepped into the stirrup.

He gripped her shoulders from behind. "Please, Nicki, don't go." His breathing was harsh in her ears.

She felt the heat of him at her back, the dampness of his hands through the thin wool of her tunic.

"I'd decided you weren't coming," he said breathlessly, without unhanding her. "I was just trying to wash off the sweat from my ride." He kneaded her shoulders, moved infinitesimally closer. "I was so glad to see you. Please stay."

He was holding on to her, totally and completely naked, begging her not to go. Nicki's heart pounded wildly when he reached around her to gently grip her foot, guiding it out of the stirrup and onto the ground.

"You don't want to go." His warm breath tickled her ear.

She closed her eyes. A riot of images bombarded

her—things she wanted and shouldn't want, things she'd almost had but could never have. "Alex . . ."

His hands slid down to encircle her waist. He moved closer. She felt him pressed up against her from behind, solid and wet and so very warm.

"Put some clothes on," she said unsteadily.

"Take yours off," he murmured.

She shoved her foot into the stirrup again and tried to hoist herself into the saddle, but he held on tight to her waist.

"No, don't! Don't! Please, Nicki. I won't touch you." He backed away from her. "I promise. I swear to God and the saints that I'll keep my hands off you this afternoon. You know I never break my oaths."

She slid her foot out of the stirrup, rested her forehead against the cool, smooth leather of the saddle. "It can't be like that between us, Alex." Christ, if only it could. If only it could. She wanted him—body and soul—unbearably. If he wanted her the same way—wanted her heart and not just her favors—she might even be tempted to yield to him, despite all the risks and the sinfulness of it. But he didn't, and that gave her strength.

"I just . . ." he began. "I just wanted—"

"I know what you wanted," she said. "The same thing you wanted nine years ago. But you can offer me no more now than you could then. Less, for I'm a wedded woman. And at least then, you loved me. Now, all you feel for me is lust."

"Nicki—"

"Tell me I'm wrong." She turned to face him, forgetting for the moment his state of undress. Cheeks stinging, she spun back around. "Tell me you want more, that the Lone Wolf has changed his ways, that he wants the attachments he used to scorn. That he's ruled by his heart, and not his cock." She bit her lip, astounded that she'd uttered such a coarse word.

She waited for Alex to laugh at her, but he didn't.

He was silent—too silent. No protestations, no denials, no promises.

"I thought so," she said soberly.

He fell silent for a long moment. "Are you still willing to teach me to read and write?"

" 'Tisn't just an excuse to get me alone, and . . ."

"Nay, I promise it's not. Didn't I just vow not to touch you? Please stay, Nicki. Please."

She rubbed at a scratch on her saddle. "Get dressed."

"All right."

She heard him retreat to the boulder on which his clothes were heaped. Presently he said, amusement in his voice, "It's safe to turn around now." She did. He tied off his underdrawers and smiled at her. "Better?"

"Completely dressed."

"Come, now. You've seen me in my drawers, and there's no one else here. And I'm wet. I'd really rather wait—"

"Then I'd really rather leave." She turned around.

"All right!" From the direction of the boulder came the soft sounds of clothing being donned. "You don't mind if I dispense with the tunic, I hope. It's turned hot."

"Of course not." She dragged the saddlebags off her mount and strode toward him, dismayed at the way his shirt and braies clung to his damp body. How would she keep from staring?

"Here, let me carry that." Alex took the saddlebags from her and brought them to a sea of ferns shaded by ancient oaks. "This seems like a good spot." He pulled out the blanket and whipped it open, laying it on the ferns and smoothing it down. Looking up, he met her gaze and smiled. "Soft as a feather bed."

Nicki groaned inwardly. Perhaps conceding to the teaching wasn't such a wise idea, after all.

*　　*　　*

Idiot. Alex lay on his stomach, carefully inscribing the Latin alphabet onto his wax tablet. *Did you have to tell her to take her clothes off, for pity's sake?*

He may as well have ordered her to lie down and spread her legs. Milo had praised his reputed finesse with the fairer sex, and here he was trying to seduce the delicate and refined Nicolette de St. Clair by manhandling her—stark naked, no less. What was the matter with him?

He was overeager, that's what—impatient to do the deed and be gone, having fulfilled his oath to Milo and saved Nicki from ruin, but his impatience had made him clumsy as a spotty youth taking a stab at his first kitchen wench.

He'd have to change his tactics. He'd have to slow down, ingratiate himself with her, make her trust him. Make her like him.

He stole a glance at her as she lay on her back gazing at the trees overhead, bathed in shadow spattered with wavering patches of sunlight. Christ, she took his breath away. She always had.

Just as she had always, he reminded himself, been other than what she seemed. An undercurrent of deceit had governed not just her actions, but her very being. How could he have known, as he wooed her so ardently in Périgeaux, that she'd squandered her precious virtue long before he'd ever met her? At sixteen, she'd lain beneath some faceless man and surrendered to his lechery, let him plant his bastard in her belly, yet now she had the temerity to play the blushing lady of virtue.

A thought occurred to him. Perhaps she hadn't surrendered to him at all. Perhaps she'd been taken against her will. Alex felt a brief surge of hope that this was so—*she didn't mean for it to happen, he overpowered her, I was to have been her first*—but promptly stamped it down, disgusted with himself.

Would he rather she'd been raped than taken a lover? What manner of low, selfish cur was he?

He shook his head, deeply ashamed.

"Is something wrong?" Nicki turned to face him, a beam of sunlight playing across her eyes, kindling a hot green fire in their depths. Alex could scarcely breathe. His hand quivered with the need to touch her.

Win her with subtlety. You must seduce her heart before you can seduce her body. He had until Christmastide to get her with child. He could afford the luxury of taking his time. And he hardly had any choice in the matter at present, with her sleeping in the great hall. It wasn't as if he could seduce her on a pallet next to her husband's bed—that is, if she kept to the pallet, rather than joining Milo, as she had last night.

Alex frowned, recalling his shock at seeing them in an attitude of such intimacy. His long, exhausting ride had helped somewhat to subdue the idiotic jealousy simmering in his belly. He shouldn't care; Milo was incapable of claiming his husbandly rights. He'd ceded them to Alex, for God's sake! Was it the fact that she still cared enough for Milo to want to comfort him that was so upsetting?

Christ, it was. Alex sank his head in his hand, dismayed to be coveting the little bit of affection she still harbored for her invalid husband.

Nicki sat up, studying him. "What's the matter, Alex?"

He laughed humorlessly. "One hardly knows where to begin."

She lifted the tablet and examined his efforts. "You're doing very well. You shouldn't feel frustrated."

There was frustration, he thought, his gaze traveling from the tablet to Nicki, and then there was frustration. Setting down the stylus, he reached over and fingered her heavy linen veil. "Aren't you hot in this?"

Alarm flickered in her eyes. "I thought you said you wouldn't—"

"I'm not touching you," he pointed out. "Just your veil. It's so hot today, and I can tell you're suffering." He trailed a finger over the sweat-dampened linen at her hairline. "I just thought you'd be more comfortable if you took this off." He shrugged and picked up the stylus. "Do as you will."

She seemed to contemplate that for a few moments, and then she removed the veil, folded it neatly, and set it next to her. Her hair was woven into a single braid down her back; moist tendrils clung to her forehead and nape. There was a damp patch on the back of her ivory tunic as well, he noticed, where it laced up with a golden cord.

Digging into her saddlebags, she said, "Would you like a peach?"

"I couldn't eat another bite." He'd stuffed himself on the meat pie and cheese wafer she'd been thoughtful enough to bring him, since he'd missed dinner.

She pulled out a peach and lay on her stomach next to him, propped up on her elbows. Riffling one-handed through the primer, she pressed it open and pushed it toward him. "Try to copy those words," she instructed as she brought the peach to her mouth.

Alex watched, transfixed, as she bit into it. Juice spilled from it, trailing over her chin and onto the blanket. "My word." Laughing, she lifted the edge of the blanket to blot her chin.

Her laughter was so rare, and enhanced her appeal so magically, that all he could do was gape, like some driveling dunce. This was the Nicki he'd fallen in love with nine summers ago, the golden girl with the enchanting laugh.

The peach's ripe perfume mingled with her intoxicating fragrance and the sweet, earthy scent of the enveloping woods, challenging Alex's resolve to maintain a chivalric distance from her. Today.

Her tongue darted between her lips to lick the juice from them, triggering a heaviness in Alex's loins. He was glad to be lying on his stomach.

Just today. He'd vowed to keep his hands to himself, but only for this afternoon. After that, if he happened to brush up against her, or take her hand in a moment of tenderness, or get swept away and kiss her . . .

"Aren't you going to copy the words?"

"Words?"

"Those words." She nodded toward the primer, then raised her astonishing, incandescent eyes to his. "Are you sure you want this?"

"Absolutely." Alex shifted to adjust himself on the blanket. "I don't think I've ever wanted anything quite as much."

Chapter 14

Nicki saw Alex as she passed the athletic field while riding through the outer bailey on her way to the drawbridge. He was teaching swordplay to a loose circle of men, something he'd done every morning for the past week.

She reined in Marjolaina, taking advantage of this opportunity to watch Alex openly without attracting notice, since she'd be but one of many doing so. Alex, with his back to her, didn't even know she was there.

Shirtless, like most of the rest of the men, he swung his big broadsword two-handed, whipping it across, up, down, around. His muscles gleamed beneath a film of sweat in the early-morning sun. His hair, which he'd tried to tie back into a stubby queue, had mostly sprung loose; wet tendrils flew as he sliced the huge blade through the air.

Gaspar stood on the sidelines, observing him with crossed arms and that studiously blank expression he sometimes adopted. Those churls who did his bidding, Vicq and Leone, stood next to him, whispering and snickering together. One of them cocked his head toward Alex and muttered something to Gaspar, who smiled.

The smile dissolved when Gaspar noticed her. He quickly scanned the length of her body as she sat astride her mount, and then glanced away as if he hadn't seen her.

It had been getting harder of late to ignore her uneasiness when he looked at her that way. In the past, she'd paid no heed. Men looked at her; they always had. And Gaspar had been subtle about it, never embarrassing her or overstepping himself. Given his importance to Peverell, she'd never thought to have Milo speak to him about it. But lately a hint of lewd menace had begun creeping into his expression. Moreover, she didn't care for the increasingly eerie reserve with which he accepted orders from her.

Alex was right; Gaspar had changed. She'd tried to ignore it, to deny it, but now that Alex had voiced his apprehensions, her own rose inexorably to the surface.

Pausing, Alex called for a volunteer to help him, and Gaspar instantly stepped forth. A young page with a pile of weapons—both real and wooden—retrieved a broadsword, but Gaspar waved it aside and pointed to a long-handled mallet with a spiked head forged of lead. He hefted the awful thing in his beefy hands, laughing at Alex's nonplussed expression.

It had been a weapon like this, Nicki knew, that had torn the flesh from Alex's hip. Gaspar knew this, too. Several nights ago, Milo had coaxed Alex into telling the story of the Cambridgeshire ambush during dinner. Gaspar had listened intently. The next morning, he was seen practicing with a mallet, and he'd even taken to carrying one around in lieu of the club he'd favored for so many years.

"This is a demonstration of swordplay," Alex said as Gaspar swaggered toward him, the mallet resting on a gigantic shoulder. "Not a tavern brawl."

Gaspar, alone among his men, did not laugh. "Might one's enemy not attack with something other than a sword? Come on—prove your stuff. Defend yourself with a sword against *this*. If you can."

Alex eyed the evil thing grimly. Nicki felt his dread as he regarded the instrument of his mutilation—not to mention the length of Gaspar's arms and his brutish strength—and wished desperately that she could say something that would put a stop to this encounter. But it was, after all, merely a demonstration, with the parties presumably intending no harm to each other. And for her to come to Alex's aid would subject him to the men's scorn. She had no desire to reawaken his hatred for her, when things between them had been fairly amicable lately.

Seven days had passed since their first lesson together in the woods. Alex, having a sharp mind, had made remarkable progress in reading and writing. His desire to learn was obvious.

Just as evident was his desire for her. He hadn't attempted any more liberties—not overtly—but often she caught him looking at her when he should have had his mind on his studies. He'd seize on any little excuse to touch her—brushing a leaf off her sleeve, hair off her cheek . . .

Perhaps it wasn't wise spending so much time alone with Alex, but she was loath to put an end to their afternoons together. If nothing else, it got her out of that dismal castle. And, in truth, she relished his little attentions, evidence of the attraction that quivered between them. She felt it every waking hour. It droned in her veins, infusing all her thoughts and actions with a kind of heady awareness.

In her case, the attraction had its basis in a hopelessly incorrigible love that she'd be just as happy to be rid of. Alex's attraction to her, on the other hand, was no more lofty or meaningful than what he had felt for hundreds of other women over the years. Although she yearned for him with every breath she took, she'd be damned if she'd add her name to the long list of women who'd spread their legs for Alex the Conqueror. Adultery was far too grievous a sin to waste on a man who didn't care for her.

Gaspar gripped the mallet in both fists and leapt at Alex, swinging it hard. Alex leapt back. A collective murmur rose from the men watching. Nicki knew what

they were saying—that it would take a miracle for a
lone swordsman to best a giant wielding such a barba-
rous weapon so enthusiastically.

Gaspar advanced, slashing the mallet through the
air with quick, powerful strokes. Alex lunged and par-
ried, sweat pouring into his eyes as he searched for an
opening, a weak spot. Sometimes he'd use his sword to
deflect a blow, steel clanking against lead; sometimes
he'd jump aside, or duck. Gaspar did not appear to
be holding back. That the men noticed this as well
became clear when some of them began urging Gaspar
to back off the beleaguered Alex, lest he do some
damage. Nicki bit her lip so hard it hurt. Might it
not be worth Alex's wrath to order an end to this
brutal spectacle?

Alex blocked a blow, slamming his sword against
the upraised shaft of the mallet. At that moment,
Gaspar looked toward Nicki, still on horseback, nodding as if he had only just now noticed her. Smiling
in a way that struck her as almost sly, he called out,
"Good morning, milady."

Alex turned to look at her. Nicki screamed along
with the others as Gaspar swung his mallet sharply
downward, ramming it into Alex's hip.

Alex dropped his sword and crumpled, roaring in
pain. It was his left hip, she saw as he grabbed it,
his body curling in the dirt. Gaspar had deliberately
attacked the hip already mangled years before by the
same weapon.

She dismounted and ran to him, yanking aside the
men gathering around him. "Let me through!"

Just as she made her way to Alex, he bellowed a
blistering oath, something she'd never thought to hear
in her presence. The men looked from Alex to her,
wide-eyed.

"Shit," Alex rasped when he saw her. "Oh, damn.
Forgive me, Nick—my lady." He struggled to sit up.

"Stay where you are," she told him, kneeling at his

side. She wanted so much to touch him—to take him in her arms and comfort him—but everyone was watching; it would be scandalous.

"Where is he?" Alex managed through clenched teeth. "Gaspar, you son of a bitch. Sorry, my lady." He groaned as he clambered unsteadily to his feet, heedless of her advice to stay put.

"Here I am," Gaspar said mildly, stepping out of the crowd with the mallet balanced on his shoulder.

Nicki leapt to her feet. "What were you thinking?" she demanded, wheeling on Gaspar. "How could you—"

"I'll handle this," Alex said quietly as he eased her aside.

"But he—"

"I said I'll handle it." He leaned over his hip, rubbing it, but his gaze connected sharply with hers. His fleeting, almost imperceptible glance toward the men made it clear: He needed to fight this battle himself, or risk losing their respect.

Conscious of the many pairs of eyes trained on her, Nicki returned to her mare and remounted her, but walked her close to the cluster of men, so that she could hear what was said.

Gaspar clicked his tongue. "You should know better than to let your attention wander in a fight, Sir Alex—especially one you're losing. If you'd like," he added, his eyes sparking with malicious humor as he glanced toward Nicki, "I'll teach you some proper fighting skills, help you out a bit." Vicq and Leone laughed uproariously.

So that was it. Gaspar was trying to take Alex down a notch, belittle him in front of her. Why should he care what she thought of her husband's cousin?

As Alex bent over to retrieve his sword, he looked toward Nicki, and her heart ached for him. She could see it in his eyes—the disgrace of having been defeated, and so soundly, in her presence. "Curious," he said. "I don't seem to have had any trouble defending myself in the past. Of course, my opponents have generally been men of honor. Such men don't tend to stoop to your tactics."

Gaspar glared at the handful of men who had the temerity to laugh at that. "I don't see anything dishonorable in taking advantage of your opponent's weaknesses," he protested. "My only difficulty in fighting with you is deciding which of your many shortcomings to exploit." His two brutish underlings guffawed. "I did use the blunt end," he said, displaying the mallet's head, strong enough to crush armor. "My point was merely to demonstrate the risks of inattention. If I were the shameless cur you make me out to be, I'd have used the spike."

"Next time," Alex said softly as he sheathed the sword on his belt, "perhaps you should. Aim for my head, though, and make damn sure you kill me. Because"—he closed his hand over the relic in the hilt of his sword, a gesture lost on no one, and nodded toward the mallet—"if you ever take that thing to me again, I swear to Almighty God you'll pay with your life."

Silence settled over the throng. Everyone looked to Gaspar for his reaction to this extraordinary vow.

Gaspar returned Alex's fixed stare, his eyes dull and flat and black. They looked like the eyes of a dead man Nicki had come upon once in the woods. She remembered standing over the poor fellow, who had been mauled by a boar from the looks of him, and wondering how eyes that had reflected light during life could absorb it so utterly upon the soul's departure.

Presently Gaspar executed one of those little bows of his; had they always set her teeth on edge this way? "I regret that the difference in our fighting styles has caused you distress . . . young sir."

Alex stiffened at the condescending term of address, but made no response.

"In the future," Gaspar continued, "perhaps we'd do better to practice our skills with other partners."

"I should bloody well think so." Turning away from Gaspar, Alex announced to the men that he was going to rest his hip for a short while, then demonstrate some finer points of strategy. The men drifted away to await the next stage in the morning's lessons, and Gaspar tossed his mallet back onto the heap of weapons.

Nicki walked her mount a few steps closer to Alex. "Are you all right?"

"I'll limp for a bit," he said, taking a few halting steps toward her to rub Marjolaina on the nose. "Won't be the first time." His sodden hair hung over his forehead. Nicki quelled an absurd urge to lean over in her saddle and tidy it.

"Perhaps you should have Maître Guyot look at that hip," she suggested. "Or at least lie down in your chamber for a while."

"There's no need for that," he said, sliding a quick glance toward Gaspar as he walked toward them. "Nothing's broken. And I'd much rather be out here in this sunshine than in that tomb of a castle."

Knowing he was trying to minimize the injury in order to salvage his pride, Nicki dropped the subject. They lapsed into silence, exchanging a look when Gaspar joined them. Why he thought he'd be welcome after his display of savagery was quite beyond Nicki.

"Where are you off to this fine morn, milady?" Gaspar asked.

Nicki bought a moment by fiddling with her reins. Seeing as she couldn't very well disclose the true purpose of her trip, she'd best keep mum about her destination—especially since Gaspar's watchfulness was gradually giving way to out-and-out prying. "I'm on my way to St. Clair," she said, keeping her gaze trained on Gaspar lest Alex look into her eyes and know her lie for what it was. "To do some marketing," she elaborated, pleased to have thought up such credible subterfuge on such short notice.

"You're riding all the way to St. Clair unescorted?" Alex asked.

"Aye." In point of fact, she was riding well beyond St. Clair unescorted. She just hoped she'd get back in time for the noon meal, so as not to raise suspicions. And, blast it, she'd have to stop in St. Clair and buy something, so she'd have it to show for the trip. Lying got everything all tangled up in knots. Alex had always said so, back in Périgeaux, and it was true.

"I'll go with you," Alex said.

"Nay. It's . . . it's not necessary."

"But I don't mind. I'd like to. I'll cancel the rest of the lesson—"

"Nay! I'll be perfectly all right. And my marketing will bore you."

"*I* don't mind marketing," Gaspar said. "You shouldn't be alone, and I've got nothing better to do."

"I want to be alone," she said resolutely. "I . . . I like being alone. If either of you insists on accompanying me, then I simply won't go."

Alex sighed. "Very well, my lady."

Gaspar fixed his dead eyes on her in a way that made her shiver. "Your lord husband must be better today, for you to travel so far from the castle."

"He is, thank the saints. He's still dreadfully weak, of course, and I don't know when he'll get out of bed, but he's sitting up for longer stretches. And yesterday I got him to eat a few bites of sausage." She raised her hand to her mouth to cover a yawn.

"You look tired," Alex said, studying her in that all-seeing way.

"Aye. That pallet is lumpy, and I keep waking up, thinking Milo needs me. He doesn't anymore, of course. After the first couple of nights, he's slept quite soundly. But I wake up anyway, and then I can't get back to sleep."

Alex frowned. "Has it been like that all week?"

"Aye." She yawned again. "Pardon me."

"You should have asked me to take over for you," Alex scolded.

"He's my—"

"He's your husband." Alex smiled wearily. "Yes, I know."

"Well," Gaspar said, "there's no need for you to be putting up with all that anymore. His lordship's resting well—you said so yourself. If you don't mind my advice, you should go back to sleeping in your solar. 'Tis nice and quiet up there, and you've got your own bed with a feather mattress on it."

Alex cast a wry look in Gaspar's direction. "I hate to say it, but he's right."

Nicki nodded. "Milo's been saying the same thing. I suppose you have a point. There's nothing to be gained from lying awake all night if Milo doesn't need me. I'll return to the solar tonight."

"Good," the two men said simultaneously.

Nicki arched her brows. "How very novel to find you two so agreeable."

Alex and Gaspar moved away from each other. Nicki chuckled. "Good day, gentlemen," she said as she guided her mount toward the drawbridge.

"Good day, milady," they called after her.

Gaspar reined in his mount at the edge of the woods and watched Lady Nicolette ride up the dusty road toward the Abbey of St. Clair. She waved to someone as she approached the entrance in the stone wall surrounding the neat cluster of low buildings.

So. Her ladyship was doing some marketing, eh? Gaspar had followed her—at a discreet distance—all the way from Peverell, and she hadn't so much as ridden through St. Clair. She'd taken the road that led around the town, not even slowing down.

The funny thing was, she visited the monastery frequently, to see that half-mad old prior, Brother Martin. No one had ever tried to stop her. Why the deception now?

No one had tried to stop her, but she'd always been given an escort—and she'd never objected to it, that Gaspar could recall. Whether her purpose for coming here was innocent or not, she was going to some pains to keep it a secret.

A secret it might be well to unearth. If he was clever, Gaspar thought, turning his horse around and retracing his route through the woods, he could get his answer tonight, while Nicolette was under the influence of the valerian. She'd be bereft of her senses, of course, but that might make her all the more malleable. He could wheedle the truth out of her if he did it right.

And then he'd do the rest of it.

Gaspar smiled in anticipation all the way back to Peverell, thinking of tonight.

Chapter 15

"**I** . . . have . . . a . . . horn," Alex said slowly, frowning in concentration over the primer as he lay on his stomach beneath the gnarled old oaks. "My horn is . . . shiny. I have a . . ." He mouthed the word as he squinted at it, stringing the sounds together in his mind. "Drum. My drum . . . is . . . red."

He scanned the rest of the page; almost done. At least it was musical instruments now. He'd hated the part about the dolls and toy soldiers. "I have a . . . I have a . . ." *Shit.*

He turned the book toward Nicki, lying next to him. "I'm sorry, but I haven't the faintest . . . Nicki?"

She was asleep, facedown on the blanket with one arm cradling her head. Her back rose and fell slowly, her breath fluttering a few stray hairs that had sprung loose from her braid and fallen over her face. Alex reached out tentatively, lifting the errant strands and smoothing them back.

No wonder she was exhausted. Not only had she slept poorly all week, but there was that trip into St. Clair this morning.

He scooped a finger under one of the earrings she'd bought there, a delicate, dangling confection of gold and pearls. A soft sigh—almost a moan—rose from her as his fingertip grazed her throat. He stilled, hoping she didn't wake up.

She didn't.

He could kiss her, he thought, laying the earring

back down carefully. Now, as she slept. It might be his only chance for a while, the way things were going.

By rights, he should be filled with happy anticipation, inasmuch as she'd be returning to her solar tonight. It *would* help, having private access to her. But the notion of bedding her with her husband sleeping downstairs felt so fundamentally wrong that he knew he couldn't do it.

He could tup her anywhere, of course—even out here on this blanket. He'd imagined it many times as they bent their heads over their lessons. The real problem wasn't finding a place, but finding a way to breach that inviolable wall of propriety she'd built around herself.

Alex rolled onto his left hip, swallowing a gasp as his old wound—reawakened this morning by Gaspar's viciousness—pulsed with sudden pain. Flopping back onto his stomach, he caught his breath and then sat up slowly, searching for a comfortable position.

A week ago, he'd resolved to be patient, to make her trust him, to win her over with subtlety. He'd done his best to be attentive without scaring her off, but it didn't seem to be working. Although in general she seemed wonderfully relaxed in his company—much like the old Nicki when they used to meet in their cave—she turned prickly the moment his touch became too familiar.

Perhaps he was doing it wrong. Alex hadn't had much practice wooing women subtly. The laundresses who trailed around after the king's retinue would raise their skirts if he but smiled at them. Some of them had a few years on him, but he liked the older ones, because they were at ease with themselves. His favorite, Margery, was nearly twice his age, but he savored her husky laugh and her stout thighs, and the way she'd lightly scratch his back while he took his pleasure with her.

Now and then he'd get bored with the laundresses

and want a fresh face. No matter where he was camped, there was usually a willing wench somewhere in the vicinity; rarely anymore did he bother with whores.

According to Luke, women liked him because he liked them. He did. He liked them enormously, all of them. Plump ones, with bodies like warm bread dough. Slight young things with firm bottoms and dainty little breasts. Old ones, young ones. He was particularly fond of the plain-faced women. Oftentimes they had cultivated some interesting quality—a whimsical sense of humor, a beautiful singing voice, sometimes even a repertoire of erotic antics—to compensate for their lack of comeliness. He adored them all, wholeheartedly, and they rewarded his devotion with that most treasured of offerings, their bodies—a gift he strove to repay by coaxing from them the pleasure they so generously gave him.

His comrades envied his success with women, and he was not unappreciative of it himself. Women were plentiful, and if he was forced, from time to time, to store his seed longer than he would like between bed partners . . . well, that only made the tupping better when it came. For years, his sexual needs had been met with a minimum of fuss and a great deal of unabashed pleasure, a boon no man should take for granted. And, although he'd genuinely liked every woman he'd ever lain with, there had never been one who'd felt special to him—which, of course, was all for the good.

Sexual frustration, if not unknown to him, was enough of a rarity to be disconcerting. And frustration of the type he'd known this past week—interminable, overriding need with no end in sight—was completely foreign to him, and absolutely maddening.

It had become too much for him last night. He'd awakened soaked in sweat, as he had most nights since his reunion with Nicki, but this time his loins throbbed with the fiercest cockstand he could remember. It actually pained him; he was desperate for relief.

He briefly considered seeking out the red-haired dairy maid who'd taken to flirting with him. But, although she was pretty in an earthy way, he found the notion of releasing his seed in her no more attractive than releasing it into his own hand. In the end, he opted for his hand, because it was less trouble and because he didn't want the dairy maid; he wanted Nicki.

He'd hated having to resort to self-abuse, a sin which his father had always counseled him to avoid, and which, for the most part, he did. In an effort to mitigate the sin, he was quick about it, concluding the deed with a few swift strokes of his fist as he imagined it to be the snug embrace of Nicki's body.

Afterward, he reached onto the floor for his money pouch, pulling out the white satin ribbon and winding it around his hand, as had become his habit when he awoke during the night. For some reason it felt comforting, and he always fancied that it helped him to get back to sleep.

Lying on his back, he'd held his hand up to the shaft of bright moonlight from the arrow slit above his bed. The ribbon glimmered softly in the silvery beam.

Never had there been one woman, alone among the rest, whom he thought of day and night, dreamt of, contrived to be alone with and touch, whose scent transfixed him, whose laughter made his heart swell with joy, who made him ache with longing . . .

Except for Nicki. His feelings were overwhelming his reason. *No attachments, remember?* His passions had gotten the better of him, just as they had nine years ago. He ought to have learned his lesson. He ought to remember her duplicity, and the fact that she was married to his cousin, and that he'd sworn to impregnate her then never see her again.

He damn well ought to seize control of the situation, do what had to be done, and ride away.

Lying in bed last night watching the moonlight play over the white satin ribbon, he'd made himself a promise. Before midnight the next day—today—he would kiss Nicolette de St. Clair. It was just a promise, of course, not a solemn oath to God, of which he'd been making entirely too many lately. But Alex de Périgeaux did not take promises lightly, even to himself, and he meant to keep this one.

But how? She bristled every time he came near her.

Alex gazed down at Nicki as she dozed beneath the cool shelter of the trees, oblivious to his roiling emotions and secret vows. He *could* kiss her now, while she slept unawares. Her mouth would be a bit of a challenge, given her position, but he could kiss her cheek. It would fulfill his promise, if somewhat ignominiously. It had been a rash promise, as are most that are made in the middle of the night. She'd never let him kiss her, not yet. His only hope was to do it before she awoke.

Alex leaned over her and slowly lowered his mouth to her cheek. He breathed in her scent, heady and sweet on this warm afternoon, imagined how soft her cheek would feel beneath his lips.

She twitched, and he saw that a lock of his hair had fallen from behind his ear to brush across her temple. It must have tickled her, for she stirred, growling in a kittenish way that sent a hot little spark of desire crackling through him.

He backed away slowly as she blinked and yawned. "I must have fallen asleep," she murmured in a voice all soft around the edges, but a little rough.

"I told you." Alex patted the cushion of ferns through the woollen blanket. "Soft as a feather bed."

Smiling blearily—God, he couldn't take his eyes off her—she sat up, absently smoothing her rumpled tunic. Her face was ruddy where it had rested against the blanket, and imprinted with little creases. Alex's gaze was drawn to her lips, which had become suffused with hot color. They would feel soft, he thought, leaning toward her, just slightly. Softer than her cheek, soft as warm silk . . .

She turned her head to drape her braid over her shoulder—probably a deliberate ploy to evade him. Alex cursed inwardly.

" 'Twill rain soon," she said, glancing at the overcast sky. "We really ought to go back."

"It's not raining yet," he said, stalling for time. "And our lesson's not over."

She lifted the open book. "Did you finish all the pages I'd asked you to read?"

"Aye. Well, almost." Taking the volume from her, he pointed to the word that had stumped him. "What does this say? I have a . . ."

She leaned over the page. "Gigue."

Alex blinked. "*Gigue?* It says gigue?"

Nicki laughed, clearly recalling King William's advice to Alex on how to busy himself during his furlough. The sound was so sweet and silly and unrestrained that it touched off his own laughter.

"It makes a most mellifluous sound," Nicki intoned, in an uncanny imitation of Berte.

"I'm quite sure it does," Alex said, chuckling. "And I'm quite sure I haven't got the slightest interest in learning how to play it." Sobering, he said, "I'm sorry about all the idiotic things she said to you that day. All that blather about . . . men's work disrupting your vital humors."

She nodded, her own mirth subsiding. "Thank you, but I've learned to disregard most people's theories about . . ." She shrugged with contrived indifference. "It didn't bother me."

He fingered the end of her braid as it rested on the blanket. "You do want children, though."

Her voice, when she answered, was low and raw.

"More than you can possibly imagine." She cleared her throat. "But it wasn't meant to be."

"But if you could—"

" 'Tisn't possible. Milo . . ." She looked away deliberately. "He doesn't want me that way."

He doesn't want me that way. Not *He can't. He won't.* She was concealing Milo's inadequacy, a kindness that Alex found quite unexpected and moving.

"If I were your husband," Alex said softly, his hand closing around her braid, "I would have been eager to see my child grow in your belly."

"I thought you disliked children."

He shrugged noncommittally.

She watched his hand as it caressed her plaited hair. "Do you have many of your own?"

"Me?" He released the braid in surprise. "I've never been married."

Her arched eyebrow spoke more clearly than words. Most men who'd been with many women had many illegitimate children.

"The last thing in the world I want is for the women I bed to bear my bastards. There are . . . techniques," he said, heat rising in his face, "to prevent a woman from quickening."

"Those vile potions that expel babes from the womb?"

"Nay. I mean before. That is, during . . ."

"Ah, yes. Edith told me about them. A woman can wear against her skin the womb of a she-goat that's never conceived. Is that the sort of thing you're talking about?"

"Aye, well, not that precisely."

"She also told me about certain herbs a woman could wear in a bundle around her neck, or preparations she could put . . . inside the opening to her belly, that will keep the man's seed from curdling into a baby." Nicki laughed delightedly. "You're turning quite purple."

"Let's talk about something else."

"Nay." She sat cross-legged with the book in her lap and addressed him squarely. "I want to hear about the techniques."

" 'Tis hardly a proper topic of conversation."

She laughed again. "And you think *I'm* priggish. Come. Tell me. Are those the types of methods you use?"

He turned away from her, incapable of discussing this while looking her in the eye. "Nay. There are . . . other means."

"Such as?"

He sighed in resignation. "The man can . . . uncouple. Before."

"Before?"

"Before."

"Ah. Is that what you do?"

"Sweet Jesus." Alex rubbed his neck. "Sometimes. Most of the time."

"And the other times?"

He cleared his throat. "It's possible to make love . . . using portals, two in particular, other than the one intended by nature."

She was quiet for a long moment. "The mouth?"

God help me. "That would be one."

"And . . . hmm . . ."

"That would be the other. Can we stop talking about this now?"

"Aren't those forms of sodomy?"

He looked away again. "I don't think of them as such." Not the first one, at any rate; he rather liked that one.

"It sounds terribly sinful to me. Not the uncoupling necessarily, but the other. Do you actually enjoy—"

"You know, I think you were right." Alex made a show of peering at the sky. "It's going to rain soon." He stuffed the tablet, stylus, and book into her saddlebags and rose, offering his hand. "We should really be getting back."

She baited him some more as they gathered their things, and enjoyed great laughter at his expense while they rode back to the castle. He shared in the laughter once his embarrassment receded, ridiculing his own chagrin and teasing her for her unladylike curiosity.

It reminded him a little of being with Faithe, and it occurred to him with a small shock that he and Nicki were talking and laughing like friends. But then, hadn't they been friends in Périgeaux, when they'd shared their afternoons together in that little cave? Not that his feelings for her had stopped there—they'd become far too complicated—but the notion that they could actually be *friends* in addition to everything else struck him as extraordinary and wonderful.

It could be like this between us, he thought. *If she were my wife, we could laugh together every day, and make love in the afternoon beneath the rustling trees, and grow fine, fat babies, lots of them. . . .*

If she were his wife and not Milo's. And if he hadn't sworn that blasted oath.

Fool! No attachments, remember? He should be coldbloodedly seducing her, for pity's sake, not dreaming of laughter and babies.

As they dismounted in front of the keep Alex realized he'd hustled them back without kissing her. How would he manage it before matins in that crowded castle?

You won't. Give it up. And don't make any more middle-of-the-night promises to yourself.

"Are you all right, Alex?" Nicki took his hand, the first time she'd done so since Périgeaux. It filled him with a ridiculous sense of elation.

"I'm fine," he said, gripping her too tightly, so gratified that she'd reached out to him. "I've just spent the afternoon with you."

"Back so soon?"

They turned to find Gaspar standing in the entrance to the keep, eyeing their clasped hands. Nicki yanked hers out of Alex's grasp, recoiling from him. "We . . . we thought it was going to rain."

"Oh, the weather's turning bad, all right," Gaspar said blandly, raising his gaze to the murky heavens. "There's quite a hellish tempest brewing. Just you wait and see."

Gaspar placed the goblet carefully in Edith's hands and closed her gnarled fingers around it. "Here it is. Now, you must make sure her ladyship drinks all of it, remember?"

The old hag stared into the goblet with that vacant expression that meant she didn't remember at all, even though Gaspar had explained it to her after supper. "What's this, then?"

"Raisin wine," he ground out with ill-feigned patience while glancing over his shoulder to make sure there was no one else in the torchlit staircase to overhear. Most everyone had retired for the night, but still . . .

There was little risk in using Edith for this mission. By tomorrow it was unlikely she would recall having brought the adulterated wine to her young mistress.

"Raisin wine," the old women murmured, frowning in confusion.

"With something in it to help her sleep," he reminded. "She's had trouble sleeping of late."

"That she has, poor lamb. Aye, but she'll be in her own bed tonight. She'll sleep like a stone." She tried to hand the goblet back, but Gaspar pushed it toward her.

"Sleeplessness can linger long after the cause for it is gone," he said. "She needs something to relax her. 'Twill be good for her."

Edith pinned him with a sharp look that reminded him of the mulish creature she'd been years before.

"She doesn't know what's good for her, that one. Never did."

"There. You see? She needs you." He patted her hands, closing her cold, twisted fingers more firmly around the goblet, lest she drop it. "You must make her drink it—all of it. She won't like the taste, but that's just the sleeping herbs. She mustn't leave a drop. I made it extra strong, so don't be alarmed if it takes effect quickly. Can you remember all that?"

"What do you think I am?" she demanded irately. "The town idiot?"

"Not at all, but her ladyship can be stubborn at times. And since she doesn't always know what's best, you must help her by making her drink all of it. Watch her and make sure she does it. Don't leave until—"

"Yes, yes! She'll drink it. Now leave me be." Steadying herself with a hand on the stone wall, Edith turned and began her torturously slow progress up the winding stairs. "I must go to my lamb. My lamb needs me."

Gaspar waited in the stairwell while Edith went through the motions of readying her mistress for bed. If anyone could get that doctored wine into Nicolette, it was her beloved maid, from whom she'd been inseparable since coming to Peverell as a child. Old age had long ago stripped Edith of her faculties, but Nicolette was unwilling to hurt her feelings by taking on another maid. The result was that the mistress more or less served the maid, coddling her like an old grandmother and indulging her every whim. She'd drink the wine just to make Edith happy.

"Well?" Gaspar said a short while later as the doddering old creature shuffled tediously down the stairs toward him.

"Who the hell are you?"

"I'm Gaspar," he said between clenched teeth. "Remember?"

"Oh, you." Grimacing as if she'd just smelled something rancid, Edith tried to push past him, but he blocked her path.

"Did she drink it?" Gaspar noted with dismay that Edith's hands were empty. Wouldn't she have brought the empty goblet back down?

Edith blinked at him.

"The raisin wine," he said slowly. "Did she—"

"I said I'd make her drink it, and I did. She always does what I tell her, because she knows I know what's good for her." She tried to squeeze through, but he held firm.

"Are you sure she drank it all?" He must remember to retrieve the goblet when he departed the solar later tonight, so there would be no evidence of his handiwork.

She let out an exaggerated huff of impatience. "Every last drop. She was swaying on her feet by the time I got her into her night shift, if it's any comfort to you."

This time, when she elbowed him aside, Gaspar let her go. "A great deal of comfort," he said softly.

Just before she disappeared around the bend of the curving staircase, Edith turned and glared up at him. "I don't like you."

"I don't like you, either, you loony old bitch."

Chapter 16

Gaspar paused in the entrance to the great hall, letting his eyes get used to the dark and the drumming of rain on the shutters, listening for sounds from behind the closed curtains of Milo's bed. All he heard was a soft, rattling snore. Beal, curled up on the floor at the foot of his master's bed like some faithful dog, was snoring as well. Presently Gaspar could make out the shapes of the servants sleeping in the rushes. Adjusting the burlap sack on his shoulder, he stole quietly across the hall, stepping carefully over the somnolent bodies.

He opened the door of the pantry slowly, lest it squeaked; it didn't. Creeping inside, he closed the door behind him and let out a pent-up breath.

It was black as hell in this little room, what with no windows to let in the moonlight. He lit the lantern hanging from the ceiling, and by its dull yellow glow shoved aside the bags of grain and meal blocking the door to the service stairwell.

Extinguishing the lantern, he ducked through the small door and ascended the narrow stairway in pitch blackness, his heart thudding with nerves and anticipation. *This is it. This is really it.*

At the top of the stairs, he peeled off his tunic and stuffed it into the sack. That left him in a nondescript shirt and braies—nothing that she could recognize as his. From the sack he retrieved the mask he'd fashioned out of an old black woollen hood by sewing up the opening and cutting holes for his eyes and mouth.

He pulled the mask over his head, filled his lungs with air, and let it out slowly. And then he turned the door handle and opened the door a crack.

He stilled then, unsettled by the golden light illuminating the big chamber, indicating that Lady Nicolette had not yet retired. Steeling himself—*she drank the whole bloody goblet, for pity's sake, and it was extra-potent*—he slowly eased the door open, smiling at what he found.

Nicolette lay on her bed, the curtains on the side facing him wide open, clad only in her night shift, writhing deliriously. The covers had been turned down, but she hadn't gotten under them. He could see all of her.

The goblet—completely empty save for a telltale crystalline residue—lay in the rushes next to the bed.

How perfect. How utterly perfect.

Closing the door behind him, he walked up to her and dumped the sack on the floor, loudly. She started, a low moan rising from her as she clutched at the mattress.

Gaspar took a moment just to look at her. The shift was nearly identical to the one he'd swiped in Rouen—a wisp of white silk that left her arms and lower legs completely exposed. Her hair was loose, like a young girl's. She opened her eyes, but seemed to have trouble focusing on him. "Who's there? Oh, God. Alex? Is it you?"

Gaspar nodded. Wouldn't that be delicious, to have Alex de Périgeaux convicted of raping his cousin's wife? Gaspar almost hoped she *did* remember her ravishment tomorrow. Milo was in no condition to challenge Alex to a duel, so most likely he'd simply be mutilated, but given Nicolette's rank, he might even be hanged. Gaspar wished he could tell her, yes, it's your Alex, come to show you a thing or two, but to speak would be risky; she might recognize his voice.

Gaspar leaned closer, relishing her look of horror when she saw his mask. He cupped her face, pressed his thumb between her lips; their slick heat made him hard. She whipped her head to the side. "Y-you're not Alex." Frantic now, she tried to sit up, but her body began to quake uncontrollably, and she collapsed under the wrenching spasms.

Her breasts pressed irresistibly against the silk of her shift as she thrashed. Gaspar covered them with his hands and squeezed. She cried out and he slammed a hand over her mouth.

Her eyes went wide as the seizure subsided. Gaspar grew stiff as a cudgel thinking about her helplessness, his power, her abject terror. Now he'd show her who was the master. Now she'd do *his* bidding, like it or not. And he'd make damn sure she didn't like it.

With his free hand, he began to raise her shift, but she went berserk at that, flailing at him with her fists. One caught him in the nose, jolting him with pain.

"Bitch!" He let go of her mouth and whipped his open hand across her face, hard.

That dazed her for a moment. "Mama?"

"Not even close." He rummaged in his sack for the rope and rags he'd brought. When he turned back, she was trying to crawl off the bed. "Not so fast." Grabbing her shoulders, he slammed her back down, immobilizing her with a knee in the stomach. She punched him in a mad frenzy, so he grabbed the rope and swiftly tied her hands to the headboard.

He'd have to gag her, too, but not right away. He had plans for that silky mouth of hers.

"Nay!" She gasped as he knelt over her face, tugging at the drawstring of his braies. "Oh, God, help! Somebody—"

Shoving a hand over her mouth again, he slid his dagger out of his boot and pressed it to the bridge of her nose. "Have you ever seen a woman without a nose? I have. 'Tisn't very pretty." Leaning close so he could savor the panic in her eyes, he said, "Just you shut up and do everything I tell you to do, exactly like I tell you to do it, and I might let you keep that lovely little nose of yours." An empty threat, of course, since he had no intention of drawing attention to what he'd done by disfiguring her, but she'd have no way of knowing that.

"G-Gaspar?"

Damn it to hell! In his excitement, he'd forgotten himself and spoken. That was careless. Now he might be forced to kill her—after he'd had his fun, of course—unless . . . "Nay, it's Alex."

Her brow furrowed. "Alex?"

"Aye." Keeping the dagger to her nose, Gaspar fumbled with the cord securing his braies. "It's Alex. You've been teaching me—now I'm going to teach you a thing or two."

There came a soft knock, and then a muffled voice. "Nicki?"

Bugger me, it's him!

Swearing under his breath, Gaspar sliced the rope off her hands and crammed it, along with the dagger and the rags, into his sack.

Alex knocked again, and this time Gaspar realized the sound was coming not from the turret, but from the service stairwell. *Sneaky bastard. He's probably been diddling her since he got here.*

The door handle turned. With no time to get to the turret, Gaspar secreted himself behind the closed curtains on the other side of the bed just as the door creaked open.

"Nicki?"

"Alex, don't," she groaned. "Don't do this."

Swift footsteps in the rushes. "Nicki. Nicki, what's—"

"Don't touch me! Don't—"

"Nicki, it's me, Alex. I'm not going to hurt you. Nicki?"

She whimpered. The leather strips supporting the mattress squeaked under the convulsive movements of her body.

"Nicki? Oh, God. Oh, no."

Alex spoke fatuous words of comfort until she quieted. "I'll be right back." He sprinted across the solar, whipping open the door to the turret staircase and pounding down the stairs.

Gaspar strode quickly to the service door while, from below, Alex shouted for Beal to ride into town and bring back the surgeon. Turning for one last, frustrating look at her before ducking through the door, Gaspar spied the empty goblet in the rushes. Hissing an oath, he went back to retrieve the incriminating item as Alex's footsteps raced back up the stairs. Gaspar made it back to the little corner door and pulled it closed behind him just as Alex returned.

Well, that's just fine, Gaspar growled as he stomped down the narrow little stairwell. He knew having that bastard underfoot would spoil everything. *Just bloody marvelous.*

"He's here." Beal ushered old Guyot into the solar, crossed himself at the sight of his insensible mistress, and fled back down the stairs.

"She caught the contagion from her husband, I see," remarked the surgeon as he walked toward them, his satchel in one hand and his bucket in the other.

Alex, kneeling at the side of Nicki's bed, nodded bleakly. "She insisted on tending to him. I tried to stop her. I should have tried harder." It should have been him, stricken down with this awful malady. He wished it had been. To see her this way, alternating between delirium and shuddering spasms, pained him to his very soul.

The old man *tsked* as he set his bag and bucket next to the bed. "No one pays me any heed." He tossed his mantle onto the bench. His green coif was crooked, the ties hanging loose, and his eyes were puffy from his sudden awakening by Beal.

"God, no . . ." Nicki moaned. "How could you do this?"

"Shh . . . easy." Alex took her hand, stroked her sweat-dampened hair. "No one's doing anything to you, Nicki. You're ill." From the corner of his eye Alex saw the old surgeon roll up his tunic sleeves, his gaze openly speculative as he watched his patient being comforted by her cousin by marriage.

Nicki twisted beneath the sheet that Alex had drawn over her, her eyes wild. When he'd first found her, she seemed to think he was attacking her. Then she'd accused Gaspar of the same thing. Other names came and went in her deranged ramblings. She said Milo's name occasionally, and also those of Father Octavian and Brother Martin. She'd spoken to Alex as if he were her late uncle Henri, and once she'd even called him "Mama."

"No one wants to hurt you," Alex assured her, taking her face in his hands. "Least of all me."

"You did hurt me, Philippe," she rasped. "How could you? I trusted you."

Philippe? "I'm not Philippe, Nicki. I'm Alex. Look at me."

"Alex?" she said in a small voice.

"Yes." Rising, he sat on the edge of the bed and took her in his arms, not caring, for now, what the old man thought. She felt so soft and vulnerable. It filled him with cold fear to see her this way. Turning to Guyot, he said, "Do something for her!"

The old surgeon was stirring something in a little bowl. Alex smelled mustard. "Sit her up so I can purge her stomach."

Wishing she didn't have to go through this, Alex

propped her up, sitting behind her for support, while Guyot got her to choke down the vile concoction. Within moments, she began to moan piteously and clutch at her stomach. "It's all right, love," Alex soothed as Guyot put a chamber pot before her. Alex held her tightly, murmuring reassurances and twisting her hair out of the way as her stomach emptied. "You'll feel much better now."

But she clearly didn't. In fact, another seizure gripped her almost immediately. Alex held her as it ran its course, and then she closed her eyes and went slack. He brushed the hair off her face and pulled the sheet back over her, lamenting her dreadful paleness. But for the rising and falling of her chest, she looked like a corpse.

"Do something that will help!" Alex ordered the old man. In desperation, he added, "If she dies, so will you—by my own hand."

Guyot shook out his bloody apron and tied it over his tunic. "I've been threatened thusly dozens of times, and as you can see, I'm still very much alive. I suggest you concentrate your energies on helping me treat your . . . lady cousin, for it you think you can strike terror into this old breast, you're sadly mistaken."

"Just see that she lives."

"That's up to God." The surgeon reached into his satchel and brought forth his small knife, testing its blade with his thumb. "And his men of healing."

Alex felt uneasy as Guyot positioned the bucket at the edge of the bed. "Is that really—"

"It's absolutely essential," he snapped. "Else I wouldn't do it."

"Aye, but she's so terrified of bloodlettings."

"More terrified than she is of death?"

Nicki stirred, murmuring something Alex couldn't make out.

"Make no mistake," Guyot said softly, "if she's not

bled, she won't live to see the morning. 'Tis the only thing that saved her husband."

"Do it, then," Alex said, wishing to God there was some other way.

"Alex?" Nicki mumbled. Her eyes glittered feverishly despite the coolness of her skin. One strap of her shift had slid down over her shoulder. Alex straightened it and gathered her in his arms.

"I'm here."

"What's wrong? Everything's spinning."

"You're sick. You've got what Milo had. Maître Guyot is going to help you get better."

She turned her head, her expression of disorientation giving way to alarm as she took in the surgeon's blood-flecked apron and knife. Alex felt her go rigid in his arms. "Nay."

"Nicki, it's the only way." But she'd begun struggling against him, kicking and clawing.

"Nay! Please, Alex, don't let him—"

"Nicki, listen to me—"

She cried out, her nails digging into him. Alex turned to find Guyot pulling a loop of rope out of his bag.

"Nay!" she screamed, fighting to free herself. "Nay, please!"

"Here." Guyot thrust the rope at Alex. "You do it. She's too strong for me. Just leave her left arm free."

"Nay!" Nicki shrieked, thrashing frantically as Alex strove to restrain her.

"No rope," Alex told the old man. "Put it away. I won't tie her down."

"But how the devil are we supposed to—"

"Put the rope away," Alex said. "I'll take care of it."

"Look at her. You can't hope to—"

"*Put it away!*" Alex roared.

Guyot complied, muttering under his breath.

"Nicki, listen to me." Alex leaned his weight on

her, pinioning her arms to keep her from hurting herself. "No one's going to tie you up. Do you hear me? I won't do it, and I won't let him do it. Do you understand?"

She nodded. "And you won't let him cut me?"

"Nicki . . . I can't lie to you. I don't want him to do it, but we don't have any—"

"Nay!" She squirmed and writhed, trying to wrest her arms free.

"Just hold her down," Guyot snapped impatiently. "You're strong enough."

"I'll do this my own way," Alex told him. "I'll let you know when it's time. Nicki, look at me."

She whipped her head back and forth on the pillow.

"Look at me, Nicki." Alex took both her wrists in one hand and cupped her face with the other, forcing her to be still. "Look at me!"

Her eyes were wide and terrified. "He . . . he tried to tie me down and . . . and make me . . ."

"No one's going to tie you down. I promise."

"He had a knife."

"Maître Guyot?"

"G-Gaspar. He was going to cut off my nose."

"Gaspar isn't here, Nicki. No one wants to cut off your nose."

"No, you don't under—"

"Look at me." Alex quieted his voice to a murmur. "Look at me, Nicki. Look right into my eyes. That's right." She was trembling, but had ceased her frenetic struggling. "Keep looking at me. Just at me." He kept up this pacifying litany until he felt her body relax under his.

"That's better." He kissed her cheek. "Close your eyes. Good." He released her wrists to trail his fingers through her hair. "Think about something pleasant," he whispered. "Think about our cave. Remember how quiet it was, way in back, where we used to talk?"

She nodded.

"We must have had a hundred candles in there at the end. They made your hair look like spun gold. Remember how the reflections from the water would shimmer all over the walls? It was like something alive."

"I remember," she breathed.

Alex took her right hand in his and gently laid her left arm where Guyot could reach it.

"We used to make up stories about the paintings on the walls. Or, you did. I mostly just listened. I thought you were the cleverest person I'd ever known. You used to read to me—poems and stories. Remember?"

She smiled. "Yes."

Alex rested a hand on her left shoulder and nodded to the surgeon, who took hold of her arm. "Maître Guyot is going to do what he needs to do now."

She opened her eyes.

"But it will be all right, because I'm here."

"Keep her still," Guyot cautioned as he positioned the knife. Alex pressed firmly on her shoulder.

"Alex—" She flinched and squeezed her eyes shut as the surgeon made his cut. "Oh, God." She clutched Alex's hand, grimacing.

"I'm here."

"Oh, God, make him stop."

"Look at me. Look at me, Nicki. 'Twill be over soon."

She winced. "I hate this."

"I know, but it will all be over soon. You're doing very well."

"Liar." She actually laughed, after a fashion. "I'm a quivering baby."

"Only about this. Everyone has something they're afraid of."

She looked skeptical. "What is the great White Wolf afraid of?"

He smiled. "Mallets."

"Aye, well . . . that's understandable."

"So is this."

"That's the worst of it," Guyot announced with a smile. "That's wasn't so bad was it?"

Alex and Nicki both cast him withering looks.

Even before Alex opened his eyes, while his mind still groped toward wakefulness, he knew something wasn't right. He wasn't lying down; he was sitting up, leaning forward on something, his head nestled in his arms. "Hunh . . . ?"

A soft chuckle, very soft and feminine.

Alex raised his head, squinting into the face looking down at him—Nicki, sitting up in bed in her night shift, her hair askew, smiling at him. "Good morning."

Alex looked around, squinting at the sun pouring into the solar through the window over the writing desk. "Good morning," he croaked as he straightened up, grimacing at the stiffness in his bad hip.

Nicki hugged a pillow to her chest and grinned. "I couldn't wake you up, of course. I considered breaking one or two of your ribs, but I don't know as I've got the strength this morning."

"No, I shouldn't think so," Alex said through a yawn. "You're much improved from last night, though. Do you remember any of it?"

"Bits and pieces. I'm not sure what was real and what wasn't." She held out her bandaged arm. "I remember this—most of it, anyway."

Alex nodded. "I'm sorry. Maître Guyot insisted we had no choice. I couldn't let you . . . I didn't want you to . . ." He combed a hand through his disorderly hair.

"I don't remember the pain," she said. "Just . . . you holding me, and talking about our cave. You were . . . you were very kind to do that, Alex."

"I didn't want you to suffer. You'd been through so much already."

"Was it the same thing Milo had?" she asked.

"Aye. You caught it from him. I knew I shouldn't have let you—"

"Hush." She touched her fingertips to his lips. "I'm his wife, remember?"

Impulsively Alex caught her hand and pressed it to his cheek. "I wish you weren't."

She fell silent, her fingers lightly scrubbing the needle-sharp stubble on his jaw. "Why did you come up here last night?" she asked quietly. "Did you know I was sick?"

Alex shook his head, wishing he had it in him to lie. "You'll think it's foolish."

"Tell me."

He closed his eyes. "I wanted to kiss you. I'd promised myself I'd kiss you before midnight, and . . . I told you you'd think it was foolish."

She gave his face one last, raspy caress and then withdrew her hand. "It's probably just as well that you didn't do it."

He opened his eyes. "But I did."

Her eyebrows rose. "You kissed me?"

"Your cheek." He reached out and touched the very spot, soft as thistledown. "Not because of my promise to myself—I'd forgotten all about that. I just did it because . . . well, I just did it. And it wasn't quite matins yet, so I suppose I kept my promise." And when Guyot left, Alex had paid him several times more than he'd had coming to him, in order to discourage him from gossiping about what he'd seen.

Nicki shook her head, smiling crookedly. "You make the most peculiar oaths and promises. How on earth do you manage to keep track of them all?"

He rubbed his neck. "It isn't easy."

"Have you ever broken an oath?"

"Never," he said quickly. "A soldier's oath is a pledge to God Himself. I would die before breaking one."

"But if you had to—"

"There could never be a good enough reason."

She smiled blearily. "Don't you think God would understand if there were? He made us. He knows our weaknesses and the impediments we face. If anyone could forgive our breaking an oath to God, it would be God Himself."

"You don't understand," Alex said. "Soldiers are judged by a higher standard of honor. We can't afford to indulge our weaknesses, or bow down to impediments. When we promise God we will do a thing, we must do it."

Slow footsteps scraped on the stone steps in the turret; something clanked softly. Alex rose and crossed to the door. "Edith is here with your breakfast."

"You do have exceptional hearing," Nicki said as Alex opened the door for the elderly maid.

"Oh, my poor lamb," Edith exclaimed when she saw her young mistress. Alex took the breakfast tray from her before she dropped it. "Serves you right, though," she added with a disapproving glare, "for not heeding Guyot and staying clear of his lordship."

Nicki just sighed as Alex arranged the tray on her lap. The lumpy porridge and watered wine struck him as supremely unappetizing, but she bolted it all down and sent Edith away for more.

"You should leave, too," she told Alex. "I want to wash up and get dressed now."

"Don't you think you're rushing things? It took Milo much longer to get over this. He still hasn't gotten out of bed."

"Milo started out sickly," she reminded him. "I feel fine, honestly. Just a bit woozy, and that will go away if I just get up and get on with things. Edith said Milo was worried about me, I want to reassure him that I'm all right."

"Very well," Alex conceded, crossing to the service staircase. "But try not to do too much."

"Alex," she said as he opened the door. "I'm very grateful to you for what you did for me last night, staying here with me, and . . . everything. But you really shouldn't have come up here. And you mustn't kiss me, even innocently, ever again."

"Nicki . . ."

"I'm married, Alex. It's wrong. If you persist in these . . . familiarities, I shall have to stop spending time alone with you. And I'd hate that. Our afternoons have been . . ." She ducked her head; was she blushing? "Please don't take them away from me."

Torn between his desire to reassure her and his obligation to seduce her, Alex found himself speechless.

"Tell Milo I'll be down by dinnertime," she said.

Alex nodded and ducked into the stairwell.

Milo could smell the wine in the goblet Gaspar held just out of his reach as he sat on the edge of the bed. It was like some madly intoxicating perfume, drifting around him, tickling his nostrils, teasing his senses. Damn the bastard for tormenting him this way. He knew how impatient Milo always was for that first drink of the morning.

"You do know he's fucking her," Gaspar said.

Milo's perceptions could not be relied on of late—he'd become nearly as muddled and forgetful as old Edith—but he didn't think he'd misheard. "Whatever are you talking about?"

"I'm talking about your wife." Gaspar swirled the wine around in the goblet, releasing more of its heady bouquet into the curtained enclosure of Milo's bed. "And Alex de Périgeaux."

Milo swallowed hard, imagining the sour sweetness in his mouth, in his belly, anticipating the dull warmth that would spread throughout him once he'd drunk enough. As if there could ever, truly be enough. "That's preposterous," he managed, mindful of how badly Gaspar would take it if he found out Milo had chosen Alex to sire a son for him.

Gaspar leaned toward him, still holding the goblet to the side. "My guess is he's been poking her every afternoon, out there in the woods, while she was supposedly teaching him how to read. Only now that she's back in her solar, he can do her in a regular bed, with plenty of privacy, while you're sound asleep down here. He sneaked up there last night, you know. He was up there the whole blessed night."

Milo fumbled with the quilt, his hands shaking even worse than they usually did upon awakening. "I . . . sent him up," he said. "Yes. Edith said she wasn't feeling well, and I can't very well make it up those stairs so I asked Alex to—"

"Don't you ever," Gaspar whispered fiercely, his teeth bared, "*ever* think you can lie to me."

Rarely had Milo seen Gaspar vent his wrath, and never at him. Christ, but he needed a drink. "I . . . that is . . ."

"There can be only one reason for you to invent such a pathetic fabrication," Gaspar said. "You're trying to keep me from discerning the truth, which is that you enlisted your cousin to do the job I was unworthy of."

How Milo craved the numbing cocoon of drunkenness. "Gaspar, listen to me—"

"Does she know he's just servicing her as a favor to you, or did he actually have to sweet-talk his way under her skirts?"

Milo licked his lips. "Give me the goblet, Gaspar." *"Does she know?"*

Across the hall, soldiers turned to stare, then returned their attention to their breakfasts.

"For God's sake, Gaspar, keep your voice—"

"Does she?"

"Nay. Of course not. She'd never go along with it. You know that."

"Not if it was the lowly apothecary castellan doing the deed. But her husband's highborn cousin—"

"Not if it was anyone. She has no idea why Alex really . . . why he . . ."

"Seduced her," Gaspar spat out.

Was it true? Had Alex already managed to coax Nicolette into betraying her precious marital vows? Milo hadn't expected such quick acquiescence. Part of him felt absurdly disappointed that she'd yielded to him so easily. Another part felt relieved, for the sooner they consummated their liaison, the greater the chance that a pregnancy would result from it.

"For the love of God, Gaspar," Milo begged, despising himself. "Give me the wine."

Gaspar stared at him for a few long moments, and then handed him the goblet. Milo gulped its contents breathlessly.

"This complicates things," Gaspar murmured, gazing in an unfocused way across the hall. "This changes everything."

"Changes what?" Milo asked.

Gaspar blinked, as if a spell had been broken. "Oh, naught that concerns you, milord." Grabbing the jug, he refilled Milo's goblet. "Drink up. That's right. There's plenty more in the buttery."

Chapter 17

Nicki watched Alex with lazy satisfaction as he hunched cross-legged over the slender volume in his hand, reading aloud from the letters of St. Jerome.

" 'I . . . gather the rose from the . . . thorn,' " Alex said, little frown lines etched deeply between the black slashes of his brows, " 'the . . . gold'?" He tilted the book toward Nicki, reclining next to him; she nodded. " 'The gold from the earth, the pearl from the' . . . well, I suppose it must be 'oyster.' What else would one gather a pearl from?"

He showed her the book again. "Oyster," Nicki said.

A warm breeze fluttered his hair and made his shirt ripple over the solid planes of his shoulders and chest. There was something about this virile, scarred soldier concentrating so diligently over his studies that made her ridiculously happy. He'd shown uncommon progress in the three weeks since their lessons had commenced. Nicki ached with pride for him.

" 'Shall the . . . plowman'?"

Nicki nodded.

" 'Shall the plowman plow all day? Shall he not also enjoy the . . . fruit of his . . . labor?' " Looking up, Alex caught her eye. "Are you sure this is about sex?"

She laughed. "Read on."

Grinning, he said, "You misled me just to make me read it. It's about . . . roses and pearls and—"

"Read. On."

Sighing grumpily, he stretched out on his side facing her. "Where was I? Ah. 'Wedlock is the more . . .' " He spun the book around, pointing.

"Honored."

" '. . . honored when the fruit of wedlock is the more . . . loved. Why, mother, grudge your daughter her . . . virginity?' " Alex cocked an eyebrow. "What the devil is that supposed to mean?"

Nicki took the book from him and picked up the train of St. Jerome's thoughts a few lines down. " 'Are you vexed with her because she chooses to wed not a soldier but a king?' "

Alex's amusement seemed to vanish. "Don't tell me this is a treatise about the folly to marrying soldiers. Well, of course, if one could have a king instead—"

"Milo's right," Nicki said, giggling. "You're so terribly literal."

"You mean ignorant."

"No!" She sat up. "No, I mean exactly what I said. You're literal. You see things for what they are, right there on the surface, instead of digging for all kinds of hidden meanings and secret messages. You're so honest and forthright yourself that you expect everyone else to be the same way."

"Once I did," he said quietly. Before Nicki could respond to that, he picked up the book. "So, what did St. Jerome mean about being vexed because your daughter chooses to wed a king?"

"*The* king," Nicki elaborated. "The king of kings. Christ."

"Ah." Alex sat up, his eyes sparking. "He's saying you should rejoice if your daughter becomes a nun— a bride of Christ."

Nicki nodded. "Because she'll remain a virgin. He discouraged marriage for the same reason."

"He must have been mad," Alex said. "Marriage is a sacred union."

"Not to St. Jerome—unless the husband and wife don't sleep together."

"Who'd put up with a marriage like that?"

Nicki felt heat rising in her face. "Sometimes one has no choice."

"Sorry," Alex murmured. "I meant voluntarily. It may be heresy, but if this is the type of thing St. Jerome believed, he sounds very much like a raving lunatic."

"His views were extreme, I suppose, but I see his point. One should learn to master one's . . . baser drives, not be forever at the mercy of them." If only Nicki could put into practice what she espoused. Her mother was right; she was weak about matters of the flesh, as demonstrated by her ill-fated affair with Philippe. If further proof was needed, there was her adulterous love for Alex, a passion so unruly that she ached with the strain of containing it. Every day she rejoiced in his nearness, his warm scent, his all-seeing gaze, his raspy-deep voice. And every night, God help her, she lay awake consumed by unholy yearnings, imagining him on top of her, inside her, one with her.

Alex was shaking his head. "Sex is a joyous act— or it should be, especially between husband and wife, because then it's sanctioned by God. And were it not for sex, no children would come into the world, and then where would we be?"

Nicki plucked at the blanket on which they sat, contemplating the predicament her own childlessness had landed her in, and the scheme she'd come up with for remaining at Peverell despite the lack of an heir. Last month, when Alex first came here, she would never had dreamed of confiding in him, but since her illness a fortnight past, she'd felt differently. They'd grown closer, although Périgeaux still weighed heavily between them and she suspected they would never regain the emotional intimacy they'd once known. But then, such intimacy would be wrong, given that she

was wed to another. Alex had heeded her wishes—
her threat, really—and suspended his amorous attentions, a relief inasmuch as she doubted her ability to
resist her indefinitely.

She cleared her throat. "Has Milo told you we may
lose Peverell?"

For some reason, Alex hesitated uneasily. "Aye."

Nicki nodded; she thought so. "Did he tell you
why?"

Alex rubbed the back of his neck. "Aye."

She touched his hand, the first she'd done so since
Gaspar caught them holding hands two weeks ago.
"Can I trust you, Alex?"

He closed his fingers over hers. "Of course."

"If I tell you something in strictest confidence, you
won't reveal it, even to Milo?"

"Not if you don't want me to."

She took a deep breath. "Because what I'm going
to tell you would make Milo very angry. He's forbidden me to . . ." She shook her head. "I'm getting
ahead of myself."

"Does this have to do with keeping Peverell?"

"Aye." Nicki tightened her grip on his hand.
"We're to be cast away from here in fourteen months
unless I produce an heir—which, of course, is
impossible."

To her surprise, Alex withdrew his hand from hers,
raking it through his hair. It almost seemed as if he
wanted to say something, but he didn't.

"So, we're bound to relinquish the castellany. I can
live with that—Milo hasn't ever really been a true
castellan—but I can't give up Peverell. You may think
the castle is old and gloomy, and I suppose it is, but
it's my home, mine and Milo's. We have nowhere else
to go."

"You have a plan?" Alex asked.

"I want the church to appoint Milo and me stewards
of Peverell. Father Octavian, the abbot of St. Clair,

would have to sign a document granting us the stewardship, and he's . . . a bit difficult to deal with. The only person who seems to get along with him is my friend, Brother Martin, Octavian's prior. I visited him two weeks ago, against Milo's wishes—"

"The day you went marketing in St. Clair."

"Aye—my true purpose was to talk to Brother Martin. I had tried to arrange an interview with Father Octavian to discuss the disposition of Peverell, but he wouldn't even see me. He said a woman had no business meddling in such affairs. So I went to Brother Martin and asked him to present my case to Father Octavian. He said he'd see what he could do, but that it might take time to get Octavian accustomed to the idea, and that I should come back in a fortnight to see if he'd had any success."

"So you're due for a visit to the monastery."

"I'm going tomorrow morning. I thought perhaps you'd consider canceling your swordsmanship lesson and accompanying me."

His gaze turned penetrating. "Why?"

She shrugged. "It does make me uncomfortable to take long trips unescorted. Bandits prowl the woods."

"Is that the only reason?"

She looked away, suddenly overcome by shyness. "I suppose I wouldn't mind your company."

When she looked back at him, he was smiling. "I don't suppose I'd mind yours, either."

That evening, a pair of traveling minstrels stopped at Peverell on their way to the ducal court at Rouen. Milo offered them supper and sleeping accommodations in the great hall in return for the evening's entertainment, which they cheerfully agreed to, erecting a little portable stage at the far end of the hall from Milo's bed. Alex and Nicki sat on a bench near Milo, while the soldiers, including Gaspar, watched from the tables at which they had supped.

Alex was grateful for this respite from his usual routine of draughts with the soldiers after supper, and at first he found the two performers—brothers from Brittany, one enormous and one small—diverting enough. The big fellow had a tiny dog that jumped through hoops. His brother juggled knives and ate live coals out of the hearth—or appeared to. But their musical offerings—a series of interminable *chansons de geste*—left much to be desired. The smaller man played the harp passably well, but his brother sang like a wounded bear. One *chanson*—about King Artus of Brittany and his Knights of the Round Table— struck Alex as curiously similar to a tale he'd heard many times in England. Others—about the Trojan War, Charlemagne, and of course, Roland—were long-winded and uninspired, a fact lost on most of the soldiers, who applauded each song enthusiastically.

The only benefit to Alex of enduring this tedious performance was that he got to sit right next to Nicki—to breathe in her fragrance and listen to her occasional laughter, and sometimes to look at her. She wore a white silken gown embroidered with gold tonight, her hair concealed by an airy veil secured beneath a golden circlet. Sapphires dangled from her ears, encircled her slender throat. She was luminous, exquisite.

He shouldn't take such pleasure in her nearness, shouldn't idealize her like some dreamy, lovestruck youth. He wouldn't, he'd decided, if he weren't so blasted randy every hour of every blasted day. All this thinking about seducing her, combined with the difficulty of following through, had escalated his sexual frustration to a level he'd never experienced before.

Alex's impetus to bed Nicki had as much to do now with his own ungovernable needs as with that damned oath Milo had made him swear. He needed sex, and he needed it with Nicki. His desire had taken on her image, her scent, her shape. No one else would do.

Seducing her had proved to be a heroic challenge. With some measure of grim humor, Alex contemplated the conundrum that had ensnared him. He couldn't hope to win Nicki's affections—and favors— unless he spent time alone with her. But if he became too familiar with her during their isolated afternoons together, she would refuse to be alone with him.

On the one hand, this past fortnight had been rather maddening, with Alex struggling to keep his distance from Nicki while trying to reawaken the intimacy they had once shared. On the other, he could not remember ever having been as carelessly content as he was in her company. There was something about being near her that set him at ease, even while it stirred his blood.

You shouldn't let her stir your blood, for pity's sake. You should do whatever it takes to get her to raise her skirts for you, and when it's done, you should ride away grateful to never see her again. Nor should he waste tears of penitence over the matter. Nine years ago she had used him to snare Milo. Now, he would use her—to assuage his lust and fulfill his oath. Where was the evil in that?

Last week, Milo had asked him point blank if he'd lain with Nicki yet. When Alex admitted his lack of success, his cousin informed him that Gaspar knew of the "arrangement" and was mightily displeased about it—one more vexing complication.

Of course, there was always the chance that Nicki's petition for stewardship would meet with Father Octavian's favor. She seemed to think there was a chance of this, and Alex had no reason to doubt her. If she and Milo could remain at Peverell without producing the required heir, there would be no need for Alex to seduce her—a mixed blessing. No longer would he have to deal with his uneasiness over finessing her into bed at her husband's behest, but neither would he get to make love to her. And making love to Nicki was simply all he wanted anymore; he longed for her with an intensity that staggered him. Sometimes he thought he'd go mad if he didn't have her soon.

Everyone was applauding, so Alex joined in. Nicki yawned as she clapped. The larger of the two minstrels noticed this. "I see milady grows weary of battles and bloodshed," he intoned across the hall. "What say you to a tale of the heart—a poignant romance which has brought tears to ladies' eyes for generations?"

Milo groaned, muttering into his goblet, "Not Tristan and Isolde."

"The timeless legend of Tristan and Isolde," the minstrel announced, "has been told a thousand times. . . ."

"And I've been there every single time," Milo grumbled, handing the goblet to Nicki and struggling to sit upright. "I say," he called out feebly, his voice thick with drink; the great hall quieted so that he could be heard. "If it's a tragic love story you want, my lady wife has penned one herself that rivals any in your repertoire, I'll wager."

"Milo, no!" Nicki whispered, grabbing his arm.

" 'Tis a poem called 'The Thorny Rose,' " Milo said, shaking Nicki off. "And I daresay my men would enjoy hearing it again."

"No, Milo, please!" she begged, but her husband ignored her. If Alex wasn't mistaken, 'The Thorny Rose' was the poem she'd torn out of his hand that first evening in the solar.

"No doubt it's an exquisite piece of verse," the big man said, "but alas, I don't know it."

"Our Sir Marlon can sing it." Milo nodded to the troubadour knight, a tall fellow of middle years who rose and strode toward the stage. "I'm sure you and your brother would appreciate the opportunity for a bit of rest and a cup of claret."

The minstrels bowed. "As you wish, milord."

"Have him sing something else," Nicki whispered to Milo. "I don't want to hear that one."

"But it's my favorite," Milo said. "Shh . . . he's about to start."

The only sound in the great hall was the popping and settling of the logs in the hearth behind Alex. No one moved or spoke as Sir Marlon closed his eyes and began to sing. He had a beautiful voice, smooth and deep and melodious. "Within the earth's most secret womb, A maiden and a soldier meet, While far above them roses bloom, Trembling in the summer heat."

Alex turned to find Nicki staring rigidly ahead, her hands fisted in the skirt of her tunic.

"Hand in hand, like bride and groom," Marlon sang, "Two souls unite with joy replete, Sheltered in this holy room, This ancient cave, so cool and deep."

Nicki closed her eyes, as if in pain; her throat moved. Alex's heart swelled in his chest until he could barely breathe.

"The maiden's love is so complete, A perfect rose with fair perfume, To treacherous thorns she pays no heed, They'll do their damage all too soon."

Abruptly Nicki rose, mumbled something to Milo, and strode swiftly toward the turret. Milo met Alex's gaze and shrugged, as if to say, "What's gotten into her?" Gaspar, sitting with his men, watching Nicki disappear into the stairwell, glanced briefly at Alex, and returned his attention to Marlon.

Alex fought the impulse to follow her, knowing how it would look and cursing the need to bow to propriety at a time like this. Marlon sang on, describing the maiden's love for her young soldier. She thought of him when the sun rose in the morning and when it set at night. Frequently her sleep was disturbed by dreams of longing for him, although he had never more than held her hand. While they were apart, she was an incomplete girl pretending to be whole. Perhaps she was mad to be so consumed by love for a man who could offer no marriage vow, no home, no future, but it was a sweet madness, and one she was powerless to resist.

"Christ," Alex whispered. For nine long years, Alex had assumed Luke was right—that Nicki had merely used him to capture Milo. He couldn't have been more wrong.

"Alex?" Milo frowned in evident puzzlement. He glanced at the doorway through which his wife had departed, and back at Alex.

Alex listened in a daze to the rest of it—the shameful secret the maiden harbored, her betrothal to another, the young couple's anguish, the soldier's desperate but futile plea for her to run away with him . . . the things she wished to God she could tell him.

In the song's final verse, a bride and groom stand on the chapel steps under a harsh morning sun exchanging vows, both deeply in love with others, but compelled for reasons of their own to wed. The bride has tucked a dainty little wild rose—one of several the soldier had picked for her their last afternoon together—beneath her bodice, next to her heart. Its petals caress her flesh, recalling a passion that will forever burn in her breast, while its thorns serve as a bitter reminder that the one great love of her life is lost to her. From this day forward, her very soul will be incomplete.

Deeply shaken, Alex did not join in the thunderous applause that filled the great hall when the song was over. Nicki hadn't wanted him to hear her bittersweet tale, he realized. She'd fled in mortification, ashamed of the feelings she'd unwillingly exposed.

Milo studied Alex with a remarkably astute gaze, given his inebriation. He opened his mouth to say something, and then closed it, looking very sad.

"Milo . . ." Alex began, but no words came to him.

Milo nodded. "I should have known."

Alex stood. "I have to go to her."

"Go." With a quavering arm, Milo reached for his goblet.

Mindful of how tongues would wag if he went racing up the stairs of the solar, Alex descended to his own chamber and then sprinted up the service stairwell. His chest was heaving by the time he reached the topmost landing.

He opened the door, finding the solar completely dark. At first he thought she must not be here, for surely she would have lit a lantern. But then he saw her, a dark form standing in front of an open window, facing the night sky, her veil clutched in her fist. Her hair spilled in a river of gold down her back.

He crossed to her, his heart pounding. She didn't hear him until he was directly behind her, and then she spun around to face him.

Her eyes were enormous in the moonlight. Tears glistened on her cheeks, making his heart constrict. "Nicki . . ."

She ducked her head and tried to turn around, but he seized her shoulders and held her still. "I love you, Nicki," he whispered hoarsely.

She stared up at him, her eyes shimmering wetly. Her veil fluttered to the rushes.

"I loved you then, and I love you now, to the depths of my soul."

She closed her eyes, fresh tears spilling from them. "Oh, God."

"Don't cry." He took her damp face between his hands. "Please don't cry. I swear to God, Nicki, I love you. I do." He pressed his lips to her cheek, salty-sweet. "Don't cry. Don't cry." He kissed her forehead, her eyelids. An agonizing gladness welled within him; it squeezed his throat, stung his eyes. "Don't cry."

"You love me?"

"Always and forever." He rubbed his cheek, wet now with his own tears, against hers, the oath Milo had extracted from him echoing in his ears . . . *You'll endeavor to sire me a son . . . You'll keep your true purpose from Nicolette, and when it's done, you'll leave here and never contact her again.* "Oh, God, Nicki."

"I never stopped loving you," she whispered, her hands in his hair. "But it was wrong. It still is."

"This can't be wrong," he breathed against her mouth. The only good thing to come out of this mire of deceit and intrigue was the love that had been born anew between them. How could a love so pure and powerful be wrong?

"I'm married."

"You were mine first." He brushed his lips over hers, tasting her tears. "We belong to each other. We always will."

"But—"

"Shh." He kissed her gently, his hands cradling her head, his mouth gliding over hers slowly, so she could savor this charmed moment. Her lips were salty and hot and sweet, and they felt like wet satin against his, and they were hers, and he was kissing her, and kissing her, softly, over and over again, and oh God, she was kissing him back.

"Nicki . . . Nicki . . ."

Her hands were cool on the back of his neck, her breath warm against his lips. She kissed him, sighing. She was kissing him. Nicki was kissing him!

Alex groaned, his joy as acute as pain. Banding his arms around her, he pressed her back against the windowsill and kissed her deeply, wanting to prolong this delirious pleasure, to make it stretch out forever and ever.

She held him as tightly as he held her, her breasts crushed against his chest, her thighs firm against his. He felt the delicate bones of her hips, and her womanly softness. Arousal pulsed in his loins, and he stepped back from her, breathless, wanting her terribly, but not here, not now.

Her gaze was knowing, her smile tender as she raised a hand to caress his face. He captured her wrist and kissed her palm. She smiled and closed her eyes, and her expression of sweet rapture undid him. He gathered her in his arms again and closed his mouth over hers and lost himself in her.

They kissed in silence, endlessly, as if time had ceased to exist . . . or as if they could make it stand still if they just kept kissing and kissing . . .

Sometimes they kissed softly, their lips barely grazing, sometimes more deeply. He kissed her temple, the exquisite curve of her cheekbone; he lightly tongued the delicate rim of her ear, making her gasp. She kissed his scratchy jaw, tipped his head back to press her lips to his throat.

A knock at the turret door startled them. "Milady?"

"Edith," Nicki whispered shakily. "I'm all right, Edith," she called out. "I'll get myself ready for bed. I don't need you tonight."

"Are you sure, lamb?"

"Quite sure." Nicki rested her head on Alex's shoulder as the old woman shuffled down the stairs. "She may come back."

Alex kissed her hair. "I should leave," he said grudgingly.

"Aye." She looked at him, her eyes begging him to stay. He lowered his mouth to hers, not wanting to leave, not wanting to lose her, dreading the notion of a future without her. They kissed with violent desperation, clinging to each other, his moans merging with her soft cries.

She broke the kiss, murmuring, "Alex, this is mad."

Sire me a son . . . leave here and never contact her again . . .

"Life is mad. We'll have to deal with it." Tilting her chin up, he bent his head to hers. "But not tonight."

Chapter 18

"**A**re you sure you're allowed to be here?" Alex asked Nicki as she led him through the abbey's large public square, bustling with servants and lay brothers, to a smaller, quieter courtyard off of it. Monasteries had strict rules regarding the presence of women within their walls.

"This is still considered part of the abbey's public precincts," she said, guiding him toward an oaken door in a low stone building. "If I were to venture into the cloister, Father Octavian would ban me from here permanently."

Alex had been disappointed this morning to find Nicki dressed so demurely for their visit here, in a heavy gray tunic and wimple. She looked very much like a nun—a stark contrast to the Nicki who had kissed him so passionately, and at such length, in her solar last night. It had been well past matins when Alex finally returned to his chamber, and far later than that when sleep finally claimed him.

Nicki knocked on the oaken door.

"Be off!" cried the voice of an old man from within.

" 'Tis I, Brother Martin," she called through the door. "Nico—"

The door flew open and an old, tonsured man in a black Benedictine robe drew Nicki into his arms. "Nicolette! My dear! Why didn't you say so?"

"I—"

"Is this him?" the old monk asked, squinting at Alex. "The one you told me about?"

Nicki's cheek pinkened. "Yes, Brother. This is Alexandre de Périgeaux, my cousin by marriage. Alex, this is my friend, Brother Martin, whom I've mentioned to you."

Brother Martin ushered his two guests through the door and shut it behind them. Alex gaped at the astonishing clutter that filled the prior's quarters. It occurred to him that the old fellow might be quite mad.

Scores of small-scale wooden models and strange devices—some recognizable, some not—were scattered over tables, lined up on shelves, and piled up on benches amid stacks of drawings and diagrams. A tabletop calculating board stood in one corner, a water clock in another, a small furnace in yet another. The walls of the sizable chamber—save for the windows and shelves—were festooned with maps, calendars, drawings of strange machines, architectural renderings, tables of the tides and suchlike. There were many representations of odd-looking ships, bridges, canal locks, and dams. One whole wall was devoted to astrological charts and sketches depicting mystifying arrangements of interlocking circles.

Brother Martin noticed Alex scrutinizing one in which the circles were labeled—if he was reading it right—Earth, Sun, Mercury and Venus. "Ah! You're interested in the motions of the planets, I see."

"Well . . ."

"This is a particularly interesting chart." From the pouch on his belt, Martin withdrew a small horn case, and from that a curious contraption fashioned of two glass disks connected by heavy gold wire. Perching the strange apparatus on his nose, he peered at the chart through it, the curved glass making his eyes look as if they might pop right out of his face. *Dear God, he is mad.* Alex glanced toward Nicki to gauge her reaction to this remarkable eye mask, but she was examining the contents of a shelf with her back to him.

"This diagram"—Martin tapped it with a gnarly finger—"is based on the observation that Mercury and Venus are always morning and evening stars and never farther from the sun than twenty-nine and forty-seven degrees respectively."

"Really." Alex couldn't stop staring at the bug-eyed old man. Was Nicki quite safe coming to see him alone?

"Whereas Mars, Jupiter, and Saturn," Martin said excitedly, "can be any distance at all from the sun, leading Heraclides of Pontus to the conclusion—quite rightly—that those three bodies revolve directly around the earth, while Mercury and Venus, being inferior planets, revolve around the sun, which in turn revolves around the earth. Pear wine?"

"I beg your—"

"Pear wine," he said loudly, as if Alex were partially deaf. "I have some pear wine. Made it myself. Quite good, if I do say so. Would you like some? Either of you?"

"I suppose."

"I'd love some," Nicki said, turning around. She displayed no reaction at all to the odd accessory adorning the old man's face. Perhaps, Alex thought giddily, it was he who was mad.

The prior removed the strange device—thank the saints—and rummaged among the debris on a work table, producing a flagon and two cups. "I first got interested in the stars in order to determine the dates of the movable feasts. But once I was introduced to the theories of the Greeks and Arabs, well . . ."

"Doesn't the Church disapprove of pagan teachings?" Alex asked.

"Some churchmen do," Martin conceded as he poured two cups of wine. "But there don't seem to be many Christians who've written about the things I want to learn." Hearing such an elderly man speak of the things he still wanted to learn made Alex feel sheepish about taking up reading at the advanced age of six-and-twenty.

Martin handed the cups to his guests. "Any thinking man ought to be able to embrace secular learning—even pagan learning—without turning his back on God. Why did God give us this wild, ungovernable curiosity, if He didn't want us to satisfy it?"

Alex took a drink of his wine, declining to point out that not all men were quite as wildly curious as Brother Martin seemed to be.

As if she'd read Alex's mind, Nicki smiled. She lifted an astrolabe from a shelf crammed with tools for studying the heavens and blew on it; dust sparkled in the morning sunlight streaming through the windows. "Brother Martin has long been fascinated by the theoretical sciences and mechanical arts," she said, replacing the astrolabe and picking up an assembly of balls, rods and bands. "Is this new?"

Martin nodded. "That's an armillary sphere. It represents the cosmos. What do you think of this?" He handed her a small brass horn. "I'm fitting it out with valves, so it will produce a variety of tones."

"How clever." Nicki studied the horn from all angles and replaced it on the shelf, sipping her wine distractedly. "Brother Martin, I was wondering if you'd had an opportunity to talk to Father Octavian about the matter we—"

"You might find these interesting, being a knight." The old man took Alex by the arm and led him to a table strewn with prototypes of siege engines and assault towers.

"What the devil . . ." Alex leaned over to examine a most extraordinary vehicle plated with iron.

"That's an armored wagon," said Brother Martin.

"I see. And the . . . thing on top of it, with the paddles . . ."

"Its purpose is to generate energy from the wind. Are you interested in energy?"

"I . . ."

"Then you'll want to see these." The prior steered Alex to a collection of bizarre creations, each more baffling than the last. "Perpetual-motion machines," he said. "Or . . . attempts at them. The point is for the device to move of its own accord, with no outside energy source, such as water or wind."

Nicki cleared her throat. "I'm naturally quite anxious as to Father Octavian's reaction to my proposal. Did you . . . happen to have the chance to bring up what we discussed?"

"Yes, my dear. Of course." The prior pointed to the largest of these machines, which featured balls rolling up and down the undulating spokes of a wheel. "I had high hopes for that one. It utilizes quicksilver. But alas . . ."

"Brother Martin." Nicki tugged on the old monk's sleeve. "Please. What did Father Octavian say?"

"He said he'd think about it. Here." He guided Alex to a table bearing an array of pots containing mysterious substances, along with a set of scales, a mortar and pestle and a slab of asbestos with burn marks on it. Opening the pots one by one, he identified their contents. "Naptha, powdered resin, niter, willow charcoal, saltpeter . . . and surely you recognize this one by the smell." He opened a leather-covered jar and stuck it under Alex's nose.

Alex choked on the hellish stench of rotten eggs. "Sulphur. What manner of alchemy is this?"

"I'm trying to concoct a missile propellant." Martin handed Alex a metal tube with a handle.

Seeing the little iron balls scattered over the table, Alex said, "This is the weapon Nick—" *Careful.* "That is, my lady cousin told me about this. It shoots those little balls."

"It will," Martin said, "when I've managed to create

a mixture volatile enough to eject the ball at a high
rate of speed without the whole business blowing up
in my hand." He rolled back a sleeve of his robe to
reveal scalding red burn marks up his left arm.

Nicki fussed over him, scolding him for taking risks,
but he chuckled indulgently. "Great ideas are worth
a bit of discomfort."

"Yes, well . . . about the stewardship . . ." Nicki bit
her lip. Alex felt for her, knowing how apprehensive
she was about the outcome of her petition. He would
have taken her in his arms and whispered reassurances
if Brother Martin hadn't been standing there. "When
he said he'd think about it—"

"Well, those weren't his actual words. Ah! You
haven't seen this, my dear." Martin thrust a small
model at her. " 'Tis a foot-powered lathe."

"It's very ingenious. What exactly did he say? Do
you remember?"

"I can't recall precisely," the prior said. "But he
didn't reject the idea out of hand. In fact, after we'd
talked for a while, he seemed to find some merit in it."

"Truly?"

"I argued most fervently for your cause, my dear.
Pointed out how well you manage the castle—extolled
your skills in accounting, and your handling of the
household staff."

"You . . . refrained from mentioning Milo," she
said.

"I thought that was best."

"If . . . if you have the chance to speak to him
again . . ." Nicki began.

"I'll continue to influence him on your behalf, my
dear." Martin took Nicki by the shoulders and kissed
her on the forehead. On the way here, she'd explained
to Alex why Brother Martin represented her best
hope for securing the stewardship of Peverell. Although very different from Father Octavian in temperament, and despite his refusal to bow down to the

abbot's will—or perhaps because of it—he was the only man within the abbot's sphere who wielded any influence at all with him.

"I'll pray for you as well," Martin assured her. "Father Octavian wants to settle the matter quickly. He intends to make his decision by Lammas Day."

"The first of August," Nicki said. " 'Tis but a week hence."

"Come back in a week and I'll give you his answer. From the looks of things, I'd say there's an excellent chance he'll grant you the stewardship. Meanwhile, I suggest you try not to fret over it. Whatever he decides will ultimately be God's will."

"Thank you, Brother. Thank you so much!"

The old monk cocked his head. "Have I shown you my plans for a vault to store snow during the summer months?" He smiled almost impishly. "One could have icy cold drinks on the hottest days." He turned and began pawing through a stack of drawings. "Now, where did I put that . . ."

From the concealing screen of trees at the edge of the woods, Gaspar watched Nicolette and Alex, on horseback, say their goodbyes to that lunatic old prior at the abbey's front gate.

Gaspar had wondered at their destination when they rode off this morning. Their lessons—if they really were lessons and not simply trysts—took place in the afternoons. Always in the afternoons. Thus, when they left together right after breakfast, Gaspar had naturally followed them.

So. Another mysterious trip to the abbey. Gaspar never did have the opportunity to find out why she had come here that other time. No doubt both visits were to fulfill the same covert agenda, an agenda that Alex was now privy to. Given the secrecy of these trips, it seemed likelier than ever that they had to do with Peverell. Lady Nicolette must have cooked up some scheme for keeping the Church from getting their hands on it—a scheme in which she'd apparently enlisted Alex's aid.

Damn that meddling whoreson to the bottommost level of hell. If not for him, Gaspar's seed might yet be sprouting in her ladyship's belly. As it was, he'd had to abandon his attempts along those lines. After all, if Alex was crawling up to the solar to tup her every night after the household had retired, Gaspar couldn't very well do the same. Three was a bit of a crowd in bed.

Gaspar had sniffed around this past fortnight for other opportunities to dose her wine and take her unawares, but none had been forthcoming. Every morning she was amongst her staff, tending to castle business, and every afternoon she retired to the woods to disport herself with Alex.

Having pondered the matter in the cold light of day, Gaspar had resolved not to interfere with young Alex's attempts to impregnate his cousin's wife. Although Gaspar didn't like to think of her submitting to the son of a bitch, she had, from all appearances, been doing so since Rouen. And, after all, it didn't really matter whose bastard slithered out of her belly nine months hence; Peverell would be saved from the Church's clutches just the same.

But as for afterward . . . that was a different matter.

Things had changed. This business with Alex had ignited a seething rancor that burned deep in Gaspar's belly, like a red-hot coal that's rolled out of the hearth and fallen into the rushes. It burns on quietly, unseen and unsuspected until at last the rushes burst into flame.

No longer was he willing to play the fawning lapdog to this highborn whore and her drunkard of a husband. Gaspar was a better castellan than Milo de St. Clair could ever dream of being. Of what import was his humble birth? He was smart and ambitious and a

natural leader. By rights the castellany should be his;
Peverell should be his.

Had not Henri's own grandfather been lowborn?
Yet he'd risen by his wits to the appointed post of
castellan, which then became hereditary—proof that
one needn't be born to the nobility to become one of
them. One simply needs the wit to see an opportunity,
and the ballocks to act on it.

And Gaspar had both.

Seeing Nicolette and Alex coming toward him,
Gaspar turned and rode through the woods, smiling
as the bits and pieces of his nascent scheme coalesced.

Oh, yes. He could do it. He could have it all—
Peverell, Nicolette, and sweet revenge. It would help,
to start off, if he knew the precise nature of whatever
Lady Nicolette was trying to arrange with the abbey.
Perhaps Milo knew. If so, it would be an easy matter
to coax the information from him tonight. All Gaspar
had to do was pour wine down his throat, and he
babbled his deepest secrets with scarcely any prompting at all. Then tomorrow, if necessary, Gaspar could
sabotage Nicolette's scheme by paying a visit to the
abbot, who'd once told him he was welcome in his
private lodgings any time.

But only if absolutely necessary. From the way Father
Octavian looked at him, Gaspar suspected his interest
in him was more of a corporeal than a spiritual nature.
The bastard made his skin crawl, but it was critical to
the success of his strategy that Nicolette's come to
naught. He must do whatever it took to convince Father Octavian to abandon her plan.

Whatever it took.

Chapter 19

"He was a mercenary knight in my uncle Henri's service," Nicki said quietly. They'd spread their blanket next to one of the giant oaks, and now she sat with her back against it, savoring the cool forest shade, the weight of Alex's head in her lap, the silk of his hair as she glided her fingers through it. . . .

And the blessed relief of revealing to him, at last, the seeds that had been planted a dozen years ago, growing into a weed that had doomed their blossoming love.

"I was fifteen when he came to Peverell," she said.

"How old was Philippe?" Alex asked, turning his head to look up at her.

Her fingers stilled in his hair. "How did you know his name?"

Alex reached up and caressed her cheek. "You spoke it during your illness."

"What did I say?"

He frowned slightly, as if trying to remember. "Something about him hurting you. What did he do to you, Nicki?"

She looked away from the compassion in his eyes. "He made me fall in love with him."

A muscle jumped in Alex's jaw.

"That is, I thought it was love. In truth, 'twas but a girlish infatuation. I didn't know what love was." Shyly she added, "I do now."

Alex brought her hand to his mouth and kissed her

fingertips. He hadn't kissed her on the mouth at all today. She wondered if he would. She hoped he would.

"He was very handsome," she said. "He was the tallest knight at Peverell, and his hair was the palest gold."

"Like yours," Alex murmured, taking hold of her single braid, which hung over her shoulder, and untying the ribbon from it.

"He had blue eyes, and quite the noble bearing. And a smile that made my knees go weak."

"Your point is made," Alex said ruefully. He wrapped the ribbon around his hand. Something about the way it looked struck a familiar chord in her.

"Do you remember that morning in Rouen when you woke up in the longship, and I was there?"

Alex groaned. "All too well. What an ass I made of myself."

"You had something wrapped around your hand."

"Ah." Fumbling in his money pouch, he pulled out a long white ribbon and gave it to her. "I've had this since Périgeaux. It's yours."

"Verily?" For some reason, she encircled her hand with it, as he had done.

"You don't think it's silly?"

"Nay, I think it's . . ." At a loss for words, she leaned down and kissed him on the lips. "Not silly."

"You kissed me." With a gratified sigh, Alex curled a hand around her neck and urged her toward him for another, more lingering kiss. "We mustn't do this," he whispered, and pressed his lips to hers again. "I want to hear your story, and if we start kissing, we'll be kissing all afternoon."

"I don't doubt it." They'd kissed for hours last night. Every time he said he was going to leave, there would be one more kiss, and then another, and another . . .

"You never answered my question," he said, gently steering her back to her account. "How old was Philippe?"

"Thirty," she said. "And a seasoned soldier. Very dedicated to it." *Like you,* she thought, but didn't say.

"What was his weapon?"

"The longbow."

Alex nodded. "It takes a tall man to handle a long-bow. And a strong one."

"He was very skilled with it," she said mischievously.

Alex rolled his eyes. "Perhaps I'd rather kiss than talk, after all."

"If you'd prefer."

She leaned down for another kiss, but he cupped her face, his expression sobering. "I need to know how he hurt you."

She straightened up. " 'Twas my fault, really."

Alex made a sound of derision. "You were fifteen. He was thirty. 'Twas his fault."

"You don't know what happened."

"I can guess. He pursued you." Alex's voice was low, his manner subdued, almost grim. "You were young and naive and incredibly beautiful, and he was determined to have you. You weren't the type of girl he could just have for the asking, though. He had to ingratiate himself with you, declare his undying love, court you. At first he seemed content to steal the occasional kiss when no one was looking. But as his passion became more demanding, he made it clear that he wanted more—needed it. He was in pain, and if you would not relieve it, he'd be forced to find a woman who would. It didn't mean he didn't love you, but he was a man, and a man had—"

"How do you know all this," she demanded in a quavering whisper. "Do all men use women this way?"

Alex sat up and looked at her squarely. "Many do. I never have." His mouth quirked. "I doubt I could manage all the necessary lies, even if I wanted to."

She nodded morosely. "He did lie to me. It was lies, all of it. He told me he loved me. He said he wanted to marry me as soon as he was landed. Uncle

Henri had already told me that he intended to leave
Peverell to me—or rather my firstborn son—and I
confided this to Philippe, but he insisted he wanted
his own land, not his wife's. At the time, I thought . . .
I thought 'twas noble of him. I was a fool."

He kissed her forehead. "You were a sheltered
young girl being manipulated by a cad. You're the
cleverest person I know—never doubt that."

She shook her head. "Mama tried to warn me.
She'd always told me to stay away from the soldiers,
that all they were interested in was the act of love,
not love itself."

"Hmph."

"She was right, Alex. I would have done well to
heed her. Especially in light of . . ." Nicki hesitated,
on uncertain ground. "Do you know anything
about . . . my father? Has Milo told you?"

"Nay. I always assumed your mother was a widow."

"She is, but . . . perhaps I should tell you about
him, and then you'll understand why my mother felt
as she did about soldiers, and why I . . . why things
turned out as they did." She hated having to look into
Alex's eyes as she peeled away these layers of the
past. "Lie back down." She patted her lap. "I like the
feel of you here."

Smiling, he did as she asked, and she continued absently stroking his hair. "My father's name was
Conon. Like Philippe, he was one of Uncle Henri's
knights. He pursued Mama just as Philippe pursued
me. She resisted him for a while, and then . . ." She
let out a ragged sigh and leaned her head back against
the tree, closing her eyes. "When she realized she was
with child, she told Conon. He tried to deny that the
child was his, but of course he was the only man my
mother had ever been with. He argued that he was
landless, and couldn't support a family."

"Your mother had no property, I take it."

"Nor was she heir to any, else I doubt Conon would

have balked as he did. Her belly grew to the point where everyone knew. When Uncle Henri figured it out, he was outraged. 'Twas he who finally forced Conon to wed her."

Alex shook his head. "This is why I . . . take measures to keep from siring children. Planting a bastard in an unmarried girl is a fine way to repay her for granting you her favors."

"I wish all men were as conscientious as you are."

"I'm glad Conon wasn't." He smiled in response to her look of puzzlement. "If he had been, you might never have been born."

"Charmer."

"So Conon married your mother."

"Whereupon Henri promptly dismissed Conon from his service and ordered him to take Mama away from Peverell. He was ashamed of her. All of Normandy knew about her by then. Conon took her to Clairvaux, where he was from. He set her up in a little wattle-and-daub hut and left to sell his services to the highest bidder. I was born there."

"I had no idea." Alex sat up again, frowning. "I thought . . ."

"You thought I was a child of privilege, that I'd been born at Peverell and knew naught but luxury my whole life."

"I suppose so."

"Lie down."

Looking pensive, he did.

"The first seven years of my life, we lived in squalor. My father never returned to us. He sent a little silver from time to time, but far less than we needed. Mama sold eggs and took in laundry."

"My God."

"It was those years of hardship that turned my mother into . . . the woman you knew in Périgeaux."

"Yes," he murmured. "I had no idea. What happened to convince Henri to let you return to Peverell?"

"Conon died—not in battle, but in a knife fight with another mercenary. The little bit of silver stopped coming. It wasn't much, but we'd depended on it. Mama threw herself on her brother's mercy and he relented. The first time I saw Peverell Castle, after having known nothing but that dismal little cottage, I could scarcely believe it. You might think it's gloomy and depressing, but to me it looked like the very gates of heaven."

"I don't doubt it." He tugged the slipper off one of her feet and caressed her toes with his strong fingers. It felt stimulating and comforting at the same time.

"Henri's condition for Sybila's return was that she must dress and act as befitted a proper widow, and that under no conditions was she to encourage the attentions of men, especially the men under his command."

"Little wonder she never remarried."

"Oh, she was completely unmarriageable when she returned to Peverell. No noble family would betroth their son to her after the disgrace that surrounded her marriage to Conon. She'd been big with child on her wedding day."

"Such transgressions are often overlooked."

"If the woman is wealthy. But my mother had nothing."

"No wonder she warned you against Philippe."

"For all the good it did her. I was wildly enamored of him. At first I refused to do more than kiss. He told me he'd have to seek out . . . a certain kind of woman. Still I held firm. I told him I was afraid of becoming pregnant, as Mama had. He promised that if I quickened, he'd marry me immediately, land or no land. After that, I'm afraid he found me all too easy to seduce. I was weak, I . . ." *I still am. My flesh hungers for yours. I have the heart and soul of a wanton, a sinner.*

"I'm surprised your mother let you out of her sight long enough to . . ." He cleared his throat. "Where did you—"

"In an empty stable stall." Nicki remembered that hasty first coupling in the straw—his grunts of effort as he'd rammed his way through her maidenhead, her whimpers of pain. He pressed a hand over her mouth to shut her up, and then his face went red, and he grew rigid as he emptied his seed in her. He sighed and collapsed on her, and then they heard someone enter the stable. Philippe withdrew abruptly, making her cry out in pain. *For God's sake, shut up,* he said, and went to check. It was only Gaspar, his confidant, whom, unbeknownst to her, he'd posted as a lookout. Lady Sybila was asking for her daughter, Gaspar said. He'd eyed her with interest as she brushed the straw off her tunic, trying to pretend her inner thighs weren't sticky with blood and semen, that she wasn't on the verge of tears from the knifelike pain in her womb. She could still recall her shame. *He knows . . .*

"After the first time," she said, "I . . . didn't want to do it again."

Alex's hand tightened on her foot.

"But," she said, "Philippe was so sweet, so contrite for having hurt me. He promised next time would be better. It was, a little. It never stopped hurting entirely, though. Within a fortnight, I suspected I was with child, because my . . ." Heat rose in her cheeks.

Alex fondled her foot with his wonderfully rough fingers. "Your courses didn't come. Did you tell Philippe?"

She sighed heavily. "Not right away. Like a fool, I kept hoping I was wrong. I waited another month, and another. Finally I had to face the truth, and I told him. He just swore and walked away. That night he rode off and never came back."

Alex sat up and looked at her.

She gazed at her hands, clutched in her lap. "Gaspar told me that he . . . Philippe, he . . . he had a wife and child in Paris."

Alex muttered something under his breath that Nicki was just as happy not to hear. He covered her hands with his.

"I was shocked, brokenhearted . . . and terrified. I'd ignored my mother's counsel, and now I'd be ruined, just as she had been. I felt like the lowest harlot."

"Oh, Nicki, Nicki . . ." Alex took her in his arms and kissed her cheek. "My poor, sweet love."

"I told my mother—I had to. She beat me, called me a whore, but I felt I deserved it. She was . . . consumed with panic. We both were. On top of the sinfulness and the scandal, there was Uncle Henri. He was almost certain to cast me out—perhaps both of us, and we'd be even worse off than we were in Clairvaux."

"Christ." He leaned his forehead on hers. "If I'd been there, I would have offered to marry you."

"Gaspar did."

Alex stared at her in evident shock.

"He came to me," she said, "and told me he felt partly responsible for my predicament, because he'd known Philippe was a wedded man. You must understand, Alex, Gaspar was different then. Not as hard. The years have changed him."

"Yes. That's all too clear."

"He said he knew he was lowborn, and unworthy of me, but that he'd claim the child as his and provide for us as best he could. I was touched."

"But you turned him down."

"Aye. I was already three or four months along. A hasty wedding at that point would have fooled no one, and all I would have gained was marriage to a man I didn't love. He probably thought I was rejecting him

on the basis of his station, and I'd be lying if I said
that wasn't a factor, but it wasn't the main one."

Alex gently pried her hands apart and took them
in his. "What happened to the baby?"

"I lost—" Her throat caught. She took a deep
breath. "I lost her."

"Her?"

" 'Twas a girl. She was . . . so tiny. Wee little
fingers."

"Oh, Nicki."

"I almost died from losing her. The midwife said it
was the most violent miscarriage she'd ever seen, and
I fell into a fever afterward. But at least my uncle
never found out. Mama just told him I'd taken ill.
'Twas curious . . . I was so sad about my little girl,
my baby. You'd think I would have been relieved,
but . . ." Nicki shook her head to dispel the lingering
image of those fragile little fingers.

Alex scooped her into his arms and held her for
a long time, murmuring soft words of comfort into
her ear.

"Mama told me I was weak about matters of the
flesh, and that this weakness would damn my soul and
destroy my reputation if I let it. She made me promise
never to give my heart to another charming young
knight. I was to find a husband who preferred hearth
and home to warfare."

"Ah. Of course." Alex kissed her temple, her cheek.
He tugged his fingers through the plaits of her hair,
loosening them.

"Shortly after that, Uncle Henri publicly announced
his intention to leave Peverell to my firstborn son.
Overnight, I was transformed from his impoverished
ward into a coveted marriage prize. Henri and Mama
tried to negotiate a marriage for me. The first candidate was old and half-blind. The second was so fat he
wheezed when he walked. They were all . . ." She
shuddered. "All they cared about was rents and mill

revenues. None of them gave a fig for me. I turned them all down."

"I wondered, back in Périgeaux, why you were still unwed at nineteen." His fingers, grazing her scalp and trailing through her hair, felt delicious.

"Uncle Henri was disgusted that I should be so fussy in the face of his generosity to me. He told me he'd arranged with the Church for the abbey to inherit Peverell if he should die before I married."

His hand stilled in her hair. "I thought his condition had to do with your bearing a son."

"That was just an ancillary condition to the first. His primary concern was that I should wed as soon as possible, to ensure that Peverell's castellany remained hereditary—that it stayed in our family. Mama begged me to marry. She said she couldn't go back to taking in laundry, and that if we were turned away from Peverell, we'd have two options—the convent or the brothel. I knew my uncle had the upper hand. Peverell meant everything to me, and to Mama."

"What about the second condition?" Alex asked.

"Henri wanted to make sure I wouldn't concoct a false marriage of appearances just to keep Peverell, and that there would be another generation to inherit it. If I failed to produce a son within ten years of his death, the estate was to revert to the Church."

Alex sighed. "He thought of everything."

"Phelis invited me to visit her in Périgeaux, and I accepted. I needed to get away from Uncle Henri and that castle."

Alex brought a handful of her hair to his face and rubbed it on his cheek. "I remember the first time I saw you, playing *jeu de paume* with Phelis and Alyce in Peter's back meadow. You were all in white, and your hair flew as you ran after the ball. It gleamed like fire in the sunlight. I thought you were the most exquisite thing I'd ever seen. I was instantly smitten with you."

"And I with you."

"Were you?" Smiling, he tucked her more firmly within his embrace.

"Oh, yes." She rested her head on his chest, comforted by the solid feel of him through the soft linen shirt, the steady thudding of his heart. "Right from the beginning. 'Twas your eyes, I think—at least at first. When you looked at me, I felt as if I were the only girl in the world, and you were the only boy."

"Boy," he murmured.

"Hmm?"

Reticently he said, "Afterward, I thought you had just used me to make Milo jealous. He was a man, a learned man, and I was just an ignorant boy."

She looked up at him. "That's the most singularly asinine conclusion I think anyone's ever drawn about anything."

He laughed and kissed her hair. "Thank you for setting me straight, my lady."

"I admired Milo. I liked him, much the same as you did, and we did share a rapport of the mind. But my bond with you went well beyond the mind. It went right through to our souls. You knew that, Alex. You felt it, that first day in the cave, when we held hands in the dark."

His arms tightened around her. "Yes."

"I knew I shouldn't feel what I felt for you. You would be leaving soon to join William, and I knew that nothing would prevent that, even me."

Alex was silent for a moment and then he said, softly, "I *was* just a boy, really. A foolish boy who thought he could have everything."

"And I was afraid," she admitted, "after what had happened with Philippe. Mama told me that soldiers revel in their conquests, and that I was the type of girl who was all too susceptible to their charm."

"What is that supposed to mean?"

"She said I had too . . . sensual a nature."

"Ah, yes." His chest shook as he chuckled. "Your supposed weakness of the flesh."

"I *am* weak. I . . . I feel things . . ." Her face stung. She pulled away from him and moved to the middle of the blanket. "I can't talk about such things."

"Even with me?" Alex crawled toward her.

"Especially with you." She tried to push him away when he reached for her, but he was far stronger, and before she knew it he had her on her back on the blanket, half covering her body with his.

"I'm delighted to hear about this terrible weakness of yours," he said, grinning.

She punched his shoulder. "Don't jest about it. I hate the way I am, and I don't want to talk about it."

His smile dimmed. "Damn that mother of yours for making you ashamed of being exactly as you should be."

"But that's just it, Alex. I'm not as I should be. Women ought not to . . ." She turned away from his all-too-direct gaze. "Women—good women—don't feel the things I fell."

"You little idiot." His kissed her soundly. "Women lust, just as men do—even good women."

She shook her head. "Not according to the priests."

"What do they know of it?"

"They're the voice of God on earth."

Alex propped himself up on an elbow. "God wants us to be fruitful and multiply, does He not?"

"Of course."

"Then isn't it possible He knew exactly what he was doing when He made sex pleasurable? He *wants* us to lust."

"He wants men to lust."

Alex smirked. "And women to submit."

"For the sake of having children."

Alex groaned. "Nicki, for an intelligent woman, you can be remarkably obtuse."

"Thank you, sir, for that instructive observation on my character."

He settled down next to her, gathering her to him so that they lay facing each other. "I wish you had told me about Philippe, that summer in Périgeaux."

"I couldn't possibly have."

He resumed combing his fingers through her hair. "Your mother swore you to secrecy, I take it."

"Aye, but I wouldn't have told you, anyway. I was ashamed of having yielded to him, deeply ashamed. And I was no fool—I knew I'd be ruined if it got out that I'd been pregnant."

He nodded. "It's all making sense now. At the end of that summer, when the message came about your uncle being close to death, you knew you'd have to marry."

"And soon. Mama told Milo about the terms of Uncle's will, and that my husband would have de facto control of Peverell. He asked me to marry him that night. I was devastated. I didn't love Milo, and he didn't love me. I loved you. I wanted you, always and forever, but you were already married to your sword."

"Aye," he said softly.

"Even if you *had* proposed, I couldn't have accepted, knowing you would never give up soldiering. You would have been gone most of the time, following William from one battle to another. I couldn't have borne having months go by—or years—without seeing you. And I would have made myself sick, worrying about you."

He nodded.

"But you didn't propose. You tried to get me to run away with you, but without asking for my hand. I couldn't be your leman. I couldn't embrace a life of shame, especially not after Philippe. But how could I explain it to you, make you understand, when I couldn't tell you about Philippe?"

"Oh, Nicki, I'm sorry." He held her more firmly in his embrace. "I was such a fool."

"I married Milo in desperation. At first it wasn't too bad, being his wife. We always got along, and he wasn't very demanding. But then the drinking got worse, and . . ." She shook her head. " 'Twas never a marriage of the heart, but eventually it became such a farce that I decided we would both be better off apart. And I thought perhaps if I could dissolve the marriage and take another husband, I'd be able to have children. I made discreet inquiries through Brother Martin, but there were no grounds for annulment. The pope wouldn't allow it."

"But you still care for Milo," Alex said, gazing at her intently.

"As a sister cares for an ailing brother," she said. "I never cared for him as I care for you."

He smiled. Nicki stroked his cheek, skimming a fingertip along the worst of the faint scars that spoiled the perfection of his face, a puckered little gash that twisted down his forehead and through his right eyebrow. "I hate to think of you risking your life in battle all these years."

He started to say something, but hesitated awkwardly.

"Don't tell me." She smiled. " 'Tis another of your many scars that weren't earned in battle."

His smile seemed sad. "That's right."

"What caused it?"

He rolled onto his back. "A club."

She winced. "And this?" She touched an old wound on his jaw.

He closed his eyes. "A club."

"And this?" She swept her fingertip over an indentation at the bridge of his nose. "A club as well?"

"Aye."

"The same club?"

He shrugged. "There were three of them, and I had my eyes closed at that point."

"Mother of God." She leaned over him, pondering that. "Bandits?"

He opened his eyes. "We should get on with my lesson. All we've done is talk."

"We should have talked like this a long time ago."

"Did you bring the tablet?"

"Who beat you with clubs, Alex?" Nicki asked, uneasy now because he was evading the subject. Alex never evaded anything.

He stroked her hair, which hung around his face like a curtain. " 'Twas a long time ago, Nicki. It doesn't matter anymore."

"Three men beat you with clubs, and it doesn't matter? You might have died. When did this happen?"

"Nicki . . ."

"Tell me!"

"Come here." He drew her into his arms and cradled her head on his shoulder. "It happened nine years ago, the morning of your wedding."

"What?"

"Gaspar and his men were lying in wait when I went to—"

"What?" She tried to rise, but he held her tight.

" 'Twas a long time ago, and it doesn't matter anymore."

"What are you talking about?" She raised her head to look at him; how could he be so damnably calm? "How can it not matter? Why did he do this?"

"To keep me from interfering with your wedding."

"Oh, God." Shaken, she let him press her head back onto his shoulder. "Oh, God. Alex, I had no idea," she said in a wavering voice.

"I know. Your mother ordered him to do it."

Shock coursed through her. "Mama?"

"Although, from what I know now of Gaspar, I suspect he put the idea in her head—or at the very least, encouraged her."

Nicki felt ill, imagining Alex's broken body, the blood, the pain. "I would have come to you," she whispered, "if I'd known. Regardless of the consequences. I would have run to you. I would have taken you in my arms and . . . oh, God." She was trembling.

"Shh . . ." He stroked her hair, her back. "It's all in the past."

"I hate Gaspar," she said with feeling. "I despise him for having done this to you. There's no excuse. I'll hate him as long as I live. And Mama, too."

He chuckled and rolled to his side, hugging her close. "I find your passion quite gratifying."

"How can you laugh about such senseless violence, especially when it was directed at you?"

"Life is senseless, Nicki. One deals with it as best one can. I'd rather laugh at my painful memories than weep fat, useless tears over them."

Nicki took Alex's face in her hands and gazed into his eyes, wondering how she'd managed to get through the past nine years without him; why hadn't she gone mad? "I love you, Alex."

He smiled. "I love you, too."

She kissed the scar on his forehead, gingerly. "I'm sorry for this." Her lips brushed the nick on the bridge of his nose. "And this." Next, the little scar on his jaw. "And this." She kissed his mouth; his arms banded around her and he returned the kiss with enthusiasm.

They lay together beneath the rustling trees and lost themselves in the simple pleasure of kissing—a pleasure Nicki indulged in with some measure of guilt, given her married state, but little shame. It was, after all, just kissing. There was, in fact, a certain purity to it, reflective of the course their relationship had taken. It was as if they'd come full circle, she and Alex, and were reliving the innocent first bloom of their love in Périgeaux.

Alex's mouth was so warm, his jaw slightly scratchy; the hard length of his body fit against hers so perfectly. Surely other women didn't feel this unbearable longing, this aching emptiness, this need to be penetrated, possessed. It must be sinful to yearn for Alex this way, but it was the sweetest yearning she'd ever felt; it surged through her like warm wine, heating her blood, making her reckless with desire.

Without breaking the kiss, Alex skimmed his hand up from her waist to cover a breast.

Her gasp became a sigh as he caressed her, very tenderly, his hand large and strong through her tunic and shift, all the while kissing her so softly, his breath coming a little faster now . . .

"You shouldn't," she murmured unsteadily, looking into his fathomless brown eyes.

"Don't make me stop," he whispered. "If you tell me to, I will, but please don't."

Alex eased Nicki onto her back, moving down slightly so he could press his lips to her throat. He closed his hand more firmly over her breast, cupping its weight, his fingertips finding the little peak and rubbing it.

Desire thrummed in Nicki's veins, settling low in her belly. His touch cast a spell on her, stole the breath from her lungs. She knew she should put a stop to this, but she lacked the will to do it.

He glided his hand downward, over her belly and lower still. "Oh, God, Alex," she moaned as he caressed her through wool and linen, his touch gentle and inquisitive—too inquisitive. Could he feel her heat, the dampness between her legs? Did he know what he did to her?

Shame swamped her. "No, Alex." She pulled his hand away. "Don't."

His frank gaze disarmed her. "You don't really want me to stop."

"What I want and what's right are two different things. If we take this much further, it's adultery."

"It would be," he said, "if you were married in more than name only."

"In the eyes of the Church," she said, "my marriage is as binding as any other, and what you want—what we both want—is wrong."

"I can't believe God considers it wrong for two people who love as we do to share the pleasures of their bodies."

She smiled wryly. "I didn't realize until this afternoon how deeply the Lord had taken you into His confidence."

"Impudent wench." Alex trailed his fingers airily over her face, her throat, her breasts. "We don't have to make love," he said, his voice deep and low. "I can give you pleasure without even touching you beneath your clothes. It wouldn't be adultery, not really." He smoothed his hand down to rest it once more between her legs.

"Alex . . ."

"Do you ever touch yourself?"

Nicki's face flamed. " 'Tis a sin!"

"Perhaps, but there are worse sins. You didn't answer the question."

"Nor will I."

He smiled. "Then I think I know the answer." His hand began to move, stroking her lightly. "All I want is to give you the same pleasure—and to show you that it isn't wrong, that it can be beautiful. I want to make you forget your misgivings and lose yourself in ecstacy. I want to hear you moan as it overtakes you . . ."

"Alex," she gasped as he caressed her more deeply, in a rhythm that kept pace with her quickening heart.

"I want to look into your eyes at the moment you come undone, and feel the tremors course through you, and know that I did that to you."

She was so close to the crisis toward which he led her, mere moments away. . . .

"No!" she cried, trembling. "No, Alex, please."

He withdrew his hand and wrapped his arms around her, whispering, "Shh, it's all right. I'm stopping. I'm stopping."

"I just . . . I can't."

"It's all right, love." He kissed her forehead, kneaded her back. "I didn't mean to upset you. I went too fast. It's just that I want you so much—any part of you you're willing to give."

"I can't give what you want me to give."

"Not yet, perhaps."

"Not ever." She felt the hard column of his erection against her belly, through their clothes, and contrition stabbed her. " 'Tisn't fair to you."

"What isn't fair?"

"This. My being here like this with you, letting you . . ."

"Letting me kiss you?"

"Not so much that."

"Ah." His hand stole to her breast.

She pulled it away. "No more. It's making you . . . want too much."

Low laughter rumbled in his chest. "I'll want too much even if you don't let me touch you." He extracted his hand from her grasp and molded it to her breast again. "At least this way, I'll have a little taste of that for which I hunger so ravenously."

"You said you'd stop if I wanted you to."

"You don't want me to." He gently thumbed her nipple, making the breath catch in her throat.

"But I'm asking you to," she said quietly.

He withdrew his hand. "Nicki, I can't help wanting you. You're all I think about, you're in my blood. But I won't force myself on you. I'll try to content myself with your kisses . . . until you're ready for more."

"I'll never be ready."

He smiled devilishly. "I could change your mind."

"I don't think so."

He rolled on top of her, grinning, and bent his head to hers. "I do love a challenge."

"You've got one," she said as his mouth closed over hers.

And so do I.

Chapter 20

"**M**y son!" Father Octavian guided Gaspar into his office, a roomy chamber on the upper level of his private lodge at the abbey. "What an unexpected pleasure." He dismissed the soft little monk who'd escorted Gaspar upstairs and closed the door.

Gaspar had never cared for being called "my son," especially by clerics, like this one, who were no older than he; there wasn't a hint of gray in the abbot's coppery hair, and his skin was smooth and unlined. It was neither experience nor wisdom that had earned Octavian the abbacy, but the sacks of gold his father had donated to the Church. His family's wealth was evident in the ornate tapestries that adorned his office walls, the massive desk with its intricate carvings, the luxurious Spanish rug underfoot—far from the Benedictine austerity of the rest of the monastery.

An observant man, like Gaspar, could see beyond Octavian's severe black robe and tonsure to the pampered creature beneath. His gestures were those of a courtier, his gaze oblique. His fingernails gleamed, and Gaspar wouldn't be surprised if he buffed them every evening, like a gentlewoman—or had that soft young monk do it for him.

"Wine?" Octavian lifted a two-handled clay bottle from his desk. " 'Twas sent to me from Gascony. A bit sweet, but worth a taste, I think."

"Thank you, Father."

The abbot's gaze slid toward Gaspar as he filled a

silver mazer from the bottle. "Pray, what glad design brings you to my door?"

"It's about Peverell, Father." Gaspar accepted the bowl of wine and sipped from it, finding it unremarkable. "I hear tell you're considering its disposition, should the lady Nicolette not produce an heir by the appointed date."

"I hardly think such an heir will be forthcoming at this point, do you?" Octavian poured a mazer for himself and nodded toward the nearest window, open to let in the early-afternoon sunshine. "You don't mind if I close the shutters. This chamber becomes an oven on days like this."

"As you wish," Gaspar said, although he didn't find the heat quite that oppressive. He rehearsed his proposal in his mind as the abbot secured the shutters on the three windows, immersing the chamber in a dusky halflight.

"I'm glad you came, for you've been on my mind of late." The abbot sipped his wine, his gaze trained on Gaspar. "I have a bit of a problem I've been meaning to enlist your aid with."

"Yes?"

Leaning against his desk, Octavian waved a pale hand toward Gaspar. "That tunic must be stifling. You needn't stand on ceremony. Take it off, for heaven's sake."

Gaspar bought a moment by crossing to a small table in the corner, where he set his mazer. Weighing in his mind the magnitude of his purpose in coming here with the distastefulness of indulging the abbot in this small way, he opted for indulgence.

Octavian watched with undisguised interest as Gaspar unbuckled his belt and pulled off his tunic, tossing both onto a nearby chair. "Isn't that better?" the abbot asked, surveying Gaspar's form through his shirt and chausses. Leaving his mazer on the desk, he approached Gaspar, who quickly moved away.

Smiling as if at some private jest, Octavian picked up Gaspar's belt and turned it over in his hands, examining the heavy buckle, stroking the leather thoughtfully. "So. You've taken an interest in the disposition of Peverell."

"I have, Father." Gaspar cleared his throat and launched into it. "I spoke to Lord Milo last night."

Octavian looked up. "How does his lordship fare?"

Careful here. Mustn't be too obvious in disparaging his master—it wouldn't look good—but it would be foolish to pass up the opportunity to reinforce the abbot's poor opinion of Milo. "He's much the same, I'm afraid. His lordship's infirmity worsens daily." That would do, since everyone in Normandy knew the true nature of Milo's "infirmity."

Octavian nodded. " 'Tis just as I feared. And her ladyship?"

"Ah, her ladyship. In point of fact, 'tis a matter concerning Lady Nicolette that brings me here." Picking up the train of his prepared speech, he said, "His lordship took me into his confidence last night." In fact, Gaspar had wrested Milo's confidences from him with a bit of coaxing and two jugs of wine, but no need to mention that. "He's most troubled by some ploy of her ladyship's to trick the abbey into letting them stay on at Peverell."

Octavian's gaze sharpened. "Go on."

"It seems she intends to petition you to appoint her and her lord husband stewards of the estate after you assume control of the castellany." She had already made the request, of course, through that old maniac of a prior, but Gaspar had decided to feign ignorance of this. "Not that you'd grant such a petition, given his lordship's . . . feebleness. And, whereas her ladyship oversees the castle itself quite admirably, I can't imagine you'd grant her governorship of the entire estate." Gaspar smiled as if this were the most ludicrous possibility imaginable.

Octavian's expression went as blank as a corpse. Gaspar realized then that the abbot had, indeed, decided to grant the stewardship to Nicolette and Milo. That sly old Brother Martin must have been damnably convincing. But Gaspar's hopes rose when Octavian said, "You have a point, of course. I daresay 'twould be risky, entrusting a woman with such responsibilities."

"Potentially disastrous. And you should know that Lord Milo wants nothing to do with any stewardship, mindful as he is of his limitations."

"Quite sensible of him."

"Aye. But as for her ladyship—"

"If women had any sense," the abbot sneered, "would Eve have taken the apple from the serpent?"

Gaspar smiled, sensing impending victory. "I knew you'd feel that way. I told his lordship there was no cause for alarm, that you wouldn't think of appointing them—"

"I may *think* of appointing whomever I please," Octavian said with chilly authority. "Don't presume to coerce me one way or the other. 'Tis true that women in general are base creatures, temptresses with corrupt souls." He rubbed Gaspar's belt against his cheek. "Have you not found that to be the case?"

"I have indeed," Gaspar said, unnerved to find himself in such complete agreement with a sodomite on the subject of women, and dismayed that he seemed to have overstepped himself in Octavian's eyes.

"However, despite the misfortune of her ladyship's gender, she may well be the best candidate for the stewardship. Brother Martin has presented her case most persuasively, I must say. He has described her managerial skills in the highest terms, extolled her learning and her authority with her staff. She's intimately familiar with the estate, having been brought up there. And, of course, one mustn't forget her connections. Martin reminded me that she seems to be something of a favorite with Queen Matilda. I can hardly ignore the importance of such an affiliation."

Father Octavian sighed dramatically, drawing his hand along the length of the belt. "If there were someone better qualified for the position, I wouldn't be forced to appoint her—and it would be her and her alone, of course. One can discount the husband altogether. But, alas, no other candidate has presented himself."

This was Gaspar's cue to say the rest of it, which clever Father Octavian appeared to have anticipated. Things weren't proceeding quite as smoothly as Gaspar had hoped. The abbot, one move ahead of him all along, was toying with him. But if he kept his wits about him, his cause might yet prevail.

"Your mention of another candidate," Gaspar said, "brings me to a matter I've been meaning to discuss with you for some time, Father." Ever since last night, when he'd hammered his final strategy into shape. "As you know, I've served in a position of considerable responsibility at Peverell for nigh unto fifteen years now. I've commanded the men and supervised the running of the estate. If it's a steward you want, I'm here to offer my services. I doubt there's anyone better qualified, including—if I may be so bold—my lady Nicolette."

"Oh, you're bold, to be sure," Octavian said in a low, almost purring voice as he walked toward Gaspar, "coming here this way to steal the stewardship out from under your mistress."

Gaspar backed up against the desk. "Father, I assure you—"

"But I rather like boldness in a military man." Octavian smiled, clearly amused to have rattled Gaspar. "You do appear to be well qualified."

"If you appoint me, I'll serve you to the very best of my ability," Gaspar said, striving for the right mixture of subservience and aggression; Octavian seemed fond of both. The point was to make the bastard believe that Gaspar craved the position and would be entirely Octavian's creature once he had it—as if he'd demean himself like this for a job as a glorified caretaker. He had more ambitious plans—far more ambitious—but first he must make sure the abbot did not appoint Nicolette as steward. And the best way to do that was to offer himself as a substitute. "Your orders will be obeyed without question."

"What an appealing prospect," the abbot murmured. "You may take off your shirt if you wish. We're all alone here, and you must be warm."

Gaspar fought down the urge to snatch the belt back, wrap it around the faggot's throat and squeeze the life out of him. It wasn't Octavian's taste for men per se that sickened Gaspar. Some of Peverell's best soldiers shared similar appetites, a fact that troubled him little so long as they kept their depravity to themselves. But there was something about Octavian that made him seem more wicked than the general run of his breed.

" 'Tisn't that warm in here," Gaspar said. "I'll keep the shirt on."

The abbot's face froze into that death mask again. "Suit yourself." He turned and strode around his desk, seating himself behind it. "As for the matter of Peverell, well . . ." He tossed the belt aside and lifted a heavily inked sheet of parchment. "This is the appointment of stewardship. I can insert the name of anyone I wish—this very afternoon if I like—but I'm afraid it really doesn't look too good for you. I require a certain level of devotion and obedience in my subordinates, and frankly, you may be too strong willed to satisfy me in that respect."

So that's how it's to be. Gaspar considered the prospect of having Peverell—and its mistress—all to himself, once his plan came to fruition. Then he considered the degradation of submitting to the whims of this deviant little worm—but just for a single afternoon, long enough to get him to insert Gaspar's name on that document.

He took off his shirt.

The abbot smiled, his eyes glittering in the semidarkness. "But, of course," he said, setting down the document and closing his hand around the belt, "if we can manage to arrive at some mutually satisfying arrangement, I may rethink things."

"What did you have in mind?" Gaspar asked, not sure he wanted to hear the answer.

"It has to do with that problem I mentioned." Rising, Octavian circled the table and came to stand very close to Gaspar. "The one I said you might be able to help me with."

"What sort of a problem is it?"

"One of a rather sensitive nature. It might surprise you to know that I have . . . impure thoughts like any other man."

This news did not surprise Gaspar in the least.

"The Devil whispers things in my ear. He makes me lust in unnatural ways." Octavian eyed Gaspar's bare torso. "When the monks under my care have human lapses, 'tis my duty to correct them, and I do. But there's no one to correct me, to purge me of these sinful thoughts." He folded the belt into a loop.

"I see."

"Who better to punish me," Octavian said softly, "than a man such as yourself—a commander of soldiers? You know about discipline, and you're not afraid to exact it . . . are you?"

"Nay," Gaspar managed.

"My flesh is weak." Octavian moved so close that Gaspar could feel the rough wool of his robe brushing against him; it took an effort of will not to flinch. "I need to humble myself, to submit to your will." He took Gaspar's hand and closed it around the loop of belt. "Are you strong enough to do what it takes to break me of my sinful longings?"

Gaspar pictured the abbot whimpering in pain, like a woman. Perhaps he'd even cry. "I should think so."

Octavian smiled enigmatically. "About a year ago," he said, "my cellarer began overindulging in strong drink—much like your Lord Milo. In order to purge him of his fixation with wine, I made him drink half a barrel of it in one sitting. I've never seen anyone so sick. But the experience left its mark. He's been sober since. You don't suppose such a method might work with sins of the flesh?"

God's bones. Gaspar wondered if he had the stomach for this. He thought of Peverell . . . and his mistress. Perhaps he could go through with it—even take pleasure in it—if he imagined the abbot to be Nicolette. He actually grew stiff at the thought of inflicting on Nicolette the indignities Octavian was so eager for.

"Well?" Octavian said. "Have we reached an agreement?"

Gaspar strode to the door and slid the bolt across.

When he turned back around, Octavian was smiling. "It would seem we have."

Chapter 21

"**B**lessed Mary." Nicki swayed as she read the document Brother Martin handed her. The color leached from her face.

"Easy, now." Alex took her in his arms and led her to a bench in the corner of the prior's cluttered chamber, hoping she didn't faint. Sweeping a pile of drawings onto the floor, he sat her down and knelt at her feet. "What is it, Nicki? What's wrong?"

Brother Martin handed Nicki a cup of his pear wine, which she accepted with a trembling hand. "That document," the prior told him, "assigns the stewardship of Peverell to Gaspar le Taureau."

"Gaspar!" Alex bolted to his feet. "God's bones!"

"How did this happen?" Nicki asked in a small voice.

Brother Martin shrugged helplessly as he took the sheet of parchment from her. "He visited Father Octavian a few days ago. That's all I know. I'm sorry, truly I am. I thought for sure . . ." He shook his head. "Clearly, I wasn't as influential as I'd thought. I am sorry."

Nicki stared, hollow eyed, into her cup.

"Drink that, Nicki," Alex said. " 'Twill do you good."

"How did this happen?" she repeated in a toneless whisper.

"Do as your cousin says," the prior urged her. "Drink that wine. 'Twill warm your belly and soothe your nerves. And then I think it's best that you two head back to Peverell. My weather clock says there's a storm brewing."

Alex thought that unlikely; it was a clear, pleasantly breezy afternoon. Still, he was eager to get Nicki away from here. Her state of shock alarmed him. He needed to comfort her, to take her in his arms and kiss her and reassure her, but he could hardly treat his "cousin" so affectionately in front of Brother Martin.

"He's right, Nicki. We should leave."

"I'd ask you to spend the night," said the prior, "but Father Octavian won't allow women on monastery grounds after sunset."

Alex squatted in front of her. "Drink the wine, Nicki."

Shaking her head, she handed the cup to the prior. "Let's just go."

They were barely a mile into their journey home when the leaves began to shiver on their branches, surrounding them with an ominous murmur that made Alex's scalp tickle. Darkness swept through the forest with demonic speed. The horses whinnied nervously.

Damn. "What the devil *is* a weather clock?" Alex asked.

Nicki, riding ahead of him on the narrow track, didn't respond. She'd spoken nary a word since they left the abbey.

A chill wind whistled through the trees, raising goose bumps through Alex's heavy tunic. His hip began to ache. "Are you cold?" he called to Nicki, wondering if they should stop and retrieve their mantles from the saddlebags.

She shook her head.

The wind blew harder, tearing Nicki's veil right off her head. It flew down into the ravine next to which they rode, a streak of white that vanished into the raging waters far below.

The first few raindrops stung their faces. "Hold on to your reins," Alex said, just as the rain slammed down in earnest, battering them like fists.

"Nicki, take it slow!" Alex shouted over the suddenly hellish storm. Her mare looked skittish.

She yelled something back, but her words were swallowed up by the roar of the rain, driven right into their faces by the wind. He saw her pat Marjolaina on the neck, which seemed to calm the frightened animal—but only momentarily.

Thunder crashed overhead, followed by a flutter of lightning. The erratic white light illuminated a horrifying scene in jittery images: the dappled mare losing her footing and toppling sideways into the ravine, Nicki flying after her.

Screams filled Alex's skull . . . the horse's, Nicki's, his.

Alex leapt from his mount, his feet sliding on the wet gravel. He tumbled down the grassy ravine, propelled by wind and rain, until a tree abruptly halted his fall. *"Nicki!"* he screamed, struggling upright. *"Nicki!"*

He half-slid, half-crawled down the rain-lashed slope, screaming Nicki's name, until a dark form materialized below him in the torrent. No, there were two forms, he saw as he scrambled closer—the mare lying on her side, half-submerged in the stream, and Nicki, kneeling over her.

Alex gathered Nicki in his arms. "Nicki! Nicki, are you all right? Are you hurt?"

"Nay."

"Are you sure? 'Twas a bad fall."

"The ground was soft. Alex . . ." She gripped his arms hard. "Marjolaina, she's . . . oh, God, Alex."

Facing his back to the rain, Alex examined the horse, who stared at him with wide, stunned eyes and flared nostrils. A swift examination revealed that she'd broken a front leg.

Alex unsheathed the sharp little eating knife that hung on his belt. Best to get this over with while the mare was still in a state of shock, before she tried to struggle upright. "Turn around, Nicki."

"Oh, God. Oh, my poor Marjolaina."

He drew her close, kissed her forehead. "You know it's the only way."

"I know. I know. I just . . . I just wish to God you didn't have to."

Alex waited, rain hammering, while Nicki bent over her beloved Marjolaina and whispered something in her ear. She stroked the mare lovingly and kissed her on the nose. Then she rose and turned her back, her head down, her arms wrapped tightly around herself.

Alex pushed the wet hair out of his eyes and positioned his knife on the mare's throat, just behind her jaw. Taking a deep breath, he dispatched her with a single stroke. He rinsed off the knife and his blood-spattered chausses swiftly in the river, then wrestled Nicki's submerged saddlebags from the dead horse's back. The saddle would have to wait until he came back to dispose of the body. Taking Nicki by the arm, he led her back up the ravine.

"Do you know of any shelter nearby?" he asked as he lifted her into his saddle.

She nodded as he settled in behind her. "My uncle had a hunting lodge near here. I'll guide you there."

The lodge, a thatched stone cottage enveloped by overhanging trees, looked huge until they stepped inside. The entire front end, Alex discovered, was an enormous byre for the horses and dogs that Henri de St. Clair and his friends would take hunting with them, and here they stabled Atlantes. A single small room in back was reserved for human habitation, and although it was hard to see much, for night was falling and the storm still raged, it appeared to have been unoccupied for some time.

This back room had one window and a door, both curtained with skins that had come loose and flapped wildly, letting the wind blow the rain onto the muddy earthen floor. Dumping their saddlebags on a rough-hewn table, Alex ducked out into the maelstrom for a rock, which he used to nail down the skins.

As he did this, Nicki built a fire in the clay-lined cooking pit, using wood piled up next to it. When it was lit, Alex breathed a sigh of relief. The openings—except for the smoke hole—were sealed, and the fire crackled reassuringly. Despite the omnipresent rumble of rain, their little sanctuary felt almost cozy.

Taking Nicki in his arms, he found her shivering violently beneath her sodden tunic. "You've got to get out of these wet things. We both do." He reached into her saddlebags for her mantle, but found it to be drenched from its dunking in the stream. Retrieving his own mantle, a long, silk-lined cape of gray wool trimmed in black lambskin, he handed it to her. "You can wrap this around yourself."

"Wh-what about you?" she asked, teeth chattering.

Alex turned his back to give her privacy and unbuckled his sword belt. "I'll be fine." Nicki's lips were blue. He would have forgone the mantle even if she'd been a man.

His hip, which had ceased to pain him during their mishap at the ravine, throbbed in earnest as he stripped off his wet clothes. His drawers were only slightly damp, having been shielded from the rain by both his chausses and his tunic. They would dry quickly if he stayed close to the fire, which was already filling the room with its blessed warmth.

Keeping his back to Nicki, he dragged one of the benches that flanked the table close to the fire, draping his tunic and chausses over it and setting his boots as close to the flames as he thought safe. When he straightened up, he found Nicki struggling to spread her clothes over the bench with one hand while clutching the mantle closed with the other.

"Here." Alex took over the chore, finding that she'd removed not only her tunic, but her linen undershift, which was nearly as wet. He laid her wet slippers next to his boots, trying not to think about her nakedness beneath his mantle. She was wet and cold and had just suffered two terrible shocks—finding out about Gaspar and losing Marjolaina—and right now she needed his comfort, not his lust.

For the past week, he'd contented himself with her kisses, as he'd promised her he would. She still balked at any hint of further intimacies, and he'd been reluctant to pursue them. At first he'd told himself that his reserve had to do with her petition to Father Octavian. Had she been able to remain at Peverell without bearing the requisite heir, his services in that capacity would not have been required. That was haphazard logic, though, because regardless of the stewardship, he would still have been bound by his oath.

He finally arrived at the remarkable, and somewhat humbling, conclusion that he loved kissing Nicki just for the sake of kissing her, without it being a prelude to seduction. He reveled in it, just as he had reveled in holding her hand those enchanted afternoons in Périgeaux. It wasn't that he didn't still desire her; he did, intensely. The feel of her in his arms—the soft weight of her breasts, the cradle of her hips, her scent and warmth—kept him aching with need as their lips caressed. But it was a sweet ache, the same ache he'd felt as a youth, when he'd learned to live with the wanting, to savor it for itself, to dream with breathless anticipation of a release that hovered always out of reach.

Nicki crouched near the fire, obviously seeking its warmth. Thinking a hot drink might soothe her, Alex fetched his tin traveling cup out of his saddlebags, filled it with pear wine from the flask Brother Martin had sent them away with, and set it on an iron trivet at the edge of the fire pit.

He limped over to a stack of straw pallets in the corner, pulled the top one off and dragged it close to the fire.

"Are you all right?" she asked. "Did you hurt yourself?"

"Nay. It's just my hip." Grimacing, he lowered himself onto the pallet and patted it. "Sit here with me."

She sat next to him, bundled in his mantle. "I hope we won't have to spend the night here."

"I hardly think we'll have any choice. This storm shows no signs of easing up."

Consternation furrowed her brow. " 'Twill be scandalous, my staying out all night with you."

"Milo won't mind."

She appeared to mull that over. "Probably not. He isn't like other men. And, of course, our marriage isn't like other marriages."

"He's your husband," Alex said. "He's the only one who matters."

She gazed into the flames, her gaze unfocused and melancholy. They listened in silence to the shrieking wind and driving rain. When the pear wine was steaming and fragrant, Alex lifted the cup from the trivet and handed it to her. She wrapped her hands around it, took a small sip.

Alex moved behind her and pulled her braids out from under the lambskin collar of the mantle, unweaving them and draping the damp tresses over her shoulders so they could dry. He rubbed her arms and back to ease her shivers. "You've had a hard afternoon, Nicki."

"Marjolaina, she—" Nicki drew in a deep breath. "She wasn't a young horse. I shouldn't take it so hard."

"You have every right to take it hard." He moved closer, tucking her up against him, his bare legs on either side of her. Circling her with his arms, he urged her to lean back against his chest. "Not just what happened to Marjolaina, but . . . the stewardship."

She sipped her wine thoughtfully. "I can't believe Gaspar went behind our backs that way."

"I can—all too easily."

"I'd release him from our service," she said, "but 'twould serve me poorly with Father Octavian. I mustn't vex him. There still may be some way to . . . to convince him to let us stay . . ." Her voice had a desperate, brittle edge to it that Alex had only ever heard in her mother's presence.

"Nicki . . ." He tightened his arms around her and kissed the back of her neck. "Don't dwell on this tonight, love."

"If I put my mind to it," she said shakily, "I can think of a way. I thought of the stewardship—I'll think of something else."

There was nothing else, of course—no magic scheme that would save her from homelessness and destitution. There was only Alex—and the oath he'd sworn to Milo. He was her only hope now.

"Yes, love," he murmured, nuzzling her. "You'll think of something. I'll help you. We'll think of something. 'Twill be all right."

"Say that again," she pleaded. Her shivers were worsening, although it was warm now in the cottage—almost too warm.

" 'Twill be all right," he whispered, and kissed her ear lightly. "Everything will be all right."

Her shoulders shook.

"Nicki?" Alex reached around to touch her cheek, damp with silent tears. "Nicki, Nicki . . ." He took the cup from her and set it on the floor, then rocked her, stroked her hair, her face, her throat. "Don't cry. I won't let any harm come to you."

"You can't prevent it," she said in a raw whisper.

"I can help." He could give her the child she longed

for, and save her from ruin in the bargain, if she would let him. And then it wouldn't matter who Father Octavian had bestowed the stewardship on, because Nicki and Milo would remain at Peverell. He wished he could tell her that. How he loathed the secrecy he was sworn to, even as he recognized its necessity. Despite Nicki's desperation, he knew she wouldn't cooperate with his true purpose.

"You help by being here. It comforts me to have you near, to feel your heat, your touch." Still weeping, she brought his palm to her mouth and kissed it. "I need that now. Just that. I've never needed it so much."

She lowered his hand, moving the mantle aside to press it to her upper chest. He felt the racing of her heart, the uneven rhythm of her breathing. Slowly she guided his hand lower still, beneath the mantle with its sleek lining, and over the trembling curve of a breast.

The room seemed to spin slowly. "Nicki . . . ?"

Her breath hitched; a hot teardrop fell on Alex's hand as she molded it to her breast, so impossibly warm, so round and perfect. She lightly stroked his fingers and the back of his hand. Knowing what she wanted, he caressed her as tenderly as she caressed him. Her nipple stiffened against his palm as he glided his fingertips over the irresistibly soft flesh.

Alex reeled with the joy of touching her this way, of knowing that she wanted him to. *It comforts me to feel your heat, your touch . . .*

It was comfort, just comfort—but the purest, most perfect kind. It was the comfort of another body next to one's own, someone's warm hand soothing, stroking, coaxing pleasure from pain.

Alex realized she wasn't shivering anymore.

With his free hand he gently eased the mantle off her shoulders, letting it pool at her waist. She was exquisite, slender and womanly, her skin luminous in the firelight. He held his breath, waiting for her to cover herself, but she merely closed her eyes and rested her hands on his updrawn knees.

"You're so beautiful, Nicki," he murmured, trailing the fingers of both hands over her breasts. "And I love you so much."

She laid her head back on his shoulder. He kissed her face and her hair as he touched her, delighting in her soft, spontaneous sighs.

Very slowly he slid one hand down over her flat belly, slipping it beneath the mantle that blanketed her from the waist down. She gripped his knees a little harder, but made no move to stop him as his fingers brushed soft curls.

Gradually he deepened his caress, thrilled to find her so wet, so ready. She wanted this. She wanted him.

He fondled her breasts more firmly as his intimate caress became more rhythmic, more purposeful. Her breathing grew harsh, her grip on his knees almost painful. She arched back against him, shaking.

Her sensual surrender was so sweet, and so unexpected. His body reacted predictably, swelling and rising as she writhed to his touch. With a groan, he pressed himself against her, instinctively seeking a joining, a completion.

Something cracked overhead, landing with a thud on the thatched roof. Nicki gasped and bolted upright. Alex gathered her in his arms. " 'Twas just a tree limb breaking in the wind."

"Oh, God." With quivering hands she yanked the mantle back up.

" 'Twas nothing, Nicki, just a—"

"What am I doing?" She wrested out of his grasp, pulling the mantle tight around her. "This is . . . God, I *am* weak. I'm just a—"

"You're not weak, Nicki—you're wonderful." Alex lowered her to the pallet as she tried to scramble away. "It's all right to want this . . . to need this."

"It's sinful," she said tearfully.

Alex took her damp face in his hands. "No real act of love is a sin, Nicki. I think you know that in your heart." He kissed her softly, tenderly. He'd never pressed his attentions on a weeping woman, but this was different. He could stop her tears forever, if only she would let him. She'd lost so much today. In her pain, she had forgotten her misgivings and reached out to him, knowing instinctively that his loving touch had the power to heal her.

"Let me love you, Nicki," he implored. " 'Twill make everything better—you'll see." It would—especially if their lovemaking bore fruit.

"It's . . . it's wrong."

"It's perfect." He dried her face with an edge of the mantle. "Look into your heart, Nicki. Doesn't it feel perfect?"

She closed her eyes. "Too perfect," she whispered raggedly.

"This was always meant to be," he whispered against her lips. "You know that. You feel it here," he said, resting a hand over her heart.

"Yes." She looked into his eyes. "Yes."

He kissed her while the tempest roared outside, and she kissed him back, drawing her arms out of the mantle to wrap them around him.

"I need to feel you," he said, loosening the mantle so that he could relish the soft weight of her breasts against his chest, the taut peaks of her nipples. They kissed again, Alex cupping her head with one hand while the other stole to a breast. She let him caress her until every breath was a sigh of pleasure, and when he reached down to push the rest of the mantle aside, she did not resist.

Alex untied his drawers and kicked them off, then rested his weight on her carefully. He was awed to be lying with her like this, to feel her naked beneath him. She felt so warm, so astonishingly right.

He settled against her, his body conforming per-

fectly to her, hips aligned, legs entwined, his rigid
length pressed against the soft juncture of her thighs.
He kissed her with all the tenderness at his disposal,
anxious to reassure her that this was good, that it was
right, that they should be together like this.

For some time he lay still atop her, but finally desire
overcame him, and he had to move. He did, but just
barely, his hips flexing slowly, measured strokes of his
aching flesh against hers. He knew she ached, because
she moaned when he thrust against her.

"Alex," she said in a wavering whisper.

"Don't be afraid of what you feel, Nicki." He
moved in a steady, deliberately slow rhythm, gradually
parting her, gliding against her slick heat. Reaching
down, he eased her thighs open and nestled snugly
between them. "Give in to it," he murmured,
throbbing with the need to bury himself in her, in pain
from the waiting.

Her breathing grew ragged, her gaze unfocused. She
whispered his name, and other things he couldn't
make out over the drumming of rain on the thatch.
Her fingernails bit into his shoulders, and he realized
she was lifting her hips to meet his.

It was too much. He was too close; there was no
turning back. His body tensed involuntarily as the crisis approached. "Let me inside," he whispered desperately, tucking his hands beneath her to tilt her hips.
"Nicki, let me in."

She threw her head back, a dark flush sweeping
over her face, and he knew she was as close to the
edge as he.

"Now, Nicki," he panted, shifting to seat the head
of his quivering sex in her. "God, Nicki, *please.*"

She moaned something.

"Nicki?"

"Yes. Oh, God, yes, Alex. Yes."

He groaned as he pushed into her, swore at the
excruciating pressure, the slippery walls of flesh so

tight around him, so perfect, too perfect, because he couldn't wait, he couldn't wait.

She cried out, bucking beneath him, her climax shuddering through her from within, squeezing his own pleasure out of him.

His body took over, arching, driving hard. He shouted as his seed discharged deep, deep inside her. Shocked at the violence of his release, he could only groan, over and over again, with each convulsive tremor.

They clung to each other, their breathless cries mingling as they rocked together, slower now, letting the pleasure subside, hearts thundering as one, their bodies at long last united, in harmony with their souls.

Chapter 22

"Wake up!" Gaspar swept Milo's bed curtains open and shook the drunken bag of bones until his teeth rattled. "Wake up, damn you."

"What?" Milo blinked, grimacing at the morning sunlight streaming in through the windows of the great hall. "Gaspar? What's the matter?"

Gaspar looked around and lowered his voice to avoid being heard by the breakfasting soldiers. "I think your wife may have run off with your cousin."

"What?" Milo struggled to sit upright. "Jesu!"

"That decrepit old maid of hers came downstairs a little while ago in a dither because her ladyship wasn't in her solar. Her bed was still turned down for the evening, and her night shift laid out. I just checked de Périgeaux's room, and his bed hadn't been slept in, either."

"I don't understand." Milo rubbed his forehead with a quavering hand. "Wasn't my wife at supper last night?"

"Nay." Gaspar sighed in irritation. As usual, Milo had passed out drunk toward the end of supper. His memory of recent events was getting worse and worse. "And neither was your cousin. They hadn't come back from their afternoon lesson, remember?"

Milo ran a hand over his mouth. "Where's my wine? Did you bring my wine?"

"Bloody hell! Do you think of nothing but your damned wine?"

"Nay. Not if I can help it."

Gaspar grabbed the bedpost and leaned in close. "Well, think about this, you worthless sot. Your wife and your cousin were last seen around noon, at dinner. Presumably they then met in the woods for their daily tumble under the guise of reading lessons. That storm hit in the late afternoon. You *do* remember the storm."

Milo frowned, as if trying to recall.

Gaspar spat out a ripe oath. "When they didn't show up for supper, it was assumed they'd gotten caught in the rain and sought shelter somewhere between the woods and here. They would have had their pick of places to stop—the mill, the church, a dozen different cottages. Everyone thought they'd show up eventually, and we all retired for the evening."

"Did you ask Edith whether she got my wife ready for bed?"

"Do you take me for a simpleton?" Gaspar demanded, a red fury mounting inside him. "Of course I asked her. And of course she doesn't remember. I'm trying to solve mysteries with the help of blithering thickwits who can't recall the last thought that passed through their moronic minds, and quite frankly, it's making me want to take both you and that crazy old bitch and slam your skulls together!"

"There's wine in the buttery, Gaspar." Milo licked his lips. "I'll concentrate better if I have some—"

"Does it ever occur to you," Gaspar asked softly, "that I might, from time to time, grow weary of playing errand boy to a pathetic wastrel who wants nothing more out of life than to lie in bed sucking on a wineskin as if it were his mother's teat? A creature who's handed over his castellany to one man and his wife to another? You make me sick."

Milo's rheumy gaze suddenly focused in a way that reminded Gaspar of the sharp-witted man he used to be. "I'll be damned. You despise me. I really had no idea."

Gaspar clenched his fists, striving for the pretense of civility when his very blood bubbled red-hot in his veins. "Of course I don't despise you, milord," he said tightly. "It's just that . . . well, my nerves are a bit frayed of late."

That was no more than the truth, of course. Yesterday there'd been that sealed letter from Father Octavian summoning Gaspar to his office tomorrow afternoon for more help with his "problem" in accordance with their "arrangement," and hinting that the assignment of stewardship to Gaspar could be ripped up and replaced with one naming the Lady Nicolette if Gaspar proved uncooperative. Appalled that what he'd thought would be a single afternoon of depravity was threatening to become an ongoing liaison, for pity's sake, and knowing he had no choice but to indulge the abbot, at least until the castellany was officially his, Gaspar had hovered since then between panic and rage.

And now Nicolette and Alex de Périgeaux had disappeared together. At best, they'd spent the night somewhere, which meant their passion had grown to the point where they risked discovery and disgrace just to tup undisturbed from dusk till dawn, a troubling complication; it would be so much simpler if de Périgeaux simply deposited his bastard in her belly and left, as Milo claimed he'd made his cousin vow to do.

That was the best possibility. At worst, they'd fled to parts unknown, a development that could devastate Gaspar's well-laid plan.

Either way, Peverell's young houseguest had ceased to be a mere irritant, and become instead a problem to be dealt with—a most vexing problem.

Gaspar smiled as the seeds of a solution to the problem of Alexandre de Périgeaux began to germinate in his mind. Best not to broach his idea to Milo while he was sober. And, too, Gaspar would be in a better position to gauge the extent of de Périgeaux's threat after he figured out where the devil they were.

"I can't believe it," Milo muttered. "I don't. Alex wouldn't have run off with her. 'Twould be dishonorable."

Gaspar laughed shortly. "He had no such compunctions nine years ago. You do know he tried to steal her away the night before your wedding."

Milo gazed at him with such stunned, watery eyes that Gaspar almost felt sorry for him. "Nay . . . I . . ." He rubbed his eyes. "I knew they'd been . . . in love. I mean, I know it now. But I didn't know . . . I had no idea he'd wanted her that badly." In a sudden flare of wrath, he snarled, "Bring me my goddamn wine and stop tormenting me, you son of a bitch."

Gaspar smirked. Big talk from a dissipated creature like Milo de St. Clair. "If he's talked her into running away with him, we may never find them. He's a clever bastard."

"They haven't run away," Milo persisted. "I made Alex swear an oath to leave here once she's pregnant and never seek her out again. I know him. He'll die before he breaks an oath. Nay, they've merely spent the night together—perhaps innocently. You mentioned a storm. Could be they got caught unawares, as you say, and—"

"Nay, they'd be back by now."

"You're assuming they were here, on our lands, when it started raining. Perhaps they were somewhere else, somewhere farther away."

Gaspar stared at Milo, astounded that such a revelation should come from the mouth of such a sorry sot. Of course. They might not have been in Peverell's woods at all when the skies opened up. And if not, he had a fairly good idea where they might have been.

"The abbey," Gaspar murmured.

"Quite right," Milo said. "She's friendly with that old . . . Where are you going?"

"To find them," Gaspar said as he walked away, "and . . . escort them home."

"What do you mean?" Milo called after him. "What are you going to—"

"Don't you want me to find them?" Gaspar asked over his shoulder.

"Aye, but I don't want any harm to come to Alex."

Gaspar just laughed; any other man would want the knave who was tupping his wife to have his balls cut off, his bowels ripped from his belly, and his head stuck on a pike. Gaspar didn't plan on going that far; after all, de Périgeaux still had to be able to get her ladyship with child, a critical component of his plan. But it wouldn't hurt to go out and meet the lovebirds on the path they'd be taking as they returned from the abbey, assuming they'd spent the night somewhere in that direction, which seemed increasingly likely. It should be little trouble to take Alex aside and explain a few things to him, using his efficient new mallet to reinforce his points—that his job was to impregnate Nicolette, not court her; that he ought to practice discretion and not make his seduction of her obvious to the world by keeping her out all night; and, above all, that he wasn't to let himself get so sweet on her that he'd decide he can't leave without her once his seed takes hold in her belly.

He thought about bringing Vicq and Leone along when he rode out to intercept the couple, but they tended to get carried away. He didn't want de Périgeaux's skull bashed in; he just wanted to teach him a lesson.

"Did you hear me?" Milo demanded in his quavering old man's voice. "I said I don't want any harm—"

"Wench!" Gaspar shouted to a serving girl just before he ducked into the stairwell. "Go to the buttery and bring his lordship some wine. Step lively!"

*   *   *

"I wish we could just turn around and run away,"
Nicki murmured against Alex's back as they traveled
along the wooded path that led to Peverell. She rode
pillion behind his saddle on Atlantes's blanketed back,
her arms around him, savoring his strength and
warmth through his soft linen shirt. Birds chortled
above the shadowy treetops. The morning was clear
and sunny, last night's storm having run its course, but
the ground beneath them was still saturated with rain;
she could smell it all around them.

"Me, too." Alex took a hand off the reins and covered one of hers. She felt his chest expand with a deep
sight. "Things have gotten . . ." He fell silent for a
moment, and then he brought her fingertips to his
mouth and kissed them. "At least we had last night."

"Mmm." And what a night it was. Nicki closed her
eyes, reliving the ecstacy of that first joining, the shock-
ing pleasure, the sense of completion, of all-consuming
bliss. Alex had groaned in pain as they separated, and
rubbed at his hip. She took over, gently massaging the
places he showed her until he sighed in relief. His
sighs turned to moans in response to her ministrations;
guiding her hand, he showed her another kind of healing touch, and then he pulled her on top of him and
showed her more. She'd delighted in the novelty of
the position, the unaccustomed sense of control, the
stimulation of looking down on him as he thrust into
her, of setting the pace by the movements of her hips.
They reached the zenith together, holding hands and
gazing into each other's eyes. Afterward, they'd slept
beneath his mantle, curled together in naked contentment.

"There's something I've been wondering about,"
she said hesitantly.

"Aye?"

"You didn't . . . that is, you told me once that when
you're with a woman, you generally . . . uncouple

before . . . and you didn't." She felt the muscles in his back tighten and regretted having broached the subject. Perhaps he felt ashamed of having lost control. The first time was so quick and explosive; how could he have had the presence of mind to withdraw? And the second time, she'd been on top, and it had been the last thing on her mind. " 'Twas foolish of me to bring it up," she said. "Forget I—"

" 'Tisn't foolish," he said, patting her hand. "Never think that. Of course you're concerned about . . . what may happen. It's perfectly understandable."

Alex must be concerned as well. Nicki knew he didn't want children; he dreaded the prospect.

"Believe it or not," she said, "Milo would probably be delighted if I became pregnant. He actually wanted me to bear another man's child in order to keep Peverell." She waited for Alex's response; none was forthcoming. Had she been hoping, deep inside, that he'd changed his mind about children, and desired one, from her?

Idiot. He'd been clear enough, on more than one occasion, about not wanting to sire offspring. *The last thing in the world I want is for the women I bed to bear my bastards.* She knew she wasn't just any woman he'd bedded. But, with a mental shake, she reminded herself that a bastard was the last thing she wanted growing in her belly. "I couldn't have whored myself, of course, even for such a cause. And if I had, everyone would have known the babe wasn't Milo's. That wasn't the way, and it still isn't."

Alex was silent, most likely appalled by the sordidness of Milo's scheme.

"If you don't want to . . . uncouple," she said, "I'll find another way. I'll ask Agatha, the midwife."

"Nay!"

"Whyever not?"

His answer was slow in coming. "Midwives are notorious gossips. You wouldn't want it getting out that you've been asking about . . . preventing babies. Everyone knows you and Milo want a son."

Nicki considered this. "I'll talk to Edith, then. She knows about such things."

"But mightn't she be indiscreet as well?"

"Edith? She can't remember things from one moment to the next. Nay, she won't talk. And she knows about the various . . . techniques. Some of them, anyway. She's the one who told me about the womb of the she-goat—"

"Sweet Jesus."

"And the herbs."

"Herbs," he said thoughtfully.

"Herbs that a woman can tie in a bundle around her neck—"

"Ah, yes," he said, brightening. "I remember. Yes, I think you ought to try the herbs."

His fervor said it all; he was adamant about not siring children. "All right," she said, fighting her absurd sense of disappointment. "I'll talk to Edith as soon as we get back."

They rode for some time in silence. "I need to tell you something," he finally said, squeezing her hand as he walked Atlantes along the muddy track. "Last night was unlike anything I've ever known. I want you to know that, Nicki. That it wasn't just . . ." He sighed again, in evident frustration at the inadequacy of words. "In the past, the sport of love has been just that to me—a game, a merry pastime. It's never been like it was last night. It felt magical, as if we were one being, with one soul and one body."

"Aye." That sense of communion with him, of connection on a higher plane, had overwhelmed Nicki's initial misgivings. How could something that felt so right, so intrinsically perfect, be sinful? She knew in her heart that their love was good and pure, and that knowledge had freed her to revel in their lovemaking.

A low, masculine chuckle tickled her ear. "Not that

it was a purely spiritual experience. Just remembering how it felt to be inside you makes me want to throw you on the ground and toss your skirts up."

As if to prove his point, he slid her hand beneath his shirt and pressed it to his manhood, distended beneath his snug woollen chausses. She shaped her hand around the thick organ, recalling the sense of invasion, of being split open, that first time, when he'd impaled her so hard and fast. He'd apologized afterward, fearful of having hurt her, but she'd assured him there was no need for contrition. The discomfort of being so rudely engorged had been lost in the astonishing pleasure he gave her. Never had she known such gratification.

She stroked him the way he'd shown her last night, remembering the second time, with her on top. He'd cautioned her to lower herself onto him slowly, gripping her hips to ensure this. Still, she'd felt stretched almost beyond endurance, and was awed at the sense of fullness once he was buried within her.

Nicki grew warm, musing on last night's lovemaking. Her breath quickened along with Alex's as she fondled him. Presently he reined in Atlantes and slid his right foot from the stirrup. "Put your foot in the stirrup," he told her.

She did as he asked. Turning toward her and shifting his weight, he caught her about the waist and swept her onto his lap, seating her sideways. Atlantes swung his big head around, regarding them with an expression of mild curiosity.

"That's better," Alex murmured, dropping the reins and prodding Atlantes into a walk again with a squeeze of his thighs. Cupping the back of her head, he closed his mouth over hers, while with his free hand he kneaded her breasts restlessly, tugging at her nipples in a way that sent currents of arousal crackling through her. He broke the kiss, gasping her name as he tilted her head back to kiss her throat. Whipping her skirts up, he reached between her thighs and slid a finger deep inside her, growling with satisfaction to find her already wet.

He ground himself against her, moaning. His desperation was contagious. She held his head still for another fierce kiss and closed her hand over his erection, caressing him through the tightly stretched wool with the firm pressure he seemed to like.

He kept his finger inside her, stroking her slowly, the pleasure building gradually but inexorably, intensified by the gentle jogging of the animal beneath them. They writhed in rhythm with each other and the horse's leisurely gait, their breath coming in harsh pants, lost in their spiraling pleasure.

Atlantes broke into a trot, jarring them out of their sensual reverie. Hissing a curse, Alex held Nicki tight and grabbed the reins, tugging on them to halt the confused beast, who's apparently misinterpreted some movement of theirs as a command to speed up.

Laughing breathlessly, Nicki said, "That was exciting."

"The excitement's not over." Gripping her waist, Alex lowered her to the ground.

The narrow dirt path squished wetly underfoot. "Alex, if you mean what I think you mean—"

"That I must have you now or go mad?" He dismounted and swiftly tethered Atlantes to a branch. "That's precisely what I mean."

"What about the herbs?"

He stalked toward her, eyeing her wolfishly. "I'm afraid I can't wait for them."

She backed up swiftly. "But the ground is all muddy. 'Twill ruin my tunic."

"Your tunic will be fine." Seizing her by the shoulders, he backed her up against a gigantic old oak at the edge of the path. "Raise your skirt."

Startled but excited by the brusque command, she

clutched her skirt in both hands and pulled it up to her thighs.

He yanked at the drawstring of his chausses. "Higher." Freeing himself, he lifted her against the tree. She clutched his shoulders and wrapped her legs around his waist, hitching her breath in when he pressed her open.

"Oh, God, Nicki, you're so tight." Supporting her hips with an iron grip, he shoved himself a little further in, pausing to let her adjust to him.

Already on the brink of release, Nicki moaned at the sweet, burning pressure of him inside her. Her heart pounded wildly as he filled her. They groaned in unison when he sank in completely.

Dipping his head down, he closed his lips over a stiff nipple, sucking so hard she could feel the warmth and wetness of his mouth through her tunic and shift. She gasped when he bit her, the sharp pressure of his teeth sending her over the edge, into a heart-stopping climax.

She heard her own hoarse cry of fulfillment as the pleasure rocked through her. A grouse raced from the brush with a furious thumping of wings.

Alex moaned her name as he drove into her, his pace growing faster, less steady, more urgent. His fingers dug hard into her hips, the muscles of his shoulders tightening beneath her hands.

"I love you, Nicki," he rasped. He looked up and met her gaze, sweat-dampened hair hanging in his eyes, his expression desperate, almost sad. "I'm sorry. I didn't know we'd fall in love. I didn't."

At a loss for words, she kissed him. He hammered into her with furious abandon, driven by this inexplicable sorrow that had befallen him. Abruptly he stilled, his body taut and quivering, his expression almost anguished. She felt a frenzied throbbing inside her, and then the air left his lungs in a low, guttural moan.

She expected him to withdraw from her and set her down. Instead, still holding her against the tree, he lowered his head to the crook of her neck and whispered her name. His face was hot and damp against her throat, his ragged breath ticklish.

His sudden shift in mood perplexed her. It was true—all too sadly true—that she and Alex had no future together. She was a married woman; Alex was still a soldier, with no desire for a home or attachments. The futility of their love—and the knowledge that it must come to an end—was a burden she carried constantly in her heart, alongside the joy of loving him. Yet never had she thought to see Alex, with his lighthearted temperament, stricken with melancholy over anything, even the aching hopelessness of their love. The possibility that he might care as much as she did astounded her.

Alex jerked his head up and stared toward the path.

"Alex, what—"

"Shh!" He listened for another moment, frowning in concentration. Nicki's chest grew tight when she saw that his eyes were wet. "Someone's coming."

"Are you sure?" she asked as he carefully drew himself out of her and lowered her to the ground.

"Yes." He swiftly tied his chausses and wiped his eyes with his shirtsleeve. Nicki brushed damp bits of bark off the back of her skirt and arranged her loose hair to cover the wet spot Alex's mouth had made on the bodice of her tunic.

"Could it be bandits?" she asked.

"Unlikely—they usually travel on foot, and it sounds like a lone man on horseback. But I want you to stay out of sight." He led her behind the big oak.

"I hear it now."

Hoofbeats approached from the direction they'd been heading, slowing down as the horseman rode into sight.

"It's just Gaspar," Nicki whispered, but when she

tried to step out from behind the tree, Alex restrained her with his arm.

"Wait."

"Why?" But she stayed put, watching along with Alex as Gaspar dismounted and tethered his mount next to Atlantes. He rubbed his chin as he walked slowly around Milo's sorrel gelding, and then he peered this way and that way into the surrounding woods.

Alex backed her farther behind the concealing tree.

"Why are we hiding?" Nicki asked. "Gaspar knows you've been riding Atlantes. He's looking for you."

Gaspar reached beneath his mantle and withdrew his mallet.

"So it would seem." Alex unsheathed his sword.

"Jesus have mercy," Nicki whispered. "What on earth—"

"Stay here." Before Nicki could object, Alex crept off through the trees, keeping himself to Gaspar's back, his footsteps eerily silent. Clearly, his reputation for stealth was well deserved. Circling around his prey, he came up behind Gaspar on the path and touched the tip of his sword to the back of his neck. "Looking for me?"

Gaspar stood motionless for a long moment, the head of the mallet resting on the ground. "My lord Milo sent me to find you . . . and his lady wife."

Nicki bit her lip, wondering how many people knew she'd been gone all night with Alex.

Alex said, "I seem to recall an oath I made once, on the relic in this very sword, to do away with you if you ever came at me with that bloody thing again."

"I haven't tried to use it against you, have I?"

"Nay, nor will you. Throw it that way." Alex pointed so that Gaspar could see, toward the woods on the other side of the path from Nicki. "As hard as you can."

"You don't trust me?"

"Why the devil should I?"

Gaspar gripped the mallet with both fists, his eyes as flat and lifeless as Nicki had ever seen them, his mouth curving in a predatory smile. She was about to call out a warning to Alex, but it wasn't necessary. Before Gaspar could act on his impulse, Alex twisted the sword slightly, which made Gaspar wince. Swearing colorfully, he hurled the mallet into the woods.

"Where's Lady Nicolette?" Gaspar asked.

Still holding the sword on Gaspar, Alex said, "She's no concern of yours. Be gone."

Gaspar walked up to his horse and turned to face Alex. "I came to tell you to be more discreet. It won't do, you staying out all night with her. People will—"

"Don't you presume to tell me what to do," Alex said.

"What of her ladyship's reputation?"

"Why should it damage her reputation to take shelter from a storm?"

Gaspar smiled salaciously. "Are you saying that's all that went on last night, after the way you and she have been—"

Alex advanced on Gaspar in two strides, pressing his sword so hard against the big man's throat that he had to bend backward against his horse to keep from being cut; fear widened Gaspar's eyes. Nicki stared in unblinking fascination. This was a side of her easygoing Alex she'd never seen—the veteran mercenary soldier who could open a man's throat with a flick of his wrist.

"Who in Hades do you think you are?" Alex demanded in a low, fierce voice. "If you ever again dare to imply such things about her ladyship, in anyone's hearing, you'll answer to my steel. And believe me," he added with bared teeth, stepping closer to slide the edge of the blade lightly across Gaspar's throat, "I'll relish the excuse to slice you open." He stepped back. "Now, get out of here."

Gaspar licked his lips nervously. "I need to get my mallet first."

"You can get it later."

Bested, Gaspar mounted up. Apparently it gave him confidence to be on horseback, because he said, "I wasn't planning on coming back this way today. Be a good fellow and fetch it for me. I can do you no damage with it from up here."

"You overstep yourself, asking me to fetch for you."

A tide of red rose up Gaspar's neck; he glared at Alex with a loathing that chilled Nicki. Alex's comment had reminded Gaspar of his station, increasingly a sore spot with him. For the first time ever, she felt truly afraid of him.

"You *will* be coming back this way later today," Alex informed him. "I want you to bring a cart and fetch her ladyship's mare. She's dead in the stream about a mile from the abbey."

Gaspar's chin jutted out. "I don't take orders from you, de Périgeaux."

"But you still take them from me." Nicki stepped out from behind a tree, to Alex's obvious displeasure.

Gaspar blinked at her. "My lady. If I'd known you were there, I wouldn't have said . . . I—"

"You wouldn't have insulted me to my face, only behind my back, is that it?"

The red stain spread up Gaspar's throat to his face. His gaze lit on Nicki's hair, hanging loose, and her wrinkled tunic. All too aware of the dampness between her thighs, she felt much the same under his scrutiny as she had twelve years ago, after losing her innocence to Philippe in the stable. But she was no longer a cowed sixteen-year-old girl, and she'd be damned if she'd surrender to her fear of this man.

"Make no mistake, Gaspar," she said. "The only reason I don't dismiss you today is that you've been assigned the stewardship of Peverell in the event my husband and I are obliged to relinquish the castellany. 'Twould anger Father Octavian if I were to remove you now, and I must endeavor to remain on good terms with him. But don't think you can push me any farther than you already have. Any more insolence from you and I'll toss you out on your ear. Or perhaps," she added with a small smile, "I'll hand you over to Alex."

Alex smiled at her in a way that suggested she'd impressed him. She felt ridiculously proud.

Gaspar regarded her stonily.

"When you come back for Marjolaina," she told him, "bring a sling and plenty of rope—and a couple of strong men, fellows who aren't afraid to work. Not those worthless curs of yours—dependable men. She's heavy."

Gaspar bowed, his jaw set. "As you wish, milady."

"Good day, Gaspar," she said in dismissal.

"Good day, milady." Turning to Alex, he added, perhaps as a parting shot, "Young sir."

Kicking his mount, he thundered off down the path.

Chapter 23

"Where have you been?" Milo called out the next evening as Gaspar entered the great hall.

Gritting his teeth, Gaspar turned to face the desiccated creature in the bed. "At the abbey."

"So late?"

"Father Octavian . . . needed my help with something, and it took longer than expected."

"You missed supper."

"I wouldn't have had the appetite for it." Not after this afternoon. Gaspar's hands curled into fists as he fought back the urge to fly into a mindless, screaming rage. He didn't know how much more of this he could take. He wanted to strangle all of them—Octavian, Nicolette, Milo, and most of all Alex de Périgeaux, whose reappearance after all these years had ruined everything. If not for him, Gaspar could have gone ahead with his original plan to dose Nicolette's wine and sire a child on her unawares. As it was, he was now forced to wait, playing Milo's compliant retainer and Father Octavian's . . . was there even a word for the role he performed behind the locked door of the abbot's office? How much longer would this have to go on before de Périgeaux's seed took root and he could implement the next phase of his revised plan?

"I was waiting for you," Milo said. "I wanted some wine, and those two won't bring me any." He nodded toward de Périgeaux and Nicolette, playing chess at the high table; but for them, the great hall was empty.

Gaspar fetched Milo the wine and poured it down his throat until he was good and soused. Drunkenness made him more receptive to Gaspar's notions, and the time had come to broach his idea regarding the problem of Alex de Périgeaux.

Softly, so as not to be heard by the couple across the hall, he said, "From the looks of it, they fancy themselves in love."

Milo gazed toward his wife and cousin with a thoughtful, rather melancholic expression, and then drained his goblet.

"Has it occurred to you," Gaspar asked as he poured a refill, "that she may not be content to remain here with you once she's carrying his child in her belly? He may find it easier to talk her into running off with him this time. Then where would you be? With no heir to inherit Peverell, you'd be cast out of here and begging on the streets before you know it."

Milo's head wobbled as he shook it. "Won't happen," he slurred. "Alex won't go back on his oath—I told you. And my wife would never go along with it. 'Twould ruin her precious reputation—and she'd be giving up Peverell. Never happen."

"You can't be sure of that."

"I am sure." Milo swallowed some more wine and wiped his mouth with the back of his hand. "I know them both—better'n you do. They'll do what's right if it kills 'em."

"Perhaps," Gaspar murmured, glancing at Nicolette and Alex as they laughed over something. "But what if they don't? People have been known to act contrary to their natures—especially in matters of the heart. What if he convinces her to follow him back to England?"

"Why should you care?" Milo's gaze was remarkably astute, considering his condition. "You get to stay on here no matter what happens. Nicolette told me

you got Father Octavian to name you steward. How'd
you talk him into it?"

Talk? He wished all it had taken was talk. Gaspar
chose to ignore Milo's second query and answer the
first. "I care because I'd rather serve as your retainer
than as Father Octavian's steward."

"Is it because of his . . . inclinations?"

Gaspar stiffened.

"They say he's a sodomite." Milo took another
drink, staring at Gaspar. His gaze when he lowered
the goblet was too knowing. "How'd you say you
talked him into naming you steward?"

"It didn't take much talking." Gaspar wanted to
punch that blearily smug look off of Milo's face. "He
wanted a military man for the job. I was the best
candidate."

"I see."

"But as I say, I'd rather serve you than him,"
Gaspar said smoothly, eager to make his point and
deflect the conversation from its present course.
"Which will be impossible if your cousin absconds
with your wife. We must prevent that."

"I assume you have a plan." Milo lifted the goblet
to his mouth. "You always have a plan."

Gaspar glanced around to make sure no servant or
soldier was creeping about. "He could take ill and . . .
keel over dead. It happens all the time."

Milo lowered the goblet slowly, his incredulous gaze
trained on Gaspar. "Nay."

Gaspar leaned closer. "Poison hemlock and white
hellebore. Very difficult to detect in spiced wine."

"Nay!"

"No one need ever know. And I wouldn't do it till
she's with child, of course—"

"*Nay!* He's my cousin, for God's sake."

"This is not the time for sentimentality," Gaspar
said between clenched teeth. "The man is a menace."

Milo sat upright for the first time all day, scowling

in astonishment. "You're telling me you want to murder an innocent man with poison, and you say *he's* the menace?"

"Innocent? He talked your wife into betraying you."

"Because I asked him to!"

"You asked him to seduce her body, not her heart. You never asked him to woo her like some moonstruck youth. You never asked him to steal her away from you."

"Alex is not going to steal Nicolette away from me."

"Your faith in him is quite touching," Gaspar said snidely, "but potentially disastrous. Spare his life and you'll end up sorry."

"I'm already sorry." Milo sank back against his pillows, a sad-eyed living corpse. "Sorrier than I can say, for ever having relied on you . . . for letting you insinuate yourself into our lives this way."

Gaspar backtracked swiftly, wary of losing Milo's trust in him too soon. He needed that trust for a little while longer. "I can't tell you how those words sting, milord." He lowered his head contritely. "I'd kill myself before I'd relinquish your confidence. What I said, about the poison . . . 'twas my concern for you, and our position here, that prompted such a rash idea."

"You won't do it, will you?" Milo demanded. "You won't go behind my back—"

"Nay, of course not!" Gaspar said, reinforcing the denial with what he hoped was a credible expression of outrage. " 'Twas just an idea, nothing more, and a foolish one. I'd never dream of going against your wishes." Not until Lady Nicolette was pregnant, at any rate. Until then, he must bide his time and put on as convincing a display of servile obedience as he could stomach—while keeping a close watch on her ladyship, lest she cook up any more clever schemes for keeping Peverell. He must not abandon his practice of following her if she rode away unescorted, especially at odd hours. So far the practice had proved most enlightening.

"Good," Milo said, but Gaspar saw it all in his eyes—the skepticism, the apprehension. He knew, or at least suspected, the truth—that Gaspar would do what Gaspar saw fit, regardless of Milo's instructions.

Gaspar might almost have been worried if he thought there was a possibility that Milo would remember any of this tomorrow.

"You're troubling yourself over nothing, milord," Gaspar soothed, pouring some more wine into his master's goblet. "Drink up and get a good night's sleep, and you'll feel ever so much better in the morning. I feel certain of it."

Chapter 24

Alex looked up from his tablet to study Nicki as she fetched their apple cider from the stream, where it was cooling. He loved watching her—her graceful walk, the restrained elegance of her movements as she flipped her braids out of the way, then crouched and pulled the string attached to the flagon of cider.

A leaf spun down from the forest canopy above and landed on his tablet. Sitting up, he lifted it by its stem and twirled it. It was the pale red of claret, with just a smudge of rust near the tip. Dozens of similar brightly hued leaves littered their blanket, strewn by a breeze that had grown inexorably cooler over the past few weeks.

At Hauekleah, Faithe would be preparing for next week's harvest feast to celebrate Michaelmas, the twenty-ninth of September, which marked the official beginning of winter on their Cambridgeshire farmstead. Faithe would supervise her staff as they decorated the barn with the last of the wheat sheaves. During the feast, she and Luke—and probably Robert and Hlynn—would dance in a circle with their devoted villeins, to the accompaniment of cowbells, tambourines, and reed flutes.

Closing his eyes, Alex could almost hear it. It had its own distinctive sound, the music of the Saxon peasants—whimsical and mellow and so oddly compelling that he only had to hear a tune once and it was burned into his memory.

Christ, but he missed England. He missed Luke and Faithe, and of course the children, terribly, but most of all he just missed England—the lush green smell of it, the damp richness of the soil, the robust people and their powerful connection to the land. Not that he'd been dwelling on it during his stay in Normandy; had it really been nearly three months already? He'd had other things on his mind, to be sure, and there could be no sweeter diversion than Nicki. But sometimes, as now, something would remind him of things English and he would feel an empty longing deep in his chest.

"What are you thinking of?"

Alex opened his eyes to find Nicki lowering herself to the blanket; she sat facing him, her knees touching his comfortably.

"England."

Nicki nodded. She knew how he felt. He told her everything—everything he wasn't bound by oath to conceal from her. They talked endlessly, here in their secluded haven by the stream, when they weren't bending their heads over their lessons or making love beneath the sheltering trees.

She uncorked the clay bottle and handed it to him. It was wet and cool; the cider filled his mouth with its special sweetness, the taste of autumn. He passed the bottle back to her. She took a sip and recorked it. Without looking up, she said, in a soft, reticent voice, "You'll be back in England for Christmas."

It was unlike Nicki to bring this up. By tacit agreement, they never spoke of the future. But then, for almost a fortnight now, she had seemed unusually subdued. Perhaps it was the change of seasons that affected her so. Winter was coming, and by the time its grip was fully upon the land, Alex would be gone.

He took the bottle out of her hand and set it aside, then pulled her onto his lap and cradled her head against his chest. Kissing her hair, he murmured, "When we're forced to part, I will miss you far, far more than I miss England now."

"You'll have other things to think about than me," she said. "You'll be back in the king's service."

"Soldiering doesn't excite me anymore," he said. "You excite me."

"Aye, but you like the freedom of that life—you once told me so. No estate to maintain, no wife and children to be responsible for. You'll stop thinking about me—"

"Never! I'll think of you every hour of every day, until the moment I die. Never doubt that."

She clung to him, and he to her. They held each other tightly, almost fiercely, for quite a long time.

"We shouldn't dwell on your leaving," she said, stroking his cheek. "We still have two months until you have to return to England."

Unless she quickened with his child, in which case he was obliged by his oath to leave immediately. As much as he wanted to give her a son—both to bring her joy and to save her from destitution—he dreaded their inevitable separation.

"What were you writing?" she asked, with a cheerfulness he knew must be feigned.

With a sheepish grin, Alex handed her the tablet, on which he'd painstakingly scratched out *Alexandre de Périgeaux loves Nikolet de Saint Clar.*

Her smile of delight warmed his heart. Locking her arms around his neck, she kissed him soundly.

"Nicolette de St. Clair loves Alexandre de Périgeaux," she whispered, rubbing her cheek against his. "And I'm so proud that you've learned how to write."

"My spelling is abysmal," he said. "Did I get your name right?"

"Almost. I'll show you how to spell it correctly, and then perhaps you can write to me after you return to England."

Alex looked away, remembering that blasted oath . . . *You'll keep your true purpose from Nicolette, and when it's done, you'll leave here and never contact her again—or the child.*

"Do you know I love you?" he asked, drawing her close.

"Aye."

"Do you really know it, all the way into your soul?"

She looked at him, her eyes like clear pools in the cool forest light. "My melancholy has rubbed off on you. I'm sorry."

" 'Tisn't your fault. Our humors are unbalanced."

She touched her forehead to his. "How shall we realign them?"

He smiled. "I think I know a way."

She returned his smile. "Do you?"

He glided his fingertips lightly over both breasts. Her nipples grew taut beneath the soft white wool of her tunic.

"Yes," she breathed, shifting to straddle him as they sat facing each other. "I believe you do."

He raised her skirt and reached beneath it; she opened his chausses. Amid whisper-soft kisses and breathless sighs, they sought each other's warmth, their caresses lingering and gentle, as if they had all the time in the world, their bodies swaying in a slow dance of passion. When, at long last, he came into her, so slick and tight, he moaned in utter helplessness. No woman had ever fit him the way Nicki did; no woman had ever been part of him. How would he find the strength to leave her when the time came?

They kissed as the dance continued, the lazy, measured cadence of it intensifying the sensations, deepening the pleasure of their joining. Alex untied the cord that laced up Nicki's tunic in front and loosened it. He tugged at the sleeves, lowering the gown to her waist and helping her to slide her arms free. But as he tucked his fingers beneath the straps of her undershift, he noticed something. "You've forgotten your herbs again."

Old Edith had made her up a tiny bundle of herbs that Nicki wore around her neck beneath her tunic whenever they were together. She wore them to prevent conception, but Alex had never known such methods to work. Their true purpose, as he saw it, was to lull Nicki into thinking there was no need for him to withdraw when they made love.

Nicki touched her chest absently. "Ah, yes. I did forget them." For a moment she just looked at him, her expression pensive, as if there were something she wanted to say. Presently, her gaze sobering, she reached behind her for her saddlebags, retrieved the bundle on its leather thong, and hung it around her neck.

This was the second time in the past week that she'd forgotten about it. Alex wondered if, perhaps, she secretly wanted to get pregnant, despite the damage to her reputation. Or perhaps it was simply that she'd been out of sorts lately.

He trailed the back of his hand lightly down her face and throat. "Do you want to talk?"

There was a glimmer of something when she met his gaze, but it was quickly extinguished. "Nay." Locking her gaze with his, she hooked her thumbs under the straps of her shift and lowered the delicate undergarment past her breasts. Alex throbbed inside her, excited by this small gesture simply because she was so bashful about undressing in front of him. He loved to watch women remove their clothes just for him, and had asked her several times to do so, only to be shyly rebuffed.

Her rosy little nipples hovered tantalizingly close to his mouth. He leaned toward one, but she whispered, "Wait." She removed the embroidered sash looped over her hips and set it aside. Gathering up her tunic and shift, she pulled both garments off over her head, leaving herself in nothing but her stockings and slippers. High color blossomed on her cheeks; she bit her lip. Alex didn't know whether to laugh at her silly modesty or weep with his aching love for her.

"Nicki, you're the most beautiful woman I've ever seen." It was true. Her body had a delicacy to it, a lissome grace, that was unequaled in his experience. Her breasts were extraordinary, not large, but high and firm and perfectly round—so warm in his hands, so sweet in his mouth. He'd never seen a narrower waist, more supple legs.

Seeing her this way, naked in her braids and stockings while he, fully clothed, was buried deep inside her, aroused him intensely. She raised herself almost until they uncoupled, then lowered herself; and again, and again. The sight of his sex gliding in and out of her undid him. Moaning, he gripped her hips and tried to set a quicker pace, but she seized his hands to prevent that and resumed her maddeningly slow lovemaking.

He captured a nipple in his mouth and suckled as she moved sinuously, her eyes closed, her head back, her breath coming faster, faster. Fulfillment approached all too swiftly. Alex groaned, partly in despair that it should end so soon, and partly because of the escalating pleasure that held him in its grip. He held off as long as he could, shuddering as he strove to make it last. When she cried out with her release, it was all over.

"Oh, Nicki. Oh, God." Holding her tight, he exploded with a suddenness that stole his breath. An anguished cry shattered the stillness of the woods, and he realized, as his climax ebbed, that it had come from him—or perhaps from both of them, together.

He gathered her in his arms, rocking her and murmuring endearments as if it were she who needed comfort, when in fact his very soul ached with the dread of losing her. "I love you, Nicki. I'll love you until the end of time. Only you, always and forever. Only you."

"Agatha?" Nicki whispered as she stood at the door

of a humble cottage on the outskirts of St. Clair early that evening. "Are you home?" She glanced around again to make sure no one saw her here. Luckily, this was a fairly remote area with few other dwellings nearby. And, too, at this hour most folks were indoors preparing their suppers, or eating them.

The deerskin covering the doorway parted, and the midwife's red, fleshy face emerged. "Go away, I'm in the middle of—" Agatha gasped when she saw who her company was. "Milady! Come in, come in!"

The corpulent woman, dressed in a homespun tunic and apron, with a rag around her head, stepped aside so that Nicki could squeeze through the doorway. The smoky one-room cottage was redolent with boiled onions and the fragrance of the many bundles of dried herbs hanging from the rafters. Agatha waved a fat arm toward an iron kettle hanging over the fire pit. "Onion stew, milady. Would you care for some?"

"No, thank you." Nicki followed Agatha's gaze to a heaping bowl of the stuff set out on the table, along with a chunk of black bread and a wooden cup filled with wine. "I can't stay long. But please go ahead and eat. You mustn't miss your supper on my account."

Grunting her thanks, the midwife crammed her massive body between the table and the bench and sat down with a great sigh. "Some wine, at least?"

"No. Thank you all the same."

Breaking off a piece of bread, Agatha said, "I haven't seen your ladyship since that kitchen wench of yours bore them twins. Has someone else at Peverell got herself with child?"

Nicki drew in a calming breath and let it out slowly. "I think perhaps I have."

"Milady!" Agatha exclaimed, her words muffled by the bread she'd stuffed into her mouth. "At last! That's wonderful! What a blessing! It's . . ." She trailed off, chewing thoughtfully as she studied Nicki's subdued demeanor. Swallowing, she washed the bread down with a generous gulp of wine. "Have a seat, milady."

Nicki sat down at the table, wishing Agatha's mother were still alive. Old Ila had been quiet, competent, and above all, discreet—the perfect midwife. It was she who had tended to Nicki when she miscarried so brutally and fell into that terrible fever. If not for Ila's considerable skill, Nicki might have died. And, if not for her discretion, she might have been ruined.

Her daughter was of a different breed—not inept, but a good deal less troubled with the more sensitive aspects of her vocation. The women of St. Clair knew better than to disclose confidences to Agatha, lest their neighbors hear it all within days.

"Am I to take it," Agatha asked, stirring her stew, "that this pregnancy isn't cause for celebration?" A rather artless way of asking whether the child had been sired by someone other than Milo. Of course Agatha would suspect this, regardless of Nicki's comportment. After all, her marriage had been barren for nine years.

Nicki smiled, mostly to allay the midwife's suspicions, although deep in her heart she was elated by the possibility—in fact, the likelihood—that she carried Alex's child in her womb. She shouldn't be; all of Normandy would share Agatha's suspicions. But she couldn't help it. To be pregnant at last—with Alex's child!—filled her with a deep and elemental joy that the circumstances could not diminish.

The fact that such a child, if it happened to be a boy, would save her and Milo from homelessness was not lost on her. She was grateful to God for what was likely a late reprieve, despite the probable blemish to her reputation.

Striving for circumspection, Nicki said, "Of course I would celebrate if I'm truly with child. My lord husband and I have waited nine long years for this."

Agatha spooned a whole onion into her mouth and

chewed it, regarding Nicki with eyes that were just this side of shrewd. "Because, of course," she said, swallowing, "if you weren't pleased about it, I could take care of it for you."

Nicki spread her hand over her belly in an automatic gesture of protectiveness. "Nay, that's not why I came here. I—"

"Just so's you know," the midwife said around another mouthful of stew, "there's no need to be bearin' babes that will do naught but bring heartache down on you. I can give you a tonic that will oust the infant from your womb."

"Agatha, I really don't want—"

"Because you're frightened." Reaching across the table, Agatha patted Nicki's hand. "You've heard the stories about such tonics. I won't lie to you. 'Tisn't a pleasant process, losin' a babe that way. 'Twill pain you somethin' fierce—but then, so will the birthin', and—"

"I don't want one of your tonics!" Nicki cried, rising from the table. "I want this baby! I've wanted this baby forever. How can you think—"

"Calm yourself, milady." Bracing her hands on the table, Agatha heaved herself to her feet.

"I think I'd better go."

"Nay, stay! I misunderstood, milady. You were just so solemn-like, I thought . . . but I was wrong, and I won't bring it up again."

Somewhat mollified, Nicki sat down. It stood to reason that Agatha would be confused about Nicki's feelings when Nicki herself felt so torn. For all the gladness it brought her to think that Alex's baby might be growing in her belly, the inescapable truth was that it would bring no happiness to Alex. He'd never made any secret of the fact that he didn't want any bastards. Indeed, he'd gone to considerable pains to avoid siring any. Although she'd suspected for the better part of a fortnight that she was with child, she had hesitated to tell him, knowing how distressed he would be, and hating to cast a pall over what little time they had together.

On top of Alex's inevitable dismay, there was the fact that this child was the product of adultery. Milo wouldn't care—he'd most likely be thrilled—but there would be whispers, perhaps outright censure. Would people think she'd given herself to another man simply to hold on to Peverell? She'd go mad if she thought about that now.

And why should she? Perhaps she was jumping to conclusions. "I'm not even completely sure I'm pregnant," she told the midwife.

Agatha crumbled the remains of her bread into the bowl. "When did your last purgation befall you?"

"On the tenth day of August." Nicki recalled her mixture of relief and disappointment when her flow arrived on the expected day. " 'Twas due again September seventh, but it didn't come."

"Two weeks ago," Agatha muttered as she stirred the bread and stew into an unsavory gray mess. "Are your menses ever late?"

"Never."

"You've never been pregnant before, have you?"

"Nay," Nicki lied.

"Have you suffered at all from stomach ailments? Any vomiting or fluxes? Choler? Putrefied humors?"

"I feel woozy from time to time."

"Let me know if you begin vomiting excessively," the midwife advised, slurping up her stew and bread mixture. "I'll make you up a binding medicine. Are your breasts tender?"

"A bit."

"Any little pains near your womb, as if someone's sticking a needle in you?"

"Aye," Nicki said. "Quite a bit of that."

Agatha smiled as she chewed. "I hope you're telling the truth when you say you want to be with child, 'cause from the sound of it, there's a child that wants to be with you."

Nicki couldn't help returning the midwife's smile, but it faded when she remembered how her other pregnancy had ended. Indeed, she'd sought Agatha out this early in large part for advice on how to avoid another miscarriage—but of course, she mustn't let on that she'd ever had one. "Are there ways of helping to keep the babe tight in the womb? I've waited so long for this. I'd hate for anything to happen."

"I'll give you a powder to cook with honey and put in your wine," Agatha offered as she scooped up the last of her stew. " 'Tis excellent at preventing such a mishap. But the most important thing to remember," she cautioned, stabbing her spoon in the air to emphasize the point, "is never to ask for something which cannot be had. For if it is not given to you, you may very well lose the babe."

"I'll try to remember." It wouldn't be hard. The only thing Nicki wanted—really wanted—that she knew she could never have was Alex. But at least now she would have a part of him, always and forever.

Perhaps, she thought as she paid Agatha for her time and took her leave, she would wait until right before Alex returned to England at Christmastide to tell him about the baby; with any luck, she wouldn't show before then. That way, they could enjoy their remaining time together without the burden of his distress at having sired a bastard on her.

That being the case, she'd better not reveal her condition to anyone, even Milo, lest it become public knowledge before she was ready to tell Alex.

"One more thing," said Agatha from her doorway as Nicki mounted her new white mare, Zurie. "If you get the urge to eat dirt or chalk, I want you to have a bowl of beans cooked with sugar instead. That's important. I don't want you to forget."

Dirt? Chalk? "I don't think I could forget," Nicki

assured her as she headed home for her own supper. "Thank you ever so much for your time."

Not long afterward, Gaspar stood in the doorway of the selfsame cottage, counting coins into the fat midwife's hand. She charged a pretty penny for her information, but it was worth it.

"You understand I was never here," Gaspar drawled as he tied the pouch closed.

"Oh, yes?" Agatha asked slyly. "I hadn't realized that."

Gaspar dug another coin out of the pouch and thrust it in her hand.

"I do now." Grinning, she poured the coins into her purse.

"Greedy cow."

A sense of well-being came over Gaspar as he rode back to the castle—a respite from the red tide of rage that had consumed him these past weeks, as he lay low between visits to the hateful Father Octavian, all the while waiting for Alex de Périgeaux to do the job he'd been brought here to do.

It would appear he finally did. Her ladyship was pregnant. Knowing this, Gaspar could proceed accordingly.

First, it would be well to deal with de Périgeaux before he had the chance to spirit the little mother-to-be to parts unknown. Gaspar could take care of that tonight; he already had the poison hemlock and white hellebore mixed up in the spiced wine—a whole flagon of the stuff.

And then finally—*finally!*—he would be free to execute the rest of his plan. In the end, he'd have not only Peverell, but its mistress. Like it or not, the high-and-mighty Nicolette de St. Clair would finally lie down and spread her legs for him.

As his wife, she'd have no choice.

Chapter 25

Nicki picked at her apple tart, making small talk with Alex, sitting across from her at the high table, as she pondered the remarkable fact that she was carrying his child. She wished she could tell him. She wished he could be happy about it.

She imagined being his wife, and giving him the news, and having him swing her around in his arms, ecstatic. She could imagine all she wanted, of course. Alex would hardly view this pregnancy as cause for rejoicing.

"Spiced wine, milord?" Gaspar asked as he filled Alex's goblet from his flagon. He'd been on exceptionally good behavior lately. Nicki wanted to think his encounter with them in the woods that August morning—and in particular with Alex's sword—had taught him a lesson, but she couldn't shake the sense that it was all an act. He was too restrained, too subservient. It made her nervous, as if he were up to something.

Nicki expected Gaspar to fill her own goblet next, but instead he disappeared into the buttery. When he returned, with a cup in his hand, he wove his way to the middle of the hall, amidst the hundred or so soldiers finishing up their supper and the servants waiting on them, and climbed atop a bench.

Alex cast a quizzical look in Nicki's direction as he lifted his goblet. She just shrugged, but a vague trepidation befell her. All she wanted was to get through this evening pretending everything was normal, unchanged. This was not a good evening for surprises.

She looked toward Milo, reclining in his bed across the hall, nursing his wine, as usual. He caught her eye and glanced toward Gaspar, holding his hands up to quiet the soldiers. She shook her head in response to her husband's perplexed expression.

"Men!" Gaspar shouted. "Pipe down, now. That's better. I've got a toast to propose." He raised his cup and the soldiers did the same. "To her ladyship, Nicolette de St. Clair." He bowed in Nicki's direction. "And to our lord castellan, Milo de St. Clair." A nod toward Milo. "Thanks be to God Almighty for the joyous event which our lord and lady have the pleasure of anticipating. At long last their alliance will be blessed with an heir, as we've all hoped and prayed . . ." His words were consumed by a roar of "Hurrah's" from the soldiers.

God, no, no . . . Not now, not this way . . .

Stunned, Nicki met Alex's gaze as he stared at her over the rim of his goblet. She could see only his eyes, wide with shock.

A movement of Milo's drew her attention. He was sitting up awkwardly, gaping at her, his goblet on its side next to him, soaking the quilt with wine.

Very slowly Alex lowered his goblet. His mouth formed her name, but Nicki couldn't hear him over the din that filled the great hall.

As the cheering subsided, Gaspar leapt off his bench and walked toward them, holding his cup in the air. "To the health of your ladyship and the babe you carry. May your child be a son, and may the good Lord bless and protect—"

"Excuse me." Alex stood abruptly and strode away, toward the turret in the far corner. Milo called to him as he passed, but he didn't even slow down.

Despair rose within Nicki. Why did he have to find out this way? Now things would never be the same between them. How on earth did Gaspar find out, and why did he choose to reveal it in this fashion—making it public to everyone at Peverell, and therefore all of Normandy, before she'd even adjusted to it herself?

Gaspar glowered at Alex's untouched goblet of spiced wine, then turned to watch him duck into the stairwell and disappear.

"Why did you do that?" Nicki demanded in a low, raw voice.

Facing her, Gaspar cocked his head as if the question confused him. "Milady? I merely wanted to congratulate—"

"Never mind." She rose and circled the table. "I couldn't bear your excuses and lies. I'll deal with you later."

Nicki hurriedly traced Alex's path across the hall, slowing as she approached Milo's bed. He was staring at her with the oddest expression. She couldn't tell whether he was pleased or saddened by this turn of events, when she'd assumed he'd be unreservedly delighted.

With considerable chagrin, she reminded herself that she had, after all, been sleeping with his cousin. Her liaison with Alex had been a union of passion; how could Milo help but feel at least somewhat betrayed? It would be different, certainly, if her pregnancy had resulted from a cold-blooded tryst of the type Milo had proposed last summer—a service performed by a man handpicked by Milo, whom she would never see again once his seed had taken. But that was not the case. Milo's relief at the prospect of an heir would, at best, be tainted with ambivalence.

Pausing at his bedside, she groped futilely for the words to account for herself, to make him understand what had happened, and why. As her consternation increased, Milo's expression softened. To her astonishment, he reached out and opened his hand, beseeching her with a gentle smile to take it. A sob rose in her throat when she closed her hand around his. Although his skin was cool to the touch, and she could feel the bones just beneath it, he gripped her with surprising strength.

"Go ahead." He nodded toward the turret staircase and released her hand. "Go to him."

Tears spilled down her cheeks as she turned and ran from the hall. She raced down the stairs to Alex's little chamber on the ground level, but he wasn't there. Thinking perhaps he was waiting for her in the solar, she sprinted upstairs and threw open the door. The big room was empty.

He must have gone outside. Leaning over her writing desk to peer out the window that faced the outer bailey, she saw him, mounted on Atlantes, leaving the stable. He kicked the sorrel gelding and tore off across the drawbridge. She watched him—a dark horseman in the twilight—until the woods swallowed him up. Nicki dried her face on her tunic sleeve, determined not to surrender to her tears, and sat at her writing desk, looking out the window.

Night descended slowly and darkness consumed the solar, but Nicki made no move to light a lantern. As she gazed out at the stars materializing in the inky sky, a strange serenity settled upon her. Her thoughts took on a focus, a clarity of vision that swept her fears and misgivings before it like a cleansing breeze.

All that mattered—really mattered—was the love she shared with Alex and the child that love had produced. The joining that had begun nine years ago as they'd held hands in a darkened cavern on a hot summer afternoon was now complete. More than their souls were linked. They'd merged themselves, created a new life with the power of their love.

What could be more important than that?

Milo awoke to his name being whispered. Opening his eyes, he saw his wife sitting on the edge of his bed. He could tell it was her in spite of the darkness because of the soft gleam of her hair.

"Nicolette," he murmured groggily. "What time is it?"

"Late," she said softly. "The middle of the night. I've been upstairs thinking."

Milo tried to sit up, but it was too much of a trial, so he just collapsed back onto the pillows. Strangely enough, he felt almost sober. He must have had less to drink last night than usual, after Gaspar's startling announcement. "Did you find Alex?"

"Nay. He went for a ride, and I haven't seen him return. I'm on my way downstairs to wait for him in his chamber, but I . . . there's something I need to tell you."

He could just make out her face; her eyes were sad. "You don't owe me anything, Nicolette. And I don't blame you—not in the least." He lifted a tendril of her hair and rubbed it between his fingers. "I can understand if you're worried about what others will think—"

"I care naught what anyone thinks but you."

Milo let out a little huff of astonishment. "What of that bloody tiresome reputation of yours?"

She chuckled. "Is it that tiresome?"

"More than you know."

"I've thought it all through, Milo. I don't care anymore. I can't afford to."

He shifted to get comfortable; damned bed sores. "You do know what they'll be whispering behind your back," he felt obliged to warn her. "They'll be asking how an invalid like Milo de St. Clair—bedridden with wine sickness for months—has managed to get that pretty wife of his with child after nine years. They won't say anything to your face, of course, but they'll wonder."

"They may wonder all they like. As you say, no one would say it to my face. No one would make a fuss.

My reputation would be tarnished, but I could brazen it out, and in time the whispers would die down, especially if you acknowledged the child as yours." She drew in a breath. "If I were to stay here."

If I were to stay here . . .

Milo let his breath out in a long, shaky sigh. "Jesu. This is what you came to tell me, isn't it?"

She felt in the dark for his hand and closed hers over it. "I'm sorry, Milo. I love Alex. I have since that summer in Périgeaux. If he'll have me, I'm going to leave with him."

"You really will be ruined then, you know."

"I know. I'll have abandoned my husband for another man, one I can't even marry, but whose child I'm carrying. I'll be the worst kind of fallen woman. The funny thing is, I find I can live with that more easily than I can continue in this marriage."

"It never was much of a marriage," Milo conceded. "But what will become of you?"

"Alex will find a way to take care of me and the baby—I'm sure of it. Nine years ago I was afraid—I hadn't enough faith in him. And there was my reputation to think of."

"It truly means nothing to you anymore?"

"I wouldn't say that. But it's just not enough anymore. I gave Alex up once in order to salvage my good name. I'm not willing to make that sacrifice again."

He squeezed her hand. Could he blame her? If his Violette were still alive, and he had the opportunity to be with her, would he remain here in this mockery of a marriage just for appearances?

"You do know," she said hesitantly, "that my leaving this way means that Peverell will go to the Church. You won't be able to stay here."

Grim laughter rattled in Milo's chest. His clever little scheme to secure himself an heir for the sake of

Peverell seemed to have turned itself against him quite dramatically. Served him right for conjuring up such shameless intrigue.

She leaned close to him, touched his face. "I want you to go back to Périgeaux. You can live with your brother."

"What? Nay!"

"Peter and Phelis will take care of you, Milo. They love you."

"I'd rather die than live under Peter's thumb again."

"Milo, you can barely feed yourself. What would become of you if I left you on your own? I won't leave until you're on your way to Périgeaux, and that's all there is to it."

"Nicolette, your concern is touching, it really is. But I'll be all right. Don't worry about me. I meant it when I said you owe me nothing. I daresay I haven't been much of a husband to you."

She ducked her head. "I don't suppose I've been much of a wife. Especially . . . since Alex came."

"The last thing that should trouble you is your conscience," he said. "Love doesn't always understand about such things as marriage vows. It doesn't always grow where we plant it. Sometimes it pushes up through the soil in some other place entirely." He brought her hand to his mouth and kissed it. "Go downstairs now and wait for Alex. You should be there when he comes back."

Milo lay awake in the dark after she left, contemplating her absurd guilt. Would it ease that guilt if she knew that Alex had bedded her with his blessing? Perhaps, but then wouldn't she feel deceived—not only by Milo, but by Alex? Milo didn't want to consider her pain should she discover that Alex had pursued her at Milo's request, for the sole purpose of getting her with child.

No . . . he couldn't tell her. He wouldn't. And he hoped to God she never found out.

Curious . . . He'd thought his conscience had long ago dissolved in a wine-soaked haze. Who would have expected it to make one last, feeble stand?

Chapter 26

Alex was exhausted and quivering by the time he returned to the keep, sometime during the night. He'd ridden for miles, guided by the moon and a sense of grief so overwhelming that it felt like the wailing of a thousand demons in his ears.

He climbed the turret staircase to the solar, never needing Nicki more, now that the end had come. On discovering her bed unslept in, he descended to the great hall, hoping he wouldn't find her in the arms of her husband, because he didn't think he could take that tonight of all nights, he couldn't stand seeing it . . . But when he parted the curtains of Milo's bed, she wasn't in there.

Milo was asleep on his side, his mouth open, his bony chest rising and falling in a hitching snore.

"God be with you, cousin," Alex whispered, and closed the curtains.

Where the devil was Nicki? Filled with disquiet, he went downstairs to his chamber. The little room was very dark, save for a ribbon of moonlight filtering through the arrow slit. The ribbon painted a silvery path across his bed . . . and over the form lying upon it. He saw a glimmer of pale gold, and sagged with relief.

"Nicki," he breathed, but she didn't stir. Lying on her back in her white gown, with her incredible golden hair spread all around her, she looked like an angel newly fallen to earth. He approached her slowly, so gratified that she had come to him; she never came to his chamber. She would have wanted to talk to him, of course, about the fact that she was with child.

Alex's gaze strayed to her abdomen, flat as ever beneath the white wool. His child. She was carrying his child.

Kneeling at the side of the bed, he very carefully lowered a hand onto her belly and rested it there, feeling the gentle rhythm of Nicki's breathing, the sweet warmth of her body, and fancying that he could sense the spark of new life glowing deep inside.

"God be with you, too," he whispered to the baby— a baby he would never see. Would it be a son or a daughter? Would it be healthy? Would it look like him? Would he ever find out? He'd sworn an oath to leave here as soon as Nicki became pregnant, and never attempt to contact her or the child.

An oath that, God help him, he must now fulfil.

Tonight. He'd come to that conclusion during his frenzied ride over the moonlit countryside. He must leave tonight, not draw it out. The anguish of parting from Nicki would only escalate the longer he stayed. If he waited until tomorrow, would he even have the strength to do it? And how could he ever say goodbye to her? How could he look into her eyes, hold her in his arms, knowing it was the last time? What would he say to her if she asked why he must leave? He was sworn to secrecy, for her own good.

This was all for her own good, he reminded himself as he lightly stroked her hair, smooth as satin beneath his palm. He came here and swore that blasted oath and sired a child on her, to protect her—not only from homelessness, but from Gaspar. He'd thought it would be easy.

No attachments . . . What a fool he'd been to think his attachment to Nicki, forged so long ago in a moment of mystic unity, had ever ceased to be. The bond between them had only grown stronger, to the point where they were now truly of one flesh and blood. Severing that bond would make his heart bleed.

But sever it he must—not only because he'd vowed to God that he would, but because it was best for Nicki. He'd done what he'd set out to do. He'd given her the gift of a child, and in doing so, saved her from destitution. Now he must remove himself from her life so that she could go on with hers—so that she could reap the benefits of what he'd sown.

It's for the best, he told himself as he shoved his clothes and belongings into his traveling satchel. For him as well as for Nicki. She was married to his cousin. Only grief could come of their love. He must ride to Fécamp and board a ship bound for England. He must leave here and never see her again, or he would surely go mad, wanting her so much—all of her, forever, not just her body from time to time—and knowing he could never have her.

He stood over her with his satchel in his hand, his throat tight with sorrow. If he hadn't sworn that oath, he might be tempted to wake her up and beg her to come with him. She wouldn't, of course. He was still a landless soldier, and she belonged to another. She'd tried in the past to annul her marriage, and it hadn't worked, so there was no way they could wed.

He would be asking her to be his leman, just as he'd unwittingly done nine years ago. Once again she would be obligated by her sense of righteousness and propriety to refuse. It was just as well that he was bound by his oath, because he couldn't bear her telling him a second time that she must choose Milo over him.

Just as he couldn't bear to say goodbye to her face. But there was, he realized, a less agonizing way.

Setting the satchel in the rushes, he opened the little corner door and climbed the service stairwell to the solar. He lit the lantern above her writing desk, sat down, and uncovered the ink horn. Choosing one of

the fatter quills—they were easier for him to handle—
he laid a fresh sheet of parchment before him, dipped
his quill in the ink, and took a deep, thoughtful breath.

How he wished he had Nicki's gift with words. She
would know how to say this; he was incapable of anything approaching her eloquence. All Alex could hope
for was that his crude, childlike handwriting would be
legible and his spelling not too atrocious.

> *To my belovid Niky, from Alex.*
>
> *When you awakin I will be gone. I am sory, Niky. I
> must leve now. I can not wate.*
>
> *It hurts my soul to be partid from you. Yet it gladens
> my hart to know that my childe sleeps inside you.*
>
> *Thank you for teching me to read and write. Thank
> you for loving me. I am sory I can not think of beter
> words for what is in my hart. I am not clevir like you.*
>
> *I will sail home to England. It is for your sake that
> I leve this way. We can nevir see eche other again. I
> am sory I can not explane. Forgiv me, Niky. Plese
> know that I love you. I know you will be a good mothir
> to our childe.*
>
> *May our childe be strong and helthy, and may God
> bless and protect you always.*

Alex read the letter over and then added, at the
very bottom, a post script: *You wood do well to dismis
Gaspar. Do it today, Niky, so that I need not wory for
you. He is dangerus.*

He blotted the ink as Nicki had shown him and
carried the letter back down to his chamber. Nicki had
rolled onto her side, although she still slept peacefully,
unaware of his presence. How he would have loved
to kiss her awake tenderly and slide his body into hers
and love her one last time. But it would not be worth
the heartache, for either of them.

He folded the sheet of parchment in half and tucked
it gently under her hand. She twitched, and he held
his breath, praying she didn't wake up, hoping she did.

She sighed, but did not open her eyes. He waited until her breathing grew deep and steady once more, and then he leaned over and touched his lips as lightly as he could to her temple. "Farewell, Nicki," he whispered, and rose.

Alex lifted his satchel, his gaze still trained on her, his heart screaming for him to stay, his rational mind urging him to leave before the sun rose and the castle woke up.

He would survive this, he told himself as he crossed to the door. He was the Lone Wolf. He'd been alone for years, and liked it that way. He'd be alone again, and he would learn to like it again. No complications, no responsibilities.

At the door, he paused for one last look at Nicki so that he could sear her image into his memory, and then he turned and walked away.

Chapter 27

"**M**ilo!"

Milo looked up from his first goblet of the morning, which Gaspar had just poured him, to see Nicolette flying into the hall. She had on yesterday's white tunic, and her hair fell in a flaxen tangle.

When she got close, he saw that she was flushed and puffy eyed, her face wet with tears. Something trembled in her hand—a sheet of parchment. "What does this mean?" she demanded in a wet, rusty voice.

"What. is that?" Milo reached for the parchment, but she snatched it out of his reach. Gaspar eyed it intently.

"It's a letter. From Alex. He's gone."

"Gone!" Milo groaned. That blasted oath. *Damn, why couldn't he have waited just one day?*

Dragging her hair out of her eyes with a jittery hand, she read from the page. " 'It is for your sake that I leave this way. We can never see each other again. I am sorry I cannot explain.' " She looked up. "And then he asks me to forgive him. Forgive him for what, Milo?"

Oh, God, she knew—or at least suspected. She must be very much beside herself, Milo knew, to have read that in front of Gaspar. He scratched his prickly chin, searching for some plausible response, praying she wouldn't find out why Alex had come to Peverell.

Gaspar cleared his throat. "I think perhaps I can enlighten—"

"You shut up!" she yelled, wheeling on Gaspar. "Just keep your goddamn mouth shut!"

Milo and Gaspar both stared at Nicolette in word-less astonishment. The breakfasting soldiers fell silent.

"Order them out of here," she commanded Gaspar, pointing to the men.

His face an impenetrable mask, Gaspar nodded to Nicolette and did as she bid him. The men, clearly sensing something amiss, filed out quickly.

"That," Nicolette informed Gaspar in a voice tight with strain, "was the last service you will perform for us."

"Milady?"

"You are no longer needed at Peverell. Pack your things and be gone by tonight."

Clearly astounded, Gaspar looked to Milo to coun-termand the dismissal. "Christ." Milo wished she wouldn't push the issue this way. It wasn't that he wanted to keep Gaspar. He'd come to view him as ruthless, almost demonic. But for that reason alone, they should be exceedingly careful in their dealings with him. "My dear," he said soothingly as he pushed himself into a sitting position, "you're obviously out of sorts today. When you're yourself again, we can talk about—"

"I want him out of here!" she exclaimed, as if Gaspar weren't standing right next to her. "I'm sick of his meddling, his brutality, his insolence."

Gaspar's hands curled into fists.

Please don't start in about the insolence, Milo silently begged, wary of the seething anger that welled within Gaspar at any hint that he was exceeding his station. "Nicolette, calm your—"

"How can I be calm?" she demanded, gesturing with Alex's letter. "He's gone! He says we can never see each other again, but that he can't explain, and that I should forgive him. For what, Milo?"

"I . . . I don't know," Milo lied, unable to look her in the eye. "Nicolette, please pull yourself—"

"Oh, for pity's sake," Gaspar snapped. "Why don't you just tell her?"

Nicolette spun to face him. "I told you to shut—"

"Your husband brought his cousin here," Gaspar said with horrible calm, "to sire a child on you."

"Jesus, Gaspar," Milo muttered.

Nicolette shook her head, fresh tears trembling in her eyes. "Liar."

"As I understand it," Gaspar said, "he was to seduce you without letting on what he was about—"

"You goddamn liar," Nicolette rasped, her face going as white as wax.

"—and then leave and never have anything to do with you again once his seed had taken root. Your husband made him swear an oath to make certain he abided by their agreement."

"Milo." She came to stand over him, her eyes wild. Not once during the course of their marriage had he seen her so distraught. "Tell me this isn't true."

Milo opened his mouth to speak, but his throat seized up. His eyes stung, he rubbed them. "I'm sorry, Nicolette."

A harsh sound came from her throat. Milo opened his eyes and reached for her with the hand that wasn't holding the goblet. "Nicolette, please listen to—"

"Damn you!" She swatted at his hand, jarring him and spilling wine all over the bedclothes. "Milo, how could you perpetrate such a . . . my God, what kind of man are you?"

"Not much of one," he admitted gravely.

She sank down bonelessly on the edge of the bed, pale and dazed. "And Alex, he . . . he came here just to . . ."

" 'Twas a favor for his cousin," Gaspar said, his eyes glinting. Milo had never hated him more. "But I don't imagine he found it too onerous a task."

"That's enough, Gaspar," Milo managed, setting down his goblet. The rebuke seemed to surprise Gaspar. Milo savored the anger coursing through his veins. For the first time in years, he felt a strong emotion, and it felt good. Leaning toward Nicolette, facing away from him, Milo laid a hand on her shoulder. "He didn't do it for me. He did it for you. You must believe that."

Gaspar snorted. "A pretty tale, but I don't think her ladyship is quite that naive, do you? Seduction is a game to some men, an amusement—like chess, or draughts. And, as with any game, there are those who particularly relish it, who become so adept at the play-acting, the little strategies and deceits—"

"Shut up," Nicolette said hoarsely.

"—that their opponents hardly even know the game is being played, and thus are all the more easily vanquished. Alex the Conqueror they call him. They say half the women in England have lifted their skirts for—"

"Shut up!" Nicki screamed, bolting to her feet.

"Don't listen to Gaspar," Milo said. "Alex didn't deceive you about his feelings. He's a man of honor."

Gaspar laughed incredulously. "Unless I'm mistaken, this is the second time this particular 'man of honor' has compromised her ladyship. If you ask me, milady—"

"I can't recall having done so," she retorted.

"You'll forget him. Anyone can see he's the lowest form of knave."

"Have you studied a looking glass of late?" she asked him acidly. Before Gaspar could summon a response, she turned to Milo. "I need to talk to Alex. I'm going to saddle up and ride north on the road to Fécamp. He couldn't have left that long ago. If I ride hard, perhaps I can overtake—"

"Nay!" Gaspar grabbed her arm. "You mustn't be riding off alone after him. How would it look?"

She twisted out of his grip. "Do you think I give a damn how it *looks*? I'm well beyond caring how things look. I want the truth."

"And you think you can get it from that lying debaucher? I can't let you—"

"Can't *let* me!" Eyes flaring, fists clenched at her sides, Nicki faced Gaspar squarely; Milo felt a surge of pride for her. "You may think you're lord of Peverell, Gaspar le Taureau, but you're not!"

Uh-oh . . . "My dear," Milo interjected gently, seeing the angry flood of red that crept up Gaspar's throat, the dull rage in his eyes. "Say no more. Just go."

"Nay," Gaspar persisted. "She mustn't."

"Go!" Milo said.

She turned and swept from the hall.

Milo let out a shuddering breath as he fell back against the pillows mounded behind him. "Nicki's right, of course. You do think you're lord here. But why shouldn't you? I've handed the castellany over to you, as you say."

"If I thought I was lord of Peverell, would I be going through all this?" Gaspar crossed to a window that would give him a view of the outer bailey and looked through it, scowling. He must be watching Nicki on her way to the stable.

Milo stared at Gaspar's back, silently repeating the retainer's words. *If I thought I was lord of Peverell, would I be going through this?*

"By the blood of the saints," Milo muttered. That was it. The bastard wasn't satisfied being Milo's retainer. He didn't even want the stewardship he'd somehow procured for himself. He wanted it all, and God help him, Milo had spent the past months in a drunken stupor in this bed, letting him play out his little schemes . . . sometimes unwittingly assisting him.

"God's bones."

Gaspar turned around. "Thirsty again?"

"You son of a bitch," Milo ground out, sitting up unsteadily. "You lying, conniving—"

"I'll be right back." Gaspar strode swiftly to the buttery and returned with a flagon. Lifting Milo's goblet, he dumped the little bit of wine at the bottom into the rushes—a slovenly gesture quite unlike Gaspar—and filled it from the flagon. Milo smelled cloves.

"I don't want you serving me anymore," Milo said. "My wife dismissed you from our service. I want you out of here—"

"You're overwrought," Gaspar bit out, his face still reddened, his hands quivering; he was jumpier than Milo had ever seen him. "This contains a sedative tonic." Recorking the flagon, he set it on the table and handed the goblet to Milo. "Be sure and finish it all. Quickly."

Milo studied the goblet in his hand as Gaspar, sparing one last look out the window, rushed from the hall. Milo heard him pounding down the stairs.

Milo's mind wasn't what it used to be, but it hadn't ceased functioning altogether. He knew what Gaspar had just handed him. For nine years he'd trusted Gaspar, relied on him, depending on him, and this was how it ended.

He should go ahead and drink it. He was less than worthless, a wretched drunk who couldn't command his own castle. He'd let down those women foolish enough to think they could rely on him—first Violette, and now Nicolette.

Milo sniffed the goblet, detecting a whisper of something ominous beneath the spicy fruitiness of the wine. Closing his eyes, he pictured Violette as he last saw her, standing in her night shift at the door of her father's shop in the middle of the night, waving to him. He could free himself of his wasted body and this sorry life and join her in eternity. It would be so easy.

He brought the goblet to his mouth and took a sip.

It tasted both bitter and sweet. It tasted like deliverance.

Gaspar burst into the stall just as the stable boy had finished buckling the saddle onto Zurie. "You're not going anywhere," he growled at Nicki.

The stable boy blinked at them.

"Off with you!" Gaspar grabbed the lad by his tunic and flung him out into the aisle. Nicki heard his rapid footsteps on the earthen floor and he fled from the stable.

"You overstep yourself, Gaspar." Nicki slipped her foot into the stirrup.

Gaspar seized her about the waist and backed her up roughly against the wall of the stall. His face was reddened; something savage flickered across his dead eyes. "It's about time I *overstepped* myself, don't you think? I've been the true lord of Peverell for years now, in fact if not in name."

"Let me go!" She tried to strike out with her fists, but he pinned them to the wall, then moved in close so she couldn't kick out. His size, his nearness, felt suffocating; her heart hammered erratically.

"Before you do something rash," he said in a low, menacing voice, "think about what you'll be giving up. Your husband's not long for this world. Once he's dead, you can marry me."

"You!" Outrage punched through her fear. "You must be mad!"

"I offered you marriage once before," he said softly, moving so close that her breasts brushed against his chest with every panicked breath she drew. "You spurned me. But it's my destiny to be your husband, and castellan of Peverell."

"You only want to marry me for Peverell. That's why you proposed after . . . after Philippe . . . isn't it?"

"Only in part. I fancied myself in love with you then, and I even entertained the absurd notion that you might learn to love me back. I wanted you for my wife as much as I wanted Peverell, but you turned me down. I wasn't good enough for you."

"You misunder—"

"Don't lie to me!" he roared, spittle flying. "You preferred the shame of unwed motherhood to me, didn't you? Your uncle would have cast you out— surely you knew that. But you would have ruined yourself rather than be bound in wedlock to a lowly apothecary's son, wouldn't you? *Admit it!"*

"Nay! Gaspar—"

"Lying bitch!" He slammed her hands against the wall with a force that jolted her to her bones. "You may have been willing to give up everything, even Peverell, but I wasn't quite witless enough to allow it. I had plans for you, and I wasn't about to let you destroy them just to serve that haughty pride of yours." He leaned in close, his voice a soft rumble, his breath hot and foul on her face. "I imagine you thanked God for saving your precious reputation after you lost that bastard you were carrying. In truth, you should have thanked me."

She stared at him, at his lifeless eyes, his horrible, knowing smile. "Nay."

"Aye. I dosed your wine with the tonic that purged that misbegotten spawn from your womb."

"Oh, God." Nicki recalled the wrenching cramps, the blood, the fear, as her body expelled her poor, wee baby. *'Tisn't a pleasant process, losin' a babe that way,* Agatha had said. *'Twill pain you somethin' fierce.* It had almost killed her. A part of her did die when she saw the tiny girl, the dainty little fingers.

"You're a monster," she accused shakily. "A devil."

Gaspar's mouth curved in a smile; his numb black gaze bored into her. Releasing her wrists, he stroked her hair as it lay over her chest. "I'm a man like any other." When his hands closed over her breasts, she flailed at him, and he captured her wrists again.

"But a man who knows how to get what he wants. I wanted you. I still do, more than ever, despite your contempt."

"I don't—"

He backhanded her across the face, hard. She gasped at the stinging pain. "I told you not to lie to me. After all these years, you still treat me like some ignorant errand boy—the apothecary castellan. You've never once looked at me the way you look at that bastard de Périgeaux. He snaps his fingers and you lie down and lift your skirts. Well, soon you'll do the same for me."

"Never!"

That chilling smile again. "Become my wife," he said, his voice a lethal purr, "or I'll tell the world that the child you're carrying was sired by your husband's cousin."

So that was it. He intended to ruin her unless she married him, thus elevating him into the ranks of the aristocracy and forcing her to submit to him—a shrewd plan, but one with a flaw. "It doesn't matter what you tell people. They'll suspect the baby isn't Milo's anyway."

"I'll confirm their suspicions. I'll broadcast the shameful details of your infidelity far and wide. How you'd run off to the woods every afternoon to satisfy your lust, while your husband waited for you in his sickbed. You'll be branded an adulteress. Your reputation will be in ashes."

Between clenched teeth, Nicki said, "I'd rather the world thought me the basest whore than marry the likes of you."

"I hate to disappoint you, Gaspar," came a ragged voice from the entrance to the stall, "but she can't marry you while I'm still alive."

Gaspar whirled around.

"Milo!" Nicki gasped. Her husband leaned heavily on his cane, gaunt and frail, his skin a sickly yellow in the dim light of the stable. She couldn't believe he'd made it here on his own. He hadn't been out of bed in two months.

Milo held something up—a flagon, looped by its leather cord over his shoulder. "No, Gaspar, I didn't drink it. If I'm not mistaken, it's been adulterated. Perhaps with . . . what was it? Poison hemlock and white hellebore?"

"You're imagining things," Gaspar said.

Milo uncorked the clay bottle and held it out to him. "Then you drink it."

Gaspar hesitated fractionally, and then sneered. "Go to hell."

"I've been there for some time." Milo shoved the cork back in and hung it on his shoulder. "I almost drank it, you know. But then I realized that I was playing into your hands yet again. I couldn't stomach the thought that my last act on earth would facilitate this putrid scheme of yours."

"How noble of you," Gaspar gritted out.

"Noble?" A wheeze of laughter rose from Milo. "Can't recall that word having been applied to me before. The only thing I'm really good at, it seems, is letting people down—especially my wife. It may be a bit late to try and break that habit, but—" he shrugged his shoulders, skeletal beneath his loose shirt "—I'm not dead *quite* yet."

Gaspar crossed his arms, his expression contemptuously amused. "What, precisely, is it you feel you can do for her ladyship?"

"I can refuse to drink this," Milo said, indicating the flagon. "As long as you're a threat to Nicolette, 'twould be a disservice to her for me to drink it. You can't marry her while I'm alive."

"Barely." Gaspar reached down and slid a dagger out of his boot. "And a condition it would be little trouble to remedy."

Milo backed up shakily, eyeing the blade. "How do you propose to explain my death?"

Gaspar, with his back to Nicki, chuckled as he advanced on Milo. "I'll think of something. I always think of something."

Grinning maliciously, Gaspar jabbed the dagger toward Milo once, twice—a cruel tease. Milo held his cane up as if to ward off the blade, but his whole body quaked just from the effort of standing upright.

Nicki looked around wildly for a weapon—anything! Her gaze lit on the mounting block in the corner, and she grabbed it.

Gaspar kicked Milo in the legs, and he crumpled in the straw. Leaning over him to seize a handful of shirt in his fist, he said, "You're a pathetic excuse for a man, you know that?"

Raising the mounting block over her head, Nicki slammed it with all her might on Gaspar's head. With a grunt, he fell on Milo, who managed to roll him off.

Gaspar muttered a curse and braced his hands as if to rise. Steeling herself, Nicki brought the block down once more on his head. He went limp in the straw.

Milo blinked at Nicki, then smiled slowly. "You've more talents than I realized, my dear."

She threw the block aside, her hands shaking, stunned that she'd managed to knock Gaspar unconscious and terrified that he'd wake up before they could get him immobilized. "I need some rope."

Milo tilted his head toward the front of the stable. "There's some hanging near the door."

As Milo struggled awkwardly to his feet, Nicki tied Gaspar's hands and legs, taking her time and making sure the knots would hold. As an added precaution, she shoved him into the aisle and tied him to a thick oak post.

Hooking her arm under Milo's shoulders, Nicki helped him out of the stable, then returned for Zurie and led her out. She closed the stable door and slid the big iron bar across, locking Gaspar inside.

Leaning on his cane, Milo extended a quavering arm and drew her into his embrace; she felt every bone in his chest. "You'd better hurry if you want to catch up with Alex."

"Are you all right?"

He smiled in that careless way he used to. "Never better." He meant it, she realized. He'd redeemed himself, to some degree, and for the first time in years he felt a measure of pride; she saw it in his eyes.

She mounted Zurie. "Don't let anyone into the stable. When I get back, I'll have Gaspar transported to the ducal prison. Go back to bed. Have Beal bring you some porridge, and try not to drink too much—"

"I'm sick to death of that bed. I'd rather stay out here for a bit. Don't worry about me." He took her hand. "Find Alex and marry him."

"I'm already married, remember?"

His expression sobered. "Look at me, Nicolette. How much longer do you think I have?"

"Milo—"

"I've been denying it. So have you. But I'm dying. We both know it."

"It could be years, Milo—"

"Find him." Milo gripped her hand almost painfully. "And marry him, and be happy. I owe you that much."

"Milo—"

"If you delay much longer, he'll be halfway across the Channel by the time you get to Fécamp." He released her hand and made his halting way to a nearby shade tree. Lowering himself wearily to the ground, he sat down with his back against the trunk, his eyes closed. "Go. And ride fast."

"I'll be back as soon as I can." She flicked the reins and rode away swiftly.

Chapter 28

Nicki rode Zurie hard on the road that led north through the woods—too hard, for as they passed a particularly rough stretch, the horse stumbled, tossing Nicki to the ground. Leaping to her feet, she grabbed the agitated mare's reins and murmured soothingly to her until she quieted.

With a sense of dread, Nicki bent down to inspect Zurie's legs and hooves, hoping she'd merely picked up a stone that could be pried loose. She moaned when she saw that the back of the animal's right front leg was sharply bowed between the knee and fetlock. Touching it gingerly, she found a pulled tendon, but no bones broken; thank the saints, for she couldn't bear to think of delivering the mercy stroke, and she *needed* this horse.

The leg swelled quickly, but some horses were rather sanguine about such injuries. Marjolaina would have cheerfully continued on three legs, and Nicki prayed that Zurie was as accommodating. Retrieving her eating knife, she reached beneath the skirt of her tunic, sliced a strip from her linen undershift, split the ends, and wound it around the leg, tying it off tightly. Once they were back at Peverell, she could stand Zurie in the bracing water of the stream to ease the swelling, and then rub her down with liniment, but until then, she'd have to keep going.

"All right, girl." Nicki mounted back up and flicked the reins. "Let's go." Zurie took a step and then stopped. "Zurie, please." Nicki did everything she could think of to urge the horse forward, wasting precious time in the process, but in the end she had to admit defeat.

Her only hope at this point was to leave Zurie there and continue on foot. She had money in her purse; she could buy another horse and send someone back for Zurie.

Dismounting, she tethered the mare to a tree on the side of the road. No one would steal an obviously lame horse, and she had to leave her where she could be seen by whomever she sent back for her.

Nicki walked on as swiftly as she could, peering through the autumn-hued trees for signs of a cottage. If she didn't get another horse soon, she'd never catch up with Alex. She began to entertain the hope that he'd slowed his journey by stopping at a tavern for a bite to eat. Perhaps he would spend the night in Rouen at the ducal palace; she hoped so.

She'd gone several miles when she heard the soft rumble of hoofbeats from behind. Alarm tightened her belly before she recalled Alex's observation that bandits usually traveled on foot. Perhaps she could ride north with this group, at least for a while. They might even be willing to sell her a horse.

Nicki turned toward the riders just as they came into view. One of them pointed. "There she is!"

"Sweet Jesus!" It was Gaspar and his men, thundering straight toward her. Nicki lifted her skirts and fled into the woods, running with all her might, her hair flying behind her. Dear God, it was Gaspar! How did he get out of the stable?

The woods were dense, making it unlikely they would try and follow her on horseback. Did she have enough of a head start to outrun them? With no choice but to try, she sprinted as fast as her legs could carry her, leaping boulders and darting between trees, her lungs burning, whispering frantic prayers.

From behind came the ominous crunching of footsteps on the dried leaves blanketing the forest floor. The footsteps grew louder as the men gained on her. Over her own hoarse pants, she heard their breathless curses and exclamations. The ground thudded as they approached. She heard Gaspar's harsh, gasping chuckle, and then something smacked her in the back and the ground slammed up to meet her.

Nicki cried out as the big man pressed her facedown into the crackling leaves, panicked as he leaned on her back, squeezing the breath from her lungs. She thrashed helplessly, trying desperately to breathe, while the three men laughed. Her vision faded; her extremities grew numb. But before she could slide into unconsciousness, Gaspar shifted his weight off her back. Her chest heaved, sucking in precious air—and dirt, for as he rose, he closed a hand over the back of her head and shoved her face into the ground.

And then he released her, standing over her with the others while she lay on her belly, struggling to catch her breath and trying desperately to think of a way out of this. She heard a lascivious snort of laughter, but ignored it . . . until she felt something cold and smooth moving swiftly up her stockinged leg, gliding over her ankle, her calf, her thigh. She flinched and rolled over, only to discover Gaspar lifting her skirt with the lead spike on the head of his mallet.

She scrambled backward, swatting her skirt back down while those two primitive louts, Vicq and Leone, gaped at her legs. Vicq held a club balanced casually on his shoulder; Leone had a dagger sheathed on his belt.

"On your feet," Gaspar ordered, gesturing with the mallet.

Swallowing hard, she looked around frantically, wondering if she could make a run for it, knowing she couldn't.

"I said get up!" Grabbing a handful of her hair,

tangled with leaves and twigs, Gaspar wrapped it around his fist and yanked her to her feet. She yelped as he dragged her several feet and backed her against a tree.

"She doesn't look so high and mighty now, does she, boys?" Vicq and Leone moved closer, their feral gazes trained on her. Her nostrils stung with the stench of unwashed flesh and clothes that had been lived in and slept in for years. They were hulking, hairy brutes with prominent brow ridges, both of them. They had about them the look of wild animals that one has tried with limited success to domesticate.

Gaspar pushed her snarled hair away from her face and rubbed a clump of dirt off her cheek. "She's as filthy on the outside now as she is on the inside—and that's pretty damned filthy." Looking down, she saw that her white tunic was torn and dirt smeared.

Something hot trickled from her nose. She swiped at it automatically, and her hand came away bloody.

"Hands at your sides," Gaspar barked. "Don't move until I tell you to. And then you'll do exactly as you're told. Do you understand?"

"Roast in hell."

In a heartbeat he pressed the spike of his mallet so hard into her throat that she could scarcely draw a breath. She grabbed it and tried to pull it away, but he only pressed harder, until she feared it would crush her windpipe.

"Hands at your sides," he instructed softly.

She lowered her hands.

"That's better." He let up a bit on the mallet. She gasped for air. He smiled thinly. "I must say I was rather put off to awaken and find myself tied up in your stable. I screamed myself hoarse before that dim-witted stable boy finally came and untied me. Your husband probably would have tried to stop him, if he were still alive."

Nicki just stared at Gaspar, his dull black eyes, his predatory smile, thinking *No. . . .*

"Aye, he was dead as a stone, under a tree, with the flagon next to him, empty. I suppose, in his own pathetic way, he was trying to do you and his cousin a favor."

Milo, Milo . . . Nicki shut her eyes against the tears that scorched them. *A favor . . . yes.* Her husband had taken his own life in a final attempt to wrest some measure of purpose and dignity from it. He did it so that Nicki would be free to marry Alex. The gesture was all the more selfless for being such a grievous sin, and Nicki promised herself that if she survived this afternoon she would pray for Milo's soul every day of her life.

"The amusing part of it," Gaspar said, "is that de Périgeaux will never reap the benefits of this favor. I will."

"If you think you can convince me to marry you—"

"Silence!" He jammed the spike into Nicki's throat until she gagged and choked, then let up on it a bit. "When I want you to use that lovely mouth of yours—" he jabbed his thumb between her lips, eliciting a gasp from Nicki and snickers from his men "—I'll let you know. Meanwhile, you're to keep it shut."

Nicki closed her eyes.

"Look at me."

She looked at him. On either side, Vicq and Leone watched in open-mouthed fascination, clearly amazed and titillated by Gaspar's treatment of her.

"You can remarry now," Gaspar said, "and you're going to marry me. Forget about de Périgeaux. He couldn't leave you fast enough once his job was done, eh? By now, he's many miles from here, delighted to be rid of you."

"Nay," Nicki whispered under her breath. How could it all have been pretense? How could he not have loved her?

But it was true that he had left her. Alex was gone, and she was at the mercy of an enraged lunatic. Gaspar had clearly crossed over a threshold of sorts. Years of frustration and imagined slights had driven him to a kind of madness, with Nicki as his target.

"You're obviously still reluctant to be bound in wedlock to the apothecary castellan," he said. "But perhaps I can think of a way to persuade you." He slid the tip of the spike slowly downward, following its progress over her throat, the rise and fall of a breast, her belly . . . She swallowed a strangled cry as he nudged it between her legs. Vicq and Leone leered openly.

"For fifteen years," he said, trailing the spike back up the way it had come. "I've imagined what it would be like to have that pretty little body of yours at my disposal. And, rest assured, I do have a rather vivid imagination. I've thought of a thousand different ways to make you scream and beg. Way out here, there'd be no one to hear you, would there? And when I'm done with you, I think it would be only fair to let Vicq and Leone take their turns—fair, and possibly quite entertaining as well."

Leone's lips stretched over a sparse mouthful of tooth stubs. Vicq just stared her up and down, his small eyes glinting with lewd anticipation.

Gaspar caressed her face with the spike's sharp point. "I almost had you once, you know. But, of course, you don't. Do you remember the night you took ill after drinking the raisin wine Edith brought you?"

Nicki had a vague memory of Edith making her drink a goblet of raisin wine that night. *'Twill help you sleep, lamb. You must drink it all.* "What did you put in—"

"Shh!" Gaspar pressed the spike against her lips. "Just something to make you a bit easier to handle while I sired a son on you."

Shock gripped Nicki. A memory surfaced . . . a man in a black mask holding a dagger to her nose. *No . . . he didn't . . . he couldn't have . . .*

"Unfortunately," Gaspar said, "de Périgeaux chose that moment to creep upstairs for his nightly poke, and I couldn't finish what I started." He smiled. "But he's not here to ruin it this time. Today I may do with you as I please. Then I'll turn you over to Vicq and Leone. If you aren't dead by the time they're done with—and you very well may be, for they do tend to get a bit carried away—I'll finish the job and bury you out here where no one will ever find you. People will just assume that you abandoned your ailing husband to run after his cousin, and that Milo consequently killed himself in despair."

Nicki began to shiver.

"That," Gaspar said, withdrawing the mallet and taking a step back, "is what will happen if you refuse to marry me. Accept me, and we'll leave now and find an agreeable priest. We could be husband and wife by tonight."

Nicki shook her head automatically, appalled by the prospect of being bound in matrimony to such a beast—but not eager to face the alternative, either. Perhaps, despite his madness, he could still be reasoned with. "Gaspar, listen to me," she said quickly. "With me dead, Peverell will go to the Church. You'll have lost your chance at it."

"If you don't marry me, I won't get it anyway, but at least I'll have my revenge, and there's something to be said for that. No more stalling. Yes or no?" He tucked the head of the mallet under her skirt and began lifting it.

"Gaspar, for God's—"

"Yes or no, bitch?"

She leaned over to push the mallet away.

Seizing her by the throat, he slammed her back against the tree. "Give me your answer!"

"I—I can't. Gaspar, listen to—"

"Is that your answer? No?"

Struggling to keep her wits—she *had* to talk her way out of this—she said, "Gaspar, please, let's just—"

"That's your answer. You stupid bitch." A red stain encompassed his face. He clenched his jaw, looking as if he might explode. "You stupid fucking bitch." With a sudden burst of rage, he swung the mallet, imbedding the spike in the tree right next to Nicki's legs. "You can't bear to think of marrying beneath you, can you, you spoiled little whore? All right. You've made your choice. Strip."

"Wh-what?"

"You heard me." Gaspar unbuckled his belt. "Take your clothes off—all of them."

Nicki's shivering turned to violent tremors as she looked from one man to the next, standing in a row watching her. Leone's tongue slid out to lick his lips; both he and Vicq seemed to quiver with excitement. Gaspar folded the belt in half and snapped it. *"Do it!"*

Something moved in the woods some distance behind them; a flash of white amid the trees.

"Now!" Gaspar screamed, shaking with fury. "Or I'll have my men do it for you."

The form in the distance took shape as a man— white shirt, dark hair tied back in a queue. *Alex!* It couldn't be, and yet it was. He moved toward them with silent, measured steps, his sword down, his gaze intent.

"What's it to be?" Gaspar demanded.

"I . . ." Nicki wrested her gaze from Alex, cautioning herself not to look that way again, lest she draw attention to him. He was trying to catch them unawares—as well he might, for it was three against one—but it would be a challenge even for someone as stealthy as he, given the dried leaves underfoot. She had to try to capture the attention of her tormenters, and hold it.

"I'll do it." Her hands shook so badly that she could barely control them, but she raised them to her throat and fumbled with the knot that secured the cord lacing up the front of her tunic. The attention of all three men was riveted on her.

From the edge of her vision, she saw Alex nod at her as he slowly approached. Clearly, he knew what she was doing, and he appreciated the diversion.

She swallowed dryly when the knot came undone. Drawing a shaky breath, she pulled the cord through the top set of eyelets, then the next, and the next, taking as much time over it as she felt she could get away with.

Gaspar smacked the belt against his thigh. "Faster."

Nicki's fingers grappled numbly with the cord until it slid free and dropped to the ground. Her tunic fell open all the way to her waist. She was grateful for her concealing undershift—until Gaspar clutched it and ripped it open, revealing a band of bare flesh down the middle of her chest.

Alex started sprinting; they would hear him for sure! "Nay!" she cried, grabbing Gaspar's wrists as he began to part the torn fabric. She risked a quick glance in Alex's direction, begging him silently to slow down; he did, thank God.

"I'll do it myself," she told Gaspar. "I will, just give me a moment."

"The more impatient I grow," he warned, stroking the belt, "the worse it will go for you."

Time . . . She needed time, Alex needed it. Her hands hovered near her throat.

"Show yourself," Gaspar said. "Do it."

She tucked her fingertips beneath the ragged edges of her shift and slowly skimmed them downward, parting the fabric just barely—enough to make all three men stare, mesmerized. The bile rose in her throat when she saw Vicq's hand—the one that wasn't gripping the club—crawl toward his crotch.

Alex was almost upon them. What would happen when he made his presence known? Despite his skill with the sword, she doubted he could take on three men at once, and Gaspar had that damned mallet of his.

An idea occurred to her. Lowering her trembling hands to the embroidered sash draped over her hips, she untied it.

"What are you doing?" Gaspar asked. "I told you to—"

"I need to get this off before I can take the tunic off." She slid the sash free and gripped it tightly with both hands, her body coiled in readiness.

Whether Alex knew what she was planning or not, he chose that moment to make his move, leaping forward, sword outstretched. All three men heard him and spun around. Gaspar swore and turned to yank his mallet out of the tree.

Nicki acted fast, whipping the sash around Gaspar's throat as he bent over the mallet. She pulled it tight, praying for the strength to hold him just long enough for Alex to dispatch at least one of the others. Gaspar made a strangled sound of outrage, clawing at the sash. She kicked his legs out from under him and knelt on his back. His astonishment alone was bound to immobilize him for a few seconds.

Leone drew his dagger as Vicq swung his club. Alex rolled beneath the club and came up behind Vicq, who wheeled around to face him. As the two men squared off, Leone darted behind Alex with his dagger. Nicki screamed a warning. Alex turned, but not before Leone sank the blade into his upper arm, yanking it out again and backing quickly away.

Vicq swung again. Slamming his sword against the club, Alex halted its progress. In a blur, he swept the huge blade across Vicq's throat; blood sprayed as he fell backward. He twitched convulsively for a moment and then went slack.

Gaspar thrashed as Nicki struggled to squeeze the sash tight, her arms shuddering with the effort. She knew she couldn't hold him much longer.

Alex whirled on Leone, who, seeing his companion's blood pumping from his throat, dropped his dagger and ran, disappearing into the woods. Nicki doubted he would ever be seen again. With a roar of effort, Gaspar hurled Nicki off of him, slamming her to the ground. He stood and wrenched the mallet out of the tree. Nicki rolled swiftly away and scrambled to her feet.

Gaspar and Alex faced each other warily, brandishing their weapons. Alex's gaze darted to Nicki. "Are you all right, Nicki?"

"I'm unharmed," she said, knowing how she looked—with her bloody nose, snarled hair and filthy, ripped clothes—and wanting to reassure him. "Alex, your arm . . ." Blood blossomed slowly on his right shirtsleeve, and the arm quivered slightly.

"It's nothing," he said, probably for Gaspar's benefit, but Nicki knew better than to believe it. That was his sword arm. He was in trouble.

Gaspar swung the mallet; Alex blocked the blow, but just barely. The problem, Nicki saw, wasn't just that Alex was hurt. Gaspar was bigger and deranged with fury, and he wielded that mallet of his with savage skill. Moreover, his reach, Nicki saw, was longer than Alex's, keeping Alex on the defensive. The two men circled each other warily, their fierce gazes locked.

"I thought you were on your way to the Channel," Gaspar said.

"I changed my mind." Alex glanced toward Nicki. "Run back to the road, Nicki. I left Atlantes there. Take him and—"

"And leave you here, alone against this monster? No!"

"You can't help me, Nicki!"

"I daresay he's right there," Gaspar said as he struck again; Alex jumped aside and countered with a lunge, which Gaspar blocked easily. "So you turned back," Gaspar said conversationally, swinging the mallet to and fro, "and came across our horses on the road. And, of course, you couldn't help trying to play the hero. But I hardly need remind you what happened the last time you tried to take me on."

"As I recall," Alex said, "I swore an oath to slice you open if you ever aimed that thing at me again." He spared another glance at Nicki as she pried Vicq's club out of his lifeless hand. "Nicki, I mean it—you can't help me. Get away from here. Ride back to Peverell and—"

"No, Alex." Nicki knew that Alex had not forgotten his disastrous encounter with Gaspar in the athletic field. And this time, the odds against him were even worse; his sword arm shook badly, and the sleeve covering it was crimson from shoulder to wrist. His facing down Gaspar this way was an attempt to buy her the time to get away; in all likelihood he expected to die.

The irony was that it was the very magnitude of Alex's sacrifice that made it impossible for Nicki to abandon him. Perhaps she could help him, perhaps not. But they were a part of each other now. This fight was her fight, too. If he fell, she would be empty, lost; she wouldn't want to go on without him.

"Damn it, Nicki, go!"

"Speaking of oaths," Gaspar said, "what of the oath you swore to Milo? You were supposed to leave for good once you'd done what you came here for. Aren't you the tediously honorbound young knight who never breaks his oaths?"

"That oath was to God, not Milo. And I've never broken one until today. But I gave it a great deal of thought during my journey this morning, and decided I didn't have any choice." Alex's gaze connected with

Nicki's for a brief, intimate moment. "And that God would just have to forgive me."

"How very touching." Gaspar whipped the mallet through the air, catching on Alex's shirtsleeve. Alex grimaced as the spike tore a fresh gash in his injured arm, but he countered swiftly, with a two-handed circular sweep that sliced Gaspar's tunic open. Blood seeped through, but Gaspar grinned. "It's just a scratch. But it looks as if I've done some real damage to your sword arm. Face it, de Périgeaux. You're done for. Give up now and I'll finish you off quick."

"Nicki, for God's sake, get out of here!" Alex yelled. "Go back to Peverell and have Milo send some of the men—"

"Milo is dead, Alex," Nicki said.

Alex fell silent for a moment, sorrow darkening his eyes. He whispered something under his breath—it might have been a curse or a prayer—and said, "Go back, anyway. The men respect you, Nicki. They'll follow your orders. Tell them to hunt Gaspar down and—"

"I'm not leaving you." She retrieved Leone's dagger from where he had dropped it. Could she use it if she had to? She thought about Gaspar's raw malevolence, and his determination to kill Alex, and decided she could. If the opportunity arose, she would shove it up to its hilt in the bastard's back and not feel a twinge of remorse. The trick, of course, lay in getting close enough to Gaspar to hurt him without falling victim to that mallet.

"Go!" Alex shouted. "Damn it, Nicki—"

"I'd rather she stayed," Gaspar said. "She's distracting you, just as she did that other time. You're easy pickings when your attention wanders in a fight." As if to prove his point, he rammed the mallet down hard on Alex's wounded arm. Alex's hand opened; the sword fell.

No! Please, God, no!

Alex crouched and reached for the sword, but Gaspar kicked it away.

"Run, Nicki!" Alex screamed as Gaspar lifted the mallet high over his head.

"Alex!" Nicki threw the dagger, which fell at Alex's feet. He grabbed it and rose, thrusting it into Gaspar's belly and yanked it sharply upward.

The mallet fell from Gaspar's hands. Alex seized him by the front of his tunic and jammed the blade in harder.

Gaspar looked down, blinking. "You've killed me, you bastard."

"I should bloody well hope so." Alex withdrew the dagger.

Gaspar sank to his knees. He met Alex's gaze with an expression of virulent loathing, but when he opened his mouth to speak, nothing came out. Presently his eyes lost their focus, and then he sighed and fell forward, landing heavily in the leaves.

Alex closed his eyes and swayed on his feet. For the first time, Nicki noticed how pale he was. His sleeve was saturated with blood; it dripped off his hand, forming a puddle in the leaves.

"Alex." She went to him, gathered him in her arms. "Alex, lie down."

He opened his eyes; they sparked with devilment. "Why?"

"Because you're going to faint."

"Oh."

With Nicki's help, he lowered himself to the ground and lay with his head in her lap.

"Aren't you going to kiss me?" he asked.

"Look at your arm! How can you be thinking of kissing?"

"I've been hurt worse than this," he said. "I never die."

"That's most reassuring." She reached into the gap

of her tunic and tore several strips from her ruined undershift.

Alex slid his good hand into the gap and opened it wider, lightly stroking her. "You have such pretty breasts."

"Stop that," she chided. "Lie still so I can bandage that arm." Nicki almost fainted herself when she got his sleeve torn off and discovered the extent of the damage. She wrapped the injuries tightly to stanch the flow of blood. Aiming for a tone of nonchalance, she said, "You'll have another scar—a bad one."

"Good. They give me character. Kiss me."

"I can't believe that's all you can think of after everything that's happened today."

His smile dimmed; his gaze grew melancholy. "What happened to Milo? Did Gaspar kill him?"

"Nay. Well, in a manner of speaking he did." She told him about the poisoned wine, and Milo's final act of redemption.

Alex touched her hand. "In his own way, Milo loved you."

"Just as he loved you."

He caressed her belly. "Are you truly unharmed?"

"The baby's fine. He's fast asleep inside me. He never knew what happened."

Alex frowned. "They didn't . . . do anything to you?"

"No, Alex. They didn't have the chance. You came in time." She smoothed an errant strand of hair off his forehead. "You came back. I'm so glad you came back."

"Every hoofbeat that took me away from you," he said, "felt like a stake being pounded into my soul. At seventeen, I'd been ready to fight for you, regardless of the consequences. I wondered what had become of me, that I was willing to give you up—and our child as well—with so little struggle. Once I was truly faced with losing you, I knew I couldn't go through with it. Oath or no oath, I had to come back for you."

"God understands about the oath."

"I know that now. Nicki . . ." He reached up to touch her cheek. "Milo gave his life for us, so that we might be together. 'Tisn't a gift to take lightly."

"If you want me to marry you," she said, "just ask."

He looked through her eyes, into her very soul. "Will you marry me, Nicki?"

"Oh, yes. Yes, I would love to marry you."

"Good." Curling his hand around her neck, he lowered her head, murmuring, "Then come here."

Epilogue

July 1074, Cambridgeshire, England

"Ah, here you are," Alex said from the bedchamber doorway when he saw Nicki at her writing desk, working by the light of the late-afternoon sun streaming in through the windows. "I should have known." He patted the baby in his arms, rooting busily on Alex's chest through his shirt, the damp little mouth blindly inquisitive. "This hungry babe is asking for something I can't give him."

Nicki turned and graced them—both of them—with one of her breathtakingly luminous smiles. Dressed all in white, her golden hair ignited by the sun, she'd never looked more angelic—and Alex had never felt more blessed. "I'm only too happy to oblige." She crossed the room to sit on the edge of their big bed and tugged at the cord that laced up her tunic.

Alex bounced the infant gently while she got unlaced. He'd never wanted children until his own child started growing in Nicki's belly. And then, so that he'd have a home to take his wife and babe to, he'd let King William grant him a substantial Cambridgeshire estate—in return, of course, for dismissal from his service, an offer Alex gladly accepted.

Their manor house was sizable enough to be imposing, but airy and full of sunlight, thanks to the many large windows. It was their bedchamber, though—their private sanctum—in which Alex felt most at ease.

The sprawling room, which encompassed the entire upper floor, bore Nicki's distinctive touch. Colorful rugs adorned the whitewashed walls, the bed was draped in buttercup curtains . . . there was even a pot of sunflowers on the writing desk.

"What were you writing?" Alex asked, wandering over to the desk.

She hesitated. "You may read it if you like."

Alex smiled at that. *You may read it if you like.* Only a year ago, she would have had to read it to him. Lifting the sheet of parchment she'd been inking, he saw that it was a letter, or rather, the start of one.

To Martin, esteemed prior of St. Clair, from your most devoted friend, Nicolette of Ravenhurst.

Beloved Brother Martin, cherished companion, how I miss you. I think of you frequently, wondering how you fare and what new marvel you have devised. Aside from the lack of your fellowship, however, I have found in England such happiness as I have never known.

Thank you for overseeing the management of Peverell in my absence. The steward you engaged has kept me well informed of all new developments, including the windmills you erected in the outer bailey and the star-viewing machine you are building in the athletic field. I only wish I could see them.

My husband and I are filled with pride and rejoicing, dear brother, for the Lord has blessed us with a strong and healthy baby. Our joy is boundless. I would, however, be obliged if you would inform Father Octavian that the deed to Peverell will be transferred to the abbey forthwith. Our child, you see, is a daughter.

"I'm ready," Nicki said, holding her arms out.

Alex returned the unfinished letter to the desk and brought young Luke to his mother. Baring one of her breasts—more ripely beautiful than ever—she set about feeding their son. Alex was captivated as always by the sweetly intimate scene. He smiled at the eagerness with which the baby latched on to the nipple, chuckled when he lifted a tiny hand to pat Nicki's full breast in a proprietary way.

Nursing generally filled Nicki with heavy-lidded contentment, so Alex was surprised to see little creases forming between her brows. "Do you think it's a very great sin to lie to a man of the cloth?" she asked.

"Brother Martin is a wise man, Nicki, and he wants what's best for you. He would understand."

"Giving up Peverell is best for me," she conceded, "but is it best for our son? Peverell is one of the most important holdings in Normandy. Are we wronging Luke by denying it to him?"

Alex sat behind her on the bed, gently easing her back until she was leaning against him. Wrapping his arms around her and their child, he tucked them up close to him. This was how he was happiest—with the three of them snugged up together. "Luke will grow up an Englishman, Nicki. He'll inherit this estate, or earn another, even better one."

"Aye, but Peverell is—"

"Old and gloomy," he finished, nuzzling her neck. She chuckled. "Aye, it is that."

"And too many sad memories are buried there," he said softly. He kissed her silken hair, inhaled a whisper of roses and spices mingled with a baby-sweet milkiness—a scent he wanted to surround him, be a part of him, always and forever. "We'll make new memories, Nicki—happy ones—right here in England."

Author's Note

Luke's little brother had the face of an angel and the well-muscled body of a soldier. His many old scars—mementos not of the battlefield but of the savage beating he'd taken at seventeen after a liaison with the wrong woman—only served to add an intriguing edge to his beauty.

That description of Alex de Périgeaux is from *Secret Thunder*, the story of Luke—a knight tormented by the savagery lurking inside him—and earthy Faithe of Hauekleah, who heals his soul. As I wrote *Secret Thunder*, I became increasingly intrigued by the amiable young Alex—and more than a little curious about those scars. Who was the mysterious woman who'd earned him that beating, and what would happen if they met again?

After *Secret Thunder* hit the shelves, I was happily inundated with mail from readers, most of whom were just as fascinated by Alex as I was, and eager for his story . . . *now!* Sorry for the wait, and I hope it was worth it.

This isn't the first time I've fallen in love with the brother of one of my central characters. While writing *Falcon's Fire*, I became helplessly smitten by the heroine's brother, Rainulf. I knew in my heart that all he needed to cure him of his angst was the right woman—and, as *Heaven's Fire* proves, I wasn't about to let the fact that he was an ordained priest get in the way!

I'm currently working on my fifth medieval novel for Topaz. As yet untitled, it's a romantic mystery set in twelfth-century London, in which a riches-to-rags heroine rents a room to a man who can offer her nothing but more trouble. And then there's the heroine's brother . . . (*sigh*)

If you'd like to be on my mailing list for news about upcoming releases, write to me at P.O. Box 26207, Rochester, NY 14626. And while you're at it, let me know what you thought of *Wild Wind*. I'd love to hear from you!